SHADOWS OF WAR

ASRIAN SKIES

ANNE WHEELER

For Daniel.

He will wipe away every tear from their eyes, and death shall be no more, neither shall there be mourning, nor crying, nor pain anymore, for the former things have passed away.

REVELATION 21:4

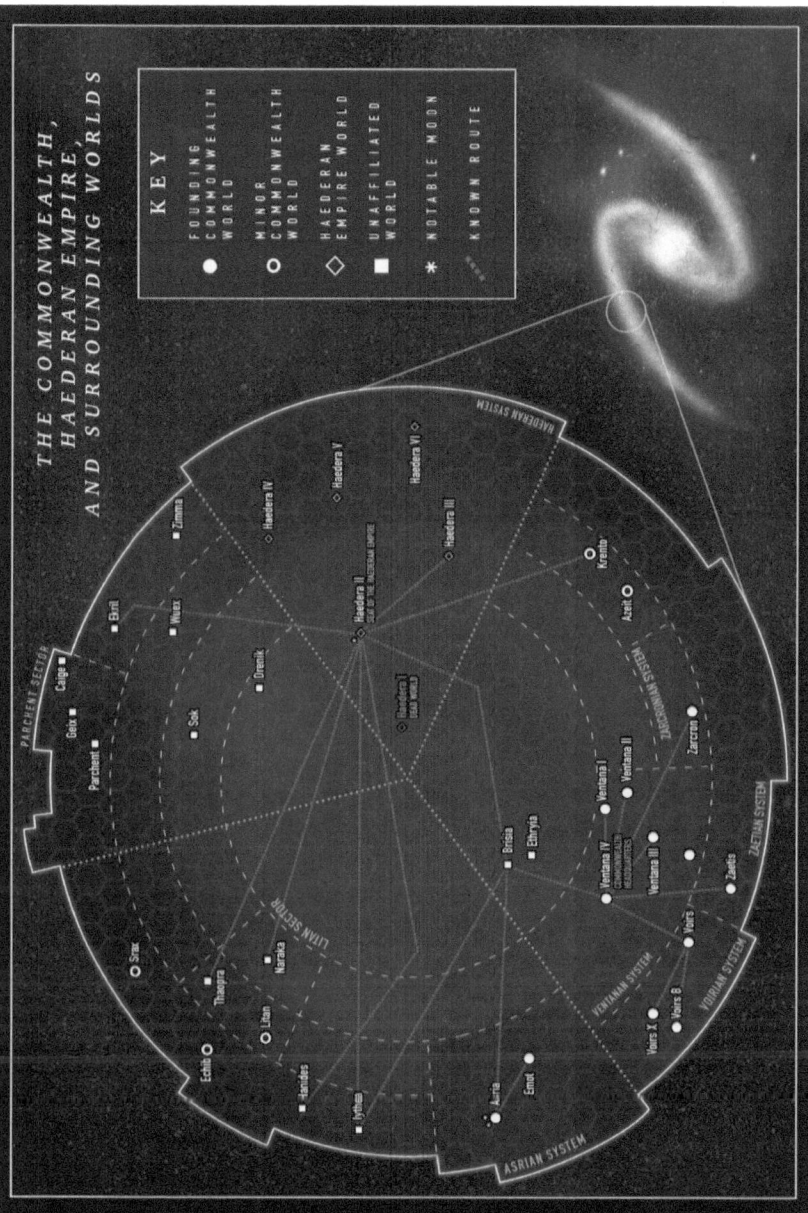

THE COMMONWEALTH,
HAEDERAN EMPIRE,
AND SURROUNDING WORLDS

KEY

FOUNDING COMMONWEALTH WORLD ●
MINOR COMMONWEALTH WORLD ◉
HAEDERAN EMPIRE WORLD ◇
UNAFFILIATED WORLD ■
NOTABLE MOON ✳
KNOWN ROUTE

HAEDERAN SYSTEM

Haedera V ◇
Haedera IV ◇
Haedera VI ◇
Haedera III ◇
Haedera II ◇ SEAT OF THE HAEDERAN EMPIRE
Haedera I ☐ HOME WORLD

Zimmia ■
Wunx ■
Bsril ■
Drenik ■
Sok ■
Cage ■
Geix ■
Parchment ■

PARCHENT SECTOR

Krontir ◉
Azeit ◉

ZACHRONIAN SYSTEM

Ventana II ◉
Ventana I ◉
Zarcron ◉
Ventana IV ◉ COMMONWEALTH HEADQUARTERS
Ventana III ◉
Zaeis ◉

DAETRIN SYSTEM

Persia ■
Ethryia ■

VENTANAN SYSTEM

Voors ◉
Voors X ◉
Voors B ◉

VOIRIAN SYSTEM

Srax ◉
Thaayra ■
Naraka ■
Lihan ◉
Handes ■
Jythas ■

LITAN SECTOR

Echilo ◉

Auria ✳
Emet ◉

ASRIAN SYSTEM

CHAPTER ONE

THE WORLD DISAPPEARED BELOW AVERY FASTER THAN SHE COULD comprehend, the horizon a bright curve outside her window, and that uncooperative life support light in the corner of her annunciator panel was flashing again.

With a grimace, she reached above her head to flick the twin-engine Dragonfly's pressurization reset switch for the second time in fifteen minutes. This *had* to work. If it didn't . . . she swallowed. Well, technically nothing much would happen. Except she would be forced to return for an early landing, and that would be unbearable, today of all days.

But thirty seconds later, the red light in the corner of her primary display resumed its blinking.

Kusir.

Childhood indoctrination kept her from speaking the Voirian curse—as did the voice recorder installed under her seat. The stars came into view as she climbed higher, a million glowing embers against velvet black, tempting her to ignore the warning and continue. The pressure suit she wore made the problem academic, but the technicians would check each system readout when she returned, and the safety regulations were clear. With two weeks left until graduation and her commissioning, she couldn't afford to violate such a critical policy.

Pressure suit or not, her breath became shallow and measured as she initialized the suborbital engines. Cursing the engineer who'd designed the switch to be behind her head, she hesitated once more before she made the call. Would anyone ever know if she changed her mind and continued on? She slammed her palm against the transmit button before she could talk herself out of the decision.

"Control, Spark 6." At least her training hid the resignation in her words.

"Spark 6, Control." The scratchy voice anchored her to the planet below once more. "Go ahead."

"I've got primary and secondary life support failures." Even after five years of flying in space, the ability to hear a voice from a hundred kilometers away sent a smile across her face, even if that voice doomed her flight this time. "Negative reset."

"Failure confirmed." A momentary pause. "Cleared for return."

"Cleared for return," she confirmed with a sigh.

With a light finger, she adjusted the thrusters, letting the Dragonfly spiral downward over the mountains that edged the eastern coast of the largest continent of Ventana IV. As unfortunate as the short flight had been, the swirling clouds and glittering seas of the planet below still took her breath away, stealing most of the disappointment along with it—but then, the wilds of Ventana were stunning from any vantage point. How could anyone think otherwise?

The Dragonfly's shadow appeared below her as she descended, casting a silhouette over the massifs where she liked to disappear for a few days of solitude whenever she earned enough leave. But that long-desired opportunity for solitude would soon be replaced by a berthing area shared with dozens of other pilots for the next three years. She should have dreaded the very idea of such close quarters, but the thought of those crowded bunks made her smile, even while she tracked the radio beacon that led to the academy's landing site.

That kind of camaraderie was exactly what she'd worked for, wasn't it? The possibility of serving on a Commonwealth cruiser had saved her from Asria, where she had nothing to look forward to but isolation and routine. Thank goodness she'd escaped her home planet—and along with it, Father and Merritt's disappointment over her growing doubts and yearning for independence. It had become too difficult to pretend to be someone she didn't want to be, too hard to pretend to believe something she wasn't sure she believed anymore. Here, on Ventana IV, far from the obligations and expectations of home, she'd found herself.

She banked the Dragonfly low over the large glass windows of the academy's library, leaving the flare assist on manual for one last landing on the planet that had become her home. It would make her approach longer, but surely she'd earned the right to extend the flight just a few minutes. The caution and warning light had turned silent once the atmosphere had become thick enough, and when the ship settled onto the pavement, she breathed an Asrian prayer of gratitude—some old rituals were impossible to ignore, much as she wanted to—and pulled the hatch open.

Early spring humidity slammed against her like hot tea as soon as she yanked off her helmet, and beads of sweat dripped down her forehead as the waiting ramp crew towed the Dragonfly off the pad to the parking area. Horrific weather or not, she would miss this place almost as much as she'd miss the mountains. Rows of hangars filled with Dragonflys ran in concentric lines on each side of the five-sided landing site—a side for each of the Commonwealth's founding planets. She was lucky to spend most of her time here and not stuck in a windowless building most days like the non-flying cadets. Did they know what they were missing?

"Rendon!"

The shout echoed from somewhere behind a nearby building,

but the culprit hadn't made himself visible yet, so when the Dragonfly came to a stop, she yanked off her gloves and grabbed her communicator from her pocket, shaking as she swiped a finger over the lock. Rumor was that post-graduation assignments would be disseminated today, and if hers hadn't arrived, if she had to wait longer to learn her fate, subjected all the while to the torture of uncertainty—she wouldn't be able to bear it.

But her heart stopped at the most recent message, even as the voice called her name again somewhere in the muddled panic that had suddenly become her reality. She scanned the text, official bureaucratic language blurring in her mind and swirling around her, until she found the one word she was looking for.

Dauntless.

Avery gave an ecstatic shriek, then slapped her hand over her mouth and read it three more times, just to make sure she wasn't dreaming. *Dauntless*, the gem of the Commonwealth Navy, was the dream of almost every cadet, but less than a handful of pilots from each class were fortunate enough to end up on the ship reputed to engage the Haederan Empire more than any other in the fleet. Second in her class or not, she'd never imagined she'd be one of them.

"Something amusing, Cadet Rendon?"

Her gaze fell on the lieutenant standing next to the Dragonfly, his arms crossed and a heated expression on his face. Was this level of irritation all because she'd ignored how he'd hollered at her from a distance? He could have used the communicator if he was that bent on talking to her. Or maybe it was something else—it almost looked like he knew she'd considered ignoring the alarm. She crinkled her nose and tried to remember if she'd said something out loud, words the recorder might have heard.

"No, sir." She slid the comm back in her pocket and forced a blank expression. "Just—"

"Whatever it is, you're done," he interrupted. "Kohren wants to see you—now. Unless you're too caught up in your messages, that is."

Avery shook her head as her heart sunk even further. There was so much accusation in his order she forgot about the system failure—and *Dauntless*. Cadets weren't called to the commandant's office unless there had been an egregious disciplinary issue —and those disciplinary issues always meant dismissal. It didn't make sense, especially after the news of *Dauntless*.

"Sir, I—that can't be right." Scrambling out of the Dragonfly, she wiped away a strand of dark hair that clung to her forehead while she tried to recall anything she might have done to draw Kohren's attention. "Did he say why?"

"No idea, Rendon, but you've got fifteen minutes. Let's go."

Her cheeks warmed at his hostility and the haste he'd put her in. Years of sweat and filth from the Dragonfly stuck to her, and no doubt anyone within ten meters could smell her, but fifteen minutes left her no time to change or shower. Disrepute wasn't the impression she wanted to give the commandant, especially now, but the lieutenant had left her no choice. With a sigh, she shimmied out of her pressure suit, lobbed it and her helmet to a waiting crewman, and followed the furious lieutenant across the landing site.

Her heart pounded as the secretary showed her into the commandant's inner office, but the warm wood décor settled her heartbeat, even as she stood at attention. Her surroundings were a welcome contrast to the steel and glass of most academy buildings—Admiral Elber Kohren was from Zaetis, a smaller Commonwealth world that usually reminded her too much of Asria. The planet was known for furniture making, thanks to the forests that stretched across the southern hemisphere, and the peikwood desk in front of her with the hand-carved designs had to be centuries old.

The age should have been a reminder of Asrian tradition, too, but somehow it appealed to her in a way she couldn't explain.

Perhaps it was simply the exoticness of it? Yes, she'd have to look into some Zaetian pieces for her home if she ever settled down—somewhere other than Asria, if she had any say in the matter. Maybe she could even do as her elder brother had done and disappear in the middle of the night. She missed Quen more than she ever thought possible, but he'd made the right decision.

Not that it mattered. If the need arose, the Asrian senate would hunt Quen down and bring him home, and his pretense at real life would be over.

Kohren cleared his throat, bringing her back to Ventana and away from a history she'd rather have forgotten. It was becoming easier to ignore the commandant's crooked nose, a gift from an overzealous cadet during unarmed combat training five years before. Rumor had it he'd refused to have the injury corrected, believing it lent him an aura of . . . well, something. It certainly made the otherwise competent admiral legendary at both the academy and throughout the fleet.

"Have a seat, Cadet Rendon." Kohren gestured toward the chair in front of his desk, so she perched on the edge and tried to shrug off her anxiety while he continued, "I just finished reading your first-classman thesis—" He gave his desktop screen a short glance. "—*The Formation of Iron-Nickel Core Dwarf Planets in the Yezru Belt*—very impressive."

"I'm sorry, sir," she replied and tucked a piece of hair behind her ear, silently cursing her lack of a shower once more. "You called me here to talk about my thesis?"

"Not exactly." He slid the screen away and folded his hands on the peikwood desk. "There's no good way to say this, so I'll be blunt. We just received word your uncle has abdicated."

Abdicated?

Her forehead creased. She must have misheard him. Of all the things Kohren—*or anyone*—could have told her, this was the last thing she'd expected to hear. More than that, it wasn't possible.

"Sir, there must be a mistake." Avery settled back in the chair, relief washing over her. "He can't do that."

"Because Asrian law prohibits it."

She tucked the insubordinate piece of hair behind her ear once more. Kohren's statement was just that—it wasn't a question. Everyone knew the history. He had to know it too, which meant this had to be a mistake.

"Of course," she replied. "It hasn't happened in five hundred years."

And five hundred years ago, it had touched off a bloody civil war that had resulted in both that prohibition and the abolishment of most of the Asrian nobility. No one, not the senate, not the royal family, and not the citizens, wanted the result of another power vacuum. The law had always enjoyed vigorous support, and although she understood the wish for a normal life more than most, even the idea of breaking it was unconscionable. If she ever ended up ruling Asria, as distasteful as that prospect was, she would follow the law.

But they'd find Quen before she had a chance at becoming queen. No matter what Quen had said, they would bring him home.

Kohren's entire face tightened. "That's probably why reports show that he fled to Haedera."

Her gut tightened.

Haedera?

But . . . Uncle Victor wasn't capable of treason. Of course he wasn't. This was bad intelligence of some sort. Her uncle wouldn't have gone to Haedera. Not the system which had been responsible for the formation of the Commonwealth itself, years ago. No, if the first news about her uncle was unexpected, this part of it had to be a joke. Did the academy play practical jokes on graduating cadets?

Kohren searched her face, and Avery suddenly knew what a pikan bound for slaughter felt like.

"I'm sorry to ask you this so directly, but has he contacted you?" he asked. "Asked for help? Told you anything?" *Especially anything about this Haedera business*, he was clearly suggesting.

"Sir, I haven't seen or heard from him in over a year. We're not close anymore." When he lifted a brow at her claim, an even more alarming thought arose. "I don't know how I can prove this, but my loyalty is to Asria. And the Commonwealth," she hastened to add as her eyes landed on the blue and silver starburst on his shoulder, the Commonwealth Navy seal she would be authorized to wear in just a few days. "Please don't dismiss me over this."

"Your loyalty isn't in question." He scratched his head, as though he was hesitant to continue, then sighed. "But we have another problem. Because of your change in . . . status, the Asrian senate has revoked your waiver."

Her jaw tightened; the formerly cool office grew hot. The Commonwealth required certain designated candidates—royalty, children of diplomats, and a few other poor fortunate souls—to obtain a waiver from their local government before attending the academy or enlisting in the Commonwealth military. Planetary forces had no such requirement that she knew of, but she'd long desired to leave Asria behind, so the Royal Asrian Defense Forces had never been an option for her. The senate hadn't let her go without a fight. And now they'd gotten what they always wanted.

They'd revoked her waiver.

No . . . not just the waiver.

Her life.

"I—I see," she said, as the room spun around her.

"Your father's coronation was five weeks ago. The courier ship stopped on Metis Station this morning to make the report," he continued, "and we'll know more once they arrive to collect you."

Swearing-in, she wanted to correct him. A common misinterpretation of Asrian law. An Asrian coronation was religious—and celebratory—so while Father might have made his solemn oath in front of the senate as soon as they approved his kingship, he wouldn't have been coronated. Not yet. Not if her uncle had truly . . . defected? It was an insignificant word for such a betrayal.

Kohren pushed a tablet across his desk toward her, and she

struggled to focus on the blurred words before her. "Your discharge authorization," he said. "I'm sorry, Your Highness, but we have no control over internal planetary matters."

Your Highness.

Avery sat frozen as the words pulled the last of the air from the room.

No longer Cadet Rendon.

Not even Lady Avery.

And never Ensign Rendon now.

Asria—not *Dauntless*—would be in her future sooner than she liked.

CHAPTER TWO

Asria.

Avery paused on the shuttle's disembarkment ramp and took a deep breath of clean, unadulterated air, her first in hours. In the shadow of the mountains, a cool morning breeze washed through Cadena, Asria's capital—though most anything was cooler than the part of Ventana where she'd spent the past few years. A few ramp handlers scurried about, unloading baggage and refueling the shuttle, but otherwise the port was quiet. It only took a brief glance around the empty terminal to assess her situation.

Father was nowhere to be seen. The snub was some relief, though it was no surprise the new king wasn't waiting for her on the landing pad. She'd had plenty of time over the six-week journey to fret over her situation, and he was the last person she wanted to see right now, even if her forced return wasn't his fault.

Instead, a grin spread across her face when she spotted Drex. How could anyone see Drex after so long and not smile? Her father's head of security was still lean, even though he was pushing sixty-five, and tall like most Asrians in the region. He looked more like an athlete half his age than a reluctant bureaucrat, and for the past few years she'd missed him more than she ever thought possible. Drex, forced into retirement from the

Defense Forces after a glider accident, would understand how disappointed she was at being called home, never to fly fighters again.

"Drex, you don't know how good it is to see you," she called out over the roar of a departing spacecraft, dashing down her own shuttle's ramp toward him. Not mentioning the white facial hair that graced his sharp chin—a fashion she never would have predicted on the professional-to-a-fault Drex—she hugged him in full view of the few employees straggling nearby. Since Father hadn't bothered to welcome her back, who cared what he would think of the emotional demonstration.

And come to think of it, Merritt wasn't here, either, and that rejection hurt more than her father's snub. Even though conflict and distance of the planetary variety had always marked their relationship and despite time apart, after ten years together as an official couple, he should have been waiting. They'd had an unspoken agreement, after all, even if he hadn't replied to her brief communication about returning home. Maybe he hadn't received it, though someone in the palace must have notified him of her arrival.

On second thought, perhaps that had done it. It would take a miracle for Merritt Parker to be caught anywhere that hinted of even the faintest suggestion of royalty.

She released Drex and looked around. "No Father. No Merritt. And not even Mother? Surely she's been wanting to see me."

"The queen isn't feeling so well this afternoon." Drex shrugged. "She's at the palace."

Her smile fell as the joy she'd first felt at seeing Drex faded away like the engine exhaust above them. His cool tone didn't hint of the turmoil Carina Rendon had been through in the past year, after the deaths of her parents just weeks apart, but Avery could read what he wasn't saying. Her mother rarely left her rooms anymore.

"Oh. I had hoped she was doing better. I'll see her first thing when I get home, if she would like." Another, more immediate, worry hit her. "But please, Drex, don't start calling me Your Highness. It's truly unnecessary."

"Request noted, Avery." Drex hesitated, hands in his pockets, as if he wasn't sure what else to say. "In private, at least. In public, things have changed."

Of course they have.

"Still, you can smile at me, you know," she replied, forcing one of her own. "I'm not angry with you."

"Don't be angry with your father, either." His dark eyes were serious as he gestured her forward. "This wasn't his call, and it's not his fault. He wants the position as little as you would."

That, she believed. She would blame the senate for this one. "Fine. I won't blame him, but I'm not happy with him, either. He didn't fight this thing at all, did he?" Drex's silence was answer enough. "What do they intend on me doing at home anyway? Sit in on committee meetings and look pretty?"

Drex laughed and pointed her at the aeroflyer parked nearby. Against her better judgment, she'd looked forward to the foreign luxury, but there was something strange about the ship with the pearlized-gold finish. That was it . . . unlike when she'd left for Ventana, it wasn't marked with the twin aster seal of the king.

Avery squinted in uncertainty at the omission. A sign of the new King Lucas's egalitarianism, extreme even by Asrian standards? No, that would be too much of a break from tradition, even for Father. More likely, the unmarked ship was an additional security measure. Animosity toward the Rendon family had to be running high in the wake of her uncle's treachery, and perhaps security had decided it was a prudent move. She shot a quick glance at her surroundings, adding that to the list of things she'd never forgive Victor Rendon for. Who was he to tarnish the Rendon name like he had?

"You don't waste any time, do you?" Drex asked. "Well, yes. I'd imagine they want you to be a liaison to the Commonwealth, too. You'd enjoy that, yes?"

"I'm not sure I'd be Ventana's first choice for a liaison after this," she said. "They think I'm a quitter. And I'm not sure I want the continuous reminders of what could have been."

"This isn't about you. It's about serving your planet, your system. You knew this was a possibility, Lady Avery."

Drex's intentional use of the obsolete title was a sharp reminder that even on Ventana, she'd never been as liberated as she liked to believe. That wasn't how things worked on Asria. Victor's wife had died just two years into their marriage, leaving him childless and devastated. Perhaps he'd thought the senate would be happy to elect his younger brother as his successor, but his reasons for never marrying again had never mattered much to her before, except as an academic exercise in Asrian futility—one she was now suffering for.

She climbed inside the transport and settled into the soft seat, marveling at how the programmed computer molded the leather to her body—a costly addition to the standard interior. The entire interior was expensive, just like one would assume from the outside, and she squirmed with unease despite the physical comfort. It had been a long time since she'd flown like this, let alone lived like this. The palace would feel even more uncomfortable after years in the dorms.

"You're wrong," she replied. "I didn't know this would happen. Quen is the one they want, not me. I thought Uncle Victor would get married again, have proper heirs. I never expected him to leave for Haedera." She packed derision into the word. "I never thought Father would accept this. It's unfair to say I knew this would happen."

Drex hopped in across from her, as comfortable in the wealth as he'd always been. "Possibly, but you can't fault the senate for this. You can't be flying warfighters with Quen gone. Especially in the current political climate."

"Warfighters?" Avery narrowed her eyes at his comment, obviously intended to tell her something while giving nothing away in public.

He cleared his throat. "Well, I suppose you've been out of communication reach for a while. You'll find out."

"We're at peace. I'd have been flying patrols in open space. Not playing games with the Haederan Empire." If Drex didn't already know *Dauntless*'s reputation, he didn't need to. "Nowhere near them, in fact, and they haven't been a threat in forever anyway, even with that situation on Echib last year. It wouldn't have been dangerous."

Finished with her argument, as much of a lie as it was, she ran a finger across the smooth ivory seat, then jerked her hand back into her lap. Her father's personal transport couldn't have been more different from the utilitarian aeroflyers she'd grown used to on Ventana. It was almost as if her palms, used to soaring in grimy twenty-year-old Commonwealth trainers, would stain the expensive material if she touched it.

"The odds of anything happening are insignificant," she went on. "Virtually zero. There hasn't been a major accident on a Commonwealth spacecraft in a hundred years. What did they think would happen? If the senate was that worried about it, I'm sure they could have found another position with the Commonwealth for me, something that would keep them happy until Father—something that would keep them happy."

Drex remained silent.

"I don't want to be here, Drex. They aren't making Quen—I'm sorry, *Prince-Elect Quen*—come home, and he's the one they should worry about." *Elect.* She wanted to laugh at the superfluous title but pressed her lips together. The senate had never elected a king or queen from outside the Rendon family. Drex knew that.

"Because no one can find Quen," Drex said. "If they could, they'd recall him just like you. Faster, in fact."

"They could find him if they wanted." Avery shook her head as the aeroflyer lifted off into the crowded aero street above Asria's capital. "They just haven't looked hard enough."

That wasn't quite true, though. Quen had sent her dozens of messages over the years, and she'd turned them over to her father like the dutiful daughter she'd once pretended to be. It might have been mostly self-serving, since Quen's presence on Asria negated hers, but each time the senate's agents reached whatever planet he transmitted from, Quen was gone. Then there was his last message, two years ago now: *If they take me back to Asria, it won't be alive.* Quen had always been a little melodramatic, but she'd believed him that time.

The aeroflyer joined a stream of traffic headed north into central Cadena, and despite her irritation, a rush of excitement filled her as the approaching skyline loomed larger and larger in the window. Cadena grew skyward instead of sprawling out, the tallest buildings springing out of the flat, dry plain along the Cadena River to touch the sky. Unusual for Asria, the design was a necessity because of its location between two mountain ranges: the high and just-about-always-snowcapped Gallis Mountains and the lower, still-hidden Pelanco Mountains, where she'd spent half her childhood wandering alone, enjoying her limited freedom.

"They're doing their best, Avery." Drex folded his arms, seemingly oblivious to the mountains. "And until they find him, we need you here."

"Hmm." She glanced out the window and narrowed her eyes at the view that had become unfamiliar. Quen's whereabouts weren't worth arguing about right now. "Where are we going? This isn't the fastest way back to the palace. I'd wanted to see Mother."

Drex closed his eyes in mock pain as the aeroflyer turned again. "Senate building. Your father and Prime Minister Baylen are waiting for you. And before you ask, no, you can't go home first. Sorry. Believe me, I've been dreading this visit myself."

Avery gazed down at her traveling clothes, the soft pearl tunic over slim leather pants—commonplace on Ventana IV but less appropriate on fashion-forward Asria. With a sharp glance at Drex, she smoothed her shirt and shook her head.

"Is this how it will be?" Her fists already ached from clenching them. "He's going to dictate every move I make? You'd think he could at least let me freshen up first after six weeks of traveling if he was going to parade me around in front of the prime minister."

"He's doing his best, and you look just fine." Drex's cool tone hadn't changed, but now his jaw tightened. "Don't be so hard on him."

"He's not doing his best if he's telling me what to do." Even as a cadet, she'd had too much freedom on Ventana IV to accept his unexpected control without a fight. "I suppose he'll have security following me around everywhere I go, too."

Drex laughed. "Just me."

"You?" Her head tilted to the side. Drex was in charge of Father's security team. He wasn't a bodyguard—not that she could bring herself to mind if Drex followed her around.

"Well, Wynne Ferran and me. She's on loan from the Defense Forces. I don't know if you've met her." At her expression, he sobered. "Your parents thought having me around might ease some of the sting of coming home, and I have to admit, it'll be nice to have something to do other than sort paperwork and hand out assignments." He glanced outside as the transport descended near the senate building. "Give him some credit—he knows how hard leaving Ventana was, and he's trying to make this better for you."

"A week," she said, a hand over her eyes. The reflected sun warmed her skin. "I'll give him a week."

Drex smiled. "Good thing I enjoy my job."

CHAPTER THREE

THAT FIRST WEEK PROCEEDED AT A GLACIAL PACE, BROKEN ONLY BY AN emergency meeting of the Interstellar Security committee—which she was determined to make a good showing at. But the door was already closed when she arrived outside the small meeting chamber in the senate building, and Avery checked her comm with no small amount of trepidation. Late for her first meeting? She would never hear the end of it. But no—she was ten minutes early. Steeling herself, she pushed open the heavy wood door and slipped inside. So what if they wanted to stare at her tardiness? If they were going to violate protocol and start without her, she didn't mind violating a small security regulation.

A shadow fell across her face as her feet hit the soft carpet inside. None of the fifteen senators turned at her entrance, their attention focused on the slight woman pacing in front of the wall of windows. Even though they'd begun without her, Sal Zarragossa, the head of the Interstellar Security committee, cut Avery a sharp look that wouldn't have been out of place in her first year at the academy. Avery smiled her politest in return as she slipped into the last empty seat.

"As I was saying before we were interrupted," Zarragossa went on, "the past two weeks have seen the attacks of four minor systems, none Commonwealth members, by the Imperial Haederan Navy. We've yet to understand where they obtained the resources for this, although we naturally suspect mercenaries."

Avery swallowed a discourteous retort. Thirty seconds into the meeting, and Zarragossa's assessment of the Haederans' military strength was already wrong. The Haederans had always had the strongest military presence in their sector. It was the reason they could stay isolated—when they chose to, which wasn't often enough to suit the rest of the quadrant.

Worse, according to the reports that had landed on her desk just the day before, that isolation appeared to be diminishing of late. Over the past decade, the Imperial Haederan Navy had built itself up to the level of the First Haederan Empire. Two new shipyards orbiting Haedera III in just the past year suggested further expansion was imminent. Why else would a four-planet system need a military that large, if not to advance their sphere of influence? It wasn't for defense, that much was certain. No one in the quadrant wanted their system.

Yes, Zarragossa was mistaken—or worse, naïve—in underestimating how badly the Haederans wanted to conquer other worlds. The Interstellar Commonwealth of Autonomous Planets and Modules—the Modules being a single deep-space habitat that had long since disintegrated—had been formed as a military response to the Haederans' imperialist tendencies, after all. Asria was a founding member, but their location tens of thousands of light-years from the remaining Commonwealth planets made them particularly vulnerable. To be sure, the distance had kept the Haederans away in the past, but technology had improved since then. Far from Haedera also meant far from Ventana and the Commonwealth's collaborative protection. The Royal Asrian Defense Forces, the interplanetary military of a small system, could only protect them so much.

Zarragossa rattled off a list of planets as she walked back and forth under the cerulean Asrian flag hanging from the ceiling above her, her dark hair a blunt contrast to the gold aster charge.

"Thaopra, Hanides, Naraka, Iythea—all atmospherically uninhabitable, all now boasting a Haederan Army land base. Recent intelligence suggests they have begun mining operations on those planets. I need not remind anyone how worrying the progress of these invasions are."

No, no one in this room needed that reminder. All four planets were in a general direction toward Asria. But why those? The Haederans had shown little interest in uninhabitable worlds before. They wanted to control people, not barren planets with zero economic value. Imperialists, the lot of them.

Then again, they were mining *something*. Asrian intelligence had to be mistaken about the lack of economic viability on those planets. Zarragossa's conclusion was wrong.

"We've dispatched a courier to Ventana IV to ask for reinforcements to our own forces." Zarragossa scowled at Avery again, as though all Commonwealth decisions fell on her shoulders. "But we are doubtful they will act on our concerns."

Avery crossed her ankles and suppressed an eye roll. Zarragossa had always been outspoken about Asria's membership in the Commonwealth and frustrated that her wish for Asria's withdrawal would never come true in her lifetime. No wonder that waiver for the academy had been so hard to come by and so easily rescinded.

"But for the moment," Zarragossa finished, "we must assume the Haederans know better than to strike a Commonwealth world. I'll open the floor up for discussion now."

"What if you're wrong?" The question came from an unfamiliar voice—probably a newly elected senator.

At least one member was nervous. *Good.* Zarragossa lacked the imagination needed for her job, and Avery was too new to say anything herself. Perhaps in a few more weeks . . .

Zarragossa motioned to her right, reluctance obvious in the gesture. "General Teruel can speak to that, I believe."

Avery sucked in a breath as Teruel stood from the front row with frank seriousness and viewed the small crowd. With what she hoped was a furtive glance, she took another look around. No, Merritt wasn't here, just as he hadn't been waiting for her at the landing pad when she arrived home. Odd that Teruel was attending such a critical meeting without his senior aide. Where was Merritt? And more importantly, was it inappropriate to ask Teruel afterward?

"We're deploying forces planetwide," Teruel began, "including scout ships on routes near and through the disputed planets. Nightflares are ramping up their patrols—we're recalling another eight from heavy maintenance to bulk up the fleet."

He waved at the projector on the side wall. The lights dimmed, and a holographic map of the system appeared, floating just to his left side.

"It won't be possible to send any ships past communication range with the Haederan fleet closing in, so we've been modifying several of the outer system modules to relay communications and extend their range. That work will be completed in another two weeks. Until then, our range will be limited to our current capability. You can see here how we've deployed our troops to keep as many shielded bases operating as possible."

His voice, along with the rest of the Defense Forces' strategy, faded into a dull drone in her mind until Zarragossa spoke once more.

"Anything else?" she asked. The room was silent, and she nodded. "Then that concludes this session. We'll reconvene in three days, unless otherwise required."

Avery took a deep breath and stood, intent on disappearing before Zarragossa could corner her with a disparaging comment about the Commonwealth. But it was Teruel who met her in the doorway and gestured her into the corridor, away from the rest. She couldn't help a grateful smile, and he laughed before she could say a word.

"Painful, wasn't it, Your Highness?"

"It was—" When the sound of Zarragossa's shoes became

fainter in the sun-splashed corridors, Avery's shoulders relaxed. "Pretty bad."

"Can I tell you a secret?"

"Of course."

"It only gets worse from here." He clasped his hands behind his back and glanced behind them. "And I must say, I'm sorry to see you back here and subjected to it."

Temper the disappointment . . .

"Yes, well—" She swallowed. "I suppose it's no secret around the senate that I'm sorry to be back here too, is it?"

"Scarcely a secret at all, and I was sorry to hear about it. I'm sure you're destined for better things here, though."

"Thank you, sir," she replied with deference instilled into her at the academy. "I hope you're right."

"If it helps, you're more than welcome to drop by any time and talk." His eyes sparkled, and something told her it wasn't at the prospect of discussing flying. "If you don't mind talking to a washed up Nightflare pilot, that is. I'll warn you though, Parker's not expected back from *Palafox* for another few days."

The sparkle in his eyes turned to a grin, and she ducked her head, desperate to regain her dignity. She and Merritt had always kept their on-and-off relationship low-profile, but her personal life was more on display in Cadena than she liked—even though she'd been gone for years. It was too humiliating for half the planet to recognize how much she loved Merritt when she struggled with the emotion herself.

"*Palafox*? The morning report said she's out past Emot right now." The *Barrancas*-class surveillance ship was tasked with listening in on any foreign military ships that came near the system. That wasn't Merritt's job now that he was working for Teruel, so it had to be his choice. "What's Merritt doing all the way out there?"

Teruel pressed his lips together as a sentry passed, then laughed. "Oh, this and that. I'm sorry for embarrassing you, but it wasn't hard to miss you looking around for him when you noticed me. And I'm sorry he wasn't on Asria to welcome you home, but it couldn't be helped. Drop by anytime—or better yet, call my office soon. We'll give you his arrival information."

* * *

She hid in her office on the seventh floor of the senate building for the rest of the afternoon and stared at the mosaic pattern in the marble floor—when she wasn't pacing the perimeter of the room, unable to focus on work or anything but Merritt. What had he done to her, that three years after she'd last seen him, she'd made a fool of herself in a senate meeting just looking for him—and in front of General Teruel, no less? She cringed inwardly at the idea that anyone else might have noticed.

They probably had, because she and Merritt had been together forever, had been well-known in Cadena, even though their future had been hazy from the first day. As a teenager, she'd made it clear to him she wouldn't be staying on Asria any longer than necessary, and she'd watched him rise from a lieutenant in the Royal Asrian Defense Forces to General Teruel's top aide. But success had its costs. He'd never had enough time for her, and she'd never planned on being planetside much longer for him. Maybe they hadn't ever had a chance. She could remember their first proper fight like it'd been the day before. It should have been a sign, but they'd pressed on, too caught up in promises and the deliriousness of childish love.

She'd been twenty and already planning her escape. Had just drafted her first petition to the senate to let her attend the academy, in fact. Merritt's career was taking off, and with the bustle of work, he'd been unaware of her unhappiness. They'd walked through the center of Sliak, along the Giftan River on Emot, the outermost planet in the Asrian system and Merritt's latest assignment as a Defense Forces analyst.

Even amid what passed for a large settlement on Emot instead of the woods they loved so much, she'd never felt such contentment, but a current of unease had settled in as they crossed another bridge. She'd only come here, had spent all that time on the intrasystem shuttle, to tell him in person about her petition. Merritt had pulled her close, his breath tickling her neck and sending shivers down her arms.

"I could spend all day like this with you," he'd said. "Longer, even."

"Me too." She said the words he expected to hear, but the unease grew as his lips grazed her ear. "Mer, can we talk somewhere?"

He stopped in his tracks and led her into the nearest café, where he ordered wine for both of them, perhaps already knowing he might need to drink both glasses. She left hers untouched and slid her handwritten request in front of him. Without a word, he skimmed through the draft, then looked up and frowned in controlled disapproval.

"I didn't think you'd really do this. Don't you think we should have talked about it first?"

"I told you I would. I want to fly, and I can't stay on Asria and do that. I can't stay on Asria and do anything I want."

"Of course you can. The Defense Forces always needs pilots."

Merritt could be so frustrating—and literal. He knew what she meant. Didn't he? Defense Forces pilots spent their time patrolling inside the system and escorting unidentified spacecraft. No rush, no flashiness, no danger, no leaving the Asrian system. Worse, he'd only done a year as a patrol pilot before moving on, and that rapid promotion would never happen to her. The Asrian military would never want it to appear they had granted her special privileges, no matter how well she flew. She'd languish—on Asria, if she was lucky, on an outstation like Emot if she wasn't—with the rest of the leftovers. The Commonwealth, on the other hand, didn't see her any differently from anyone else.

Except for the waiver.

"You know why the Defense Forces isn't an option," she said. "There's so much more out there for us. Don't you ever wonder?"

"Not really. I've seen other star systems. I choose to stay here."

Avery swirled her drink as they sat in silence, too stubborn to take a sip of the wine Merritt had selected and too disappointed that he felt staying on Asria was a realistic future. Didn't he understand how limiting it was? She'd been explaining it over and over, for years. Building a life where people knew her for what she did instead of what family she belonged to was the only route to happiness.

"I thought you'd be happy I took the first step," she finally said. It was a lie, mostly. She'd been afraid he'd react like this. "I didn't know it was going to ruin the entire day."

"You've been talking about it since I met you. But that was all I thought it was—talk." He looked away, out the window toward the river, then closed his eyes and sighed. "I didn't think you'd really do it now. That's at least three years on Ventana and then who knows how long away from here."

"What if I agreed to only one term? That's only five more years on top of the academy, right? Easy. It'll be over before we know it." She reached for his hand, but he refused the invitation.

"You don't get it, do you? I don't want you light-years away from me!" Merritt ran his hands through his hair. "I wanted— dammit, Avery, while you were here, I was going to ask—"

He was going to ask what?

Her stomach dropped, and it wasn't from her untouched wine. *This isn't how this is supposed to happen.*

But if a proposal was what he meant, his feelings made sense. He was five years older than she, more than ready to settle down. They'd known each other for two years. Her throat closed up. She hadn't toyed with him or led him on, so that couldn't be it. She'd always been open about her desire to leave Asria. To do something important with her life.

She placed her hand on his, but he jerked it away. Self-consciously, she pulled hers into her lap.

"I didn't know you felt like that." It came out as a whisper.

"How did you think I felt? I love you, Avery, more than I ever thought I could love someone. I'll love you for the rest of my life, and I want everyone to know that." His gray eyes flickered away from her. "I didn't know you were one foot out the door already, and now I feel like a fool."

"Mer, it's just a petition. They'll probably deny it."

"And you'll request it again and again until you get out of here!"

Her eyes widened. "I hadn't yet thought about what I would do if they denied it. I suppose I'd assumed I would request it again, yes."

Merritt stood without a word, and they walked back to his flat in silence, where they sat in even gloomier silence on his small sofa.

"I know this is awkward, but I can't leave for another two days," she whispered. "The intrasystem shuttle—there's no departure until then."

"It's fine." He didn't even look at her. "The guest room is open. You're welcome to it."

"That's not what I mean." Frustrating as it had been when they'd first met, Merritt's overly principled ban on intimacy had never mattered less—not when their entire relationship was on the verge of falling apart. "I wish I could explain everything, but there's no good place to begin."

If she accepted his proposal, she would never fight the senate for her waiver. She'd never leave Asria if that happened, but she had to see through her dream of flying before she started with another. And if they agreed to wait for each other, what did an engagement matter? She couldn't explain any of that to him when it scarcely made sense to herself.

Beside her, Merritt shifted.

"You don't need to explain. I'm sorry for what I said earlier. I was too harsh." He pulled her close, and she leaned her head against his chest, too ashamed she'd interrupted his planned proposal to look at him. "If you're not ready, you're not ready.

We'll keep on doing what we've been doing. You need to follow your dreams."

"But that's not fair to you," she said to his shirt.

"It's not about what's fair and what's not. Reality dictates life, sometimes, and no matter what it brings, I love you. I'll wait."

And he had. He'd been transferred back to Asria six months later, and she'd been thrilled to see him back home, though she'd hadn't been as ecstatic at his less-than-eager reaction to the senate's eventual approval of her waiver and, later, her departure to Ventana.

But that was over now. They were both on Asria at long last, and there was no reason to wait.

Well. Technically, there were quite a few, but none of them mattered anymore, did they? She and Merritt had overcome everything before now, and they'd overcome everything else that came up.

Shadows grew deeper in the corners of her office as she mused it over. With a sigh, she flicked the desktop with a finger and reached for the communication card to call Teruel's office.

* * *

The curls slipped from Avery's hands one more time as she wrangled them into some kind of style Merritt would appreciate. She gave herself a baleful look in the mirror, tossed the handful of pins to the side, and let her hair fall over her shoulders. If Merritt was happy to see her, it wouldn't matter how she looked. If he had misgivings about their overdue reunion—well, she wouldn't spend more time on her appearance. She'd spend it worrying about how the evening would go instead.

Merritt had wanted to meet at Cadena's public launch site, but Drex, who'd assumed that meant a flight in whatever experimental aircraft Merritt was building this time, had refused to allow it. No amount of arguing or threats—and there had been many—had persuaded him. He wouldn't allow her to die in a crash two weeks into his new job, he'd said, and Avery had sent word, not without a bit of resentment, for Merritt to meet her in one of the palace gardens. Drex, of course, was correct about what Merritt had planned, but this was just the situation she'd feared when they'd called her home.

Her father could not make decisions for her, the senate could not make decisions for her, and Drex could not make decisions for her.

Except they could and they were.

After three years coming and going as she pleased—normal academy restrictions notwithstanding—Drex now had her on a short rope, like a child who couldn't be trusted on her own. That would have to change, and so would the guards who trailed her as she made her way downstairs. Somehow, she would find a way to make it change.

Merritt was already waiting on a bench by the reflecting pond when she arrived, and she could tell with a glance that he was uncomfortable. He'd always hated the palace's formality, even if it was imagined, and she hated that she'd made him come here, but she'd been unable to come up with another choice to satisfy Drex and Wynne.

She smiled hello as she approached, and he stood and grinned in return. Oh, he hadn't changed a bit in three years. Or was there now a bit of gray in his light brown hair to match his solemn gray eyes? Cut as short as it was, it was hard to tell. Thirty-three was too young for gray hair—she hoped for her own sake—but working for someone like Teruel had to accelerate it. He wore it well though, and even though the new maturity stressed their difference in ages, he was hers. He'd always been hers, ever since that cold autumn day so long ago when they'd first met. How had she ever walked away from him?

She stared a moment longer than appropriate, taking in everything about him, from the new hair color to the new fatigue lines around his eyes. How his shoulder was at the perfect height on which to lay her head and how polished and pressed his clothes were, even though he was just home from weeks away on *Palafox.*

"Hi," he said.

"Hi."

Something fluttered in her chest at the sound of his welcome, earnest and innocent. She could do nothing but repeat his greeting, an automatic and instinctive response. Seeing him took her breath away, and the awareness of how she reacted to him flustered her more.

"You're staring." He looked amused, on the verge of laughter, but he was still more composed than she had any hope of being. Dignity, that was Merritt.

"Am I?"

She held a hand to her cheek. *Please, don't let it be red.* The heat beneath her fingers told her otherwise, and she ducked her face to the side. He knew just what he did to her, and now he was doing it on purpose. Teasing her. The infatuation she'd felt when she first met him was back. Only this time . . . he was already hers.

His laugh escaped, and he held out a hand. "I missed you. It's been a long time."

"I missed you, too. Congratulations on the promotion."

She edged toward him and linked her fingers with his. Had it been too long? She'd been the last to find out about Merritt's promotion to lieutenant colonel over a year ago, just like she was the last to find out about anything that happened on Asria. But that had been her decision.

"Thank you." He sounded pleased, then ran a hand across his head. "I was afraid you wouldn't make it tonight."

"You know me better than that."

"I know." Was it her imagination, or did a shadow cross his face? He drew her into an embrace, his lips tickling her ear. "I missed this, too."

A jolt of arousal sparked through her and she drew back, though she didn't let go of his hand as they walked along the edge of the pool. Merritt swung it between them as he cast sideways glances at her, but she couldn't move closer to him. Not yet. Maybe never.

"When did you get back?" she asked, glimpsing a sentry up on the second level. The pleasantry was innocent, but the heat inside of her was uncomfortable and foreign after so long. And now they had an audience.

"This morning," he replied.

"Oh. You must be tired."

"Not really." He sounded so short with her. Had she upset him, or was it something else?

"I would be." She swallowed, then the nervous prattling spilled out. "You know, it was almost two weeks until I adjusted back to Asria's gravity after being in space so long. It was exhausting. I thought I'd never become used to it again. They actually kept the gravity on *Rascal* a little higher than usual on the way back since there were a few Voirian passengers on board, but you know that always doesn't—"

"Avery." He pulled her against him. "Stop."

"Am I boring you?" Her heart skipped. In truth she was prolonging the inevitable, because the inevitable was terrifying. Jumping off a cliff and trusting him to catch her was the most frightening thing she'd ever experienced.

"You're doing something to me, but boring me isn't it." He laughed again, lower this time. "And I think you're well aware of it."

His eyes turned serious behind his dark lashes, all pretense at flirtation gone. A breeze caught her hair and whirled it about her face, but before she could grab it, he caught a strand. He ran his finger along its length then tucked it back behind her ear, a gesture that always made her melt.

"Mer—" An ache began somewhere deep inside her. There were no excuses this time. What if she wasn't ready for him, for *them*? It'd been so long.

"Why are you looking at me like that?" he interrupted.

"Like what?" she whispered.

"Like you're terrified of me."

"I'm not terrified of you."

He leaned toward her and brushed her lips with his, and she was certain it was only her grip on him that kept her upright. His kiss—all of him—was softer and warmer than she remembered. Was that what three years apart did to a memory? Did time shatter memories into tiny pieces that were unrecognizable when put back together?

"There," he said to the side of her face. "That's nothing to be afraid of, is it?"

"No." Shivering, she took a deep breath. "But you can't tease me like that."

"Who said anything about teasing?" His eyes sparkled, and he wound his hand through her hair. He'd be able to feel her heart beating this close, but she didn't care. She'd needed his kiss for three years and hadn't even known it. If this was the reward for being forced home, she might not care about being trapped here. Her eyelids drifted closed, and she braced herself for the next onslaught of unfamiliar sensations.

A cool breeze washed between them.

"I can't do this." Merritt untangled himself, leaving her empty and alone.

"Can't do what?" she asked. She reached for him, but he took a step back. He tried to dart around her, and that time she grabbed his arm. "Mer, what's wrong? What—what happened?"

"I'm sorry. This isn't you." A flash of fabric disappeared around a column above them, and he shook his head, then waved at the lush plantings, the trickling fountains. "This isn't me."

Kusir. Sentries were prowling around now, interrupting, *watching.* Drex had insisted on interfering tonight, but he knew better. He knew Merritt had grown up in what might as well have been a shack, that he hated all of this, felt uncomfortable around the wealth and trapped by the security precautions.

"Then let's go somewhere else. I'll talk to Drex, right now. Maybe we can go somewhere else. I know it's too late to find your favorite spot in the mountains, but maybe tomorrow we can plan something, or whenever you have some time off, we can spend all day together like we used to, and—"

"No." This time the interruption was cold. "I'm sorry. I have to go, Your Highness."

Her throat closed up.

He couldn't mean that. Merritt had never been comfortable with her family's position, but—but no. They should have moved past this. Merritt should have moved past this. He didn't understand, and she needed to make him understand somehow.

But how?

"Avery, Merritt." Her voice broke. "It's Avery. You know it's me. Nothing's changed. Please don't do this."

He didn't look at her again. Only a single cough from somewhere in the distance interrupted his retreating footsteps, and when he disappeared through a doorway at the end of the garden, she fell to the nearest bench and cried.

CHAPTER FOUR

The silence woke her, heavy and still. Disoriented by the quiet, Avery jerked awake and waved at the sconce by the side of her bed. It refused to light, and she waved at the overhead lights with the same result. The insistent darkness had to be a power outage, but the low hum of the background generators was missing, too. Those would have turned on automatically if the main power grid to the palace had gone down, which meant . . . what? A major technical problem or something more ominous? She burrowed under the covers, pretending the childish action would change things, but a hot flash pulsed through her as if her body knew something her brain hadn't yet grasped.

Something was wrong.

Voices sounded in the parlor, and she jumped from underneath the warm covers to look for another light—something, anything, that worked. Her feet had scarcely hit the floor when a furious banging on her door added to the voices. She didn't have time to answer before Wynne flung the door open, a flashlight pointed at the floor.

"Get dressed." Wynne, fully dressed, didn't appear as though she'd bothered with anything as banal as sleep in a long time.

"Half the Haederan fleet just dropped out of hyperspace right outside Emot."

"What?" Ice squeezed Avery's chest as she dug through a stack of freshly unpacked clothing and pulled on a pair of velvet leggings. That was why Wynne was so awake—it was impossible to be anything else anymore. "When?"

"Ten minutes ago," Wynne replied. "They didn't shut everything down until five minutes later. I hope they weren't too late. We've got to get you downstairs."

Too late. Without the power, the Haederans could see some targets, but it might be enough to confuse their targeting systems. Even so, Emot was too close. How had they gotten this far, well past the Defense Forces outer system defenses?

And what else had Wynne said?

Downstairs?

Holy One.

Wynne was talking about the bunker. As a child, Avery had played in the network of underground shelters built before the Asrian Civil War, but it was only as an adult that she'd realized the full purpose of them—to protect the royal family from assassination and worse. The idea of hiding in one of them, waiting for an explosion to bury them under a kilometer of rubble, froze her more than anything she'd have done in the Commonwealth Navy.

"Wynne, don't send me down there," she protested. "Please. Where are my parents?"

"For once in your life, can you do what you're told without arguing?" There was fear in Drex's voice as he entered her parlor and held the door open behind him. "Your parents were already halfway to Sabino when we heard, and they've taken shelter elsewhere. They'll be fine. Worry about yourself now, please."

"All right." It was a straightforward thing to agree to most anything when Drex was afraid. She could pray for Mother and Father later. And if it came down the worst . . . she could mourn them later, too. "All right," she repeated.

Wynne fell into place behind her as she crept through the

palace behind Drex. It was dark and silent, except for the confused shouts of guards outside. The Haederans would have surely planned to take out the palace and senate buildings second, right after they dealt with Alcaris, the Defense Forces headquarters just outside Cadena. And Merritt would be at Alcaris now, would have returned as soon as he received word of the invasion.

Please let him be safe.

Drex keyed a code into the pad near the doorway and pushed her toward the stairwell. "Down. Quickly."

Avery took the stairs two at a time, and the upper levels of five-hundred-year-old brick faded away into new with smooth, fortified steel sides. Drex and Wynne's footsteps echoed in the stairway behind her, and her breathing slowed as she reached the bottom. Everything would be fine. Safe underground was better than in danger up above.

Drex shut the bottom door, and her ears filled with pressure as he sealed the room in. The ceiling of reinforced steel wasn't quite twice her height, lower than she remembered, and the rest of the shelter wasn't that big, either. Avery paced off the longer wall—seventeen short, confining steps. Small, but then again, it wasn't meant to shelter more than a few people at a time. She flipped open one door of the floor-to-ceiling cabinets that lined the free wall, dismayed at the amount of field rations packed inside that would allow for an extended incarceration. It would be possible to stay here for weeks if the Haederans didn't have weapons that could penetrate this deep, if the environmental systems stayed functional.

Weeks.

Her stomach churned, and she gasped for air, suddenly short of breath. Staying in this small underground room for weeks was the last thing she wanted to do. Some of her classmates had dropped out in the first few weeks of training, unable to handle the small cockpit of a Dragonfly. It had never been an issue for her since space—wide, open space—was just on the other side of the windows. But small rooms with no escape—yes, those would be her undoing. Best to die now if it came down to it, instead of starving to death in a tiny hole underground.

Clearly unaffected by the limited space, Drex settled himself in front of a console across from the entrance, and black screens whirred to life. Avery leaned over his shoulder and pretending the ceiling didn't exist as he brought up a patch to a Defense Forces system. The main screen told the story, or at least all the story she needed to know: two cruisers, a dozen heavy bombers, two troop ships, and one command and control ship.

"Drex, that's—" She worked her jaw back and forth, trying to remember. "That's got to be more firepower than our entire fleet!"

"It is. More fighters than we have, too."

"But how did they slip by the nets?" The surveillance nets should have provided advanced notice of such a situation, light-years from the two populated planets in the system. "They've never made it past Emot before."

"They've never made it anywhere close to Emot, if we're being technical. And if we live through this, we'll have to figure out how that happened." Drex waved a finger at the controls, and the display changed from an orbital readout to ground-based surveillance. "They're launching Nightflares from Alcaris now. Again, too slow."

Not Merritt.

Avery sank to the chair beside him as a low rumble shook the shelter. Merritt couldn't be flying, not now. He had to be safe at home. He couldn't be flying into this—but there was no question he was. Hand over her mouth, she turned away, unable to watch. Ten hours. She'd seen him just ten hours ago.

"Is that orbital?" Wynne asked from across the room.

Another explosion sounded, louder and longer the second time, echoing in Avery's chest. Any other day, it would have sounded like thunder. Odd how something so life-changing could sound exactly like something so mundane—something she'd never be able to experience again without thinking of this attack.

The Haederans weren't just stealing Asria itself, they were stealing the tiniest joy that a summer thunderstorm brought.

Drex shook his head. "Those are low altitude bombers. They know where the fleet is based, and they're trying to make sure our interceptors can't reach orbit. I can't believe they've gotten this close already."

Avery closed her eyes. Teruel could spread assets all over the planet, but there were only so many places to send them, and Uncle Victor would have known about all of them. He would have directed the enemy where to strike.

Have mercy on us.

"I wish—" she began. Drex would have a lot to say about what she wished, but she rushed on. Anything was better than sitting here staring at those screens, even spilling her greatest desire right now. "I wish I was up there. I should be up there. Merritt tried to talk me into it for so long, and—I said no. It should be me. It shouldn't all fall to him."

"You're safer here," Drex replied.

"I don't want to be safe. I should be doing something, not sitting here and waiting to die."

"Should you?" He raised his eyebrows. "I would think you have other responsibilities right now."

"Perhaps," she snapped. "Even so, I wish you'd stop telling me what I should think and want and do. You don't know me as well as you think you do."

"I know you well enough. I know sometimes our desires are selfish. Maybe you were called back to Asria for a reason."

He sounded all too certain about her fate, but at least growing anger was overtaking fear. She could handle anger. Anger wasn't humiliating. And there was enough anger to go around. Victor—the Haederans—even Merritt for walking out on her, not caring that it was the last time she'd ever see him.

"You're being ridiculous, Drex." Avery ran her hands over her face and gulped in air that seemed to grow thinner by the second.

"I'm only here because my family couldn't follow a law that's been in place and followed for hundreds of years. Nothing more."

"Are you sure about that?" Drex leaned back in his chair and regarded her with a look she knew all too well and hated.

"I'm very sure. And I'd rather appreciate it if you didn't imply I'm meant to die under a building's worth of rubble."

"Death isn't the end, Avery. Your parents taught you better than that. I taught you better than that."

Not this again. She stood and paced toward the bunk in the corner, wish she could hide under the covers like a child and never come out. Another explosion, louder than thunder this time, echoed above them as though to argue his claim. How could he talk of eternal life now? Didn't he understand how many Asrians were dying tonight?

"Stop scaring her, sir." Wynne sounded sharp—and on her side since the first time Avery had met her. "It's not helpful."

"Most would be comforted."

Despite her fear and anger, Avery's soul softened a bit. Drex meant well.

"I know what you're trying to do," she replied. "And I appreciate it. But right now—I'm just not in the right frame of mind."

Drex nodded and leaned forward, his elbows on the console as the lights in front of him flashed alarm after alarm. His eyes were closed, though, and she knew he was praying.

CHAPTER FIVE

THE CHRONOMETER ABOVE THE DOOR DECLARED IT WAS THE SECOND day of the orbital siege, but in some ways, it might as well have been a week. In other ways, the attack might have begun five minutes before. The shields at the two air bases on the far side of Asria had somehow held throughout the previous day. Neither had effective ground-to-space offensive systems though—only small contingents of atmospheric aircraft, and those had been all but destroyed in the first hours of the attack. The same had happened to the fighters from Alcaris. The Commonwealth base at Rincon, halfway across the planet, had unquestionably been damaged, if not obliterated.

After reviewing the damage, Avery paced the small shelter that was more like a prison cell—or a tomb. She tried not to think of Merritt, but not thinking of him was a losing battle. He had to be safe. Had to be. And perhaps he was.

With no Asrian interceptors left, the Haederan fighters had retreated to space hours before. The thunder of orbital shelling still filled the bunker, no doubt still directed at Alcaris, Rincon, and the other Defense Forces bases. It was quieter than the atmospheric battle the day before, but she wasn't close to hoping it was over.

Drex remained hunched over the communications equipment as she paced, trying to raise someone, anyone. The crackle of an empty radio line said everything. No one at Alcaris had responded since the day before, and the small comm station under the palace didn't have the power to reach any other Defense Forces base.

"It doesn't necessarily mean anything," he insisted to her and Wynne once more, rolling a stylus between his fingers. "Their communications might be destroyed—or the Haederans are jamming them. Or they might shut everything down intentionally."

"False optimism." Avery's hands hadn't stopped shaking for hours, and the tea she'd abandoned after spilling it down her shirt had gone cold. "You can't really believe that—Alcaris is gone."

"Sometimes optimism is warranted, much as you would prefer to believe otherwise." Drex tapped a few more keys. "It looks like they're staying away from civilian targets, and Alcaris has the same shelters we do. Knowing the Haederans, I think they're clearing the way for an occupation, not a complete destruction of the planet."

"That's supposed to be a better outcome?"

"It's a better outcome for Asria."

Better for Asria, worse for her.

She started to pace again. Was it quieter than before? Her breath quickened, but the new silence couldn't be the end. Still, no planetary defense force in the Commonwealth had ever been forced to repel an attack of this magnitude, and Asria was too small to defend against such a large military. The attack had to end *sometime*.

Wynne looked up, as though she could see space from her spot on the floor. "I think the shelling's stopped."

"It appears so." Drex massaged the back of his neck. He moved between computer systems, muttering under his breath, then raised a finger. "The Haederan fleet is trying to raise Alcaris again, threatening further offensive action unless we respond to their requests for surrender."

Avery closed her eyes, decided the move made her a coward, and opened them again. So many hours of battle, but the end was too soon at the same time. Minutes ticked away, and when there was no answer from anyone at Alcaris, she sat on the bunk and waited for the bombing to begin again.

"There," Drex rubbed his face, bristly from two days without a razor. "Teruel's responding." He pressed his hand against the earpiece and listened with his eyes closed, then shook his head. "All we could've expected, I suppose. Unconditional surrender. Then, if we cooperate with their initial demands, they may agree to other terms."

Unconditional surrender . . .

Her stomach dropped. "What demands? Teruel isn't really going to agree to this, is he?"

"It's not completely up to him." Drex held a hand up to silence her while he listened and repeated the highlights.

"They want a contingent to sign the agreement aboard one of their cruisers. You won't like the names they've named. They want to know where we stashed the royal family. We have one hour to launch the shuttle and one more to produce you and your parents."

"I'll go," she whispered. It hadn't been three days since she'd stood waiting for Merritt to arrive at the palace, so certain life would go on even though she was back on Asria. So certain her future included him and joy and freedom. "But Drex—I'm afraid."

Drex stood from the console where he'd spent so many hours, his face whiter than she'd ever seen it. "Wynne and I won't leave you for a second." He sank down beside her. "And I don't believe they have anything to gain by harming you. Everything will be all right."

But she could see in his eyes that he didn't believe his own lie.

* * *

Avery hadn't bitten her nails since she was five years old and her mother had bribed her to stop, but now it took all her concentration not to resume the childish habit. Not because of her mother's disapproval, this time—in deference to her emotional fragility, the Haederans had allowed her mother to return to and remain at the palace, now secured by Haederan troops—but because chewing on her hands would make her terror apparent. Instead, as she waited outside the main senate chamber with Drex, surrounded by a dozen Haederan soldiers, she dug her nails into her palms.

They sat for over two hours, and with each minute that passed, the thought of what was being discussed inside turned her stomach to ice. Her father and Grant Baylen were meeting with the Haederan occupation governor, Taln Perrin—a high-ranking general in the Imperial Haederan Army, Drex had informed her under his breath before a soldier had noticed them speaking and put a stop to it.

She stared at her feet and tried not to imagine how horrific the general could possibly be. Instead, she summoned up a shred of courage every few minutes and glanced at the soldiers, trying to figure out the people who had attacked her home. Drex had been correct about an occupation, for the troops in the lobby were not Imperial Haederan Navy, the ones who had executed the attack and overwhelmed the Asrian military, but regular Haederan Army.

That was all she knew about them. Ground personnel of any planet's armed forces had never been relevant enough for intense study at the academy, and that shortsightedness was catching up to her now. She finally decided the stylized supernovas on the shoulders of their dark moss fatigues meant they were Zeta Division infantry, and it was an inexplicable relief to see professional soldiers instead of deranged mercenaries—even if they were Haederan. Maybe they wouldn't execute the royal family after all.

Some of them looked bored, kept pointing around the building and laughing with each other, while others stared at her and Drex like they wanted them dead. It wasn't difficult to decide which group offended her more. The bored ones, certainly. Had Asria put up so little of a fight the Haederans weren't worried about resistance? Maybe they just weren't concerned about guarding a young woman and an older man. That had to be it. It was certainly a more desirable explanation for the indifference.

"Lady Avery—he wants to see you now."

Avery jumped as the door to the main chamber opened. A green-clad soldier beckoned her inside, and she stood on legs that insisted on shaking. Drex moved to follow her, but the Haederan shook his head.

"Just her."

Drex nodded reluctantly, and her heart raced as she followed the soldier inside the chamber and sat beside Father at a large table in one of the side alcoves. Wrinkles creased his traveling clothes, and dark circles smudged the skin under his eyes, but a bit of smugness pushed away some of her fear when she recognized the relief on his face. Had it taken an invasion for him to show an ounce of feeling for her? Well, she wouldn't give him the relief he seemed to want.

She turned her attention to the Haederan occupation governor, a tall man older than her father, whose emotionless eyes matched the color of his uniform. No casual working fatigues for the general, he wore pressed trousers and a dress jacket covered with ribbons she didn't want to guess the reasons for. His choice of clothing bothered her more than his cold eyes—clean and crisp and formal, it didn't appear that invading a planet had disturbed him one bit. Asria was just another blip in his day of invading planet after planet, and he would go on doing the same thing the next day and the next.

Her cheeks flushed. How *dare* he look as though nothing significant had just happened?

"Your Highness," the governor began, with no small amount of derision in the title, "I'm sorry our first meeting had to be in a situation like this. But I'll come straight to the point," he went on. "We are quite concerned about your ties to the Commonwealth. I'm told they are especially close and recent."

Well, it wasn't surprising he had *that* bit of information. Uncle Victor had certainly talked quite a bit once he'd arrived on Haedera, not that her academy attendance was any kind of secret.

"General—" She would never give him the courtesy of calling him Governor, but a military leader wasn't able to intimidate her after three years at the academy. Who was he to her anyway? A virtual no one. *Polite but indifferent.* "If you know my background, then you also know that while I graduated, I never received a commission. My sole loyalty now lies with Asria."

Perrin quirked one side of his mouth. She'd been wrong about the emotionless eyes. There was arrogance there, and his words confirmed it.

"You mean the Haederan Empire," he replied.

She wiped her palms on the dingy velvet leggings as Baylen, ever the politician, stepped in.

"You assured us," he began, "that none of the royal family would suffer any consequences for any prior associations. This line of questioning seems unnecessary, Governor."

Avery shot him a grateful look, but Perrin gave him an exasperated hand wave.

"That was the intent before we learned of her history," he replied. "Of course, we would worry about your loyalties less if the royal family would consider pledging their loyalties to Haedera."

The blood drained from her face, and she dug her nails into her palms again. Anything to keep herself from saying what she wanted to say. Anything to keep herself from looking at the resigned look on the king's face. Her background couldn't be news to the Haederans. It wasn't news to anyone on Asria. This general was only trying to intimidate her.

"Well, we can revisit that idea at a later time." Perrin laughed, a shockingly inappropriate and pleased reaction. "I wouldn't want you to pass out right here over a simple request. Go home and think about it, Your Highness—but not for too long."

Avery stood, nodded at Father and Baylen, then stalled for a moment. Once she decided her legs would continue to support her, she turned and fled the chamber.

CHAPTER SIX

AVERY TOOK A DEEP BREATH AND PUSHED HER UNTOUCHED TEA toward the tablet containing the surrender agreement. Breakfast was the last thing on her mind, and even the familiarity of the casual family dining room next to the palace kitchen couldn't soothe her worries. Not this morning. Not with Father looking the way he was. Not with what she'd just read.

"I know you don't want to talk about it right now," she began, twisting her fingers together, "but we can't just sit here and not do anything."

Father made a valiant attempt at a frown from across the table. "No, we can't sit here and do nothing, and we won't—but you will. In case you didn't notice, they don't trust you at all." The creases around his eyes grew deeper. "I don't want anything to happen to you, and I don't know why you insist on bringing more attention to yourself. Forget the Commonwealth, Avery."

"It's too late to hide from them. They know where I've been for the past three years. I don't know why I should pretend otherwise. And I don't know how you can sit here and take this. You didn't even get a vote in this! How could the senators approve this agreement? A protectorate! Dissolution of the senate, of the Defense Forces!"

She ran a finger across the tablet's dark surface, and the hateful wording reappeared. She'd been worried about Merritt before reading that last section, but now her imagination was in overdrive. He'd been unreachable since the invasion, and though she refused to believe the worst, the worst was looking more and more likely.

What had the Haederans done to him?

A flash of fire cut through the fatigue in Father's eyes. "You would prefer to live the way they're living on Naraka, on Thaopra?" he asked. "Like the rest of their new colonies? You would prefer internment camps, secret police, shortages of necessities? The senate did what they thought was right for all of us, and you will not criticize their decision in my presence."

The mention of the Haederans' other occupied planets mollified her enough to forgo an impolite retort. No, she would not prefer to live like that. Starvation, executions, disease . . .

Asria had suffered that way during their long civil war and subsequent famine, when over twenty percent of the population had died of malnutrition. But things were different now. The Imperial Haederan Army which now patrolled the streets of Cadena didn't treat the average Asrian nearly as poorly as they treated internment camp prisoners on the other planets. That, at least, was something to be thankful for.

She was even more thankful for the presumed absence of the Haederan secret police. Even on Asria, everyone knew how the Imperial Security Command maintained control on Haedera and its conquered worlds: raids, arrests, coercion, and torture. The cameras that filled public spaces on Ventana—cameras she'd always cringed at—couldn't compare to the surveillance the Haederans kept on their own politicians, suspected dissidents, and ordinary subjects who might have crossed a security officer.

Still, it was no way to live. Not that she would risk mentioning it to Father. There had to be *something* she could do . . .

"You're right," she replied. "I don't want to be treated like that. But they're not Commonwealth members! It's supposed to be different here. The senate conveniently ignored our existing treaties, and I'll criticize them all I want."

He slammed his fist on the table, spilling his tea in his lap. "I don't want to hear anything from you about any existing treaties!"

Her eyes grew wide. Emotion wasn't acceptable in the Rendon household, and she'd always defined Father's parenting style—and ruling style, as short as it had been—as disinterested. Though he'd prepared for the throne in case of his brother's death one day, he'd always preferred his agricultural businesses, even over his own family. After Quen left, he'd become more distant, adding her mother's family estate in Sabino to his holdings. Not that Avery blamed him for retreating with her mother to that quiet piece of land. Her father had seen Quen's betrayal of the Rendon family as his own failure.

"I see breakfast is over, sir." Drex strolled in at the sound of an impending argument, and Father looked relieved at his appearance.

"Carina and I leave for Sabino in an hour," he replied, avoiding Avery's questioning gaze. "I don't know if we'll be back. She may accompany us if she wishes." He gave her one final disappointed look and stalked out.

Avery stared at his retreating figure and turned, open-mouthed, to Drex. "He's just going to walk away?"

"It's probably safer for everyone involved if he does what they want." Drex perched on the edge of the table beside her lukewarm tea and chewed on his lip. "Do you want to go to Sabino with them?"

"Did the Haederans ask him to leave?" she asked. "Can I stay here?"

"They suggested you may, but I'm worried at their willingness to allow it when your father is all but being forced out of the capital." Drex rubbed his eyes. "They might be wanting to keep a close eye on you."

She laughed, but the forced humor didn't dispel the sudden chill in the air. "I'm not sure what they think I'm going to do."

Amusement turned to bitterness as she dragged her tea toward her and swirled it around. "They can suspect me all they want, but I'm not a Commonwealth officer. That's ancient history. Someone else's life."

"They don't see it as ancient history, especially since it was just a few weeks ago. They see you as a threat. Not to mention that five minutes ago you said you weren't going to sit around and do nothing."

Her eyes flew open in shock.

"Oh, yes. I heard the entire argument, and don't think for a second that I'm going to listen to you speak like that either. That kind of talk will get you arrested. Is that what you want? I can't protect you from everything. Certainly not Imperial Security, and make no mistake, they've arrived here along with the army."

"I want them gone." She stood and headed for the summer parlor off the family dining room. It had become suffocating inside since Father's outburst, and Drex's certainty that the Haederan secret police were skulking around Cadena made her head spin. "They already know how I feel about them. Why should I bother hiding it?"

Drex, never deterred by family politics—or any other kind—followed right on her heels.

"Because, as you said," he replied, "it might as well be ancient history. You can keep fighting against your present life all you want, but you are not a pilot and you are not a military officer. You aren't doing yourself or your planet any favors by wishing you were. We cannot live in the past. Move forward. They will harm you if you don't."

She inhaled the heavy scent of roses, and the flowers made it easy to indulge in the garden's normality. "I can't believe you would talk like that. You're fine with them being here?"

"My job isn't to overthrow them. It's keeping you safe, and I can't do that if you won't stay quiet. Please? Let things settle. Can you do that for me?"

Avery pinched a bright yellow flower off the nearest rina bush and pulled its petals off one by one. What he was asking was too hard. She was too outspoken and cared too much about loyalty. Her father and uncle had pounded it into her head—and her years on Ventana IV had reenforced it. The petals dropped to the stone walkway, and she ground them in with her foot, focusing on the color bleeding into the stone.

"Your Highness?"

She jumped. Two Haederan soldiers stood in the doorway to the garden, eyeing her and Drex with curiosity. How much had they heard?

"Governor Perrin wants to see you." One of them glanced at Drex. "And alone."

Alone? And so soon after their first conversation? She looked to Drex with more confidence than she felt. He crossed his arms and nodded his unsought consent.

"Go ahead. It'll be fine."

She wasn't as certain, but she followed the soldiers through the foyer of the residence section of the palace. Palace guards would have staffed the foyer in normal times, but it had been unprotected since the Haederans had arrived. The emptiness made her shoes echo on the marble, and the clatter filled her head. Had it always been so loud? It was curious how life amplified some aspects now, like the quietness that paradoxically made life louder, while other feelings were dulled.

To her annoyance, the Haederans led her through the large breezeway that ran to the newer, more public section of the palace, where the offices and meeting rooms were located. The breezeway entered the formal, vaulted three-story main entrance of the palace, directly across from the ballroom used for official planetary events. The intricate gold leaf doors were closed and, from what she could tell, locked. There would be no more celebrations there for a long while, if ever again. Not unless—until—they overthrew the Haederans.

Perrin stood outside those intricate doors, staring at the line of paintings of past monarchs. He turned at her when she arrived, arrogance still plain in the glint of his eyes.

"It's a fascinating history you have," he said in greeting.

She skimmed the paintings of ancestors who'd never so much as seen a spacecraft, then focused on him. "I'm sure you already know everything about it."

"Of course, but being able to see it in real life is something else." He gestured to the space to the left of her grandfather's portrait where Victor's had hung. It had already been removed when she'd returned from Ventana IV. "What's missing here?"

"You know what's missing." She didn't bother to keep the hatred out of her voice. "We do not honor traitors."

"Is that so? You should consider honoring this one. His requests are partially responsible for what we're about to discuss." He waved down the hallway. "This way—we'll discuss it in private."

Avery glanced at the dozens of troops milling about. Would they stop her if she fled back to Drex?

"You're safer with me than with them, I assure you," Perrin said. "Quite a few of them wish we were still shelling you from orbit."

Not news, from the looks some of them gave her.

"And you?" she asked.

"I follow orders, and right now those orders don't include shelling you from orbit."

Comforting.

He was polite enough to let her lead him into what she'd called the Blue Room as a child, and Avery watched in silence as he circled it, inspecting the glass sea dragon miniatures that were the only part of the room she'd ever liked. Quen had liked to chase her around the palace holding them, and now Perrin was running a hand over the smallest one, a little green monster with a secretive smirk. The man was intolerable.

"Picking out trophies to take home?" she asked.

He spun around, a disdainful look on his face. "And if I am?"

Suddenly too tired to fight him, she shook her head.

"Good." He turned around again. "This room is beautiful."

"It's the King Mauris Room," She would push harder next time, when she wasn't so exhausted. Verbal jabs were the only rebellion she could manage—for now. "Named after—"

"Your ancestor who took the throne after the Asrian Civil War."

This Haederan had done his research. She had to respect that.

"He was a minor noble," she said, "but the people loved him. They'd have loved anyone who ended that war. And they loved his son—enough that our family has served Asria longer than any other."

Perrin's lips curved at her resolve. He stabbed a finger upward, and somehow she knew it wasn't in reference to the ceiling medallions. "Until now. You've forgotten the bombers?"

"No." In her anger and sudden fatigue, she had. "But we can make life miserable for you no matter what armament you have up there."

You would prefer internment camps, secret police, shortages of necessities?

At the moment, she couldn't decide which was worse.

"I don't doubt you could," Perrin said. "But you won't."

"You don't know that." She shook her head. Was it unfathomable that Asria would accept this occupation? There had been uprisings on every other planet the Haederans had taken in recent months, and they'd treated those planets much more poorly. "Even King Mauris's policies would cause an uprising today."

"Unlikely. People want normalcy. We'll give it to them, and they won't care enough anymore to launch any meaningful resistance movement." Perrin paused. "Most of them anyway. We can easily handle the ones who choose to disregard our generosity."

"You haven't allowed us to leave the palace since your troops arrived on the surface, and I doubt you're treating the rest of Asria much better. I don't call this normalcy."

"Not yet, but we'll get there. A few weeks, maybe a month,

and I'll allow businesses to open again. Limited public assembly, perhaps. Call it a test. We'll give it a bit of time to see what happens. When people are desperate for the freedom they lost, they'll take what's given to them."

She hated to admit he might be right. Everyone knew what was happening on other Haederan-occupied planets—and the average Asrian citizen would be so relieved it wasn't happening to them that they might accept whatever restrictions the Haederans imposed on them. That might not be the end of the world, though. If things on Asria settled down, it might make it easier for her to—to do what?

Nothing.

Drex was right. That part of her life was behind her now.

"And my uncle?" she asked. "What requests did he have?"

"It seems he doesn't want his planet destroyed, nor his family harmed. The emperor has seen fit to grant him that request. You should consider yourself one of the luckiest people on Asria right now."

Perrin stepped toward her, and she stumbled over the edge of an antique rug as she backed away from him.

"There's one condition, though," he went on. "You lied to me, and I know you did. I know if you had half the chance, you'd be back on Ventana in one of those fighters, and I won't tolerate any dissent from you. I'll allow you to perform your duties as before, so long as I approve of them. But if you so much as think of opposing us, not only will I hold you personally accountable for your actions, but I will revoke Asria's protectorate status. Immediately. Believe me when I tell you that isn't something you want to happen. Is that understood?"

She gripped the table next to her. "You can't threaten me."

Perrin smiled and ran his fingers over the little smirking dragon before shoving it in his pocket.

"I just did."

* * *

A few weeks later, though she found it hard to believe, Avery had to admit Perrin had kept his word. Life hadn't been normal for her, but Cadena—and the rest of the planet, for all she knew—had settled into a distrustful calm. Even the small, ineffective protests had grown smaller each day. As much as she prayed each night for open revolt, the odds of rebellion grew slimmer each day. The Haederans had learned from the insurgencies that had plagued their other territories, it seemed. Give them a little hope, and they would stay controlled with little effort. The heavy bombers that remained in orbit helped too. She couldn't blame her people—much—for wanting to live.

She could blame Merritt for his continued absence though—and did, even though she knew he'd blamed her for much the same during her years on Ventana IV. But it wasn't the same anymore. She'd come home, had expected to rekindle their relationship and move forward. Instead, she'd found emptiness and heartache where she'd expected talk of marriage.

She frowned as she tapped a fingernail at his most recent communication. Her first two messages and one personal visit to his home in Cadena had gone unanswered—but perhaps the latter had more to do with the Haederan soldier accompanying her. Her stomach had been in knots when she'd shown up on his doorstep with their enemy, but Perrin had kept his word that he wouldn't allow her outside the palace by herself. He'd relented on permitting Drex or Wynne with her most of the time, but he'd made it clear he wouldn't allow to meet with a former Defense Forces officer alone. So, the Haederan escort it had been.

It was no wonder that Merritt had replied after that with a brusque note telling her not to contact him again. He'd survived, yes, and that was a relief, but . . . it wasn't the outcome she'd wanted.

But she wouldn't cry over him again, no matter how much her heart was breaking. Not here in her office with the Haederans watching her and so much work to do. With the government in shambles, she was cooperating with any work requests the Haederans sent her way. It made rebellion easy—and almost entertaining. Bad data here, a wasted effort on obsolete intelligence there. Anything to make their lives more difficult. If nothing else, it made her *feel* better.

The tablet flashed, heralding a new message, and hope surged through her veins as she flicked it open.

Not Merritt.

Of course not.

Her forehead creased. In fact, it wasn't a message from anyone at all, just random strings of numbers running down the screen. The auto-decryption had failed, or more likely, whatever the Haederans were doing to read their communications had fouled the system. Bastards. How was she supposed to perform her duties when she couldn't even read her messages?

She was about inform Wynne of this newest surveillance when her eyes landed on the numbers once more. Familiar, almost, the sequences reminded her of . . . Dragonfly data standards? She'd spent hours studying how to hand-decode the numbers the training spacecraft used for guidance and control—then decided the useless ability was just another way to torture the cadets.

Rolling her shoulders to ease the tension which had appeared, she pulled the tablet closer. No, the numbers meant nothing, but she could test her skills, keep her mind sharp, even on random digits. She worked through the thirty-two-digit groupings, scratching solutions in the air and then on a notepad without thinking much about them. The error message was longer than any real data she'd ever worked, and by the time she finished, her mind was too tired to be angry about much of anything anymore. Drained, she examined the notepad for the first time.

She had jotted down a set of terrestrial coordinates.

In Commonwealth notation.

Her breath caught. It had to be a coincidence. She'd only been playing with the numbers, but the configuration was too specific for this to be chance. She placed the notepad in a locked drawer, then began decoding the numbers once more on a blank sheet. It didn't come as easily the second time, and it was another half hour before she verified her initial work.

The results were the same.

She rubbed her eyes and flipped the pad over, the Haederans outside her door ever so close. What to do with coordinates now? There weren't any Commonwealth maps available in the senate building, so she'd have to convert them to the Asrian system. She tapped a finger on her forehead and started the painstaking process, pausing every so often to check her math in the conversion tables she'd pulled from her bookcase.

There.

Finished, she grabbed a different, standalone tablet, typed the converted coordinates into its stored planetary map, and frowned. The location was a small shop in the ancient part of Cadena, a part of the city she hadn't visited in years. Before the Haederans, before Ventana IV, before Merritt. Dozens of scenarios flew through her head at once, none of them pleasant. Drex had warned her often enough—was this a Haederan trap?

Her gut said yes. Her mind said it was possible—but unlikely. They didn't need to resort to subterfuge, especially where she was concerned.

The one thing that was certain was that there was no way to know what was waiting for her as long as she sat in an office.

No matter what Drex said.

CHAPTER SEVEN

The lights of Cadena glittered in the pre-curfew sun as Avery crept along the crowded street, her head down and hair falling across her face. So far, no one had recognized her, which she'd expected. Before the academy, it had been different, but memories and recognition of the king's niece had faded over the past three years. She'd never been a focal part of the capital's socialite scene anyway—to her mother's dismay—and she was counting on that anonymity tonight.

It helped that all too many women in the capital shared her looks—she and Quen both had the higher cheekbones and green eyes typical of the Rendon family, but otherwise uncommon on Asria. She'd resented those light eyes forever, jealous of the brown that otherwise filled Asria, but it was a resentment not shared by most. Paradoxically, Cadena's desire to maintain the looks, if not the power, of the old nobility had led to a persistent green-eyed, dark-haired population, taller than those in communities on the other side of the world. Merritt had always sneered at the way people based marriages on such a desire, but that desire was also the reason he hadn't picked her out as a member of the royal family when they'd first met.

But he could sneer all he wanted, because if he hadn't recognized her, an unobservant Haederan soldier wouldn't either. They hadn't noticed her leave the palace, after all. The guards had left a side door near the servants' kitchen unguarded, and the second she'd ducked through it, an explosion had sounded in a park across the street. Yet another small protest had erupted ten minutes afterward, and it had distracted the soldiers enough that they hadn't witnessed her escape.

She checked her notes again—another two kilometers. With each step, the feeling of eyes on her back grew heavier. Haederan eyes, or had someone friendly followed her from the palace without alerting Drex?

No one is watching you.

No, the sensation was nothing more than paranoia. She reached into her pocket to touch the small dagger hidden there. Hidden under a desk, it had slipped through the Haederans' many searches, and for that she was thankful. The humiliating memory of having her personal rooms searched again and again by Haederan security kept her fears at bay until she reached the wall that separated the ancient part of Cadena from the modern capital. Mixed with steel and other modern materials the builders had chosen over the past five hundred years, the way the metal wound in and out of the stone and brick was artistic. Had her ancestors who'd built a wall to protect themselves against local invaders ever imagined an invasion from space?

Unlikely.

The alley she was headed for, a dark void in the evening light, was easy to find once she reached the Old City. Relieved for the shadows, she stepped off the main road and counted four doorways south to the shop with the coordinates in her notes.

Chimes sang in the wind as she pushed open the door to reveal an empty store. There was no question the place was a traditional Asrian healing shop, with shelves lined with dozens of bottles and the pungent smell of incense and herbs. Asria never changed. Shouldn't traditional medicine have gone the way of the popular ancestor worship, gone for a thousand years now? But freshly cut plants hung in bundles from the ceiling, confirming her suspicion that the shop wasn't abandoned, or at least hadn't been empty long.

A light in the back room caught her eye, and she crept toward it with a hand on her dagger. From the security of her office, it was easy enough to believe that a Commonwealth code meant a Commonwealth contact, but she wouldn't bet her life on that. No, halfway across the city, it seemed even more unlikely.

Her heart threatened to stop when a man came out of the storeroom, back-lit and unrecognizable. She drew the knife, but before she could move again, he slammed her face-first against one of the large cabinets. A cry escaped as he yanked her arm behind her, tearing her loose tunic at the seam. She spun toward her attacker, but he released her arm as soon as she did. Off balance, she crashed into the cabinet as the dagger clattered to the concrete floor.

Kusir, why was she so out of breath?

Despite the pain in her knee, she readied herself for another kick, then gasped in recognition. There was no question who the intruder was—even though shaggy blond locks had replaced the light brown military cut she'd last seen on him. He'd almost broken her arm and gotten himself stabbed, but the eyes looking her up and down glinted the same as they always had on Ventana.

"Captain Hadley. On Asria." She caught her breath as the past caught up to her. Zenos Hadley, assigned to the academy when she'd left, was one of the most flirtatious men she knew—but his way of charming women was innocent. *Unless he needs something.* "That explains everything."

"And even so, you almost stabbed me." His Voirian drawl was unmistakable, and it brought back a rush of memories. He grinned down at her, then picked up her dagger and handed it over. "Who else were you expecting, Your Highness?"

"I certainly wasn't expecting you." She shoved the knife in her pocket and examined the rip in her shirt. Nothing to be done about that. "Not on Asria. Were you at Rincon during the invasion?" One never knew with Hadley—he had a reputation for disappearing from the academy for weeks on end.

"Not during the attack, no." The denial—and his grim expression—said everything there was to say about how Rincon had fared. "We were fortunate."

"We?"

"What fun would it be if I shared all my secrets right away?" Hadley's eyes twinkled, but turned serious in a heartbeat. "Come on down and let's talk. Drop the 'Captain', too. Ears, you know."

Avery ground her shoes into the floor. "I have the feeling I'm not going to like why you're here—or what you have to say to me."

"You won't, but it doesn't matter." Hadley held out a hand toward the door. "Come on, we've got grafa tea downstairs. Can't stand the stuff, so someone might as well drink it."

She wrinkled her nose in an interrupted sneeze as he led her down a wooden ladder into the cellar, then through an earthwork tunnel to another cellar. Shielded with copper mesh, unlike the rest of the dirt-lined sublevels in the Old City, it was one computer short of a military command center. A small rashat-mallow plant in a chipped indigo pot, pilfered from the shop upstairs, was the only soft touch.

"I'm impressed," she said, running a finger along the old pottery. "You could practically run a war from down here."

At her comment, another man stuck his head around the back corner, holding a steaming cup of the promised tea at arm's length. Graying temples lent an air of experience to an otherwise boyish face; he could have been thirty or forty-five years old for all Avery could judge. His quiet appearance was the perfect complement to Hadley's buoyant enthusiasm, and despite his apparent aversion to one of her favorite drinks, she liked him before he said a word.

"So Zenos talked you into it, did he?" He held out both the tea and his free hand. "Elex Feye."

She narrowed her eyes as she shook Feye's hand and took the cup. "He's persuasive."

"That," Feye replied, "he is."

* * *

An hour later, Avery sat open-mouthed, the tea forgotten. An unfathomable heaviness had taken over the room, stealing her words and indeed, her very thoughts. She tried to breathe through it, steady and slow, but Hadley's appeal and the sheer horror of her potential fate had made the cellar shrink around her. Did he— could he possibly understand what he was asking?

"No," she said, her hands gripping the edges of her chair. The refusal came out a whisper, and she steadied her voice. Anger helped. "You've got to be kidding me. I won't do it."

"You don't have a choice." Hadley rocked back in his chair and kicked it forward again. The feet hit the floor with a clang.

"Funny, I've been hearing that more and more the past few weeks, though I have to say, I never expected to hear it from the Commonwealth. And actually, I have a choice. This is the most foolish plan I've ever heard. You think that not only can I collect intelligence for you—and why you're involved in this as a personnel officer, I can't figure out—but also smuggle it out of a complex crawling with Haederans. To you two. People who think they can wander around the city, around the planet, without proper identification and then, somehow, get that information off-world. Well, you can't do it, and I won't help you fail."

"Personnel officer?" Hadley's smirk grew. "I thought you were smarter than that."

Her teeth ground together. It was an open secret at the academy that Hadley was Commonwealth Navy Special Operations Forces and used his position to hand-select recruits for his service when he wasn't on missions himself. That made Feye the same, though it amplified the difference in their personalities.

"Then it's true." It was as close to a confirmation as she would ever receive. "And let me guess. The explosives used tonight at the protest weren't Asrian." She received no answer from either. "Fine. Whatever. Look, Captain Hadley, they trained me to fly. I'm a pilot. I'm not intelligence and certainly not special operations. I wasn't trained for this, I don't have the skills, and I won't do it."

"What difference does any of that make?" Hadley's face was unreadable, but any pretense at friendliness was gone. Feye was still silent.

"It means I'm not doing it, end of story. It's a death sentence for me. I would die for Asria and the Commonwealth, but I don't intend on walking straight into an execution, which is what I'd be doing if I agree to do this. Perrin's made that clear."

Hadley kicked back in his chair again, unfazed by her glare. "You're scared," he said after a moment or two. "You fly those things with a mere micron of metal between you and a vacuum that would kill you if you had a bad day, and you're scared of sneaking around a bit of information?" He laughed. "That's absolute nonsense. Besides, we're betting your position will keep you safe. They won't ever suspect you, and if they do, you have a better chance at surviving than anyone else."

She swallowed.

"Well, you're wrong about that. They told me—Perrin himself told me I'd regret it if I oppose them. That Asria would end up like the others. These are my people. I won't do that to them. I won't. Find someone else, anyone else. The fleet must be halfway here by now. Let them handle things!"

Hadley's expression changed to something that might have been compassion had he been anyone else.

"You've been isolated," he said softly. "It's no wonder you haven't heard. Just before Rincon evacuated, we got word the fleet has been engaging the Haederans all over this quadrant. We will come, but not yet. Not soon. There aren't enough ships. We need time, and while we wait, we need information. I'm not the enemy here. Remember that."

Her stomach dropped. The Commonwealth fleet was

supposed to arrive any day. The Defense Forces couldn't over-throw the Haederans alone, and especially not without the Night-flares. That type of military action wasn't what they'd been created for.

And Perrin was right. As long as they treated the Asrians with some semblance of respect, her people wouldn't take the risk of open revolt. They had to wait on the Commonwealth, and that was what she would do, too.

"If that's true, then nothing I do matters." She rubbed the bruise Hadley had left on her forearm. "Nothing I can do or offer will help. I'm deciding for myself now, and I won't do this. Go back to Voirs if you can, and if you can't do that, at least get out of Cadena and leave me alone. Asria is a sovereign planet, and you do not decide anything for us. Neither does the Commonwealth."

"I'd hardly call a Haederan protectorate sovereign," Hadley replied with matter-of-factness.

"You—" She stood up to leave. Hadley was the same as he'd always been. "I had no control over the senate's decision, and you know it."

"You might not have had any control over their decision. But you have some control over the way things go now." Feye waved a piece of paper in her direction. "You need to read this before you go."

She grabbed it from his hand so violently the corner tore. The shred of paper fluttered to the floor, and she watched it fall, frowning.

"What is this?" she asked.

"Don't make him ruin the surprise." Hadley leaned back and folded his arms behind his head. "Just read it."

The letterhead—the Special Operations Forces seal—grabbed her attention first, and the crease between her eyebrows grew deeper. She looked up at Hadley, who grinned in return, his eyes sparkling.

Lieutenant Avery Rendon,
You are hereby ordered . . .

She skimmed the rest, the dread that had been building since she'd followed Hadley down here twisting into all-out terror. The letter, signed by General Lew Torin, the Commonwealth's head of Special Operations Forces, granted her a Commonwealth commission—and ordered her to cooperate with Hadley and Major Feye's deranged operation.

They had trapped her.

"He can't do this. Can he?" She dropped the paper to the table and placed a palm over it. Maybe it would disappear if she pretended it was gone. "I don't understand how he can do this."

Hadley looked at Feye and chuckled. "Don't you mean, 'He can't do this, sir?'"

"You're insufferable." She tried to collect her thoughts. "The senate made their feelings on my service with the Commonwealth clear, and I will not disobey them. I don't care what General Torin wants. I'm done with them, and him. Believe me, those are words I never thought I'd say, but I'm saying them to you."

Hadley reached across for the paper and tossed it into a small incinerator on the floor next to him. "The Asrian senate is no more. As far as General Torin is concerned, we're not bound by their earlier desires any longer."

"And if I refuse?"

He folded his hands on the table and tilted his head. "Then I suppose we drag you back to Ventana to face charges when this is all over. You took a vow to serve three years ago when you arrived at the academy. Did you think the wishes of a defunct political organization voided your oaths?"

Her mouth dropped open. Hadley was using her own words against her, and she would never forgive him for that. He couldn't possibly think he could just show up and bully her into doing what he wanted. General Torin either. He was nothing to her, not anymore. There had to be a way out of this.

"Do you think your intimidation is any different from theirs?" she asked, her palms sweating.

"Probably not. But I know you're dying to help me, and I'm

not asking you to do anything you weren't thoroughly prepared to do six months ago when you were about to commission."

"It was my decision back then. I planned on flying, not slinking around an occupied planet and spying for you."

"So?" Hadley blinked in confusion, looking mystified for the first time. "What does it matter whose decision it is?"

"It matters."

She took a step toward the ladder. Hadley would never understand that helping him because she'd been threatened was the last thing she wanted to do. But maybe he was right. She was furious at his manipulation, but maybe he was right. She'd meant what she'd told Drex—she wanted the Haederans gone. What if this was her chance to do something about it? Her only chance?

Her pulse quickened as her imagination tore off in a dozen different directions. It wasn't flying. It wasn't anything she had any background in or natural talent or skill at, and it might get her killed. *Dying to help* was more accurate than Hadley had meant.

But she couldn't deny she wanted to help Asria. That she needed to help her people. Maybe Hadley's way was the only way—it wasn't as though she had a better idea.

With a frown, she sat back down and folded her arms, ignoring how the left one still throbbed.

"Fine," she said. "You win."

"I knew I would. You should just trust me on these things next time. It would save time for both of us, and a lot of frustration on your part. Now"—he reached for a tablet that Feye handed over— "can we have a rational conversation about this, Lieutenant Rendon?"

CHAPTER EIGHT

No matter how many times she wiped them on her skirt, her hands wouldn't stop sweating. She stared out the window of her office. The view of the temple and the tree Feye had made sure she knew about didn't help her nerves, and neither did the Dragonfly model in front of her. Hadley must be crazy to ask her to do this. Crazy or desperate, and she preferred him crazy. Desperation meant things were as bad in the quadrant as she suspected they were, and she needed someone to be optimistic for her. If not Hadley, who?

She picked up a silver pen and debated. True to form, Hadley hadn't given her much direction at all, so she scrawled the first thing that came to mind.

I wish I had never met you.

Hadley would think it was amusing, and it allowed her to vent her aggravation at him. Even more important, if one of the Haederans found it first, she could pass it off as a note to Merritt. It was a curt message, yes, but even an invasion hadn't stopped rumors about their relationship. It might work.

That task complete, she shuffled through a stack of public works data she could afford to lose. She selected four random disks and slipped them inside a transport folder along with the handwritten note, grateful the Haederans hadn't yet seen the need to sit inside her office and keep a close eye on her all day. Drex had left an hour before, and she glanced at Wynne, who'd been sitting in the corner ever since.

Wynne, not the Haederans, was more likely to be a problem today. The idea of a woman on her security team had been appealing when Drex had first mentioned it, but Wynne took her job too seriously. Her piercing brown eyes didn't miss a thing, and Wynne's safekeeping would have comforted her if it hadn't been for Hadley's assignment.

"I don't suppose it's worth asking if I can take myself home?" she asked. "Drex has never had an issue with it."

Wynne looked up from her tablet where she was no doubt researching how she and Drex could further restrict Avery's life.

"If you're ready to leave, we'll go now," she replied.

"Wynne." Avery gave her a pleading look. "I've lived here for years. I know where I'm going, and I'm not in any danger anymore, you know that. The Haederans have loosened so many restrictions. Please, just let me have one hour to myself." If not for Hadley's work, then to prevent herself from suffocating under the constant observation.

"No." Wynne made her way in front of the door, trapping her inside.

Exhaling in frustration, Avery scooted around her and out the door, not waiting for her to follow. With any luck, the Haederan corporal in the outer office didn't have Wynne's tenacity and would have grown tired of waiting and left.

He had not.

"What's this?" He held out a hand, boredom turning to wary interest in a second.

Avery handed the envelope over. Self-preservation kept her quiet as he flipped through the disks, though he'd be able to read the anger on her face if he looked up.

"Hmm?" he asked, when she didn't reply. "That's a question that requires an answer."

"Infrastructure information." She forced reluctance into her response. "Reports on the increased demand of the Cadena power grid. I'm taking it home to work on this evening."

He pressed his lips into a thin line. "You've never hand-carried anything before today."

The self-preservation fled. "I wouldn't have to start if you'd stop reading everything we send through our own communications systems. General Perrin wanted this kept quiet, and I'm acting in accordance with his wishes."

There. Perrin had become useful.

"You're forgetting that you're allowed to carry on your business at our discretion, Your Highness. Next time be more forthcoming, please."

Wynne grabbed her arm hard enough that Avery had to take a step toward her to maintain balance. "That's enough," she said. "Don't argue with him. Let's go."

Oh, please.

The corporal flung the folder at Avery's chest. Wynne pushed her out the door and slammed it shut.

"What did you think you were doing in there?" she said under her breath. "You are not to argue with them!"

"They can't do this, Wynne." She looked around and lowered her voice, though the hallway was empty. The corporal was probably rifling through her desk now. "How can we live with them watching our every move, telling us what we can and can't do? We have to do something."

"You had better not be up to anything." Wynne looked back at the door, still blessedly closed.

"I'm not up to anything. I swear." But on second thought . . . Wynne could be an ally if she could only convince her. Hadley's plan would be easier if Drex or Wynne were on board with it. "But I want to do something," she went on. "If you'd only listen—"

"If you do anything else to antagonize the Haederans, Drex and I will make sure you don't leave your rooms for the next five years. I don't care what your father has to say about it. You will not risk your life or his with some childish plot." Wynne hissed the words in her ear and Avery believed she'd make it happen. "Now go."

* * *

The car was already waiting outside, and Avery wanted to scream at the latest obstruction. Did Wynne distrust her so much that she wouldn't allow them to walk a half kilometer back to the palace? It wasn't even worth asking again, and she ground her teeth together as she approached it. Who needed a ride for such a brief trip?

Wynne opened the door for her, and Avery slid across the backseat to the opposite side.

"As soon as she gets in, leave and don't stop for anything," she blurted to the driver without thinking.

Rank has its privileges. Sometimes.

Wynne slipped inside the car. As her eyes met Avery's, she slipped out the opposite door and slammed it closed. The car sped off like she'd hoped it would, Wynne's shouts disappeared in the distance, and Avery darted back inside the senate building, hoping no one had seen her.

It was empty this time of day—the Haederans hadn't allowed the senate to meet since the dissolution, but she'd seen a few of the senators here and there in the past few days. Grant Baylen had even stopped her a few times to say hello, but his acceptance of the Haederans' occupation told her he wasn't to be trusted.

We need to do what they want for now, he'd told her a week ago, after cornering her outside his office. She'd started taking the long way to hers after that, avoiding any staircases where she might run across him. Yes, if she saw the prime minister now, she'd have to call off today's intrigue, for he was one person she would never ask for help. Her uncle had appointed him after all, and she couldn't help but think the Haederans allowed him to fulfill some of his functions because they trusted him.

The very idea made her sick to her stomach. But luck was on her side tonight, for there were no senators, no untrustworthy prime minister, and no Haederans, and she walked through the public area of the senate complex to the temple without being seen. Oh, there were the few people cutting through to or from work—the gardens were beautiful and there were a few shrines where anyone could pray—but no one said anything to her. That was promising.

The senate temple, the five-story granite building that filled her entire office window, stood in stark contrast to the modern senate complex. In the temple's case, the resemblance to a pair of praying hands was unquestionable, even to her. Open to the public, it was in reality only used by the senators—even her father and uncle had preferred the small chapel at the palace. She preferred neither the temple nor the chapel, tired of one more shackle that tied her to Asria and the limitations that came with it.

Not much had changed in three years, she immediately noticed as she snuck inside. The soaring ceiling still made her feel small beneath it, and the candlelight was still warm. Not as warm as it should have been, though—something was missing. She took a deep breath of fresh air as she searched for the omission.

Incense.

It was the intoxicating aroma of incense that was absent, so she climbed the marble stairs to light some at the altar. The traditional temples like this one only allowed matches, so she struck one on the side of the circular altar, worn dark from so many before her.

Round, with no beginning and no end, just like the Holy One.

The smoke drifted up toward the center vent hole high above her. Feeling somewhat comforted from the familiar aroma, she slunk into the third curved row from the altar and bowed her head—more out of nervousness than devoutness, although some of that emotion crept in, too.

What would the Haederans do if they caught her? The answer

75

to that question was all too easy to answer, for her status and her uncle's wishes could only protect her so far. The executions on Asria were no secret, and the Haederans had their own means to quash insurrections on their other conquests. On the uninhabitable planets, they forced uncooperative subjects out of the habitats to die of exposure. Whether that was immediate death in Thaopra's near-vacuum or a slow death from carbon dioxide poisoning on Iythea, it wasn't a fate she wanted to meet. Neither were possible on Asria, of course, but a one-way ride into low orbit would provide much the same ending.

Her breathing grew shallow, just like it had as she'd gasped for air during low-oxygen training at the academy. But worrying about this was futile—they wouldn't do anything to her, because they'd never find out what she was involved in. She wasn't carrying anything suspicious or acting suspiciously, merely visiting a temple to pray and worship like almost any Asrian would.

She steadied her shaking hands and removed the handwritten note from between the disks in her folder. Hadley had been certain the Haederans wouldn't come anywhere near the temple, viewing it just as sacred as her own people did, but what if someone else had seen her? Someone who wasn't loyal? Without looking around again, she leaned over and placed the note under the loose left foot of the bench in front of her.

Will You protect me? Am I doing the right thing? Help me figure it out.

Her raw nerves sparked the unscripted prayer that drifted skyward along with the incense. Relieved that Feye's test was halfway done, and eager to leave before Haederan security arrived, she all but skipped out the side door, pausing only long enough to light a single red candle on the rack outside.

* * *

That night, she switched between lying in bed staring at the ceiling and pacing in front of the windows in her parlor, waiting for the knock on her door. Alternate versions of her immediate future streamed through her mind, merging into one horrifying fate. Any minute now, Imperial Security Command officers would arrive to arrest her for espionage. Drex had warned her. Perrin had warned her. And yet, she'd done what Hadley had asked of her. That meant something, didn't it? Would they remember when she was gone?

The quiet ping of the tablet by her bed distracted her from visions of torture and death. She rolled to her side, bracing herself for whatever bad news came next, then drew her brows together.

Merritt?

Why would Merritt be messaging her now? Had he forgiven her? A familiar giddiness arose, then turned to disappointment as a flick of her finger provided the answer.

I'm hurt. But I'd still like to see you again. Same place, same time, two days?

Her shoulders sank in relief. She could now add network infiltration to Hadley's skill set. It was clever, really. The Haederans were monitoring everything sent through regular communications channels, but the enemy wouldn't give much importance to messages between her and Merritt—for a little while, at least. Perrin had been irate when he'd found out she'd tried to visit Merritt and had made it clear to her he didn't want her trying it again. She'd have to warn Hadley and Feye of that, but for now, she was safe.

Well . . . safe, yes, but unsuccessful. It didn't matter that she'd been victorious at dropping a test message, because she'd never have another chance at leaving any critical information. Drex and Wynne had cornered her as soon as she walked back through the senate building. Judging by Drex's reaction, Wynne's threat of confining her to her rooms for the next five years wasn't so far off. She'd told him she'd been praying in the temple, but he hadn't believed a single word she said—she'd been too vocal with him in the past about her dwindling faith.

But even with Drex's fury, her limited success thrilled her—though she was less happy with Hadley's method of communication, and at a loss of how to tell him she wouldn't be going anywhere to meet him soon. Two days would never be enough time for Drex to back off even a little. She typed out a quick reply, letting Hadley-as-Merritt know it would be another week before she had free time, and sleep overcame her.

CHAPTER NINE

"DON'T GET COCKY." FEYE SHOT HER A LOOK THAT MADE HER FEEL AS tall as an Asrian burrowing snail. "For all you know, they have half the army out looking for you right now. Or worse, Imperial Security."

"If they are, they are. I'll take my chances with the Haederan Army." Avery shook her head and looked around the small cellar. The smell of tea that had permeated the air the first time was gone, and its absence lent the atmosphere a troubling seriousness. "But I honestly don't think the army cares what I do as much as Taln Perrin likes to imply. They aren't supposed to leave Drex and Wynne alone with me but they do, all the time. They think he's too old, Wynne's too feminine, and I'm too incompetent. Have since they first landed here."

"It's true." Hadley rocked back in his chair in a motion she was beginning to recognize as confidence. "Oh, the good general might not trust Her Highness at all, but the good news is that he's too busy to keep track of her himself—and his men think she's nothing more than a daft young woman." He grinned as she glared at him. "Wait, let me be more specific—a daft young woman who can't finish anything she starts. It works in our favor."

"You don't have to imply you agree with them!" For a moment, her annoyance overshadowed any fear. "It wasn't my decision to come back here. You know that. I had no choice."

"And if you hadn't come back to Asria, where would I be now?"

"Threatening someone else into doing your work for you?" The rashatmallow plant was wilting in the dark cellar, so Avery crumpled a few dried leaves onto the table and breathed in the calming scent, ignoring how Feye's forehead wrinkled at the ancient technique.

Hadley waved a finger at her. "None of that. Besides, it seems you have a bit of skill at this. Maybe I picked the right person."

Avery blew out a breath. "I haven't done anything except test your plan—and I think luck is more accurate than skill, because I can safely say that was the most terrifying experience of my life. Not a fear you would understand, I'm sure."

"I remember my first mission." An apologetic look flashed across Hadley's face. "I was sure that everyone who came within two meters of me could hear my heart racing. You either get used to it or think your own mother is about to turn you in."

"If that's supposed to be reassuring, try again."

Feye showed her the note she'd left, then dropped it in the incinerator. "Any major issues with the plan so far?"

She rubbed her eyes. "My security team is the problem. The Haederans might have loosened their surveillance on me for now, but Wynne and Drex haven't. I'm only here tonight because she's sick and he left me alone for ten minutes for a telemeeting with my father." Another meeting about her deserting Wynne, no doubt. "If you want to worry about anyone seeing me, worry about them."

"We could take care of them for you." Feye shrugged. "Permanently."

"Kill them?" She inhaled sharply. "You can't do that! Hadley, he's not serious, is he?"

"Calm down." Feye waved her off. "It was just an idea."

"It's a terrible one." Her eyes went wide. "Are you sure you're on our side?"

"He's not serious, and taunting her isn't accomplishing anything, sir. As unfortunate as that is—it truly is entertaining." Hadley turned serious, his focus shifting to Avery. "It's a temple. They won't let you in there alone? To do whatever it is you people do in there?"

She sighed.

Right.

There it was, that reputation Asria had among the other Commonwealth worlds. She hadn't known the extent until she'd met her second-year roommate, the otherwise distant Voirian who had taught her to curse, then explained that people were surprised Asria was a member of the Commonwealth to begin with. After all, didn't Asrians keep themselves isolated because they thought their religion made them better than everyone else? Why were they willing to volunteer for military service anyway? It had taken weeks for Avery to convince her that not all Asrians were fervently pious.

And Hadley was also from Voirs. Reputation, indeed.

"I can explain it away," she replied, rubbing her eyes. "Somehow."

"There you go." Feye pumped a hand in the air. "Success."

"Not yet." As much as she was warming up to the potential, he was still too optimistic. "Now what?"

"We'll start with easy information. See if you can get the exact damage to your own bases. We'll need to know the Defense Forces remaining capabilities for when the time comes. We already know about Rincon, so don't worry about that. Try to get the number of Haederan troops in Cadena and planetwide. The number and type of their ships remaining in orbit. How they got past your defense nets, especially. That's fairly alarming. Whatever else you think looks interesting."

"Oh, is that all? You have a fascinating definition of easy." Avery pushed the crushed leaves into a pile, then drew a finger through them. "Hold on a second. How are you two planning on getting all of this information out of here? They'll intercept any signal you send. That has to be what happened to the distress signals the Defense Forces had sent the night of the invasion."

"Hmm." Hadley considered her a moment before turning to Feye. "She's bright."

She frowned at him. The Asrian couriers were some of the fastest in the Commonwealth, owing to the planet's distant location, but the Haederans would never allow an unauthorized ship into the air. Certainly not into orbit. Even if they managed it, it was a six-week trip to Ventana, crossing dozens of Haederan-controlled routes.

"And they can determine the source location from any transmission, and you would never risk that," she went on. "You also can't be planning on escaping on a courier ship—you'll never make it into orbit."

Hadley shared several apprehensive looks with Feye before replying. "They can't jam our signals if we're hijacking their own."

"You can do that? But that only gets the signal to orbit, so—" Her brain caught up. There must be a Commonwealth scout ship parked somewhere outside the system. It would have to be out of Haederan range, yet close enough to pick up the transmission and relay it to Ventana IV. What other explanation could there be? "Never mind. I'll take your word for it."

Hadley nodded. "And one more thing."

Her shoulders sagged. He'd already asked too much of her. The Commonwealth had already ordered too much. There was no way she'd agree to more.

"Don't come back here," he said. "In fact, forget you ever knew where this place was. If we need you again, we'll find you."

It was the easiest request he'd ever made of her.

* * *

Feye's instructions had sounded simple in abstract talk, far from the watchful eyes of the Haederans, but learning anything of use was another matter. Despite Hadley's claim that the Haederans didn't see her as a threat, they were understandably uncommunicative around her. But the Blue Room? The Blue Room would be the key. She still disliked the parlor, formal and strange, but it was the perfect location for overhearing their discussions, since the large hallway just inside the main public entrance to the palace attracted all sorts of conversations.

Tonight though, there hadn't been discussions of anything other than social arrangements. It infuriated her that the Haederans were enjoying their time on Asria, so infuriating she wanted to storm upstairs and hide. But she waited, seething inside. If nothing else, eavesdropping would teach her the patience her mother had always said she lacked. Curled up on a chair with a silk throw draped over her, she was half-reading a tedious recollection of ancient Asrian history when the words outside caught her attention.

". . . won't be able to do anything with those fighters."

Avery stifled a yawn, clawing herself back to full consciousness, then sat up and leaned toward the open door. The response was still too quiet to hear.

"No, but the central launch pad is too damaged for them to take off, even if someone could get to a ship—which they can't."

Alcaris.

They had to be talking about Alcaris, but once again, walls muffled the response. She rose from her chair, kicking her shoes off as she did, thankful for the deep carpeting that quieted her footsteps. The speakers couldn't be far down the hallway if she was hearing even half of the conversation, and as she moved closer, the muted response became clearer.

"Still, we should have destroyed them all. It's risky to keep any of their equipment around. What happens if they're lucky enough to get to it?"

"That won't happen. Alcaris is locked down. Anyway, they can't take down the entire fleet with a few Nightflares."

A pause.

"If you say so. I don't trust any of them."

They hadn't destroyed all the Nightflares? That was surprising. Were the Haederans planning on using the Asrian interceptors for something? It made sense if they were. They'd also taken losses during the invasion and appropriating a few enemy aircraft for their own use was better than nothing.

"Me either. Good thing for them that none of this is my call. This protectorate business is bullshit. Do what we're doing on Naraka, that's the best way."

Avery leaned her forehead against the wall, her jaw tight.

"Who wants to patrol an internment camp on a barely habitable planet? Asria's a better gig than Naraka, that's for sure. Especially Cadena. Even more especially, this palace. Been in this room yet?"

Heart pounding, she darted back to her chair and unfolded the tablet.

In the decade after the Great Flood, the first interstellar explorers appeared. Called "star people" by the early Asrians, these explorers brought—

"What are you doing?"

Avery jumped at the Haederan accent behind her, as he would have expected of her.

"What?"

"I asked what you're doing in here." It was the one with the deeper voice. The one who wanted them in camps.

She lifted the tablet and flashed him a polite smile. "I'm reading. This is still my home, and no one told me I couldn't be here."

Get off my planet.

"For now." He leered at her, and the expression made her skin crawl. How she loathed them and their obvious contempt. "And I'm telling you to get out, Princess."

"Fine," she said, tossing her hair over her shoulder. They'd think she was nothing more than a foolish girl, and that belief would be her best protection. Wasn't that what Hadley had told her? "But I'm taking the tablet with me."

She could feel their ogling eyes on her back as she sauntered out and dashed to her rooms. The rest of her reservations about working for Hadley flew off into the distance as she copied the information about the Nightflares and damage to Alcaris to a disk. It only took another hour to talk Drex into a trip to the senate complex—where he was obliging enough to wait outside while she left the information in the temple.

CHAPTER TEN

AVERY SAT OUTSIDE PERRIN'S COMMANDEERED OFFICE IN THE SENATE building and drummed an impatient foot on the tile floor. It had been twenty minutes now without a single word from him, well past their appointment's scheduled time. Not that the wait was surprising. The delay was purposeful on the governor's part—he'd never waste an opportunity to let her know just how little he thought of her and her planet.

Not that she cared what he thought about Asria or even how long he kept her waiting either, because waiting gave her a brilliant opportunity to watch Haederan ships coming and going through the windows behind the low bench on which she sat. She couldn't ask for a better view of the senate aeroflyer site below her, and if she squinted, she could glimpse the Alcaris hangars far in the distance. She hadn't yet determined a pattern to the arrivals and departures at the senate building, but at least she was becoming more observant, honing surveillance skills she never thought she'd need. Even better, Perrin's office had the same large windows with a better view of the former Defense Forces base in the distance. He might see a lot more of her than he wanted. Still, she was beginning to think it wasn't worth waiting any longer when he stuck his head outside.

"You've got five minutes. I don't have time for your problems today."

Avery bit back a snort and followed him inside. The governor delegated his more distasteful work to everyone around him—his haste was just another instance of his disdain for her. He was so blatant about his dislike for her that she and Drex had laughed about it the day before, in fact. They felt the same about him, they'd agreed, but hid it better. They couldn't let themselves forget who had the upper hand, Drex had pointed out—for now.

She rested back in the soft velvet chair across from his desk, for once unbothered by his office décor that had been transported from Haedera, including the picture behind his desk—bare sand dunes that rippled every few minutes with the timbre of his voice. How could he consider a planet that included such desolate topography home? Asria had nothing like the immense ergs that covered Haedera's equatorial regions, and Perrin had once told her that was yet another deficiency of his conquered world. Not culture, not religion, not even Asria's admitted absence of varied cuisine—but a lack of sand dunes, of all things.

Ridiculous.

"What do you want?" Perrin swiped an idle finger across a touchpad as he spoke.

His rudeness was so obvious that she couldn't help but smile. At best, she'd stumble across significant intelligence, and at the very worst, she'd waste his time. Both ideas were appealing.

"There was a concern brought to my attention yesterday," she replied, "about a mining operation your people have begun in Tarragona. I thought it best we discuss it in person before something serious happens there."

He swirled a glass of scarlet-colored liquor in reply and didn't quite bother to stifle a yawn at her declaration. He usually looked bored around her—when he didn't look hostile—and it was a mannerism that was growing old.

"Tarragona?" he asked. "I don't know it."

He had to be lying, but she couldn't know for sure. Tarragona was a small enough settlement, on the other side of the world from Cadena, that even most Asrians had never heard of it. Maybe he was telling the truth.

"It's a small village," she said, "but the residents are alarmed. Their repeated requests for information went ignored, and when a group of them showed up at the mine looking for answers, your troops met them at gunpoint. Shots were fired, and while no one was injured, I still find the report disturbing."

"They should stop asking so many questions, then."

"They're civilians. Innocent people."

"There's no such thing as an innocent civilian. Not on Asria."

"It's their home, General. They just want some answers."

She sat forward, forcing the unease to the back of her mind. This had been a terrible idea. Perrin would never fall for her line of questioning, and he was growing more suspicious every time he saw her. But the local government *had* asked for her support, and she might get some information for Hadley, too.

"They're not entitled to those answers, nor are you." Perrin resumed his liquor swirling and tapped at the desk with a stubby finger.

"You asked for my help in keeping my people—compliant." Her skin crawled. "To that end, I am informing you that secretive mining operations and threatening the local citizens is not the way to encourage that level of cooperation."

Perrin crossed his arms and studied her.

"Perhaps you're right." Perrin stood to refill his glass. "All right. It's erlite. You can let them know there is no cause for concern—it's nothing more than routine security." He shrugged. "You know how people can overreact. I'll contact the commander there and tell him he can back off with the threats. I require cooperation in return, however."

Erlite?

She wrinkled her nose. Perrin couldn't expect anyone on Asria to be happy about the Haederans mining the combustible material for their spacecraft, but it wasn't an activity they should feel the need to hide. They'd known the Haederans would use their planet for economic purposes, hadn't they?

"You don't look happy with that answer, Your Highness."

"Hardly. I should think you have enough erlite in your own system to keep your ships supplied for the next thousand years."

Insolent, yes, but she wasn't about to hide her feelings for him now. Not when there was a Haederan fast corvette lifting off from Alcaris in the window behind him. She had to keep him talking—this was a better view than she'd expected, and she'd just learned the central launch pad was operational again.

"Maybe we do. But you have to admit it's a good use for our new territories, don't you think?"

"No." She folded her arms across her favorite shirt to wear to meetings like this. Dark blue silk, with silver edging along the sleeves. Commonwealth colors. He'd finally learned to temper his visible rage at the sight, but the vein in his neck didn't lie. "I don't."

"Well." Perrin beamed at her over his cup. "It's a good thing your opinion doesn't count for much. And your time is up."

Avery didn't make a move to leave. "The prefecture government has asked me to visit them in Tarragona to discuss the situation."

The cup hit the desk with a thud, and he stood. "You won't leave Cadena. And if you insist on interfering in matters that don't involve you, I'll have you confined to the palace."

As if he was the first to make that threat. Wynne would love it if he did.

"I don't believe this doesn't involve me," she replied, settling deeper into the chair.

Perrin jerked the door open and loomed over her. "Leave now, or I'll have you removed."

She gave him one last contemptuous look and left without another word. Was he hiding something, or was this his usual bluster? It was so hard to tell with Perrin. But no, they weren't mining erlite in Tarragona, she was sure of it. The Haederans were up to something. That thought stuck in her head as she headed for the lift tube on the other side of the building. Her imagination was running scenarios when someone called her name behind her.

"He wants to see you again." The young corporal's face was red with exertion—or fear.

"Now?" She blew out a deep breath of frustration and followed him back. She'd only left five minutes earlier. Nothing significant could have happened in five minutes—could it have?

"Where are they?" Perrin's ruddy face had gone all-out mottled by the time she stepped through his doorway once more.

"Who?"

He narrowed his eyes. "Your parents. Don't pretend you don't know where they are."

Avery's mouth dropped open. "They're at the estate in Sabino. Or they're supposed to be there. I haven't spoken to them since they left Cadena." Her gut twisted. Perrin's question meant they weren't there any longer. "What happened?"

"What happened is no one has seen either of them in over a day, and a search of the area came up empty." Perrin shouted so loudly the corporal disappeared out the door. "What do you know? Who helped them escape?"

"I don't—" She sank into the chair she'd vacated just minutes before and put her head in her hands. "I don't know where they are."

"I don't believe you."

"You can believe me or not, but it's the truth." Just to antagonize Perrin further, she added, "But I'm glad they got away."

"You won't be, if we find them. And if I find out you had anything to do with this . . ."

Perrin's thread dangled in the air, and it occurred to her, randomly and idly, that it wouldn't matter if the Haederans could prove she had anything to do with it or not. The king could be drinking his morning tea in Sabino that very moment, and she'd have no way of knowing. For all she knew, Perrin could be simply looking for an excuse to keep her confined to the palace as he'd promised—not that he'd need an excuse to do so. And he was too agitated to be acting. No, something had happened.

"I didn't. I don't know anything." She needed to calm him down before she became trapped at home and useless to Hadley. Needed to calm herself before she cried. The shirt she'd taken such pleasure in pulling over her head this morning had suddenly become a liability. "I swear to you, I had nothing to do with it."

"I hope that's true." Perrin took a breath. "And if you hear from them?"

"I'll let you know."

A lie. He couldn't believe she meant it.

"I hope so." He turned to the corporal who had crept back in, perhaps deciding Perrin's wrath was unavoidable. "Take her home. She's not to leave the palace until you hear otherwise from me."

She stood, her legs liquid. A light blinked on his desk before the corporal could show her out and to safety, and Perrin swiped a finger over the top.

"Wait." More swipes, then he looked back at her. "You wouldn't happen to know a Jon Gavni, would you?"

"It's not familiar," she said, a hand on the doorframe. It was the only thing keeping her upright. Had someone helped her parents escape? What was Perrin playing with now?

"He was arrested two nights ago. Sabotage, it says here in the report. Apparently, they found him placing explosives near one of our barracks outside of town." Perrin rocked back in his chair. "We disarmed them before any explosion took place."

Alarm bells.

They rang in her head, turning her thoughts into a murky cloud.

"I don't—"

"Know what that has to do with anything? Of course you don't. It doesn't have to do with much of anything, really, except that his execution was scheduled for next week. I think we should move it up a bit, and that it would be rather educational for you if you attended. This afternoon."

* * *

She spent the entire aeroflyer ride imploring Perrin to spare Gavni's life, but he refused her every appeal with a ghastly smile. As they landed, as he stepped out with a curt nod to the guards waiting there, Avery realized he'd enjoyed every single entreaty she'd thrown at him. It was hard to keep her hands off his neck as she followed him through the civilian prison outside Cadena, her hands balled into fists at her sides, but the soldiers behind her guaranteed she'd never have enough time to kill him before they grabbed her.

They passed through one last set of doors on one of the lower floors. A contingent of guards on the opposite side disarmed Perrin and the lieutenant with him, then searched her thoroughly. The humiliation took her mind, for a minute at least, off the icy concrete walls and floor of the room they'd guided her into.

The combination of sweat and something more metallic made her stomach twist. Asria had banned the death penalty in the wake of the civil war hundreds of years before, so judging by the stains on the floor, this could only be a cold storage room turned execution chamber. The room had embraced its macabre change in purpose already—and frequently, it appeared.

Avery stared at the bloodstains, trying to come up with another argument, anything to change Perrin's mind, when a set of guards led Jon Gavni in, hands and feet shackled. His mouth opened in silent surprise when he recognized her, and he managed the subtlest of nods.

It was so small that the Haederans couldn't have noticed, but she did, and desperate tears flooded her eyes. Oh, he was so young, despite the maturity and despondent wisdom on his face now. Someone's child. Unless his parents had been arrested with him, they'd be distraught, never knowing what had happened to their son. Maybe he had a younger sister who would be heart-broken over his death for the rest of her life.

Gavni's shock turned to tranquil hope as he stared back, like she could do something about his fate. How wrong he was. He would die because of what she'd said to Perrin, but she would beg once more anyway.

"Governor—" Yes, she was so desperate for amnesty that she'd call Perrin by that despicable title, if that was what he wanted. "Governor, please don't do this. He's just a child! You've scared him enough. He didn't kill anyone. No one was hurt, and you know he won't act against you again. Let him go. Let him go and he can still be a warning for everyone else."

Gavni gave a tentative cough, cut off by a sharp blow to the back of his head from a guard.

"He's nineteen," Perrin said. "Old enough to know what he was getting into when he helped put those explosives down. Quite the disorganized rebellion you all have going on in the city, it turns out. He gave up most of the rest of his cell, and if you don't stop arguing with me, you'll have a front seat for those executions as well."

"Rebellion? There's no rebellion going on in Cadena, and you know it!"

She pressed her lips closed. Perhaps that wasn't true. At least, Hadley hadn't mentioned anything—either he didn't know, or he was trying to keep her out of it. It was disheartening to hear they were disorganized. But Cadena's fledging resistance movement mattered little to her at the moment, because Gavni, his face covered in fresh bruises, and with what looked like a broken arm, was still begging her with his eyes.

"General." Her chest ached at the look of utter despair on his face. All the arguments, all the games, nothing mattered anymore. "I am begging you. Don't. Please."

Perrin waved a hand at the soldiers behind Gavni. "Do it."

The ridicule in his order was real. Avery clenched her fists at her sides, lest they find Perrin's throat on their own. Would it matter if they did? What else could the Haederans do to her? Shoot her along with him?

They pushed Gavni to his knees, and she silently pleaded with him to move, to get up and fight them. But what would be the point in that? He looked like he'd done plenty of fighting already, and it hadn't made a bit of difference for him. It was two of them against seven Haederans anyway. But as the soldier behind Gavni raised his pistol, she took a step forward. Perrin twitched his head at the sergeant next to her, and he grabbed her before she could take a single step.

"No!" The scream came out before she could stop it, and before she knew what was happening, there were two of them holding her back. She tried to twist away, but they held firm. "Let me go!"

Her interruption had distracted them, but it was only for a second. A sudden stillness filled the room, a strange quiet at odds with what was about to occur. Gavni pressed his eyes closed, his lips moving in what she recognized as a plea for mercy to the Holy One, then the pistol shattered the surrounding air. He fell face forward to the ground and lay motionless in the numb silence that had returned.

Perrin said something to the soldier next to him, like nothing had happened, but whatever he was saying, Avery couldn't understand it over the roar in her ears. She took one last look behind her as Perrin waved the group out and back down the hallway, hoping beyond hope that Gavni would stand up. When he didn't, she tried to shake off the guards on her arms, but they didn't let go.

Finally, she let them drag her—they were the only thing keeping her upright. Her entire being needed to be out of the building, and overwhelming relief filled her as Perrin led them back toward the aeroflyer landing pad they'd arrived on. She could forget everything as long as she was home.

But Perrin stopped before the group reached the landing pad, just outside the holding cells meant for incoming prisoners. She moved a foot toward the exit and tried not to shudder in impatience.

You will pay for this. Monster.

"I think the ride over was a little crowded," he said to her, his head tilted in deliberation. "I also think a night here might do wonders for your attitude toward me." He turned toward the soldier on her left. "Sergeant, give her a blanket or something—I'd hate for any complaints about her treatment to reach Haedera. I'll send someone tomorrow morning for her."

He disappeared down the hall before she could argue with him. But what would be the point? Even Victor wouldn't care about her spending a night in a holding cell as punishment. Drex would, but how could he fault her for this? She'd done nothing wrong.

The sergeant opened the door to the nearest cell, and she stepped slowly inside. Despite her all-consuming desire to leave the prison, it was hard to hide a laugh. It was bare, yes, but hardly smaller than her meager barracks room at the academy—*Dauntless*'s berthing would have been even worse—and the smoked glass door kept the crushing claustrophobia away. Gavni's execution might have been an effective deterrent if she were less determined to help Hadley, but this portion of Perrin's warning was a complete failure.

A night alone to consider her next move.

A night alone for the hate to build.

It could be worse.

"By the way," the sergeant said, just as she was feeling rather smug about her indifference. "This was the kid's cell when he arrived yesterday." His mouth curled in a twisted impression of a smile. "Have a pleasant night."

CHAPTER ELEVEN

No matter what mundane or complex topic Avery thought about, Gavni's face haunted her for the next few weeks, as she was sure it would for the rest of her life. His eyes pleaded with her in her dreams and hung in front of her vision when she was awake. She'd done everything she could to save him, short of throwing herself in front of the soldier with the gun—although she'd just about done that as well—and it hadn't been enough. Nothing would have been enough, and the futility ate at her. Execution would have been in Gavni's future regardless, but Perrin had only done it with such speed and cruelty to prove a point to her. He'd been a victim of poor timing and his alleged crime.

The Haederans would pay for what they'd done—somehow.

Pushing Gavni from her mind, at least temporarily, she took a deep breath and stood from what had become her favorite chair in the Blue Room.

"I need fresh air," she announced to the soldier in the corner, a stocky sergeant who hadn't bothered to introduce himself when he arrived at the palace two hours before. Since Father's disappearance, the Haederans' watch over her had become suffocating.

This one had been polite and indifferent though, so he was an easy target.

"Go sit in the summer parlor." He waved a dismissive hand at her and returned his attention to the small tablet even she knew he wasn't allowed to have on duty.

"Sergeant—" She smiled at him, trying to end any suspicion before it began. Charm him, that might work. She could lose him if she was out of the palace. How hard could it be? "I'm sorry, you never introduced yourself."

He grunted. "Keating."

"Sergeant Keating, might you"—she nearly choked on the request—"accompany me into town, perhaps? I need to get out of here for a while. Even the summer parlor is still so confining."

"It's not safe to be out in Cadena." He tossed his tablet to the side and eyed her with . . . well, not quite suspicion, but no small amount of doubt. "You know that."

Right. *Not safe.* The Haederans had been consumed with the protests that had exploded in Cadena within the past week, protests they hadn't hesitated to break up with violent force. Still, Keating's worry was comical. There was no reason she should be afraid of her own people protesting their occupiers. She'd be out there with them if she thought she had half a chance of getting away with it. If Perrin kept pressing her, she might attempt it anyway.

"I'm not worried," she replied. "Are you?"

Keating rolled his eyes at her challenge, and she knew she had him. He stepped outside in the main hallway, but she could still hear him on the comm, asking permission. While he waited, she made her way into her private rooms and retrieved her latest data package, loaded onto a thin plastic disk. It wasn't anything other than the latest gossip and rumors from the Haederans stationed around the palace, but Feye would find something of use in it. She ran her hands down her hips, dismayed to find no pockets.

There was nothing to be done. Keating would find it suspicious if she changed, and the dove gray of her knee-length dress allowed her to blend in with everyone else. Her shoe, perhaps? The noise of voices somewhere outside startled her into action, and she shoved the disk under her foot without thinking. It cut against her bare skin, and she headed to the foyer with an affected limp, hoping she wouldn't damage it. Keating scrutinized her as she entered, the same doubtful look on his face.

"Did you hurt yourself?" he asked.

"On the stairs." She stared him in the eye, daring him once more to challenge her. The doubt that remained in his expression suggested he wouldn't. How had someone like him ended up in one of the most critical security positions on the planet? "Twisted my ankle. I think a walk would do it good—keep it from getting stiff."

"Whatever you say." He motioned toward the corridor. "Let's go."

* * *

The streets were quieter than in the past, but a fair number of commuters, the ones who were more worried about making a living than protesting the occupation, hurried about. She had timed her request to match the heaviest foot traffic in the area around the palace, but there wouldn't be much time. Keating was cooperative so far, but that would only last as far as the peace in the city did. And these days? That could be for the next five minutes, and not a second more.

She pointed down a side street, toward one of the most crowded areas, in the opposite direction from Hadley's shop. "There's a small park down that way. It would be a nice place to stroll for a bit."

Keating looked at her like she was up to something, and he knew just what. Her attempt to visit Merritt had helped her in that regard—the Haederans seemed to think every strange move she made was an attempt to see him again.

"You could have stayed at the palace to sit in a park," he replied.

"Not sit," she corrected. "Stroll. It's something we do on Asria, if you weren't aware."

With that piercing reprimand, Avery walked off, silently begging he would follow at a discreet distance. He sighed and turned to follow, and his footsteps were lost in the normal noise as she ambled onward. She breathed in the city air, sharp and clean, like it always was this time of year. Winter would come sooner that she liked, yes, but for now she would enjoy the forthcoming autumn, Haederans or no Haederans. It was easy to do so here, away from her royal prison.

After they'd walked a half kilometer, she caught their reflection in the windows of an empty building. Keating was a half-block behind her, so she stopped and pretended to favor her ankle —but really to catch her breath. Her heart began to race, and for the first time that evening, she admitted to herself she had no plan.

A yell caught her attention, and she looked toward the plaza a block south where a group of people had gathered. Protesters already surrounded the small fountain in the center, and more were rushing up. Was this her chance? She glanced back at Keating, but he was watching the same scene. Without thinking, she stepped backward and into the nearest shop doorway.

Outside, the sun had been bright, leaving her half blind in the dim shop. The smell of fish hit her as soon as she entered. There were no windows to let fresh air in, only the open door of the store, and she choked down a gag at the haze of brine that surrounded her. The shopkeeper behind the counter must be enjoying the weather or airing the place out. He stared at her in confusion as she pressed herself against the wall, then his eyes creased in recognition.

"Lady Avery?" he asked, the lines in his forehead growing deeper.

Avery put a finger to her lips and edged away from the doorway. He must have understood her predicament because he gestured her behind the counter without a word. She darted across the store and knelt behind the counter, hoping Keating hadn't seen her enter. If he hadn't, she could either wait him out or lose him out the back.

But if he had . . .

The heavy metal door crashed to the floor and the electronic lock engaged with a click. She leaned back and rubbed her eyes, releasing a shuddering lungful of air. The shop went dark except for a small lamp on the counter, but even the abrupt sanctuary didn't stop her shaking.

The shopkeeper knelt down next to her and brushed his hair from his eyes. "There's a protest beginning in the plaza across the street," he whispered. "I'd be foolish to leave my store unlocked during that kind of demonstration, no?"

"Thank you for this." That time she managed to smile. "You don't have any idea what you just did for me."

He nodded. "Anything else I can do to help, let me know."

"I need to shake my guard." Part of her wanted to lie, but it was too late not to trust him now. "He's waiting right outside, and I know he must have seen me."

"Haederan Army?" The shopkeeper shook his head. "I saw a few soldiers when I locked up. They seemed to be focused on the demonstration, though. Let me check the security tapes."

Her aching knees reminded her she was too sore to remain crouched like this. Without making a sound, she slid to a seated position and waited for him to return. Her racing heart refused to calm. Should she pray? Yes. The Holy One always listened to prayers, they said, even though she didn't believe it.

Help me.

The shop owner came back with the view card sticking out of a tablet, interrupting her prayer. Avery watched herself and Keating come into view in front of the shop, saw herself stop and roll her ankle back and forth. Keating was looking at her for a while, but as she turned to survey the demonstration, he did too. She twisted through the open doorway into the store, but Keating's focus was still on the plaza—and when he did notice she was missing, he couldn't do anything but make a call on his comm.

"Good enough." She put her face in her hands, then took a breath. "And thank you. But I need to get out of here now."

He didn't ask any further questions but nodded and led her to the back exit.

"Sando Road is to the left," he said, pointing. "You know the way? If you hurry, their attention may still be on the protest, and you can get to wherever you're going."

"Yes. I can find it. I can't thank you enough for this."

The evening air raised the hair on her arms as she pushed open the door, looked around, then stepped aside to let her out. A few scavenging birds scurried about the deserted alley searching for discarded fish, their talons clattering on the uneven stone. The quiet would have made her nervous any other time, but tonight she was grateful. It was so empty that she could hear her own footsteps as she slipped away, which meant she'd be able to hear any Haederan troops chasing after her, too.

She blew out several deep breaths as she walked, though she wanted to scream. Once she returned to the palace, the Haederans would never let her out of their sight, not after she'd slipped away from Keating. What had Hadley expected from someone who had no training, no experience, and who was chaperoned everywhere she went? He had to have seen this outcome.

The plastic disk rubbed against the sole of her foot, and she wanted nothing more than to reach down and move it. Instead, she moved south from the palace, taking the long way to the senate grounds. She needed to get as much distance between her and Keating as possible before she turned back toward the temple and Feye's drop site. It would take more time than she could afford, but she couldn't chance running into Keating again.

The main street grew closer, and the shadows in the alley disappeared along with her relative safety. Time to circle back north. Avery glanced both ways around the corner, but the Haederans must have still been busy trying to break up the demonstration, because there wasn't a single soldier in sight. The usual city traffic was blessedly heavy on the main road though, and she could use that as a cover.

Good.

She stepped around the corner, head down, hoping no one noticed her—

Only to slam into a figure dressed in Haederan green.

Kusir.

She gasped, then lowered her head further and mumbled an apology. The figure grasped her arm before she took another step, and she knew in an instant Keating had found her. Hot fear shot through her, but there was nothing to gain by fighting, so, with the greatest reluctance, she looked up at her captor.

To her surprise, it wasn't Sergeant Keating who stood there, but a Haederan military police captain in his early forties, looking at her with an expression she couldn't quite identify. The expression transformed into a disarming smile, a strange visual on an enemy officer wearing a uniform that would have otherwise made her recoil in disgust. It softened his features, striking but ever so Haederan, and she relaxed in relief as he dropped her arm.

He was only a glorified policeman then, no different from the rest of them who roamed the city breaking up protests and enforcing the nightly curfew. This man was no threat to her, not really, especially since he lacked even the lightweight armor the rest of the Haederan military police wore. So, just a captain out making sure the rest of them did their questionable job of harassing Asrians. Still, he was an aggravation she needed to rid herself of as soon as possible if she had any hope of delivering Hadley's information.

"I'm sorry." The words wavered as she stepped around him. "I really should pay more attention to where I'm going. Excuse me."

"Your Highness, wait, please. We've been looking for you."

Avery deflated in defeat. Just her luck. She'd been so close, but there was no chance of eluding him if he already knew who she was.

"Keating said you were caught up in a protest," he continued, that odd expression on his face again. "It must have been pretty bad for the two of you to be separated."

"It was," she replied curtly.

So, Keating had made up a story, not that it would do him any good when his superiors found out. Well, she wouldn't contradict whatever flimsy excuse he'd invented. At least his ineffective attempt to protect himself would also protect her, with the extra advantage of never having to see him again. She looked the captain in the eye in an effort to look unconcerned, but by the way his smile hadn't faded, her affected composure wasn't working.

"Is that so." It wasn't a question. "You know you're not permitted outside the palace alone, no matter what demonstration you come across."

His straightforward manner sent a pang of annoyance through her, as did the way he'd trapped her against the wall. That was her own fault for not paying more attention to her surroundings, but she would take her frustration out on him anyway.

"What I do is none of your concern, Captain—" She glanced at his waist. No, he might not be carrying a rifle like most of the other soldiers, but he was wearing a sidearm, of course. He wouldn't let her go then, and Gavni's execution was too fresh in her mind for her to challenge him further.

"Gareth Chase." He smiled again, and even as shaken as she was, she recognized it as the look of someone who was not accustomed to being defied. "And that's where you're wrong. As of today, General Perrin has me handling security for the royal family. That's just you, until we find your parents, so what you do is very much my concern. I'd hate for my sole responsibility to be injured in a protest. And you know Asria's protectorate status is predicated on the behavior of certain individuals. It would be unfortunate if that status were to be revoked because one of those individuals refused to follow policies agreed to in good faith by her own government."

Good faith? Her cheeks grew warm despite the cooling air.

"They shouldn't have agreed to those policies!" she snapped at him.

"Perhaps not, but that's irrelevant right now. Neither one of us has control over what happened in the past, but I have my orders now." Chase paused, then said under his breath, "Your Highness, I'd really like to not make a scene here."

Avery looked around again for an escape route, but gray dusk filled the streets; glass and steel blocked the sun as it finished its race below the horizon. On the corner where they stood, the crowds from a half hour before had faded. None of the remaining people would want to get involved, even if they saw something wrong through the shadows that grew deeper every minute.

She wouldn't be able to overpower him, and even though she was nearly certain his sidearm was only a stun pistol, he would find the disk if she were unconscious. She spread her hands in defeat. No, there was no option but to go with him.

"Good." His tone turned friendly. "Where do you want to go now?"

"Go?" He didn't plan to take her back to the palace? Perhaps her luck had held just a bit longer. "I don't understand."

"You must have wanted out badly to pull that stunt. I can't let you wander around Cadena alone, but if you don't want to go home yet, I'll go with you anywhere you want to go. Almost anywhere." He laughed, and she was unsuccessful in hiding a smile in response. There was something about that him that lowered her defenses, and it felt *good* to laugh once more. "A ship off the planet isn't an option."

Well, wasn't that interesting? He was aware she'd slipped away from Keating and still had no plans to do anything about it. Had she found an ally in the most unexpected place?

"I don't know," she said. The lure of freedom, false as it was, was appealing. Even standing here on the corner with a Haederan soldier was better than being sent back to the palace like an errant child. Wasn't it?

"I've heard the temple by the senate building is spectacular," he said in a conspiratorial tone. "I just arrived on the surface a few days ago and haven't seen it yet. Maybe you could show me?"

Her heart fluttered in panic, and she pretended to consider his suggestion while she tried to calm herself. Hadley had been convinced the Haederans would never go near that building. Was it possible Chase knew she'd been on her way there? He couldn't have known where she'd been headed, could he?

No. Everyone on Asria, even visitors to Cadena, heard the same thing about the temple upon arrival, and it was true. It was just a coincidence. And panicking would only make him suspicious.

Avery glanced down the alley again, trying to hide the guilt that must be plastered across her face, then looked at him and forced a smile. "If you want."

* * *

The temple was empty, as she'd hoped it would be. Chase poured the sanctified water from the cup on the altar over both his hands, then lit four candles, murmuring a prayer as he did. Avery glared at his back from four rows behind, arms crossed in her only opportunity at defiance. Drex would be furious if he found out she brought a Haederan here, but Chase hadn't given her much choice.

Well, that wasn't quite true. She could have refused his suggestion if she had wanted, but she hadn't wanted to go home. And maybe, just maybe, she missed the temple—actually worshiping in it. Drex would never believe that, and he would question her at length about her newfound, non-existent faith—a conversation she never wanted to have—so this was the next best opportunity.

She forced her gaze away from the seat with the loose leg as Chase turned toward her.

"You don't approve of me being here," he said.

"No." Lying took energy she didn't have after an evening spent sneaking down alleyways. "I don't approve at all."

Well, he'd asked. She wouldn't apologize for her honesty.

"We believe the same thing, in case you'd forgotten. I belong here as much as you do."

Her eyes widened at his presumptuous comment. No, she hadn't forgotten. It was a cosmic joke, the way Haedera and Asria were two of the few planets in this part of the galaxy that worshipped the Holy One. Or more likely, they were just on the way for the priests of old who'd traveled between star systems. Still, his remark was intolerable.

"I know what you believe," she said. "And I know you only believe it because your emperor forces you to. Why someone who's clearly only using faith for control would pretend to love Him is something I'll never understand. And you're too blind to see it. Or don't care." She took a breath, amazed at her outburst. "So yes, I know what you believe. And I think you should go believe it back where you came from. You don't belong in this building—or on Asria."

"I could arrest you for saying that." Chase's expression was unreadable in the dancing candlelight. "All of it."

"Then do it." Certain he was goading her for a reaction, and tired enough of the threats to be flippant, she flopped on the nearest bench and pretended to examine a fingernail.

Chase stared at her, like he couldn't believe she'd been so bold, then burst into laughter, the incongruous sound echoing off the arched stone ceiling.

"Not this time. But if you talk to him like you talk to me, I'm beginning to see why Governor Perrin doesn't like you very much." He sat down next to her and leaned forward, elbows on his knees. "You hate us, don't you?" he asked, sounding disenchanted by the idea.

He was an Imperial Haederan Army officer. Didn't he feel the same way about her? Avery scooted away and stared at him, noticing his eyes for the first time. They weren't brown as she'd first assumed, but dark blue, a legacy of his planet's decades-long occupation of Voirs so long ago.

"You attacked us, unprovoked," she replied. His laughter and the unintentional vulgarity of those eyes had made her bold. "You destroyed our world, our lives, our way of life. Wouldn't you if you were in my position?"

"I probably would." Chase shrugged. "I might even be angry enough to do something about it."

"That would be foolish." Her scalp prickled a warning, and she resisted the impulse to slide a little farther away from him.

"It would. But desperate, angry people do foolish things sometimes, don't they?"

"I wouldn't know."

"No?"

Avery took a deep breath and looked him straight in the eye. Her nerves were fraying more and more with every second they sat there, with each prying question he asked.

"I hate every single one of you for what you've done to Asria," she said. "Angry doesn't come close to how I feel about it, but I'm not reckless."

"Good. Because I'd hate to see what would happen if you were."

He stood to look at the nearby winterberry vine climbing up the inside of one of the inset glass windows, and she swallowed the lump in her throat. Her performance could have been better, but he was nothing to worry about. At most, it was a caution given by someone who was projecting his own ideals onto her. It was the atmosphere that bothered her more now, being somewhere she wasn't welcome.

"Something wrong?" Chase didn't bother to turn around.

"Nothing's wrong."

A lie. He smelled like the incense burning over the altar, the expensive kind made from the becariana trees that grew up north, the kind only used in this temple, and she hated him for it.

"Still me or something else?"

She shook her head, unwilling to admit how much being there with him bothered her. "I don't like being here. I don't believe much anymore." She cringed at her frankness, though her claim wasn't completely true. Why was she telling him this? The loneliness of the past few months was catching up to her. But a Haederan? She could find anyone to talk to but him.

"I think it's comfortable. It's holy." At her skeptical look, he added, "You thought I was acting earlier?"

"Yes, I—I suppose I did. Can you blame me?"

It didn't make sense, though. It wasn't as though there was another Haederan in the building to report him, so why had he bothered with the ritual? Even most Asrians weren't devout enough to always symbolically wash their sins away before lighting the altar candles. The only other explanation was that he *did* believe, but her enemy couldn't be more faithful than she. It wasn't possible. She struggled with her convictions, and he didn't? That wasn't fair.

"Not really." Chase gave her a small smile. "Although I'll admit this is all a little more ornate and ritualistic than I'm used to. I felt like I was acting. I'm curious though, why don't you believe anymore? And if you don't, why does it bother you so much that I'm here?"

He had a point—it was like he'd zeroed in on her soul. His presence wouldn't bother her so much if she truly believed the temple was just another building, and for the second time since they'd been sitting here, his insightfulness bothered her. This Haederan had just called her on a lie she told herself.

"I said I don't believe much," she said. "It's not as big a part of my life as some would prefer. It's just another way for them to control me. My thoughts. My actions. And I suppose the concept of another life with the Holy One, free from pain and misery, is just too outlandish to believe." She looked at him with the least amount of malice she could manage. With the threat of arrest hanging over her, insulting him would be ill-advised—though it would feel so good. "But at least I'm not a hypocrite."

He chuckled. "Outlandish? Hardly. You're not afraid of being controlled at all. You fear death."

How dare he make her fear sound childish? What did he know of death? His people had invaded her planet, along with a half-dozen others. Asrians knew death. This man, who had observed the attack from a protected troop ship above the planet's surface, did not.

"Of course I fear it," she replied. "Doesn't everyone?"

He didn't answer right away, and she turned her gaze to the flickering candles at the side of the aisle. Everyone dreaded death. It was a frightening, unknown thing, with no guarantee of everlasting life afterward, no matter what Drex said. And it was closer than ever since the Haederans had arrived. It would be years before the sounds of bombs falling from space and the fighters just above Cadena faded from her memories.

Still, what came afterward, if it wasn't life? Probably nothingness, a black, empty void with no awareness. That wasn't reassuring either. Or was it? It was better than the alternatives they talked about. But she knew what she'd been taught, and it wasn't that.

"Not everyone. There's no use in believing the truth if you don't believe every part—especially something as simple as eternal life." Chase crossed his arms and regarded her with interest. "And it's never too late. Didn't they teach you that? He'll wait for you as long as it takes . . . He wants reconciliation."

Drex's gentle words were one thing, but there couldn't be anything in the galaxy more infuriating than an arrogant Haederan officer lecturing her on theology. Anyway, he was wrong. If the Holy One existed, he would never forgive her doubts. Deities were about punishment, not mercy.

She turned back to Chase, her jaw tight.

"Anyway, by the time I turned twenty," she said, ignoring his lecture, "I'd mostly left that part of my life behind, and it felt good. Freeing."

"Then let me guess—you left for Ventana IV as soon as possible."

A shock of unexpected dread exploded in her chest, and she pressed her palms to the bench in a vain attempt to center herself. He was prying now, and her openness with him didn't extend to his mentioning the Commonwealth.

"I'm not going to discuss that with you," she replied.

Chase laughed again. "Innocent question, Your Highness. I promise."

She doubted that. There was no such thing as an innocent question with this man—that much was obvious.

CHAPTER TWELVE

IT WAS DAYS BEFORE SHE COULD MUSTER THE NERVE TO CONSIDER leaving her rooms. The mood in the palace, and in most of Cadena, for all she could tell, was increasingly somber. Mother and Father were still missing, and while she tried to hope, even Drex's requests for information went ignored. Perrin threatened her more and more with each message he sent, and while she was certain most of his warnings were nothing more than intimidation, they certainly had a detrimental effect on her own morale.

And then there was Captain Chase. Though she'd destroyed the inconsequential disk in a palace incinerator after her conversation with him, the very sight of his Haederan uniform filled her with dread. The streets of Cadena, filled with them in turn, were the last place she wanted to be.

But Drex knocked on her door one morning, whistling a folk song and trying unsuccessfully to hide a broad grin. He claimed he felt guilty that she'd never been able to see Merritt's plane and knew just where Merritt was hangaring it.

In the wake of her run-in with Chase, going anywhere at all sounded risky, but Drex had been so excited about his news that she'd relented. Not that Merritt would have let her fly it, even if all Asrian air and space traffic hadn't been shut down since the invasion. No, she'd given up on contacting him and wasn't sure she wanted to see him either—though Drex had assured her Merritt wouldn't be there.

Yet knowing Drex, she wasn't all that surprised to see Merritt in the hangar when they arrived, polishing one wing of the Banshee. Avery turned to protest this new set of circumstances, but Drex slipped out the door with a grin. A grin and, presumably, some sort of believable story to tell their waiting Haederan escort. She spun around to face Merritt, attired in a brown jumpsuit stained with grease and oil, even though she wanted to follow Drex out and never return.

"Mer—" She held out her hands, pleading. "I didn't know. Drex said you wouldn't be here, and I—"

Kusir, Avery, that sounds even worse . . .

"Sure." He tossed his sanding equipment on a nearby table and crossed his arms, his displeased expression foreign to her. She didn't want to argue with him, but if he was just going to stand there and look at her like that . . .

"It's true. He told me he was taking me to see the Banshee, and that you wouldn't be here. But I don't care. She's beautiful, and I'm glad to finally see her."

And you. And you, Merritt.

But his expression was too painful to focus on, so she patted the silver gloss composite on the plane's nose, marveling at the craftsmanship. She might be capable of flying it, but she wouldn't be able to design and build anything like this if she worked at it for a hundred years. But that was fine. She'd fly it one day—if the Haederans ever left them alone.

"Thank you. I'm happy with how she turned out. What do you want?"

"I don't want anything. Only to talk to you, maybe. Come on, Merritt. This might not have been my idea, but I'm still happy to see you. I've missed you. Even if you still feel how you did that night, you could at least ignore your feelings and be polite to me." His mouth twitched in a gesture she recognized as impending capitulation, so she swallowed the rest of her misgivings. "Ten years together! I think I deserve a little respect for that, if nothing else."

"All right." He uncrossed his arms and tossed a rag to the floor. "Thank you. What do you want, Your Highness?"

"That's not—" She was about to snap at him when his eyes sparkled. "That's not funny." It was scarcely the reprimand she'd had in mind, but her Merritt was almost back now, and she wouldn't break that tenuous thread.

The twitch turned into a grin. "I thought it was. I also think we were set up."

Avery glanced toward the door. The low drone of the Haederan transport reverberated beyond it, but Drex was gone.

"No doubt about that," she replied, squeezing her eyes shut in mock pain. "But please don't be angry with him. You know Drex means well, even if he gets a bit conspiratorial."

"I'm not angry. Not really. He was right to do it. Right to make me talk to you." Merritt blew out a breath. "I was wrong. Waiting around for you to decide the Commonwealth Navy wasn't for you was the hardest thing I've ever done, and then in the end, you didn't even come back for me. You only did because they forced you to. And that hurt. I felt like I didn't know who you were anymore. I let myself get intimidated by where I was, and who you are now, and I shouldn't have."

"I'm sorry." She tried to smile. It was a shallow apology when they'd always sworn nothing would come between them. Had it been a foolish promise between two people too young to know genuine commitment? "I broke your trust, and you don't owe me anything for that, least of all your forgiveness. But I'm the same person I've always been. You know—stubborn and driven to a fault."

"Love, you don't need to apologize for that. But there was something else you need to know." He ran a hand through his hair, longer now than the day he'd walked out on her. She'd been right about the gray, too. "They were grooming me. Preparing me to take Teruel's place. It was a surprise, and I didn't know how badly I wanted it until they proposed the idea."

"That's not a bad thing. It's—"

She stopped herself just in time. Congratulations would be inappropriate when he'd never be taking Teruel's position now.

"Avery." He held out his hands, mirroring her earlier plea. "It would have looked bad if they promoted me like that. People would have believed it was only because of my connection to you that they chose me."

Her hand hit her mouth.

"You'd have chosen a job over me?" She hadn't meant to raise her voice, but it echoed in the high metal ceilings of the empty hangar as she dropped her palm. "You wouldn't have fought for both? You coward! I thought you loved me!"

Merritt's face turned as red as if she'd slapped him. "I wouldn't be the first one of us to do so," he said in clipped tones. "I can't believe you've forgotten so soon."

"That was different!"

"Was it? And since you weren't listening the first time I said it, I'll say it again. I made a mistake. I had planned to come back the next day and tell you it didn't matter what they offered me, that I would rather be with you."

She took a step back. "That's a convenient explanation now that it's no longer an option, isn't it?"

"Stop it." He closed the space between them in less than a second and grabbed her hand. "I'm sorry. I wish I'd never said anything about it, but I can't turn back time, and you deserve to know. How can I make you believe that?"

She fought the feeling arising in her chest, but his touch calmed her. It always had that effect, and she couldn't control it. Furious that she was reacting to the warmth, she made a perfunctory effort to pull her hand away, but he held firm.

"I don't know that you can." Surrendering to the affection that had never once completely disappeared, she wound her fingers between his, even though she couldn't meet his gaze. "You avoided my messages for days. I was so afraid for you, and when we received word that everyone had been released and yet you still didn't contact me, I was angry. What was I supposed to think?"

"It couldn't be helped. I was—incommunicado for longer than I would have preferred." The smile in his eyes faded as he focused on the floor. "But I'm sorry for not replying to your messages afterward."

"Are you? I'm not sure I believe that. You could have sent me a single communication and let me know you were safe. Mer, I've been so worried about you. When you just disappeared like you did . . . I just wanted to make sure you were all right."

"I'm alive. About all we can ask for right now, right?"

He picked up a fiber patch and turned away to lay it along the edge of the silver tail, but not before she glimpsed sadness on his face. Sadness and something else.

Fear?

A pit formed in her stomach, warring with the heat in her cheeks. The Haederans couldn't have treated him well, even if he'd survived the initial attack unscathed. How had she ever grumbled about the delicate way in which Haederans had treated her so far? Even the night she'd spent in that prison on Perrin's orders couldn't compare to what Merritt must have been through as Teruel's senior aide and one of the few Defense Forces' officers who knew more about Asria's defense systems than anyone else.

"I'm so sorry," she said, resting her hand on his forearm. "Sorry for everything."

"You have nothing to be sorry for." Merritt fussed with the patch on the tail, ignoring her touch. "Do you want to sit in her?"

She frowned at him, but his attention was elsewhere.

"I—I suppose I do." He was changing the subject, and she wasn't finished discussing them, but she would go along with it for now. Somehow she'd hit on something painful, and she was certain it had nothing to do with *them*. "I was wondering if you were ever going to offer."

Merritt unlatched the canopy and held it up while she scrambled into the pilot's seat, then he hopped into the copilot's seat behind her. The compartment was so small, she was all but wearing the plane instead of sitting in it, but it felt so *natural*. How she'd missed the delirious freedom that came with flying. Adrenaline surged through her limbs, almost like her body couldn't believe it was still on the ground. Merritt flipped on the power, and her soul became weightless in the glow of the instrument screens. The illuminated speed dial that floated just in front of her caught her eye first, the limit faster than anything she'd ever seen in a civilian aircraft.

"How fast can she go?"

Merritt dangled a languid hand over the side of the cockpit and picked at another loose piece of composite. She was starting to think he was damaging it on purpose in order to have something to repair—an activity that would fill his empty days and keep his mind off the past.

"I had her to five hundred once."

"Five hundred!" Avery gaped at him. It wasn't surprising. The silver and black Banshee was the sleekest thing she'd ever seen; the tail-mounted engine took up half its length, the pointed nose a dangerous knife. It was pure Merritt—always pushing the limit, unafraid of anything. A year before she'd left Asria, he'd been playing test pilot when the new interceptor he was flying all but exploded on takeoff. She'd sat next to him for two weeks, waiting for him to regain consciousness. "You're lucky you aren't dead."

He laughed at her admonishment. "Well, it was in a dive."

"Still. That's more exciting than anything I've done in the past year. This thing makes a Dragonfly look like a plodding cargo starship. Not that you'd know anything about flying something so mediocre." She laughed in return and reached for his arm. Even Nightflares were more exciting than what she'd flown at the academy. "I wish I could fly her."

It was a statement any pilot who sat in such a plane would make, but his shoulders slumped at the remark.

"It's my fault you can't," he replied.

"Your fault?" She must have misheard him. With his back turned to her and the whir of the equipment, she couldn't hear him well. "That's ridiculous. None of this is your fault, Mer. It's the Haederans' fault, Perrin's especially. It's Drex's fault for treating me like a child and Father's fault for ordering him to do so. I'd have been flying her the day before the Haederans got here if they'd simply trusted me more."

Merritt twisted around to look at her and propped one knee against the hatch, his movement awkward in the small cabin.

"Love, we never saw them coming."

Oh.

Her mouth parted, then the Banshee felt like it was falling, like they'd hit a sudden burst of turbulence, and she was falling with it. She leaned back against the velvety black leather and gasped for air that didn't exist any longer, ignoring the harness latches that stabbed her back.

"Oh, Mer," she whispered.

There wasn't anything else to say. The guilt of his failure was all over his face, and there was nothing she could say to soften it. Nothing she could do to allay the devastation in his eyes. And she'd called him a coward. She would give anything to take that one word back.

"There was no notice." His voice broke. "There's no way they should have been able to slip through the nets and every other early warning system we have. We've always been able to see them coming from light-years away."

That much was true. The Haederans continually played war games just outside other systems' space, provoking and baiting and posturing. In Asria's case, the Defense Forces had always seen them coming and had days to scramble fighters and chase them away. The Haederans had always left.

Until now. This time they'd gotten too close.

"We screwed up," he went on to himself. "Missed something. I don't know. It was just like they appeared out of nowhere, and now we're all paying for it."

"How is that possible?"

Her question sounded too matter-of-fact, even to her, but it was that or scream. She had to attack Merritt's problem head-on, if only to keep emotion from overwhelming her. Because it shouldn't have been possible for the Haederans to appear out of nowhere. Their ships were hard to see in hyperspace, like every ship, but it wasn't impossible. Even while traveling faster than light, a ship left an unmistakable ripple in space, like when she'd thrown stones into the frigid lakes outside Cadena as a child. Any ship was visible if you knew what to look for, and the Defense Forces were experts at detecting the most hidden ones. They had to be.

"It shouldn't be. You know that."

"Unless—" She gasped out loud. "Merritt, you don't think—"

"Your uncle gave them enough information to shut us down?" He'd always been able to read her mind. "No. I wouldn't worry about that. He never had access to anything that classified, and everything was functional. It was like they just—one minute everything was fine, and the next, they were right in front of us." He paused. "Avery, if they've found a way to make their ships untraceable in hyperspace, there won't be any stopping them."

"Stealth?" Irritated by the harness, she yanked it from behind her back. It clattered against the side of the cockpit. "We've been working on that for two hundred years. The Commonwealth even longer. It's impossible."

"I know it's impossible." His voice was sharp again, and for a moment she feared they'd lost any progress they'd made on their relationship. "I was throwing out an explanation. Because I just don't know otherwise."

That, she could understand. Anything to explain what had happened, anything to take some of the guilt away. Still, Hadley might be interested in Merritt's theory, however crazy and self-validating it might sound.

"Well, ignore the Haederans for now, as difficult as that might be. Is there anything I can say to convince you that this isn't your fault? Because however this happened, it's not." She shifted forward and put her hand on his shoulder, not caring if it was too forward. He grabbed it and shook his head, and she wound her fingers around his. "Mer, I'm not angry with you. I don't blame you. No one does. You have to believe that."

"That helps."

"And I need to see you again."

Merritt shook his head. "That's not a good idea."

"Why not? Have the Haederans told you to stay away from me? Well, I don't care what they think about it." Working with Hadley had made her bold. "I'm sure we can work something out."

He hesitated. "I'll talk to Drex and see what I can do. But don't count on it," he warned, growing serious, just as a grin spread across her face. "If it came down between seeing you again or keeping you safe . . . I'd say goodbye first."

* * *

Merritt's stealth theory, as offhand as it was, troubled her for the rest of the afternoon. What if the Defense Forces hadn't missed something? What if the Haederans had developed some new technology that had hidden them from the Asrian early warning systems? If they had, it wouldn't be long until they could take most of the systems in the quadrant. The idea kept her thinking until she got home and unpacked disks of her old academy texts. Faster-than-light travel had never been one of her academic interests, but this practical application? There would be no rest for the remainder of the day with this kind of learning curve.

But after three hours of delving through history and engineering texts, she rubbed her eyes and groaned out loud. The astronomy research she'd done for her thesis was one thing, but some of the engineering books were so advanced she could barely make sense of the sentences, much less the equations. There wasn't anything here. No connections. She couldn't link Merritt's concern to any new research. He was just . . . wrong.

"A little light reading?" Drex asked, as he entered her private parlor and pulled the door closed.

"Just research." Chewing on her lip, Avery pointed at the stack of disks. Drex would be suspicious if she asked, but he was her best chance at getting more information. "Drex . . . I know how preposterous this sounds, but you don't think the Haederans developed stealth technology, do you? Some kind of technology that would make them undetectable in hyperspace? We've been working on it forever, and—well, suppose someone did it?"

Drex pulled up an armchair and looked over her shoulder. "Parker suggested that? He's reaching, isn't he?"

"I don't know." She rubbed her eyes again and yawned. The golden rays of a late sunset cast shadows across the books, and seeing Merritt for the first time in weeks had all but shattered her. Who knew a reconciliation she'd desperately wanted could be this exhausting? "I think he is. But you have to admit, it's strange that we didn't see them coming at all."

He stretched his neck back and forth, then shook his head. "The simpler explanation is that someone wasn't paying enough attention. It happens, as much as no one wants to admit it. Don't read too much into it."

"But humor me." Twenty-one years in the Defense Forces meant he knew more about this than she did, but accepting it was something different. "What kind of technology would make it possible?"

"Why are you so curious?"

She flushed. She'd never been able to lie to Drex well.

"Merritt feels guilty," she replied, "and I would do anything to lessen that."

Not a lie, but not the whole truth.

"He's not responsible for what happened." Drex searched her face while she tried her best to appear more innocent than she felt.

"All right. Yes, we've gotten close in the laboratory. Large quantities of verium added to standard spacecraft fuel can mask the signature. And I mean enormous. No one's ever been able to make it work on an actual ship."

"Successful experiments? But verium is highly unstable, especially in large amounts, correct? So how did it work in the lab?"

"I honestly couldn't tell you. It's not my field, and the experiments were decades ago. We gave up, and the Commonwealth gave up." Drex shook his head. "I'm sorry Parker feels guilty about what happened, but you're trying to put something together that's just not there."

Her eyes grew hot as she focused on the texts. Merritt didn't just *feel* guilty. Drex had to understand that.

"But I'll tell you what," he added. "I'll ask around and see if anyone has better information. Maybe it's something else. Who knows? Will that make you happy?"

"Really?" Abrupt relief flooded her. Drex had more freedom of movement than she did, and much better contacts. More than that, he could ask the right questions without arousing suspicion. "Yes, thank you—I could kiss you for this!"

"Two conditions." He raised his brows and two fingers. "One, you keep whatever you discover close. The Haederans can't know you're looking into this."

"Easy enough. I've been worried for hours that one of them would walk in and start asking questions about my new hobby. What's the second?"

"I do this for you, and I'm off the hook for what I did earlier today."

"You did look quite pleased with yourself for setting things up —but you were never on the hook for that one." Avery stifled a laugh. "Not with me anyway."

CHAPTER THIRTEEN

The snow atop the highest peaks of the Gallis Mountains glittered in the distance as Drex's private car came to a stop beside Merritt's in the meadow across the river from Cadena. Avery might have forgiven him, but he'd worked hard at getting himself off the hook with Merritt as well—even sneaking her out of the senate building earlier that afternoon. It was a chance, especially with the military police in charge of her security now, but she would happily deal with the consequences if Captain Chase found out. Seeing the mountains like this, immense and near and holy, went a long way toward healing her soul.

"You two probably have quite a while before they realize you're gone and come looking for us." Drex looked all too proud of his deception as she jumped out and threw her arms into the sparkling mountain air. "Enjoy. Behave."

"Always," she told him. "Thank you."

"I'll have her back before then," Merritt added, giving Drex a goodbye wave before pulling her close. "You made it," he said into her ear, but there was no darkness in his features today. This time he'd trusted her to show up. "I can't believe I missed you so much in just a week."

"We won't wait this long again." Avery kissed his cheek in return. "I promise."

"And I'll hold you to that."

They hiked another ten kilometers to their favorite picnic spot, a clearing that might as well have been another world. A thick cover of low clouds chilled the early autumn day, and Merritt threw her a blanket as she settled onto a lichen-covered rock to watch him unpack his rucksack. She tugged it around herself as he busied himself with a bottle of Rendon wine, and her eyes filled with inexplicable tears at the sight.

So much wasted time.

"Do you know how much I love you?" she asked as the cork flew off into a clump of wildflowers, dark and brittle in the coming cold.

"I know it's not nearly as much as I love you." Merritt abandoned the wine and jumped up beside her. Avery offered him the blanket, and he wound it around both of them. He put a finger to her lips and grinned. "No, don't argue. I'm sorry, but it's just not possible."

How she'd missed that smile. She thumped his shoulder with her palm and laughed, then leaned into him. In the cocoon of the blanket, she was warm and safe, and somehow, it made the emotions of the past month too much. Her eyes welled up, and she turned away from him, brushing them dry.

"Hey, don't do that. I was just kidding. If it means that much to you, then you can love me more." The grin faded away. "What's wrong?"

"I can't tell you." She spoke into his shoulder. "If I say it, it'll make it real."

"Tell me." His voice was soft. "If that makes it real, then we'll deal with it together, I promise."

She swallowed.

"My parents." Her gaze bounced between the mountains in the distance and dried flowers at the bottom of the rock. "They're dead. I just know it. I don't know what happened, but I know the

Haederans killed them. I never got the chance to tell them how much they meant to me. And with my father gone . . ."

"I had no idea." Merritt ran his free hand through his hair. He'd always respected Father, even through his unease with royalty and wealth, and that was something else to love him for. "Ah, love, I'm so sorry."

"I thought they'd be safe in Sabino. I don't know what happened, but I just know it's something terrible." She wasn't making any sense, but it was too hard to formulate a thought that did. "And with Quen gone . . ."

"The senate can handle things for a while once we boot the Haederans off the planet. We'll be fine until they find him."

Merritt didn't understand. Her future, the one she'd seized from Quen, however unwillingly, was in the hands of . . . well, not Father anymore, but certainly Grant Baylen.

"There's no finding Quen anymore," she said. "Drex keeps saying they will, but how can that possibly be true? And even if they manage it, there's no chance the senate will ever approve his kingship after he went away. I'm here, he's not. I was responsible and came home when ordered; he ran off. It'll be me. Merritt, they're going to choose me!"

Saying it, the one thing she'd feared too much to verbalize before now, left no doubt. No matter what power the Haederans thought they had, she would be the next ruler of Asria, if she wasn't already. For who knew what they discussed in the more clandestine senate meetings and electoral assemblies she wasn't allowed to witness?

Understanding dawned in Merritt's eyes, understanding and fervent endorsement.

"Then I think you'll do a wonderful job. And I would be honored to call you my queen."

She leaned her head against his and tried to blink against the future. Was he speaking as an Asrian—or as her Merritt? It had to be the latter. Had to be. She hadn't known until this very moment how one could be so desperate yet so terrified to hear an answer to a single question. One question whose answer meant everything.

And she had to know.

"But I'll lose you if that happens," she whispered, clinging to his hand. "And I don't think I can handle that."

There.

It was said. The fear, her entire existence, laid bare before him. Whatever the Haederans would do to her if she took her father's place didn't matter, but she couldn't lose Merritt again. He would have to sacrifice so much if she became queen—had already, just for loving her. She worked her fingers in between his as if she could keep him from fleeing just by holding on to him.

"No." His lips grazed the side of hers, and the sensation and his declaration chased away a bit of the chill that had settled into her soul. "You won't lose me. I told you I would rather be with you, whatever your title is, whatever it does to my career." He held up a hand before she could say anything. "Yes. Even if this had happened six months ago, and I'm sorry I ever made you doubt that. Because I do love you more." He laughed and squeezed her so tightly she let out a high-pitched squeak.

"No, you don't." She laughed back at him as he released her, but the heaviness of duty settled deep in her bones. "Mer . . . I've never been this scared in my life. Everything that's happened, it's too much. I don't know how much longer I can handle it. The soldiers in the palace, in Cadena, following me all over the place." Any hint of a smile that might have remained vanished. "You probably think I'm a coward."

"Love, you're not a coward. You're the bravest person I know. Drex says you're holding up brilliantly, especially having to deal with them day in and day out. I know I couldn't do that. And I know it won't be much longer."

Her smile, artificial as it was, slipped a bit more.

"You're far more optimistic than me—though it's hopeful to hear someone who believes things will change soon. Even Drex doesn't hold out much hope." Father hadn't been optimistic, and even Hadley wasn't confident the Commonwealth Navy would reach Asria soon. Merritt's hope, solitary as it was, was a balm. "But let's talk about something else. I won't let the Haederans ruin our entire day together."

"Something else . . . well, let's see." Merritt pulled her closer and feigned deep thought. "Do you remember the first time we came up here?

"You wanted to show me another clearing somewhere up here that you claimed was covered in wild cylva," she said, sliding onto her back, her head in his lap. She couldn't forget, even though it had been a lifetime ago. "And you thought you knew where you were going, but you got us hopelessly lost instead."

She laughed at the memory as he twisted a piece of her hair around his finger. Almost strangers, they'd gone too far into the thick alpine forest searching for his meadow that day. The narrow dirt trail became obscured by ferns, and they'd circled the valley for hours in the dwindling light. They had only spent the night after Merritt had navigated them past the same misshapen tree a half-dozen times.

"Hopelessly lost about covers it."

"The look on your face that night when I told you who my uncle was—I thought it was the end of everything before it had even begun."

"Yeah." Merritt chuckled. "You thought I'd be used to the idea by the time we got out of there. Clearly, you were mistaken."

"I'm just glad you forgave me for lying about it. And I'm even happier you brought a map the next time we came up here."

She closed her eyes, remembering. The ghosts of the past were too near, too present, and there wasn't much else to say. Ignoring the wine, they stared out into the meadow for another hour before the wind picked up, bringing a sudden chill to the higher elevation. She shivered again, and Merritt checked the time.

"We'd best be getting back," he said. "Drex must be worried, and I don't want to know what he'll do to me if I let you freeze to death up here."

He left the real worry unsaid as he pulled her to her feet, but it was obvious he was worried the Haederans had discovered she wasn't at the senate building or the palace—they'd been on the mountain almost twice as long as Drex planned. Still, it was hard to pry herself from the warmth of Merritt's arms as they trudged downhill in the stiff wind. It hadn't been this cold in Cadena when they left, but tomorrow's forecast storm seemed to be making an early appearance. Drex's car would be warm though, and they couldn't reach it soon enough.

Exhaust blew from the engine as they approached, and Avery thawed at the prospect of heat blasting on her skin. But as they drew close, Drex was nowhere in sight, and her blood turned cold in a way that had nothing to do with the coming storm—a squad of Haederan soldiers lingered around his and Merritt's cars, clad in moss green anoraks and pacing in circles around their own transports.

She dropped Merritt's hand and stepped in front of him.

"What did you do to him?" she called out. "Where is he? If you've hurt him, you'll answer to me."

Captain Chase stepped around from the back side of the car, rubbing his gloved hands together against the chill, and her heart sank further. Drex wouldn't have brought her up here if he hadn't truly believed they had a chance to slip away, but it looked like he'd underestimated her new jailer.

But then again, so had she.

"I sent him home," he said easily. "You'll see him tomorrow."

Avery relaxed enough to glance at Merritt. "Mer, you go home, too," she muttered sideways at him. He'd never been afraid of anything, yet the dread that had appeared on his face at the sight of the soldiers tore at her. "Now. Please."

He grabbed her hand and yanked her to his side, probably harder than he'd intended to. "I'm not leaving you here with them."

Warmth rose in her body at his touch, despite the wind and the dozen Haederans who surrounded them, but she had to do this alone. Even being escorted back to Cadena with a dozen enemy soldiers was better than seeing Merritt staring at the gloomy skies and blackening mountains like he was.

"It's fine. Really. Just go home." She turned toward him and whispered against the wind. "Look Mer, they waited for us to come back instead of searching for us. That means something. They won't harm me, and Captain Chase seems to be harmless enough, so please go. This isn't your fight."

Chase's gaze landed on Merritt, cold and predatory. "Mr. Parker, why don't you come back to Cadena with us?" he asked with contrived politeness. "It won't be a problem to give you a lift, too."

Mr. Parker?

"His car is here," she said, grinding her teeth together in irritation. No one had called Merritt Mr. Parker since long before they'd ever met. "Have some respect, if you're capable of such a simple thing. You can't expect him to just leave it on the side of a mountain."

"One of my men will take it home for him. It's the easiest thing for all involved." Chase shoved his hands in his pockets. "It's getting cold. Can we get inside before we all freeze?"

She glanced at Merritt, pleading with her eyes for him to ignore Chase and walk away. He shook his head, his gray eyes dull, and gestured toward the open back door of Drex's car.

Resigned and unwilling to argue with him in front of the Haederans, she slipped into the back, and Merritt followed without saying a word. He wouldn't look at her, wouldn't even take the hand she placed over his. She twisted her fingers through his, feeling the cuts from his work on the Banshee, and prayed her presence would calm him—but she'd known him long enough to know it wouldn't work. Merritt could live in the past, and it was clear he was doing so now.

The sun fell below the horizon as they entered the city, and a cold rain fell as the glittering lights extinguished one by one. They rode in silence through the empty streets for close to half an hour before Avery realized they were driving in circles through the central business district. And then—and then past the office tower just outside Alcaris where it was rumored the Haederans held the more vocal opponents of the occupation. The ones who weren't slated for immediate execution, that was. Had Chase heard the rumors, too? Was he confirming them? Was this a not-so-subtle threat?

Merritt made eye contact with her as the car slowed in front of the tower. She squeezed his hand tighter—by his wide-eyed, unblinking stare, she could tell he knew the significance of their location, too. Personal experience? Maybe. She'd never ask unless he mentioned it first.

Chase twisted back toward them as she fought to control her unease. "Home or somewhere else, Mr. Parker?"

Merritt's jaw tensed. "I'm not getting out of this car until she's home safely."

"You needn't worry about her safety," Chase replied. "Not while she's with me."

"I'm supposed to take your word for that?" Merritt gave a short laugh.

"I don't see that you have much of a choice. But yes, you're supposed to take my word for it."

"Your word isn't worth much, Captain."

That cutting quality in his voice and the way he'd set his chin promised a fight. She was caught between two men who plainly weren't used to having their orders ignored, but this wasn't Merritt's battle. She couldn't let it become his battle—even if he wanted it to be.

"Look, there's no reason we can't stop at the palace first if that's what he wants," she broke in. "He can find his own way home from there."

"The palace isn't on the way."

"You—" An audible scoff escaped her lips. "I'm supposed to believe you're worried about an efficient route after you've driven us around half the city?"

Chase didn't reply, so she looked at Merritt and raised a palm up in reluctant capitulation. He nodded likewise in reluctant agreement and appeared to satisfy himself with a hostile glower at the back of Chase's head.

"Very well," he said after a calm breath. "But if I find out she didn't make it back safely, you will pay. Personally."

"Merritt!" Avery sucked in a gasp of air through her teeth. Had he just threatened a Haederan soldier? Right after they'd driven past that—that building? Chase could arrest him right then and there, and there'd be nothing she could do about it. Merritt *knew* better.

What? Merritt mouthed, apparently not caring what Chase thought about anything.

Avery glared back at him and pulled her hand away in silent censure. Really, he needed to be more cautious about what he said and who he said it to.

"Understood." Chase ignored her warning, apparently not caring about what Merritt thought of anything, either. She wanted to scream at them both. "Then what will it be, Mr. Parker? I'd hate to drop you right here on the street."

"Take me home." Merritt didn't sound as resigned as she expected he would, but he didn't say another word when they pulled up in front of his home fifteen minutes later, sparing her only a brief glance as the car came to a stop. Avery smiled good-bye, trying to look more confident than she felt. Merritt got out and gave Chase a look that announced he would make him pay later.

If only that were possible.

As the door shut behind him and Drex's car moved again in the palace's direction, she leaned forward and cleared her throat. "Was that necessary, Captain?"

"Was what necessary?" Chase asked.

"Do you practice that innocence in front of a mirror each morning? You know what I'm talking about."

She sat back and choked down her rage as a high-speed train

flew by them on its way to Sabino. Was anyone on it? It was racing past them too fast for her to tell, a white blur in the silver twilight. An empty white blur, another false normalcy. The automated trains ran on schedule, like only Asrian trains could, but the Haederans had forbidden Asrians from riding them past curfew. They themselves did, of course.

"A ride back? That was a favor. His car wouldn't start. We checked twice."

The comment chilled her despite the overheated car that had been so comfortable just five minutes before. There was no doubt the Haederans would do something to Merritt's car before they dropped it off at his house. Install a tracking device? Destroy it out of sheer vindictiveness? Leave it parked halfway up the mountain where he'd have to work a miracle to get it back? Who knew what they were up to, but Merritt was unlikely to have a functioning vehicle at the end.

"A ride back to town that included a tour of the entire city, yes. I live here, you know. I could have given you one." She was close to shaking when she thought of the building, though Chase *had* all but confirmed the rumors with his little show. Hadley would be interested in the information, even if there wasn't anything anyone could do about it. "Don't treat me as if I'm a child. It wasn't a favor. It was a threat, and it was unnecessary."

"Unnecessary? You don't know what you're talking about." Chase shot the driver a quick glance. "Pull over. We'll walk the rest of the way."

"No. I don't care what I told him, I'm not walking back with you."

But the car had already come to a stop on the side of the empty street. Avery stared out the nearest window at the next train that rushed by. Chase opened her door, and she ignored him as he waited for her to step out, more patient than she'd assumed him capable of.

"Don't you think you've tested me enough for one day, Your Highness? Get out of the car. Now."

Maybe not so patient, then. Well, he could wait a little longer. She counted to twenty before getting out, just to let him know he couldn't order her around, then headed toward the palace without waiting for him to follow. The streets, both ground and aero, were now empty, the sparkling buildings now shadowy against a leaden sky.

"Are you going to tell me now why you kicked me out of the car?" she asked as he appeared beside her, his boots almost silent.

"Because I like the city, and I thought a walk sounded nice. Exploring my surroundings takes a bit of the homesickness away."

"Homesickness?" She shot him a disgusted look. She had never expected civility from the Haederans, but Chase had been more courteous than most, and his lack of tact was disillusioning. She'd never give him that much credit again. He was lying anyway. There was no doubt he wanted to lecture her, away from the ears of the driver. "I have a solution for your *homesickness*."

"I'm sorry. Was that insensitive of me?" He grinned when he noticed her frown. "It's true, though. I like Cadena, even if it's a little cold. If it was twenty degrees warmer, it would remind me of where I grew up. Well . . ." His grin turned thoughtful. "It's not as big as Cadena, and there are fewer people back home, but the traffic is just as bad somehow. Maybe we just have worse drivers on Haedera."

Wonderful. She was walking home with the friendly, talkative version of Gareth Chase, and he was going to ramble on and on about Haedera, undoubtedly for no other reason but to aggravate her. Well, he could talk as much as he wanted, as long as he didn't expect her to volunteer anything about her life.

"I doubt Asria is anything like where you grew up," she replied.

"And I doubt you know anything about Haedera beyond what you learned in whatever Commonwealth-biased schools you attended. Let me guess—we're all imperialist conquerors, yes?"

She made a disdainful sound at his defensive tone. Was he that oblivious? Maybe not. Maybe he was just bitter the Common-wealth worlds hadn't tripped over each other in a race to say yes to Haederan annexation the second time around.

Arrogance, oh yes . . .

"You're the ones who invaded us, so I don't think what I learned is that far off." Rage welled up but subsided as she glanced at him once more. He was provoking her on purpose, and she wouldn't give in. Still, being able to vent her frustration to a Haederan with more culture and humanity than Perrin was tempting. "What you did to Asria tells me all I need to know about you and your people. I don't need to know anything else."

Not that she didn't know more. As isolated from the core of the quadrant as Asria, Haedera had developed faster-than-light technology before most other systems. They'd then used their new capability to conquer dozens of planets and expand their reach far beyond their own. It had taken centuries for those so-occupied to throw off Haederan rule, and another hundred years to form the Commonwealth. Asria was the only founding member to have not been controlled by the First Haederan Empire, its isolated location protecting them, but they hadn't so much as questioned the creation of a collaborative defense organization.

"And Asria has never wanted to expand its borders? I find that difficult to believe."

His inability to comprehend their desire for undisturbed isola-tion was clear. No, the Haederans hadn't changed enough in the past centuries if he couldn't understand Asria's desire to rule their own system and no one else's. Even if Asria had wanted to expand, they'd had too many internal problems over the centuries to care about conquering other systems. Their violent civil war, hundreds of years removed but never far from anyone's memory, was proof of that. Their internal problems were a price to pay for the freedom they had compared to Haedera and most other plan-ets. True freedom meant having the freedom to make evil choices and moral ones. But she wasn't about to let Chase know Asria was anything but a utopia, even if it was, compared to his militaristic homeland.

"If you're so educated about Asria, then you know we've never conquered any other planets. Why would we want to?"

"Everyone wants more power, don't they?"

"No. They don't."

Let him think Asrians had the moral high ground—though no society could claim that. And she didn't want power for herself, if that was what he was trying to imply. She just wanted to be left alone with Merritt, left alone to fly, but being born to the wrong family meant those wishes were nothing more than a dream now.

"I see." Chase paused. "Well, you're missing out. It's an intoxicating thing, I'm told. Not that I would know myself."

"Are you trying to indoctrinate me? Is that why you're following me around?" She wasn't successful in suppressing a hysterical laugh, more out of fear than amusement. It would make the Haederans' occupation easier if the Asrian royal family believed Haedera was a paradise.

"Maybe." He grinned at her again. "Is it working?"

"No, it's not." He was earning every disgusted look she gave him tonight. "And it never will."

"That's too bad. I think you might enjoy Haedera. Maybe in a year or two, once this mess settles down, you can visit and see for yourself."

"I don't think so." She blurted out the words, horrified by her sudden curiosity of such a foreign world. Would he not stop talking? Why was it taking ten times longer than usual to reach the palace?

"No?" Surprise laced his question. "Well, perhaps you're right. You speak your mind a little too freely for a Haederan. That kind of candor drastically shortens one's lifespan back home."

He was silent after that, and she prayed he'd stay that way until she could bolt into the palace and hide the rest of the night. They walked along on the quiet street in silence for another few kilometers, and when the palace came into view, she quickened her step.

Almost free.

Chase caught her by the wrist, then stepped in front of her before she took two paces.

"Not so fast, Your Highness." His voice turned cold. Their earlier conversation in the car was clearly about to resume. "You and Lieutenant Colonel Parker were both warned before today—several times, actually—and I can see the prior counsel didn't take. So I'll tell you this myself, and you would do well to listen to me this time: you are not to see or communicate with him. I hope it won't be necessary to give him another reminder, too."

"Don't touch me." She jerked her wrist from him and backed away, trembling at his change in demeanor. So they *had* threatened Merritt, just as she'd feared. No wonder he was so tense around her and so anxious around the Haederans. "And leave him alone."

"You first."

"Why?" She raised her hands in front of her, a pleading response to his flippancy. "Do you think we're going to start a revolt together?"

Chase cocked his head at her, a gesture that was becoming all too familiar. "I know you're not going to. At least, you claim to not be stupid enough to try, and I try to believe people. And frankly, I'm the last person who wants to impede love. But General Perrin doesn't want you around him, so it's my job to make sure it doesn't happen."

And with that, she understood. This was punishment—for being Asrian, for being unlucky enough to have been the target of the Haederans' latest attack, for being her father's daughter. It was Perrin's way of showing her he had absolute control over every part of her life. He'd give her just enough freedom to let her think she had some say over her future, then take it away, all to make certain she knew he was in charge of Asria and indeed her very life. And he was punishing Merritt too, for doing nothing more than defending his home and loving the wrong person.

The senselessness of it all made her want to scream. Not words as such but merely to scream—at Chase, at the Haederan sentries patrolling the palace, and at the empty streets. The city shouldn't even be empty and dark, and that made her want to scream too. It was either scream her pain away or pummel the arrogance off Chase's face.

Instead, she gulped the emotion down and steadied herself. "Are you going to tell General Perrin what happened today?"

"I don't want to." Chase shook his head, relaxed his shoulders. "No. Not if you give me your word that it won't happen again."

She glanced up the street as the sentries disappeared behind a palace wall. Anything to delay what she had to say. Because she needed them away from Merritt. She needed to protect him, even if it meant she'd never see him again.

"Fine." The street seemed to blur into a haze of pain and grief. "You have my word that I won't do it again. Just leave him alone."

"Consider it done."

CHAPTER FOURTEEN

THE CONTACT DREX HAD INTRODUCED HER TO, A PHYSICIST ONLY FIVE years older than herself, was younger than Avery expected the scientist would be, but Cameron Pernella's girlish appearance and animated manner worked in their favor. When she'd arrived at the palace earlier that afternoon, the Haederans hadn't suspected she was anything other than an old friend of Avery's from Sabino come to gossip like they assumed women were inclined to do. They had been so convinced of this that the guards had been scarce since Cameron arrived, evidently believing the cheerful young woman was nothing more than she appeared.

Cameron handed over the research, a dozen tiny disks of data, before parking herself cross-legged on Avery's velvet settee, unfazed by the surrounding wealth. Avery suspected she didn't notice her surroundings most of the time, as captivated by her work as she was. She was desperate to learn how Drex had found her, but there was no good way to ask, since even though the Haederans didn't appear to be listening, they had to be. She and Cameron couldn't risk talking out loud, not even in her private parlor.

"Do you remember him?" Cameron asked.

Head down, she wrote a fast explanation of her research on

her tablet, then laughed out loud, bubblier than anyone in Cadena had any right to be these days.

"Tall and blond, right?" Avery replied, taking the tablet. "I think we had an Asrian history class together. You can tell he made little impression on me."

But all this is theoretical, Cameron had written. *None of it matters because it assumes the Haederans can get the verium they need for the fuel.*

Avery shook her head at the ending note. *Which they can't,* she wrote out and erased.

"Well . . ." Cameron lowered her voice and giggled like a woman trying to hide the details of her most recent love affair from anyone who might be eavesdropping. She scribbled again.

Right. Not found naturally on most planets. Too unstable, and when it exists, it's in small quantities. That's what the research has focused on in the past few decades. Making it stable enough to use. We can't make it work except in the lab.

That was discouraging, but it was just as Drex had said. Merritt was wrong, and someone had missed something that night. It wouldn't come as a surprise to anyone. Disappointed, but curious, Avery scrawled the question.

Deposits on Asria?

"Yes." Cameron pulled up a map on her tablet and pointed.

Only one, the finger she held up indicated.

Avery leaned closer.

Tarragona.

She scratched furiously. *The Haederans are mining erlite there.* Or so Perrin had claimed when she'd confronted him about it. She'd doubted him from the start, but now—now it was even more unlikely. *What are the odds?*

Cameron pinched the bridge of her nose and shook her head as Avery erased her comment and handed the tablet back. *There's no erlite in the Paseo Formation,* she scribbled. *Base rocks are too old. Just verium.*

Avery's eyes went wide. *You're sure about that,* she wrote.

The Defense Forces thought about mining it there years ago, Cameron added on the tablet. *You can find the records of them buying up land over there, if you're curious. But there was no point, and ultimately, they backed off. That's all classified, though. The locals think they were looking for a new launch site.*

"How do you—"

You're not the only one who wants my expertise. Carmen laughed. *Just don't tell anyone, not even Colonel Langley, all right?*

Telling anyone, even Drex, was the last thing on her mind. Her heart thudded. Could the Haederans hear her shock? She could, for it echoed in her mind and hears, tumbling about the day parlor. Because it was impossible to believe what Cameron had just told her—and yet, there wasn't any other explanation for it.

It was verium that the Haederans were mining on Asria.

There was no other explanation. It explained the heavy security at the mine in Tarragona. The Haederans could claim otherwise all they wanted, but they wouldn't have bothered firing on the villagers over erlite. It was verium. They'd found a way to make it stable, and they were using that stable verium to hide their engine signatures in hyperspace.

And they'd used their new technology to take Asria.

"Cameron—" she began.

Cameron stiffened in understanding. "They made it work, didn't they?" she whispered, her cheeks flushing. "How?"

Avery nodded, hand over her mouth.

Where else can you find verium? she wrote. *What other planets?*

Cameron's smile slipped. She was, likely, finally seeing how this discovery had affected her planet.

Nowhere on Asria. Just near Tarragona. Off-world, you're looking at Hanides, Iythea, Naraka, others. I could get you a better list, but geology really isn't my thing.

"No," Avery said out loud. "That's all right. You've named enough. This is bad, Doctor Pernella. Really bad."

Haedera now held all those uninhabitable planets. They'd been the first systems taken in their new bid for control of the quadrant. And now she knew why. The Haederans were mining verium on those planets now, too. Merritt's wild speculation had been correct, and if it had fooled the Defense Forces—

That meant it would fool Commonwealth, too.

"Apologies, Your Highness." Cameron took the tablet back, and her dark eyes sparkled. "But it's not the disaster you think it is. That's the best part about all of this."

She hesitated, like she was preparing for a grand finale.

Adding verium to their fuel isn't as foolproof as they think. If a ship traveling faster than light shows as a clear ripple in a lake, then a ship using verium might look like—she bit her lip, probably trying to dumb the theory down enough for her uneducated student—*something like natural, local variations in gravity. We don't know for sure because we've never seen it that we knew of. Tracking ability might fluctuate in and out. If you aren't looking for a ship that way, you'd never notice. But they're not invisible. You just need a longer track to determine destination is all.*

I need to copy all of this right now, Avery wrote.

Cameron nodded. Avery wiped the tablet clean, then stared at the stack of disks in her palm. It might be months or years before the Commonwealth could duplicate the Haederans' efforts, but they needed to be aware of their enemy's capabilities now, and she could give them that.

But right now, she could give them enough. Even more perhaps, for the second piece of Cameron's news was more critical. Even if the Commonwealth couldn't make the verium-enhanced fuel work for themselves, they might have a chance of defending other planets against the Haederan fleet.

No mistakes this time.

* * *

Raised voices woke her the next morning.

Avery raised her head from her desk and glanced at her chronometer. *Seven hours.* She'd slept seven hours without moving or waking, Cameron's disks still on her desk next to her head. As the voices grew louder and the tension in her shoulders grew tauter, she tossed all but one data disk into a nearby transport storage container—the Haederans would have to be desperate to once more search through her belongings that had been shipped home from the academy. The final disk, the consolidated, critical data that needed to find its way to Hadley first, went under her desk, into a small cut-out she'd made with her dagger the week before.

The argument, if it was an argument, had quieted by the time she crept into the foyer, though every light was at full brightness and her anxiety had become a tsunami that threatened to drag her under. Drex stood there, his arms folded in a gesture she recognized, along with a half-dozen Haederan troops, Captain Chase in front of them.

Her entire body tensed. The Haederans couldn't know anything, could they? No—they hadn't paid any attention to her conversation yesterday. It *had* to be coincidental. But it was so early, and there were so many of them . . .

"It's not even sunrise," she said to Drex. "I'm sure there's a reason for this commotion."

And I hope no one asks why I'm wearing the same clothes as yesterday . . .

Drex ground his feet into the floor and shot her a look that was cautioning and mocking at the same time.

"They're just delivering word that Wynne and I are relieved of our duties here. Permanently."

"What? Why?" Avery forced herself to take one shallow breath, then turned her frantic attention to Chase. "You're not . . . you're not arresting them!"

"Is there any reason we should?" At her panicked look, he smiled. "No. It's because Governor Perrin wants it this way. He's displeased at the lax security here, especially after the situation with your father. They're permitted to visit, but they're not to be alone with you."

The situation.

It was so unpleasant to describe her parents' disappearance like that, and there was no doubt Chase had been the one to inform the governor of her guards' permissiveness. She'd been expecting something like this for weeks, but as each day passed, she'd hoped the modicum of freedom the Haederans allowed her would become permanent.

"Fine." It was the only thing she could say. Her voice would betray her if she argued with him further—but then again, perhaps sounding outraged would hide her fear. "But in the future, I'd prefer if you wait until later in the day for anything like this. I'm going back to sleep for another hour. Then I'm going to my office."

With one last glare at Chase, she turned to go, too incensed they were standing in her family's private quarters to say goodbye to Drex.

"You'll go to your office when and if I say you can," he replied, then smiled as she turned back toward him. "You're free to do what you want in the residence only, and I'm leaving two guards here to make sure you stay."

More and more restrictions. They were planning something. She didn't know what, but something was coming, she was sure of it. Whether it had something to do with Mother and Father or her own doings didn't matter—there wouldn't be much time to get to Hadley.

"You do what you need to do," she replied.

She stalked off before her face turned redder.

Before they realized she had something to hide.

* * *

No matter what she'd claimed, she'd never intended to go back to sleep. For two hours, she stared at her parlor door without seeing it. How could life be this unfair? After months of enduring an occupation, she had information worth all of their efforts, and now there was no chance she'd ever get it to Hadley. The Haederans didn't know what she was doing, or they'd have arrested her by now, but they were making her life miserable and her job hopeless.

Was it time to let Feye know they were onto her? Warning him required a signal at her senate office, and Chase didn't seem like he'd allow her to go there anytime soon. Did she dare sneak out? *Could* she sneak out past his new and more vigilant guards? That had only been successful once, and now she knew her presumption of the guards' incompetence hadn't been her imagination.

The unrelenting chime of the intercom roused her from the whirling of useless thoughts in her head. Ignoring it, she paced her parlor in the dappled morning sun, ignoring the tea a servant had brought in, wishing she knew what to do, wishing she could ask Drex for advice. Or even Father. Would he have understood? Not likely. Not with his undisguised apathy to anything political.

The intercom chimed again, three rings in a row this time, infuriating her with its incessantness. Drex would have knocked on the door or come straight in, and Wynne was enjoying her newfound freedom from her problematic charge, so it had to be one of the Haederans. Instead of answering, she stormed out of her room and back down to the foyer where Chase stood, a contrite look on his face.

"I'm sorry about what happened earlier," he said in greeting. "Governor Perrin didn't give me much of a choice."

"Do you expect me to believe that? I think you always had the option of not barging in here in the middle of the night."

The contrite look turned to remorse. "Not this time, unfortunately. One of my men told him what happened last week with Colonel Parker, and I'm afraid he was rather furious about it. I couldn't hide the fact my men haven't been the most diligent lately."

For what felt like the hundredth time that morning, rage faded into fear.

"Rather furious probably didn't begin to cover his reaction, I'm guessing," she replied. "What exactly did he say?"

"Oh, quite a bit. He was most vocal about wanting Parker arrested. The rest isn't repeatable in polite company."

Avery took a reflexive step toward him, prepared to beg for Merritt's release. The idea of him in that prison because of her . . .

"Did you?" she asked.

"No." Chase nodded to the side, remorse turning to something else. "I stopped by and told him he might want to consider making himself scarce for a while." He reached for the door, then stopped and turned back to her. "Believe it or not, I'm sorry about this. I can't do anything about the increased security, but perhaps I can make it a little better today?"

Not likely. Maybe she could use his offer, though.

"How?"

* * *

No matter what she'd told Chase earlier, she didn't need to be in her office. But he'd offered, and she needed to get out of the palace. Needed a change of scenery. Needed to go somewhere she could think and plan her next move. And her rooms at the palace, which were crawling with Haederans, were not the place that was going to happen.

She spun toward the window in her float chair, and her eyes landed on the large Dragonfly model behind her, a gift from her parents when she'd been selected to fly. It would be a straightforward matter to move the spacecraft in front of the window and be done with Hadley for good. He'd expect her to do it if he knew what had happened that morning—but that had to have been a coincidence. The Haederans were acting off Father's disappearance and her visit with Merritt, nothing else.

Stiff from her pretended hours at work, she stood and wandered toward the window, gazing down at the street below. A few children were running through the garden shrines, screaming and laughing, though she couldn't hear them, of course. Security would chase them out soon, and her heart melted for them in advance—they deserved a bit of fun, even if in an inappropriate location.

The temple was scarcely visible through the trees, their leaves changing in the fall sun. It would become cooler soon, the temple would grow large in her window through the bare branches, and Cadena itself would be awash in color. She'd missed autumn on Ventana. Missed seasons. Missed how the city's developers had loved nature enough to include it in their plans. It wasn't something all Asrians cared about, for the first time that day, she smiled as a single red leaf drifted downward. One child picked it up and held it above her head, and their game of chase became a game of catch the leaf.

For a moment, at least, the enemy in her outer office didn't matter. Avery pressed her hand over her mouth and laughed as she watched. Maybe Asria would survive after all. Where there was youth, there was hope, wasn't there? Even she and Quen had played like this, another lifetime ago. Another leaf fell to the ground, and a young boy picked it up this time, drawing her attention to the tree behind him.

Her smile faded when she noticed the deep gouge in the bark.

CHAPTER FIFTEEN

DEEPENING SHADOWS OF RED SPILLED ACROSS THE FLOOR AS AVERY stared out the window of the palace's main observation deck, set with an unspoiled view of the mountains and glowing orange clouds in the distance. On any other evening, departing spacecraft from the palace and city launch bays would have marred the sunset, but since the invasion there had been nothing but the mountains, their tallest peaks already blanketed in snow. Was snow always there so early in the season? After so many years away, she couldn't remember how long it would be until the cold made its way to Cadena. Six weeks, perhaps?

Six weeks.

For the first time in her life, the future was frightening. What would Asria be like in six more weeks? Would it be like the other Haederan-occupied planets, with the Imperial Security Command sweeping through the city? Contrary to Drex's anxiety, there had been no sign of the Haederan secret police so far, even though they must be on Asria by now, if only to wipe out the small insurgencies Perrin complained about each time she saw him. No one was better at suppressing political dissidence than they.

Or would someone organize a significant resistance before that happened?

It would be the latter, if she had any say in things. Their enemy could be gone in less than six weeks, though that outcome seemed as unlikely as the winter snows leaving Cadena untouched. Time continued on, and she couldn't stop it or control the future.

Her inability to do anything had kept her on edge the whole day, and the anticipation that ran through the palace didn't help her nerves either. Anticipation of what, Avery wasn't sure. Since seeing Feye's signal on the tree the day before—the scratch that marked the temple drop site as compromised—she'd been trying to find a way to his secondary location. But the Haederans had stopped her at every turn, and she'd all but given up. Getting out of the palace itself seemed impossible.

And why had Feye marked it in the first place? Was he being too cautious, or had the Haederans become suspicious of him? Had he had an altercation with the Haederan military police? They were so hard to avoid in the capital nowadays. Captain Chase was proof of that.

The heavy doors to the observation deck creaked open, and her breath caught. Because the figure who slipped between them—

Merritt?

"Wynne helped," he said under his breath as he entered. A non-explanation if she'd ever heard one. "Can we talk somewhere else? It's urgent."

"The garden?" Trembling with unrelieved strain at Feye's clandestine message and giddiness at seeing Merritt, she led him down the outside steps into the expansive garden just outside the observation deck—the same garden where he'd walked away from her a lifetime ago. Except for a few birds taking shelter in the leafy paradise above them, the silence was ominous.

"Not here." He sounded tense and rushed. "The creek."

Avery furrowed her brow as he clutched her hand and led her onward. The sound of the small creek that meandered through the garden soothed some of her nerves, but that wasn't Merritt's purpose. That sound would camouflage their conversation and thwart any listening devices. The Haederans had placed them in the palace a few weeks ago, some openly enough as a warning, but others more surreptitiously. She'd not dared to look at or dismantle the ones she saw. But even the good models weren't capable of distinguishing quiet speech from water rushing over the arranged boulders.

She focused on those boulders, waiting for whatever Merritt had to say that was so important that he'd consider coming to the palace. Even with Wynne's help, it must have been difficult for him to make his way inside with no one noticing, and Chase's warning hummed at the front of her mind.

. . . you are not to see or communicate with him. I hope it won't be necessary to give him another reminder, too.

And there was something else. Something worse, something she could scarcely verbalize, even in her mind. If Merritt had slipped by the Haederans, that meant they weren't paying much attention to the palace, and *that* meant they had directed their attention elsewhere. Merritt's rush told her he knew the reason for the Haederans' distraction, and the dread that flickered through her told her the reason would devastate them both.

Merritt rummaged through a pocket with one hand while his other clung to hers.

"There's so much I need to say," he began, "but I need to give you this first. I've been carrying it since Emot, praying it would eventually be the right time."

She inhaled as the flicker of dread became a brilliant fire. There was only one thing he could have carried around since Emot, and she gripped his hand so tight her knuckles paled. But now? What was he thinking?

"Then you know what I have here." He smiled at her reaction and pulled a plain silver ring from his pocket—the only ring he had been able to afford so many years before. "I've wanted to give it to you so many times, but it always felt wrong. You were always leaving, or talking about leaving, or coming home for such a short time. And now, it's the right time. The only time."

The only time?

"I don't know what to say." Avery reached for it, then pulled her fingers back. The fire grew deep inside her, but this time it wasn't a pleasant heat. "I wasn't expecting—Mer, it's impossible to keep up with your feelings anymore. Just a few weeks ago, you made it clear you wanted nothing to do with me, and now you're standing in front of me holding a ring?"

"I know you weren't expecting this, and I'm sorry to spring it on you now." He pressed the ring into her hand and closed her fingers over it. "I won't be able to follow through on this promise. I wish I could, more than anything, but I—I can't, and this is yours. It's always belonged to you."

"What are you talking about?" She rolled it between her fingers and stared at the delicate metal. Eight years. He'd carried it for eight years, even after she'd declined his first marriage proposal on Emot. She didn't deserve that kind of love. "Why can't you follow through? I'll marry you this instant. I've always loved you, I've always known we'd be together like this someday, and now—now you're saying you can't follow through? Mer, I don't understand what's going on."

Merritt pulled her into his arms, and the heat in her chest turned to a cold sweat. His body against hers set off that familiar longing, but something was wrong. This wasn't like him. Even embracing her, he was too distant and too cautious for someone who'd just handed her a ring.

Like his mind was somewhere else.

"There's something I have to do tonight, and it's best if you don't hear anything else about it. I shouldn't be telling you this much." He drew a shaky breath, and when he spoke again, emotion filled his voice, emotion that destroyed her soul. "All you need to know is that I love you, and I will love you for the rest of my life. Even if—even if the rest of my life is only today."

"Merritt, please don't do anything rash."

She grabbed his arm and clung to him, holding him back, as if she could keep him from doing such a reckless thing. For now she knew—the Defense Forces had planned an attack, something that they couldn't possibly get away with. That had to be it. Because yes—there were Nightflares at Alcaris.

Functional ones.

No.

Her legs went wobbly, and the rush of the creek turned into ocean waves, threatening to wash her off her feet. Convincing him not to do it felt like treason, but she couldn't let him do this. It wasn't as easy as taking a few interceptors and destroying the Haederan ships left in orbit. Merritt's plan was suicide.

"Listen to me," she went on. "You don't have a chance. They've been acting so strangely the past few days. They know what you have planned, they must."

"I don't have a choice. We have to try. We can't live like this." He stroked her hair as he spoke to the top of her head, too careful not to whisper in her ear. "I love you so much. I wish—so many things. That everything was different."

"I love you too."

There wasn't anything else to say. Merritt kissed her forehead, his lips gentle, and fury engulfed her. How could they be so close to forever and not make it? She breathed in his warm scent, trying to memorize the woodsy undertones, and tears ran down her cheeks. After all these years, he was still the one she loved. The only one she would ever love.

"I have to go now, love." He wiped her tears with a thumb, looking better than he had earlier, more composed than she would ever be again. "Don't cry for me, please? At least not after tonight. I'm not afraid of this, and I don't want you to be, because whatever happens, everything will be set right. Remember that. Remember that promise. No mourning, no tears, no pain. No death."

He was wrong. He was so wrong. How could he say these things and not understand how wrong he was? How could he not understand that this was the end of the world? His meaningless platitudes were just that, especially tonight. He couldn't really believe death was temporary. He couldn't have said what he'd just said.

Everything will be fine. The Haederans will be gone shortly, and I'll see you tomorrow, love—that was what he was supposed to say. Not this. Not a promise of more death.

"Please don't go." She grabbed him tighter, as though holding him back would stop his leaving. "Don't do this."

"I have to." Despite his earlier strength, his voice cracked as he pried himself away from her grip. "Goodbye, Avery."

Merritt had never said goodbye to her. Not once, not ever, not even during any of their many separations. It killed her to hear the finality in his voice, how he sounded a thousand times surer than she'd felt about anything in her entire life. Her world shattered into a million pieces as he stood, and watching him walk away for the last time, so sure of what he was about to do, destroyed her soul more thoroughly than she'd ever thought possible.

* * *

Avery didn't know how long she sat there, wishing their conversation had never happened. The heady smell of rina, still blooming in the protected garden so late in the year, brought heat to her cheeks. It wasn't from fear and devastation, either. It was *anger*. Weren't the flowers aware of what had just happened? What *would* happen? She ripped off a blossom and tore it to bits, then tossed it to the ground as Drex's footsteps sounded behind her.

"Please, Drex, give me a minute," she said to her feet.

"No time." He sounded sympathetic but determined as he sat down next to her. "You need to leave before this whole thing blows up."

"You knew?" Her voice cracked. "Am I the last to know everything?"

"Only since this afternoon. Parker wanted to say goodbye and tell you what's going on himself. As for you, there's a shuttle waiting just outside the city in one of the civilian launch sites. The Haederans think it's been deregistered for scrap, but the site owner is reliable and claims it's spaceworthy. It's risky, but it's our best shot."

"We could have tried to escape Asria weeks ago. Are you that desperate now? You know we'll never even make it into orbit. I'm not about to get in a shuttle they'll shoot out of the sky."

Especially if it meant she'd never get her data to Hadley.

"It's your last chance to leave before things get bad."

Avery shook her head. "I'm not leaving."

Drex's eyebrows shot up. "Oh, yes. You're leaving, even if I have to knock you out and carry you the whole way there."

He probably meant it, and Wynne would be thrilled to help him, too.

"I can't leave." She lowered her voice. "I need to take something to the Old City. Please don't ask what, or to who, or why. I can't leave without doing this, even if it means I never leave Asria again. Even if it means—look, it's that important, Drex."

He surveyed the creek without looking at her. "Parker thought it was safe to talk here?"

"I think so. I mean, yes."

"Then talk."

The *or else* remained unspoken. Drex's threats were legendary to her and Quen, but she threw her hands up in frustration. He couldn't intimidate her now.

"I can't."

"Why not?" he asked.

"Because I can't. Don't ask again."

Drex swore under his breath. "So help me Avery, what are you playing at?"

"They—" She kicked at some loose pebbles under her feet. "They came to me just after the invasion, wanting my help."

She didn't bother mentioning who they were, or that they'd started off by coercing her. She needed Drex on his side, and it wasn't as though Hadley had talked her into something she hadn't wanted to do to begin with.

"And I agreed. I've been passing them information for over a month. Nothing that important until just now." She took a deep breath. "Merritt was right about how the Haederans surprised us. It was a guess, but it turned out he was right. That research you had Cameron bring over? It proves everything, at least as far as anyone can prove it. They're mining verium out in Tarragona and probably on dozens of other planets. It's part of why they're here, and it's why they've taken the planets they've seized already. I suppose they thought it would be easier to mine it on Asria than on an uninhabitable world where they need to worry about building shelters. The Commonwealth needs to know, Drex. They need to know how they can do it, too, and I have the data on how to make it work."

"You can't be serious." His voice was flat. "Tell me you're not serious."

"About which part?" She hadn't even mentioned the Commonwealth would be able to circumvent the new technology and track the Haederan ships in hyperspace, but that would stay her secret for now. Some things didn't need to be said out loud, even in front of a creek.

"Dammit—all of it!" Drex swore again, more vulgar than before. "Do you know what the Haederans will do to you if they find out?"

"I've had nightmares about Imperial Security finding out since the very first day," she confessed. Nightmares and a vivid imagination were an anxiety-inducing combination, but she would never admit that to Drex. "But I told you we couldn't sit around and do nothing."

"Yes. You did mention that." Drex fell quiet, and that was worse than the shouting. Quiet Drex was someone to be afraid of. She and Quen had always known that. "And I thought we had come to an understanding that sitting around and doing nothing was exactly what you would do. Do you know how much harder you've made my job? How much danger you've put yourself, your parents, and whoever you're working for in?"

"You may have thought we'd agreed on that, but things changed. And I can't change that now. I'm sorry."

"I suppose it's too late now to argue with you more about this." That damage control expression was on his face. "But no more. You're done. Done," he repeated as she opened her mouth to argue with him once more.

"No. Drex." She turned toward him, hands up in appeal. "I have to get this information out tonight. Please help me. I won't do anything else like this ever again, I swear to you."

He jumped to his feet and began to pace, his footsteps loud on the stone pavers. "How much did Parker tell you? Do you know what's going on right now?"

"Specifically?" She reached in her pocket and slid Merritt's ring on her hand. "He didn't say."

"Good. Then he hasn't completely lost his mind. I can't imagine what they're thinking, but this won't end well. If you don't want to leave—and I suppose it's not worth trying to force you to go—you'll have to get somewhere safe, at least for the night. And after that, we'll discuss what else we can do."

"Not the bunker." She'd never go there again. "Please, anywhere but there. I don't care how risky it is, I can't go back down there again. You don't understand the claustrophobia. And I still need to—"

"No." Drex held up a hand as she protested. "Look. I think what you've been doing is ill-advised and reckless, but I'd have probably done the same thing at your age. Perhaps even now, had I known about it." The drawn look on his face contradicted his assertion. "I'll take you to the old chapel to wait until this is all over, then I'll take whatever you need wherever you need it to go. Whatever else I think about the Haederans, even they won't damage it on purpose."

Avery exhaled. Hadley wouldn't like it, but she couldn't get past Drex—and if she had to trust anyone with this assignment, it was him.

"Everything is on a chip, hidden under my desk," she said. "Can you get it out of the city? Don't tell me where right now. I'll find you—and it—when things blow over."

"Don't want to tell me who and where your contact is, do you? All right. That's fair enough. I'll find someplace to stash it and try to get word back to you. If not—"

Avery smiled with more bravery than she felt. "I'll deal with it then."

"I know you will." Drex sighed. "But Av—" He hadn't called her that in years. "There will be retribution for what Teruel's people are planning to do tonight, and I can't protect you from that."

"I understand."

"Do you? I need to hear that you won't provoke them more than you already have. You know what it means for you if your father is truly gone. Keep yourself safe, at least for now. Do what they want. Promise me that."

She'd never seen Drex this frightened. Never. Not even on that night when the Haederans had arrived and everything had changed. Now his eyes were dark with worry. The shadows there seeped into her soul, and for a moment, she wished she'd listened to him before. Still, she hesitated to agree. Do what the Haederans wanted? It was too much of Drex to ask of her.

"I'm not sure I can promise all that, but I'll try. That's all I can promise you. I'm sorry."

"Then that's all I'll ask." He threw a glance at the running creek, then back up the steps to the darkening garden. "We need to get out of here while we still can. I'll try to come back for you soon, but if not . . ."

"I know. And thank you—for everything." She leaned over and kissed his cheek. "I'll see you soon."

* * *

The outline of the wooden altar was scarcely visible in the dark. Avery ran her palm over it, searching for matches, until a shard of uneven timber stabbed her in the hand. She should have known better. She'd always considered the small stone chapel on the edge of the palace grounds ancient, but as she searched the gloom with eyes that refused to adjust, she realized it was still well-kept. Mostly. The candles were new, although the chalice was empty and felt like it had been for some time. Had Victor been responsible for the upkeep himself? The timeline of abandonment felt right.

With a sigh, she made her way to the cold spring outside to fill the cup and rinse her hands. It wasn't consecrated water, but the Holy One wouldn't mind, would He? Her fingers found the matches, more cautiously this time, and she lit a few of the short votive candles for light, then stepped back.

A prayer.

She was supposed to pray, but her mind remained blank as the candles flickered, casting eerie shadows on the walls. Black holes. Nebulas, where unsuspecting starships became lost. And less natural pictures—Haederan cruisers and bombed-out Asrian cities.

In the silence, Drex's fears assaulted her. The small chapel began to cave in on her, the stone collapsing onto her, and she sagged against a window. The darkness outside didn't help, though rational thought told her it would take more than her fear to make the sturdy, stone building fall. What was happening to her?

Nothing is happening.

Nothing was happening to her, and nothing was happening outside, and nothing was happening at Alcaris. Maybe nothing would happen—there was always the chance the Defense Forces had called off their plan. Or maybe it was already over. She'd know if it was over and Merritt was dead, wouldn't she? Didn't people feel when the ones they loved were gone? No. Of course not. Knowing in your gut that someone you love was dead was a silly, romantic notion, not a belief based in reality.

She was wrestling with the temptation to go back to the palace —against Drex's orders—when the shouts began. They were too far away to make out words or to tell which direction they were headed, but she tiptoed to the altar and blew out the candles. Without them, the darkness was so heavy she flirted with the idea of lighting just one, but the light in the windows would alert anyone halfway observant to her presence. She sank to the floor, whispering a prayer, pretending the walls weren't as close as they felt.

Without warning, the door swung open. There was no way to explain why she was sitting in the dark, so she sat where she was and blinked against the beams of light pointed at her. For a moment, she hoped it was Drex, but it was Chase who stepped inside.

Her entire body slumped. Hope was—hope was a useless emotion. What had Drex once said? That the Holy One gave them hope? That the Holy One *was* hope? Drex was wrong. Drex was so naïve.

"What are you doing?" Chase sounded startled, but his shoulders sank in relief at the same time.

But of course he was relieved. Perrin would have his head if they lost her tonight. That idea made her want to dash out the door and try to lose them in the woods, but she'd never make it past all of them. She could, however, annoy him, no matter what she'd promised Drex.

"What do you think I'm doing?" she asked. "It's a chapel. I'm praying."

"You? In the dark?" He sounded astonished, and she wanted to laugh at his reaction, but he composed himself before she mustered up the emotion. "Whatever you're doing, it's time to go. There's been an attack on Alcaris. There's concern they may strike the palace next."

Oh, Merritt.

Her stomach lurched at Chase's confirmation. Still, something obviously had him worried. What was happening at Alcaris? Did the Defense Forces have a chance?

"Do you really expect me to be worried about that?" She scrambled to her feet and brushed the dust from her hands, pretending she wasn't on the verge of falling apart. So much for promising Drex she wouldn't provoke them, but Chase had asked for it, and she was hardly afraid of him. "I don't think I'm the one in danger from anyone attacking your base."

"I don't care if you're worried about it or not." His expression changed to one of concern. "You're leaving now."

Her palms began to sweat as she took a step toward Chase. What had Drex said about retribution? What if this was the start of it?

"Where are we going?"

CHAPTER SIXTEEN

If they didn't stop asking questions, she was going to scream. Some she refused to answer, and some—like where her father was —she didn't have the answer to. Even if she did, the Haederans would never believe her anyway, no matter how much Chase gently prompted her to answer truthfully. Nothing she could say mattered. Mother and Father were dead. She knew that deep down, knew she should mourn, but her relationship with them had been superficial for so long that she couldn't bring herself to cry. Not yet, at least.

Drex was another matter. For years, he'd been there for her, and he'd risked his own life for her in the end. If something had happened to him, she wouldn't be able to live with herself—and if he hadn't gotten the chip out and the Haederans found it in her rooms, she was dead.

Those two thoughts overwhelmed her with fear as Chase disappeared into the ballroom across the corridor, leaving her with another Haederan Army captain who still wouldn't stop asking questions about Merritt's whereabouts. He stormed off at her continued silence, but not before raising a threatening hand to her. She stared at the floor of the central palace library as he exited, her cheek stinging where his palm had hit, and the unwanted memory came slipping back.

She was four years old, visiting the palace for the first time, and she'd slipped away from her parents. Awe had overcome her as she'd pushed open the library doors. Three stories tall and lined with thousands of books and pictures of Asrian royalty, the room couldn't have been more different from the sprawling country estate on the coast where she'd grown up. She'd lain on the floor and stared in wonder at the ceiling, decorated with an artist's interpretation of an ancient map of Asria, the icy marble floor chilling her back and making her giggle.

She'd just found Sabino when Mother had marched in, followed by Father and Uncle Victor. Furious at her mischief, Mother threatened to drag her back home right then, but the young King Victor had laughed at his sister-in-law and said, *Let her be. This might be hers one day.*

Avery had grinned at the idea of such a magnificent room being hers, unable to understand the full significance of his remark. Maybe Victor had always had some idea of what the future held for her—and him. The future she'd never wanted until now.

Still, the memories of her mother, Sabino, and happier days were calming this time, and she'd stopped shaking at long last when Perrin appeared through the wide double doors that led from the main corridor. The soldiers by the door and on either end of the couch straightened at his entrance, and the chill of the library's white marble floor filled the entire room.

Without preface, he held out a thin tablet. "You'll read this over the worldwide Asrian networks tonight."

Avery didn't reply as she took it, just skimmed the brief speech with growing dread, each section worse than the earlier one.

An admission that Asria was withdrawing all ties to the Commonwealth as a territory of Haedera.

A declaration of her own loyalty to the Haederan emperor.

And an announcement that her parents had been assassinated

by Asrian insurgents for her father's soon-to-be announced allegiance to his brother and the Haederan Empire.

Hot tears welled up but didn't fall. Ignoring Perrin's sharp inhalation, she dropped the tablet to the floor, indifferent to the repercussions of that minor act of rebellion. It shattered into a million dazzling pieces on the cold marble, and she pushed the toe of her shoe into it, mesmerized at how the remains sparkled in the light of the chandeliers. Silver glitter, gold swirls in the marble. Like fine jewelry. Like Merritt's ring.

"I won't read this," she said. "If you think I'll help you, you're going to be very disappointed."

"I didn't give you that option, Your Highness." Perrin's cheeks flushed, but his fury didn't spill into his even voice.

There will be retribution . . .

"I won't read it, and even if I wanted to, I can't." It was too late to pretend to care what Perrin thought of her. She focused on the one statement she could do something about, even as Drex's warning rang in her ears. "You know I can't authorize the dissolution of any treaties, especially regarding our status as a Commonwealth planet. Only the senate can, and—"

"Oh, yes. The senate. They held an emergency session early this morning and voted to cancel all existing treaties and unions, including Asria's membership in the Commonwealth specifically," Perrin replied. "You'll just announce it."

Her head spun. The senate had met? She hadn't heard a word about it. Had Drex kept her out of the vote on purpose?

"That's not possible. You haven't allowed them to meet, and even if you did, you can't tell me they unanimously agreed to withdraw. You can't tell me I wasn't allowed a vote."

"Your vote is ceremonial, Your Highness. It doesn't count for anything. As for the rest, who said they voted unanimously? There may have been some hold outs, but we handled it."

His sneer and his words chilled her more than the hard library floor.

"That's coercion." *Or murder.* She shook her head before she could ask for details. "It doesn't matter anyway, if you're trying to prevent a strike by our fleet."

Our fleet.

She cringed at her slip, but Perrin appeared unaware of her meaning. Or perhaps her unintentional display of allegiance to the Commonwealth wasn't surprising enough for him to comment on.

"As far as the Commonwealth is concerned," she continued, "we're still a member planet, ready and willing to uphold our responsibilities. They don't know anything different, and they won't. You cutting off our communications has finally benefited us."

"Right now," Perrin said, "A shuttle carrying Brendin Larris is leaving the boundaries of the Asrian system. He's hand carrying a letter affirming Asria's vote to cancel their agreement with the Commonwealth."

"Senator Larris?" He'd supported her desire to leave for Ventana. "He wouldn't do that."

"His wife and children were arrested this afternoon. I don't think he felt he had much of a choice."

Without thinking, she lunged toward him, but the two soldiers flanking the sofa caught her by the shoulders. Realizing the futility of her attempt, she stopped and shook them off. They backed away, but not by much.

"You can't keep threatening us." Her heart thumped. "I won't allow it."

"And you can't keep ignoring my demands."

Perrin's lecture was cut short as Grant Baylen walked in, surrounded by Haederan soldiers. The prime minister was dressed in casual but expensive clothing, and no sleep lines creased his face—far from the rumpled appearance she'd have expected this time of night. How much of the senate's latest vote had been his doing? Baylen was known for bending the senate to meet his own whims, after all.

Avery glared at them both as she sank to the sofa again, but even from across the room she could tell that Baylen looked as unhappy as she felt. Perrin waved him over, and Baylen sat next to her as she gazed at him, mystified by his expression. The faint red mark on his jaw and his cerulean shirt, the exact color of the Asrian flag, sealed her judgment, and a strange relief flooded her at the sight of this unexpected ally. Baylen wasn't cooperating with the Haederans after all.

She picked at a loose thread on the sofa in relief, ignoring his silent question.

No. I am not all right, Prime Minister.

"It's disappointing to learn that we don't have the support from the Asrian government that I thought we might," Perrin said, pulling up one of the reading chairs across the low table between them. It was Mother's favorite, a garnet damask armchair that matched nothing else in the palace and so had been relegated to the library years before. Avery wanted to knock him out of it.

"Although perhaps not very surprising," he went on. He glared at Baylen. "Regardless of what I'd hoped, I have a problem now. We're aware the royal family is well-liked, particularly in Cadena and among your military, and I'm becoming increasingly doubtful of our ability to maintain peaceable control of Asria without your backing."

His unspoken allusion to her relationship with Merritt sent a wave of dizziness through her, and she pulled out more of the thread than she'd planned. Where was he going with this? Was he simply drawing out his little speech? Well, he was right about one thing. He wouldn't get her support tonight. He wouldn't get it at all. Nor Baylen's, if she had anything to say about it.

"The backing you're not giving me tonight," Perrin continued. "That's going to change, right now, because I have a proposition for you both. You might remember, Your Highness, that when we first met, I suggested an eventual oath to the Haederan Empire, and I think that time has come. You both sign it, one of you gives the speech, and things go back to how they were two days ago.

Refuse, and . . ." He held a hand out to the library door. "Well. I'll leave the consequences to your imagination for a while. I don't think you'll find them desirable."

"No."

Her reply was without hesitation, and so was the shake of her head.

"I have to say, I'm surprised." Perrin's eyebrows shot up, so Baylen must have done the same. "I think it's a foolish and short-sighted choice, but the offer's open when you two decide it's time to come around. I don't think it'll be too long." He raised a finger, and the soldier behind him approached. "We're done here."

Avery stood. Whatever came next, it had to be better than being in the same room as Perrin. Another slap on the cheek? It certainly couldn't be worse.

"Oh!" Perrin snapped his fingers, and his face lit up in a grin more suitable for the king's birthday ball. "I forgot one thing. I believe you both know a Merritt Parker?"

Her knees went weak, and she fell back to the sofa without a word. Perrin wouldn't come into focus, and as she fought to clear her vision, Baylen's hand slipped over hers. With that gesture of comfort . . .

She knew.

"You know we do." Baylen sounded livid for the first time that night.

Perrin reached into his pocket and pulled out a small item, clutched tightly in his closed hand. "Lieutenant Colonel Parker led the attempt to take back Alcaris tonight. An ill-conceived and futile plan, I might add. I can't imagine what your Defense Forces were thinking."

He smiled at her, drawing out his news one more time. Toying with her because he could.

"Fifty men, against a heavily guarded base?" He shook his head in mock regret and glanced at his fist again. "Even if they'd gotten in the air, even if they'd made it to orbit, it wouldn't have mattered. But they never even made it to the ships. Foolish."

"Just say what you're going to say." The venom in her own voice shocked her, and she didn't care if Perrin did anything about her contempt. He could do anything he wanted to her now, because without Merritt, her life was over.

"It sounds like it won't surprise you to hear we knew they were coming." Perrin sounded all too pleased with himself. "None of them survived."

The floor dropped out from under her, and suddenly she was falling through space, the library spinning in sheets of color she couldn't identify. As she plummeted, Perrin opened his hand and slid two rounded, silver stars across the low table between them.

The fall into nothingness slammed to a halt, like the stars were a solid steel wall.

Royal Asrian Defense Forces lieutenant colonel rank.

Her hand reached out on its own, but she pulled it back and dug her fingers into the fabric of the sofa. She couldn't touch them. Touching them would make it real.

But it was real. From now on, her life would always be split into two halves—when Merritt was here and when Merritt was dead.

"Where did you get these?" she whispered.

"Don't be ridiculous, Governor. Those could belong to anyone." Baylen's cool assertion broke into her irrational emotion before Perrin could reply, and a sliver of hope took its place.

He was right. Those didn't belong to Merritt. Perrin was only tormenting her. Merritt wasn't dead. How could he be? He was supposed to be around for the rest of her life.

"They could, but they don't. This doesn't, either."

Baylen sighed as he held out his hand, and Avery tore her stare from the stars to see Merritt's authorization token laying in his palm, his picture staring up at her. He would have never given up his system access, and even the Haederans wouldn't have taken his identification from him—unless he was gone. The gold swirls on the floor spun again, and something Perrin had said jolted in her mind.

"None of them? But that doesn't make sense." Even a last-minute attack wouldn't have resulted in the deaths of everyone. Merritt wouldn't have attempted something like this without a firm strategy, and the Haederans must have taken at least a few prisoners. She turned to Baylen in a panic, a hand over her mouth, as a horrifying suspicion swept her away. "They murdered them."

"Is this true?"

Baylen's smooth politician act returned as he spoke, his question as unwavering as any he'd have asked on the senate floor, and Avery clenched her fists beside her before she struck at him. Before she hurt him as much as Perrin had hurt her, even though physical pain could never compare to the emotional kind. The kind that ripped out your soul. How could Baylen sound so rational when her world had just shattered into a million pieces for no reason at all? No reason except revenge.

That infuriating smile appeared on Perrin's face again. "I warned you both that any resistance would have grave and immediate consequences. You could have accepted this annexation without a fight, but you wanted to test us militarily. Again. You're seeing the consequences of that decision now." He stopped to look at Baylen. "I assume you ordered this?"

Avery found her voice, if only to divert Perrin's attention from the prime minister. "You murdered them! You killed—you can't have killed them all!"

She couldn't say Merritt's name, but the next thing she knew, she was on her feet once more, and it was Baylen, not the soldiers, who was pulling her back. Why was he bothering? Perrin needed to die for what had happened to Merritt and the others.

Perrin looked astonished that she'd argued with him. "Can't? Haven't you learned yet, Your Highness? We can do anything we want." He waved at the guards. "Get them out of here."

CHAPTER SEVENTEEN

There shouldn't have been any tears left, but they continued to fall as Avery wrapped her arms around herself and looked around the cell. They'd blindfolded her on the short flight to wherever she was, but the long elevator ride suggested she was deep underground, likely in the same building with which Chase had threatened Merritt and her. The cell reminded her of the bunker, and of the invasion, and of Drex. For the thousandth time since they parted, she asked the Holy One if he was safe. If he'd managed to get the chip out of Cadena. Or had everything she'd done been for nothing? Likely it had been, and that meant she'd forfeited her life for no reason at all.

But sitting and praying solved nothing, so she explored the entire cell, more to keep warm and occupied than out of any hope of escape, for she'd already decided there were no weak points in the concrete box. As she ran her fingers along the walls, she cried over Merritt until the headache outweighed the pain in her heart. When that proved fruitless, she searched her pockets once more for any useful escape tools, but the Haederans had taken everything, even Merritt's ring. The empty place on her hand, where she'd already become used to the weight of that small piece of metal, was something else she'd never forgive them for.

Exhausted and too frustrated to do much else, she stood on the bench and studied the ceiling once more. It was at least three times her height, with nothing but a light and a small vent at the very top. An irregular breeze blew from the vent—the Haederans must have changed the programming to prevent her from having any sense of time—and it wasn't large enough for her to fit through, even if she climbed the wall. She placed a foot on the wall to test it anyway, but it was too slick to gain any traction.

The door beeped as she was considering her chances at carving handholds into the wall with her nails. Caught, she jumped to the floor and backed into the farthest corner. Was Perrin that impatient for her or Baylen to read his speech? By now he must be, and she didn't know if she was strong enough to say no again.

But when the guards outside pulled the door open, it was Chase, not Perrin, who stood in the doorway, a package under his arm. Curiosity and relief replaced fear, and she stepped away from the wall—if anyone was to visit, best to be him. He was more of an ally than anyone else in this place, wasn't he?

"What do you want?" It sounded rude, but how could she blame her for that? Relief and politeness only stretched so far.

"Just to give you this." He stepped inside and held up a small package.

The door closed behind him, and he walked farther inside. But instead of handing her the package, he reached into his chest pocket and brought out a few small objects. Even in the dim light, she could see it was her silver ring and Merritt's stars. Tears threatened again, and she dug a nail into her palm to stop them. Her enemy couldn't see how his kindness affected her, not even one as sympathetic as Chase.

"I'll just leave them here, then," he said, motioning to the bench.

"No." He must have noticed the look on her face. The obvious emotion was even more humiliation she couldn't stand, and she wasn't sure she could take much more. "Please. I'll take them."

He handed them over without a word, and she slid the ring on her finger, relishing the very weight of it. The Haederans wouldn't get it back. Ever. "I—I appreciate it." Thanking him made her feel as traitorous as her uncle, but Chase was likely acting against Perrin's orders, and that had to mean something.

"It's no problem." Chase unwrapped the package under his arm and glanced inside. "Sennyl. And water." He took a step back, and the consideration calmed her enough to take the items from him. "You're still going to have one hell of a headache."

How long had he been watching her sob over Merritt? To cover her unease at the obvious surveillance, she rolled the pills between her fingers and scrutinized them. If they weren't pain medicine, they were a perfect copy of it. Taking a chance, she tossed them in her mouth. The package had been sealed, after all.

"Where's Prime Minister Baylen?" she asked. He'd been on the shuttle here—at least, she thought he'd been—but she hadn't heard him exit with her. So many lives were in jeopardy because of her. "Is he all right?"

"He's thinking things over, just like you. But if you're ready, I can take you back to Governor Perrin now. I can't promise how much more time he's willing to give the two of you."

"No." Avery sat the water on the floor and rubbed her temples. The headache had ebbed, but now it had blasted right back with his suggestion. "It's not going to happen, so if he sent you here to talk me into it, you can tell him that."

Chase gave a short laugh. "Believe me, you don't want to know what he'll do if I tell him you said that, so I'll forget I heard it. I'm curious though—why not just do what we want? Things would be a lot easier for you if you'd stop fighting this. You had to have seen his request coming a long time ago."

She sank to the bench and stared at Merritt's ring. Why indeed? She knew, and Chase had to know, but *saying* it was something completely different. A confession, perhaps.

"Because I'm Asrian," she replied, never looking up from the ring.

It was the only explanation she was willing to give, even to Chase. Because if he didn't already know the answer to that question, he had no concept of allegiance, and there was no chance of making him understand. Not that he deserved any kind of justification for her decision. Not that any of them did. She wasn't going to give Perrin his oath, and that was all there was to it.

"You're that certain?" he asked.

She didn't even nod.

"I wish you felt differently." His shoulders sagged as he turned to go.

I bet you do.

As the door closed again, she traced a shaking finger around the stars in her palm. They were shaped just like Merritt's favorite flower, the wild cylva that grew in the alpine meadows outside Cadena. She'd never agreed with him about the resemblance before now.

They hadn't made it that high the night the Haederans had interrupted them, but they'd hiked through the same field years before, the week before she left for Ventana IV. Merritt had tucked one of the pale violet blooms behind her ear, and the intensity in his eyes had frightened her. She hadn't wanted to fall in love with him back then, hadn't wanted to fall in love with anyone, hadn't wanted anything to tie her to her own world. She'd loved him—but she'd wanted off Asria. What she wouldn't give to change that now.

She shoved the stars in her pocket and kissed his ring, and the weight of her hand against her mouth muted her cry.

She was dreaming of Merritt again when the heavy door slid open once more, jolting her from a restless sleep. Even though she hadn't seen Perrin since his ultimatum in the library days before, she'd expected him soon, and when four Haederan soldiers entered instead, an unexplainable panic bubbled up inside of her.

They weren't here to take her back to Perrin—somehow, she knew that. The dread in her soul couldn't be wrong.

No, today they were here for something much worse.

They'd left the door open when they marched inside, and without thinking, she darted straight at it, her feet as heavy as lead. She made it halfway before one soldier grabbed her by the arm and flung backward. Still exhausted, she didn't put her hands out in time and landed with her weight on one shoulder. Agony sparked deep within her, and when she reached up to rub the sting away, pain exploded in her side.

"Don't move, or I'll do it again. Put your hands on the back of your head."

A rifle pushed against the back of her neck. She gulped for air as she tried to catch her breath and will the pain away. It didn't work, and she couldn't suppress a whimper, the sound of her own fear tangible as it bounded off the walls.

"I told you to shut up."

The soldier kicked her in the side, harder than the first time, and a blinding pain flashed through her. Through the haze, she wanted to argue that he hadn't told her to shut up, and that she hadn't moved, just as he ordered. Instead she stayed silent, the gray floor cool and soothing beneath her cheek. She focused on the comforting feeling, trying to ignore what must be at least one broken rib, as his boot moved into her field of vision and toward her face.

Images flashed into her mind, bruises and blood and electricity. The soldiers didn't understand. The Holy One didn't understand. She couldn't survive this. There was no way. Would they not just shoot her and be done with it? Was Perrin so enraged with her that he had ordered her to be tortured first?

A breeze fluttered across her cheek, and Avery squeezed her eyes shut, bracing for another blow. Another set of footsteps echoed into the cell, and when she opened her eyes to the sound, the boot had stopped in midair, a hair's distance away from her jaw.

"That's enough. Get her up."

The new voice was familiar, but so strangely cold she couldn't identify it from her position on the floor. She tried to raise her head to make out the owner, but the smallest movement sent a shock of agony through her body, and she froze, flat on her stomach. Two soldiers jerked her arms behind her, and when they pulled her to her feet, she kicked backward—making contact with one of them, if the string of curses he let out in some obscure Haederan dialect was to be believed. Thrilled she'd hurt him, she braced herself to try again when the other pressed a stun pistol against the back of her neck so hard she gasped.

"I'd stop now, if I were you," the familiar voice remarked with a casualness that felt out of place. "You won't like what they do next."

She looked up at that, and her mouth went dry in horrified recognition at the man who stood in front of her. The man who looked and sounded exactly like Captain Gareth Chase . . . but who now wore the uniform of a colonel.

An Imperial Security Command colonel.

She blinked at him, trying to free herself from the disorientation that had settled around her like a thick fog. It clung to her as she stared at him for a minute that seemed to stretch on for hours; she was powerless to throw it off. She blinked once more, and in a flash of understanding and certainty, the confusion vanished.

They knew.

He knew.

Somehow they knew, somehow he had found out. How long had they known? How long had he known?

Her eyes flickered around the cell as she tried to focus on the still-open door, on the floor, on the walls, on her feet, on anything but Chase. But focus evaded her, and her focus drifted back to him again and again, back to the small crossed swords on his collar, the Imperial Security Command insignia that signified her worst nightmare. She couldn't formulate any further coherent thought. Only one word.

"Please."

Chase took a step toward her. "I'd rather they not do that again, but that depends on your cooperation." Another step. "And that cooperation starts with you not attacking my men."

Eyes wide, she shook her head as much as she dared, needing to get away from him more than she needed to breathe—though that had become almost impossible. The pistol pushed harder against the base of her skull as she shifted to the side, and she wished she hadn't moved.

"No?" He turned away just long enough to wave the door shut. "I think it's an easy request. But maybe you're right. You don't know what else I want."

She did. She wished she didn't know why he was there, but she did. The door to the cell loomed behind him, mocking her, and she closed her eyes. The loss of her only escape route had suddenly become worse than his presence.

Chase laughed softly. "Or maybe you do." He must have gestured at the men holding her, because the pressure on her neck disappeared. "Sit down."

On trembling legs, she walked to the hard slab, then put her head in her hands so he couldn't see the fear on her face. No one said anything as she sat there, so she counted off the minutes pausing too often to focus on the numbers and not the sweltering terror that swirled about her.

One.

Two.

Her shoulder didn't hurt as much anymore, but bolts of pain shot down her side, making it hard to breathe and harder to keep count. Maybe if she didn't look up, they would leave. Or maybe it was a dream. Yes. That was it, just a dream. But if it was a dream, where was Merritt?

It was a nightmare, then.

No, even a nightmare would be better than this reality.

Three.

Four.

Five minutes.

She was about to count to six when Chase spoke, scattering any possibility it was a bad dream.

"Aren't you even a little curious?" he asked.

He was so conversational. So casual. And so close to where she sat.

"A—about—" Her voice shook, and no matter what he had just asked, she sat without speaking until she could control it. "About w—what?"

"Who I really am."

Avery shook her head and focused on his boots. Black, like the ones she'd worn for three years at the academy. Just not as polished as the Commonwealth Navy had required of hers. She'd sat in her room each evening and buffed them until they'd gleamed, an activity Chase clearly found beneath him.

How irrelevant.

She started to pray—if she prayed hard enough, wouldn't she disappear? Maybe Chase and the soldiers would. Why didn't prayer work that way? What good was it for if it couldn't save her from this horror?

Holy One, make him go away. Protect me.

"Then you already know."

Avery glanced up long enough to see the strange expression she hadn't recognized the first time they'd met on his face. It disappeared in an instant, but now she knew him well enough to see he couldn't quite hide the fact he found the situation entertaining. She resumed her study of his boots, the terror building into a crescendo of hate. Her fear *amused* him?

"Look at me." Chase grasped her chin and forced her to look up at him, tightening his grip as she fought to twist away. "Why are you so worried?"

Her heart was beating so fast she thought it might splinter right there in front of him. He was playing games. He knew exactly why she was so afraid, and he knew the bruises he was leaving on her jaw were the least of it. She couldn't meet his stare

—could only focus on those crossed swords—but she kept her voice steady, if only a whisper.

"Because I know what you are, Colonel."

She tried to pull free from his grip again. He would have been someone to fear even if she hadn't spent the past few months working for Hadley. Even if she'd done everything the Haederans had ever asked of her. But she hadn't cooperated with them. She'd opposed them instead, and even as a cadet, she'd heard the accounts of how the Haederans treated those they considered spies. Back then, the stories hadn't affected her much—she was more likely to die a quick death in space, after all—but now each one rushed back in an instant. Did Hadley know or even care that they would torture her before they killed her? Or had he used her as he'd used dozens of other operatives?

"Oh? Yes, I suppose anyone educated on Ventana IV would." He released her chin and looked at her with alarming appraisal, a frown forming. But there was a glint in his eyes, and even in her terrified state, it was clear the frown was merely to keep himself from laughing. "And that frightens you this much?"

Avery looked away again, and that time, he didn't force her attention back toward him. It had to be a nightmare. He knew too much about her. She had already told him too much. Another minute ticked by as she tried to remember everything they'd talked about over the past few months.

Too much. It was entirely too much.

"I asked you a question."

He still sounded as patient as he always had, but an icy undercurrent in his voice pricked at the back of her mind. Desperate to keep the tears from falling, she looked back at him. The humor in his eyes was gone.

"Yes," she whispered. "It does."

"Good."

His reply sent a shiver down her spine, as she assumed he intended it to, and she couldn't keep from crying any longer. It was humiliating to let him see her like this—the exact opposite of the courageous façade she needed to show—but she couldn't make herself stop. He'd frozen her so thoroughly with his unspoken threat that she couldn't even move to dry her eyes.

"Although I can't imagine why it would," he continued, ignoring her tears. "You certainly weren't afraid of me the night we met—the night you couldn't wait to tell me how much you hated me. I've shown you quite a bit of leniency and consideration since then, given the circumstances. Much more than you deserve." He narrowed his eyes at her. "Yet you're sitting here acting like I'm about to torture you."

Torture.

The word hung in the air between them, intentional and harsh. Yes, he'd been decent to her, kind, even, but it had all been an act. Now he was scaring her half to death for his own entertainment while pretending he didn't know he was doing it. She knew what came next, could only manage a whisper.

"You will."

"I would prefer it doesn't come to that." Chase's voice was still cold, with an edge that hadn't been there before. "But I'm glad we have an understanding now."

Avery shifted back against the smooth wall to put the last bit of distance between them. There wasn't anything else to say to him. He'd left no doubt of what he would do if she forced him into it.

"We'll talk more later," he added, visibly more relaxed than when he'd entered. "I only wanted to introduce myself again, but it looks like you did my job for me. Thank you for that." He smiled as he headed toward the door. "Tomorrow, then."

CHAPTER EIGHTEEN

DESPITE HIS PROMISE—OR THREAT, AS SHE KNEW IT WAS MEANT TO BE —Chase didn't come back the following day, and though Avery was thankful for each hour that passed without him, being forgotten about deep underground grew more terrifying than whatever he had planned for her.

The cell they'd left her in was a tenth of the size of the bunker under the palace, and unless her eyes were closed, she was certain the walls were falling down. The murky claustrophobia became unbearable as memories washed over her, each breath harder and harder to fight for, so on the second day, she stretched out on the floor in front of the door. It was sealed tight, but through the panicked heat that flowed around her, she could imagine a hairline crack at the bottom. That small vision of freedom eased her fear enough that she thought she might survive, but the guards made her move as soon as they discovered her technique—forcefully. The bruises they left had been worth it, though.

The terror came back in earnest after that, so heavy she could do nothing but sit in the middle of the dim room and scream until no more sound came out. That breakdown earned her a visit from the prison medic, who mended her two broken ribs just enough to take the edge off. The medical attention was a relief, but what the Haederans hadn't known was that focusing on the physical discomfort had been the one thing keeping her sane. She hadn't known either until it was gone, and her full concentration was diverted to her circumstances. Her only protection after that was sleep, but sleep was almost impossible to come by, achievable only in small bursts of utter fatigue. She would die if they didn't let her out soon.

But when they did . . .

When the lock beeped on the third day, she was close to sobbing in relief and exhaustion, but in a surge of clarity, stopped herself before the door opened. Chase had planned all of this. He knew just how to push her, knew just how to terrify her. Her gratitude was what he wanted now, and she was shivering with that realization when he appeared outside, polished and fresh.

"Let's take a walk."

He spoke like it was a perfectly natural extension to their last conversation. Like it'd never ended. Like he didn't know she'd spent the past three days in a panic.

Her mouth was so dry she couldn't swallow. "A walk?"

"A walk." Chase's eyes skimmed the small room as he drew a blindfold from his pocket. "I don't like being here anymore than you do."

Avery shook her head, drawing her knees up under her chin. The motion sent fresh pain through her healing injuries, but going anywhere with him was the last thing she was going to do. He would have to drag her out, and she wouldn't make it easy for him when he did.

"What did I tell you about cooperating?" At her silence, he added, with a gentleness she didn't understand, "We can do this the easy way or the hard way. It's up to you, but you're not staying here."

The bruise over her ribs throbbed. Half her brain screamed that she should fight him, and the other half was too scared of him and the soldiers behind him to do anything except sit frozen in one spot.

No, whatever she decided didn't matter—in her condition, the end would be the same. She lowered her head and allowed her hair to fall across her face, but the dark curtain of hair didn't help much. Battling the part of her will that wanted to fight, she rose and staggered toward him.

He smiled his approval as she came closer. "Taln Perrin said you were a slow learner, but I suspected otherwise. I can't wait to tell him how wrong he was."

His praise sent a hot wave of shame through her. Second-guessing the traitorous half of her brain that'd suggested she listen, Avery glanced toward the back of the cell. She should have remained seated, but no matter how much she feared the dark-ness that blindfold would bring, her legs wouldn't let her turn around.

"Will I need their help?" He waved the fabric over his shoulder toward the guards. "Or will you continue to cooperate?"

Internal heat turned to ice as she stared up at him. *Trapped.* She'd never been so trapped before. Couldn't move backward, couldn't move forward. If only time would stop.

"No." Her voice grew stronger, even though she could scarcely breathe. Perhaps she just needed to keep using it. "But I want to see where I'm going. I don't—I don't want to fall. I swear I won't run. I swear I won't fight you."

A flash of pity crossed his face. "The blindfold is nonnego-tiable. I'm sorry. But if it helps, I don't plan on letting you fall."

Sorry.

The word echoed in her mind as she nodded, fighting the gesture the entire time. Chase took one last step toward her, and the cell disappeared beyond dark fabric. Dizzy and lost inside her own body, she wavered from side to side until he took her by the arm and guided her forward.

She counted her steps as she stumbled along beside him, attempting to memorize each turn, but it was impossible to keep track of the continual meandering through corridors and lifts. He must have figured out what she was doing, because he led her in circles for what had to be an hour, until up and down ceased to have meaning. As they turned left and right and then left again, the futility of planning an escape route enraged her.

"Relax." His voice broke into the darkness as they entered another lift tube. "I want to make this fast, but I can't if you keep counting like that. Stop now, or I'll walk you around this place for the next week."

Avery tripped over her own feet, and his hold on her arm grew tighter.

You've failed again.

Worse than that realization was her sudden awareness that his voice grounded her, helping her stay calm in the blackness. She hated him for his unwitting reassurance. She hated Hadley for putting her in this situation. By the time they stopped walking fifteen minutes later, she even hated herself for what Chase would force her to say.

But when he removed the blindfold, she wasn't standing in her imagination's version of a torture chamber—it was an ordinary office, one that might be found in any number of Cadena's business districts. The army uniform Chase had been wearing before she'd seen him last was folded next to a military-issue cot in the corner, a stack of data disks on top of it. But after the days of darkness, it was the floor-to-ceiling window overlooking Cadena that caught her attention.

He let go of her arm and stopped by the desk, so she walked over to look out, even though the light hurt her eyes. The sun was scorching on the glass, the trees below her a blaze of red and gold, and the claustrophobia of the past few days melted away. She stood motionless, not wanting to move in case she was imagining the outside world. How could you be homesick for a place you never left?

The traffic was non-existent though, the usual ground cars and aeroflyers gone. This wasn't the Cadena she remembered. Despite the warmth of the sunlight, her skin chilled at the sight of the empty streets. Perrin hadn't been lying when he said things would change if she didn't play along. How much worse could it get?

"It finally stopped raining for more than an hour at a time. It's been so unpleasant here for the past week. The time of year, I'm told."

Avery jumped. How had she become so caught up in the panorama that she'd forgotten where she was and who was behind her? Chase sounded tired, and she wanted to lash out at him. He had no right to be tired after what he'd already put her through. As though the weather on Haedera was perfect all the time. As though she was supposed to care what he thought about Asria's seasons. As though he'd brought her here to talk about rain. Would he not just get on with it?

"Why am I here?" she asked.

"We have some things to talk about. I thought we'd try it the civilized way first." He leaned on the edge of his desk, arms crossed, watching her for a reaction.

"Civilized?" Her heart thudded. "Nothing about this is civilized, Colonel."

She turned back toward the window and searched for the small teashop where she'd first met Merritt all those years ago. He'd smiled hello that rainy night, and before he'd said anything, her world had changed. She twisted his ring on her right hand, her last link to him, but even thoughts of Merritt couldn't calm the tension that rushed through every part of her body. It curled even harder around her ribs at the clinking noise behind her, as if Chase was sorting data cartridges.

"We can still make it so," he replied, "if you're willing to talk about what you've been up to over the past few months."

Avery leaned her forehead against the window and concentrated on the splashes of warm color outside. Cadena had a distinct smell after a rain, clean and limestoney and spicy. *So many memories.* Chase might find the cold autumn rain unpleasant, and any Haederan probably felt the same, but to her it was home.

Home? That was a new description for it. When had she started thinking of Cadena as her home again?

"I've been quite busy." She blinked back tears, tears Chase couldn't be allowed to see. The clinking noise continued, and her voice broke. "Perrin assigned me work, and I have my own responsibilities, of course. None of it is anything that concerns an intelligence officer."

"Is that what you think I am?" There was a quiet laugh behind her. "Actually, it's just one of your activities I'm interested in."

"I don't know what you're talking about."

If she kept thinking it and kept saying it, she might believe it, and then he would have to believe it as well. Wasn't this how this worked? Yes. False bravado was better than nothing. It was better than crying in fear, even though she was right on the brink of that and he knew it.

"I think you do. You wouldn't be so afraid of me if you didn't." His tone was light, as if he saw right through her attempt at indifference. There was more shuffling and clinking, then his voice hardened. "I'm not going to keep talking to the back of your head. Why don't you have a seat?"

She tore herself away from the view and settled into a small chair by the window, as far away from Chase as she could get. No matter how politely he had phrased it, it wasn't a suggestion, and it wasn't a battle she'd win.

His eyes crinkled in amusement as she sat. In the sunlight, a smattering of distinctly Haederan freckles was evident across his nose. They hadn't been there until that day, and their appearance unnerved her.

"I have to admit, I was surprised when I first met you, Your Highness. I couldn't believe you were the sort for this. But facts don't lie."

The title, spoken with such casualness by someone who rejected the very idea of her having any status on Asria, spurred an idea, one last hope. There wasn't anything to lose by telling him now, was there? Perrin had shown he didn't care how prisoners of war were treated, but Chase had always seemed more reasonable than the governor. For the most part, he'd been kind. He'd always, before now, seemed to have some kind of honor. Maybe the truth was a way out of this horror.

"It's—" She licked her cracked lips before tossing herself over the edge and onto his mercy. "It's actually Lieutenant Rendon."

"Is it now?" He eyed her for a long moment, his amusement just hanging on. "Commonwealth or Defense Forces?"

"C—Commonwealth."

"I thought as much." His smile grew genuine. On any other person, at any other time, it would have been reassuring, but this certainty of his made her heart ache. "Did they tell you that would protect you? That any kind of military status would make a difference if you were arrested? It doesn't, you know. Not to me. They didn't warn you about Imperial Security, did they?"

Avery opened her mouth, shut it again.

Chase spun a pen around the desk with a finger, then used it to push the cartridges away one by one. "So whose idea was it? Yours or theirs?"

She grasped at Merritt's ring, silent.

He shook his head. "You can keep this up as long as you want, but you're only making it harder on yourself." He moved to the window next to her, staring outside at a view he had no right to be looking at. "I already know most of it anyway."

Fear of him crashed back in a wave that threatened to pull her under and hold her down, and she struggled to breathe through the heaviness of it all. It was no wonder he knew most of it. He'd followed her around for weeks, and she'd been too reckless to suspect him. Too certain he was as harmless as he acted. Her pride had gotten her here. Now she was sure it hadn't been a coincidence that he'd suggested they visit the temple that first evening. No, this hadn't started five minutes ago. It had started the very day she'd run into him on the street.

A chair screeched along the floor. He sat in front of her, his knees almost touching hers, looking straight into her eyes. She flinched, then looked away, out at the intense blue sky. It couldn't be this blue right now. It just couldn't. Not when this was happening.

"I warned you, you know." He waited until she looked back at him before he continued, and his patience scared her more than anything else. "It was the least I could do in light of your uncle's request that you be treated fairly. I hoped you would listen to me, and that would be the end of it—I was willing to let everything go if you'd stopped immediately. Against my better judgment, I even gave you one last chance to confess a few days ago, just so we'd be able to avoid this unpleasantness."

He paused, tilted his head toward the floor, and by extension, she assumed, the prison below.

"But you didn't listen to that either, and now Perrin is furious. He feels you took advantage of his generosity and deliberately ignored his repeated warnings to cooperate with us. He won't let your continued defiance go, especially when it comes to this. I doubt those on Haedera with any say in the matter will be inclined to show much clemency either. I could convince them to keep you alive, but I need you to give me a reason to help you."

He was lying. He had to be lying. It was too hard to concentrate on any of his words to be sure.

"Maybe I'd rather die," she said.

"I don't think you would. You told me as much, remember?"

Yes, she remembered.

How could she have been so naïve? She'd had no business talking to him the night they'd met, and instead of shutting up and going home, she'd given him all the information he needed to manipulate her. He knew the very idea of dying terrified her, and it was the easiest thing in the world to use against her. The right thing to do swirled around her head, but as hard as she tried, she couldn't catch the thought. It wouldn't stop moving, only flitted and darted about, and she could bat at it all she wanted, but she couldn't trap it in her hands to study it and examine it and figure out what she needed to do.

"Whose idea was it?" Chase repeated. He paused, like he wanted the question to sink in this time. "Your Highness, I want to help you, but there's nothing I can do if you won't talk to me."

He doesn't want to help me.

That was the only thing that was clear in the chaotic jumble of thoughts orbiting her mind. This had nothing to do with Perrin or anyone else. It was him, all him. It had always been him. If only time would stop, just for a minute, so she could collect her thoughts and figure out what she was supposed to do and say. She reached for the answer again, and again it darted away.

"Please don't." Sudden nausea overwhelmed her. Chase was lucky her stomach was empty, because she was five seconds away from throwing up on those not-so-polished boots otherwise. "I can't—"

"It was theirs, wasn't it?" He didn't wait for an answer. "The Commonwealth asked you to pass information to them, knowing how dangerous it would be for you, never warning you of what you were up against. Now they've abandoned you here. And you would still protect them? The ones who put you in this position? They don't deserve your loyalty." He grew quieter, thoughtful. "Why would you protect them?"

She squeezed her eyes shut and wiped damp palms on her knees. When he explained it like that, it didn't make any sense. He was right, the people she had trusted, had been loyal to, they'd left her here. Hadley, Feye, and the Commonwealth had thrown her into this situation against her better judgment, and now they'd abandoned her to certain death.

"I don't have anything to say to you," she whispered.

She glanced up at him once more, the first step toward betrayal making her weightless with fear. He wasn't between her and the door anymore, and maybe she could get past him and outside, then past the guards. Maybe she could find her way out of this building, wherever it was. Maybe Hadley and Feye would be gone before she told the Haederans where they were. Maybe they would never find out she knew about the verium.

Maybe, maybe, maybe.

"You have plenty to say." His amusement was gone now, and a resolute calm took its place as he leaned forward and lowered his voice. "And you'll tell me all of it."

CHAPTER NINETEEN

The cell door slid open while Avery was running a finger over a bruise on her forearm—she wasn't sure where this one had come from—and she blinked in the intense light that spilled across the floor in front of her. The two silhouettes in the doorway weren't Chase, and her initial relief turned to apprehension when they stepped inside. The soldiers had hurt her before. Chase hadn't, and she found herself wishing for his presence. He was, at least for now, somewhat predictable.

"Get up."

She faltered as she stood, her knees stiff from being pulled under her chin for so long. But sitting with her knees up against her chest was the only position that seemed safe, and standing . . . standing made her feel more vulnerable than she'd ever felt in her life.

One soldier remained in the doorway while the other circled behind her. Avery could hear him exhaling in between her own ragged breaths, but he didn't strike her this time. Didn't even touch her.

Just stood.

And breathed.

Her eyes adjusted to the artificial light streaming inside, and she lifted her chin, meeting the gaze of the soldier in the doorway. Arrogance. It was so evident.

So it was more psychological torment, then. Well, fine. The other one could stand behind her for the next hour if he felt like it. She didn't care. As long as they weren't breaking more ribs, she didn't care what they did.

His fist slammed against the center of her back just as she swallowed, and she took a step forward, catching herself just in time—both from falling and spinning around in anger. She'd learned the hard way that confronting them over their treatment only led to worse.

"On your knees."

She bit the inside of her cheek as she sank to the floor, letting the hatred overtake the fear. It was sharp and hard, and simply handling it by the edges cut into her soul, but she clung to it, pretended there was nothing to be afraid of, that no emotion existed for her but absolute loathing.

"I catch you standing"—a hand wound through her hair, yanking hard enough to draw a gasp—"and you'll be doing nothing but standing against that wall for the next week."

He released her, but she didn't bother asking how long she was supposed to kneel here—she'd also learned the correct answer was *until they returned and told her otherwise*. Maybe that was how she'd gotten the bruise, but she couldn't be sure, for the dark holes in her memory grew deeper every time she woke up.

Boots thumped around her, and the door slammed shut once more, leaving her kneeling alone in the gray darkness, staring at the gray sleeves of the jumpsuit they'd given her a few days before. Did any other colors still exist? Was the blue sky she resented so much out there somewhere? She hadn't seen it since that day in Chase's office, and that day could have been yesterday or a week ago, for trying to keep track of time in this dark, unchanging place was impossible.

Still, even though time had no meaning any longer, they couldn't leave her like this forever. A few hours, maybe. She'd lost count last time after thirty-five minutes. Ordering her about like this was just another game, another way to break her resistance before Chase brought her back to him. Before he finished wearing her down completely. Before she told him everything he wanted to know.

Hadley.

Drex.

Cameron Pernella.

The verium.

Tears dripped onto her thigh, soaking through the thin material. The jumpsuit was worn, and it hardly kept the chill from sinking into her muscles. Muscles that were cramping already. And yet, as bad as the physical discomfort was, the psychological part—which Chase was clearly experienced at—was even worse.

There's only one way out of this—out of seeing him again. You know what you have to do.

Avery shifted on the concrete as the familiar thought intruded once more, the soldiers' latest game of *how can we scare the hell out of her this time?* almost forgotten. She'd been arguing with herself about the same thing for what must have been hours, ever since they'd dropped off her latest meal, flavorless field rations she couldn't bring herself to touch.

I don't want to do it. It'll hurt, and I'm afraid.

She'd never been stunned. She wished now that she'd had the opportunity, just so she'd know what to expect. Still, anyone could guess how unpleasant it would be—the initial feeling of a hot lightning strike, followed by a blinding headache and muscle weakness that could persist for days afterward.

It'll only hurt for a moment, and then you'll have escaped. For a while, at least.

Yes, for a moment. Were there long-term effects to being stunned more than once in a short amount of time? Had anyone researched it? She didn't know and hoped she wouldn't find *that* out the hard way as well, because getting them to stun her repeatedly was exactly what she was going to do.

The soldiers came back sooner than she'd expected, and in that instant, she didn't care how badly they hurt her so long as she ended up unconscious. Avery sprang forward as they entered, catching nothing more than a glimpse of their startled faces. They would learn if there was a next time, but right now she might as well have caught them sleeping.

Shadows turned to luminosity as she darted into the corridor. Heavy doors lined each side, and for a fraction of a second she wondered who else might be behind them.

Then she caught sight of the door at the end.

Escape through the door would be an even better outcome than being stunned if she could make it that far. She hurled herself toward it, the heavy-booted footsteps of the soldiers right behind her. Her hands shook as she felt for the handle, and it took more seconds than she could spare to get a firm grip on it.

When she did, she cried out in frustration.

Locked.

She clawed at the touch pad on the side of the doorframe, but flashed red, coded to the guards' fingerprints, she now realized. A great force smashed her into the door, stealing her oxygen, and she turned her head just in time to avoid breaking her nose.

Fight him.

She twisted around and kicked at the guard, but he slammed her against the wall a second time as she raised an elbow to his chest. Her teeth jolted as the back of her head hit the wall, his face all too close to hers.

This was it.

She hadn't made it to freedom, but they'd have to shoot her now, and she'd avoid another visit with Chase. She wouldn't be able to tell him anything. Not about Hadley, not about Cameron, not about Drex, not about the verium.

The other soldier raised his stun pistol.

Avery took a deep breath, bracing herself for the heat.

Sleep . . .

The pistol slammed twice across her face before she could exhale. Light turned to shadows as she collapsed forward on her hands and knees, unable to move. Her knees ached, had ached forever, it seemed. Her head pounded, a dull, aching throb she couldn't understand. She struggled to catch her breath, bewildered by the guards' forceful reaction, and the one who had hit her lifted her head up by her hair. An involuntary moan escaped, and he yanked harder.

"Do you think I don't know what you're trying to do?"

The floor swirled underneath her, and for a moment, she wondered if one could vomit on an empty stomach.

"Well, you're not getting out of it that easily. He wants you conscious."

There went that brilliant plan. For every tactic she devised, they were one step ahead of her, and now Chase would subject her to some punishment or another for her attempted rebellion. Her stomach rebelled at the very idea.

They yanked her to her feet. Avery fought them with every step, but her feet scarcely touched the ground as they dragged her to a bright, windowless room—not nearly far enough from her cell for her liking. Her eyes were still blinking away the unfamiliar light when the soldiers let go of her arms without warning. She crashed to the concrete in front of Chase, too dazed to take advantage of the sudden freedom.

"What happened?" Chase peered down at her, sounding as surprised as she felt.

"Sorry, sir."

The response was almost inaudible, as were the rapid footsteps leaving. The door slammed without further explanation, sealing her inside.

They're afraid of him too.

She pushed herself up and eyed Chase with apprehension, but he only looked startled at her unorthodox manner of arrival. It was a long second before he collected himself enough to order her to her feet, but she shrank away from him instead, a hand on her already swollen eye. The sticky warmth suggested blood as well, but she couldn't bring herself to confirm it.

He sighed as he knelt in front of her, as though she'd frustrated him more than anything else.

"Let me see," he said.

He hadn't said anything about her refusal to stand, but it had to be coming. The guards would have never stood for even the slightest rebellion like this, after all. And if he hit her now—she recoiled from him at the very thought. If he hit her now, she wouldn't be able to stand it.

"Hurts," she replied, though it was only a whisper. Her throat tightened at the sweet perfume of . . . incense? It was unmistakable in a place that smelled of nothing else but sweat and fear. He'd been at the *temple* before coming here?

"I'm sure it does. Let me see it."

She searched for compassion in his words, but there was none, only emotionless agreement. He pried her hand away as she stared unblinkingly at him, and his eyes widened in faint, satisfied astonishment at what she could only guess had turned into a remarkable welt already. It was not an encouraging reaction.

"Why did they do this?" he asked.

Why did you make them do this to you? was what he really meant, and she wasn't going to confess to anything. Her explanation wouldn't make a difference to him anyway. As far as he was concerned, she'd asked for what the guards had done to her and for whatever else he would mete out as punishment for her escape attempt.

Avery pressed her lips closed.

"Answer me."

His cold demand and the fragrance of betrayal clinging to his uniform sparked something recalcitrant in her. The response winding through her mind was akin to poking a stick at one of the venomous takairs that stalked the mountains outside Cadena, but she couldn't stop herself.

"Because I didn't hit them hard enough first," she managed to stammer.

Stupid, Avery. He's much more dangerous than a takair.

Chase stood and folded his arms.

"I suppose it's time to have a discussion about your lack of cooperation. I've been tolerant of this for far too long." He regarded the floor with more interest than it could possibly warrant, then reached for the handcuffs on the table behind him. "Get up. If I have to tell you again, you'll be begging me to send you back to the guards."

CHAPTER TWENTY

TIME SLOWED TO A CRAWL; THE DAYS AND WEEKS BLENDED INTO A haze of beatings, interrogations, and sparsely provided field rations. She hadn't known hunger until now—hadn't known actual exhaustion either, the kind that stole entire days from her memory.

But more troubling than both the hunger and fatigue were the Haederan Army guards, who had apparently decided that any hesitation on her part to their instructions was to be considered defiance, an act forbidden by their Imperial Security master and punished as such. It never mattered how quickly she complied with their demands—it was never fast enough. They never struck her as hard as she feared, so she guessed Chase wanted her *able* to talk, but her resolve slipped away each time they came to bring her to him.

Today, when they dropped her in a chair in what she assumed was the same room they'd brought her to so many times before, she struggled to stay upright. It was only the ache from the blindfold, wound against her injured eye, that kept her awake. True, her hands were cuffed in front of her, and she could remove it if she wanted to, but she'd only needed to make that mistake once—it turned out the pain from being hit across the face with a stun pistol a second time was worse than this minor discomfort. There were soft murmurs in the background before the door closed, then Chase's voice, too close.

"They tell me you didn't fight much this time." He untied the blindfold, and she blinked in the unwelcome glare. "I'm glad to hear it. I hope that means you're finally starting to realize this pointless struggle is a waste of time. A waste of . . . well, a waste of everything, no?"

He ran a light finger across the bruise that threatened to cover the entire left side of her face. The pain should have become something easy enough to ignore, but she flinched and tried unsuccessfully to hide a sob. His touch made her bad eye water, and she closed them both in defense. The darkness . . . oh, it felt so good. She slumped against the chair, ignoring his presence. If he would only forget about her for five minutes—

A slap echoed in the closed room, and her eyes sprang open in search of the sound. Stinging pain followed, and she braced her feet on the floor to keep from sliding off the chair. Closing her eyes had been one more mistake in a long series of them. Of course Chase would never let her fall asleep, just like the guards hadn't allowed her to sleep for more than an hour or two at a time in her cell.

"Am I boring you already?" he asked as she swept away the pain with her fingers.

It was difficult with one eye swollen shut, but she gave him her best attempt at a fearless stare. Today she wouldn't say one word to him, no matter what he did. Still, his patience was frightening. Didn't he have superiors demanding an update from him? Surely they wouldn't give him this much time. Chase himself knew her tales about her involvement with the Commonwealth—innocent half-truths some days and brazen lies on others—were just that. He told her as much each time he ordered her back to this room, a room that would forever haunt her dreams. How long would he wait?

"Or have you not been getting enough sleep?" he added.

I hate you. I hate you. I hate you.

"You know I haven't." So much for staying quiet, but he knew just how to provoke her.

"This is a Haederan Army prison, not Imperial Security. I don't have any say in what goes on down here." He looked at a tablet on the table behind him, then set it aside. "Only whether you stay. And so far, you haven't given me any reason to have you moved to better quarters."

She ignored him yet again and stared at the wall. Did he honestly expect her to believe he hadn't given the guards implicit freedom to beat her? He must be trying to keep his own conscience clean. Still trying to gain her trust.

"In fact, just before you came in," he went on, "I replied to another request for your transfer to Haedera, asking for more time. I can safely say that won't be the better treatment you want."

"What?" Her eyes met his, hot and imploring.

"You didn't think they'd give me forever to do this, did you?" He pulled a heavy metal chair opposite her. She wanted to slide away from him, but every part of her was too heavy to move. "I can't put them off much longer. You have to give me something I can use. No more stories. No more lies."

"When?" Her voice broke. Just a single word, and she couldn't say it without falling apart. And why couldn't she stop shaking?

"They've called me up tomorrow to discuss this." He made a vague gesture upward at what she assumed was one of the Haederan ships in orbit. "I need to have something to tell them before that. If they don't like what I have to say, I suppose you would leave the next day, on the first courier ship out. That's not up to me."

The world tumbled around her, like a ship spiraling out of control through space, and the nausea she always associated with zero gravity advanced. She wavered, trying to balance on the chair without the use of her hands.

"I can't go there."

Holy One, I can't go there.

"I would tend to agree with that." He looked at her with compassion, the expression she hated to see on him more than the hard, cold ones. Was her future so terrible even this Haederan officer was worried for her? "I don't want to send you there either, but the decision will be out of my hands soon."

Upright, she was still upright, feet on the ground, and a sudden clarity she hadn't felt for weeks crept into her mind. She could still do something about this. As long as she stayed on Asria, she could do something about this. Chase had wanted . . .

What had he wanted? She could barely remember anymore. He'd asked so many questions over the past few weeks . . . questions she hadn't answered. Questions she'd pretended to know nothing about.

"I'll show you where the second location is."

Her mouth spoke before her brain caught up. But yes—if she could only get there, she could leave Feye a message, and he and Hadley would be out of Cadena before she knew it. It didn't matter if the Haederans knew where it was or not, did it? If they went poking around there without her, Feye would be suspicious, and she couldn't imagine a suspicious Feye would stick around long enough for the Haederans to catch him.

"Show me?" Unblinking, he raised one brow. "That won't be necessary. You'll tell me. Now."

"I don't remember until I'm walking there." Oh, this had been a terrible idea. "It's in the Old City, and the streets are confusing—"

Chase's chair clanged against the hard floor as he stood, and she jerked at the sound, slamming her back against the chair. He strode to the door and called two of the guards back inside while she stared at him, wide-eyed.

"Take her back," he told the lieutenant. "I'll comm further instructions tomorrow evening."

The lieutenant's reply vaporized in a buzz of terror. If she didn't talk to Chase, he'd tell his people she wasn't cooperating with him, and then they would take her to Haedera, and then she would tell them everything anyway, somehow, and then they would kill her.

No. Stop!

Why wasn't Chase listening to her? She couldn't speak, couldn't find the words to make him listen. The soldiers grabbed her by the arms and lifted her out of the chair, and her knees gave out.

"No! Don't let them take me!"

Chase didn't appear to have heard her—or perhaps he'd ignored her—even though she'd screamed the plea that time. She couldn't force herself to say anything else. They dragged her limp body toward the door, the door that was the entrance to the end of her life. They were a step from it before she could speak again.

"It's a warehouse in the Old City." The tears fell harder as she fought to free her hands so she could cover her face.

"Shut up." The lieutenant's voice was right in her ear.

She scarcely felt his weak slap to the side of her head, too used to the harsh treatment of his men, but his words cut into her soul. Didn't he understand? She couldn't go to Haedera. She *had* to talk now, had to tell Chase—

"Let her say what she wants to say." Chase appeared at her side, staring at her with expectance, as if by some miracle she might say something of consequence to him after all this time.

She took a ragged breath. "On Ameto Road. There's a loose brick on one side of the building, and—"

"The signal?"

"I was supposed to leave the window in my office at the senate building tinted open that night."

Ice stabbed her heart.

She'd forgotten. She'd been too terrified to remember.

The Dragonfly model.

She'd forgotten it was the signal to advise Feye she'd been compromised. Why hadn't she thought of it before she spoke? It would've warned Feye away, saved both him and Hadley. Chase would have moved it in front of the window just like she told him to, never the wiser—at least until Feye never showed his face anywhere. And by then, it would've been too late to find him and Hadley. She could have protected them. But he would never believe her if she changed her story now. Sluggish, she pressed her lips. Everything she did made things worse.

"Don't ever lie to me again," he said, eying her carefully, no doubt deciding whether to crush her throat.

He jerked his chin at the lieutenant, and they dropped her back into the chair. Avery watched them leave, then focused at the wall across the room, unable to look at Chase. How had he known she was lying?

The room was quiet for a long time, with only her soft hiccups to break the silence.

And then Chase sighed.

"You know you've been here too long for that information to be of any use to me," he finally said. "They won't trust a single piece of intelligence you leave there now. If you'd been up front with me from the beginning, told me the truth, things might have been different. But now . . ." His voice was soft as he leaned against the table. "You're going to have to do better than that. I'll call them back in otherwise. Last chance."

The world spun again. She'd used every bit of energy on ignoring her loyalties, and now he was saying it meant nothing? What else did he want from her? She couldn't remember anything. Couldn't even remember what she wasn't supposed to tell him. She wasn't supposed to tell him anything, was she? It was too late for that now, but there was one thing he couldn't know above all else.

Not the verium. He can't know anything about the verium.

Chase glanced back at his tablet as she panicked inside, that same indifferent expression back on his face.

"You've already told me enough that the Commonwealth won't want anything to do with you ever again," he said. "If that's what you're worried about, you might as well tell me everything. It doesn't matter what you do any longer as far as they're concerned."

"I—" Avery wiped the tears away, but they kept falling. "I don't know what you want anymore. I don't know anything."

He appeared to consider that for a moment. "I'm sure you know where your contact is."

The world stopped spinning, and a clarity she couldn't believe took over.

He was right.

She had betrayed everyone. Asria, the Commonwealth, Hadley himself. Had ruined everything. Why would anyone trust her after this?

She swallowed, even though the movement hurt her throat.

"Yes. I know where he is. I'll tell you where to find him."

Not *is*, though.

Was.

It had to be *was*. Hadley and Feye would have to be gone by now if they had any sense at all. If they were still there, she'd never be able to live with what she'd just said.

"That'll do. For now." Chase held out the tablet, then laid it in her lap when she didn't take it from him at once. "Write it down. I want details. When I get back, we'll pay him a visit."

With bound hands that shook more with each word, she scratched directions to the safe house under the herb shop, then, at Chase's prompting, a poor rendition of Hadley's looks. Was it poor enough that the Haederan Army wouldn't be able to recognize him if they saw him on the streets of Cadena?

She handed the tablet back once she'd finished, unable to look at him. The lights on the side flashed, transmitting her betrayal, but there were no more tears.

Tears were for the innocent.

CHAPTER TWENTY-ONE

CHASE MIGHT NOT HAVE BEEN WILLING TO ORDER BETTER QUARTERS for her before he left Asria, but he had ordered the soldiers to leave her alone, for just a few days. Only Avery wasn't sure she cared what they did to her anymore. He was right. She'd betrayed everything and everyone she'd ever cared about. Hadley must know what she'd told Chase, and that was why he'd deserted her. Her father had left her to rule Asria alone, even by dying, but she wouldn't survive long enough to do so, because even Drex had abandoned her. If anyone would've been able to save her, it would have been him. He'd sworn to protect the Rendon family so many years ago, but now there was no one.

And Merritt. Just thinking of him bent the physical pain the Haederans had inflicted into something deeper, something she would never heal from. He'd been so convinced there was life after death. Another life. That the Holy One waited for them, in a place with no grief, no more pain. He'd been so convinced of this that he'd gone to almost certain death, not fearing it at all. That alone had to mean something.

She curled into a ball in the shadows and cried for the loss of everything she'd ever known and loved. Chase was gone now, meeting with the people who had power of her life, and his temporary departure had set the last segment of this nightmare into motion. Her death on Haedera would be the only way this would end now.

Death.

The word filled her mind. Chase had mocked her for being afraid of it, and even then, she'd been able to tell he wasn't afraid —likely never had been. More than anything he'd done to her here, she hated him for that devoutness and lack of fear. She was supposed to forgive him for what he'd done on Asria, but she'd never forgive him for making her confront her shaky belief. For taunting her over it. For worshiping in her people's temple even as he destroyed their lives.

Who did he think he was?

She lifted her head from the icy floor and stared at the door, solid and dark.

Or it meant nothing, because the Haederans were coming for her again—over the past few weeks, the dread that seeped into her bones at the faint noises outside had never been wrong. Was she the only one here? Were the guards quieter when they came for any other prisoners? And was Chase back so soon?

The lock beeped, confirming her fears, and she struggled to sit up against the wall, fighting fatigue and shame. The guard who pulled the door open looked down at her, as impassive and silent as always, but the Haederan Army major next to him—

She gasped out loud. "Ha—"

Hadley strode across the cell and struck her jaw so hard that her head snapped back against the concrete. Blood trickled from her lip, tickling her chin, but she couldn't risk a move to wipe it away. Couldn't give him another excuse to strike her. Instead, she pushed herself against the wall and let it run down her face as the man she'd thought she knew addressed the guards.

"Imperial Security's transferring her. Orbital shuttle's waiting, so we'll have to be fast." The major gazed down at her, and she looked away. "If she fights, knock her out. I don't have the patience for these games that others seem to."

Her head fell to her chest as he turned on his heel and stalked out. It hadn't been Hadley at all. The major's accent was unmistakably Haederan, and Hadley's drawl was anything but. And Hadley would never hit her. Would never terrify her. Whatever she'd ever thought of him, he'd been on her side.

A heaviness overcame her as they pulled her to her feet and snapped metal around her wrists. She'd betrayed everyone, and it hadn't saved her. That resignation and the exhaustion which embraced her made it difficult to walk fast enough to keep them from dragging her along. Focus meant nothing when she couldn't concentrate on anything except putting one foot in front of the other. By the time they reached the top levels of the building, it was a struggle to complete even that simple action.

Her foot slid on the slick floor of an aeroflyer pad, and she gasped out loud, then tilted her head up, trying to see under the blindfold, hoping for a way to escape. One soldier shoved her head back down, then pushed her up a ramp and onto a hard bench. They'd brought her to an aeroflyer for sure—an automated one, judging by the engine noise. Firm hands shoved her back in her seat and buckled her harness.

"Move, and I'll make sure it's the last thing you do, understand?" the major asked. Avery kicked at him, but he only laughed and swore at someone behind him as he sidestepped her blow. "I told you we needed that clearance five minutes ago. What's keeping them?"

"Sir, I requested it. Perhaps the authorization was lost somewhere along the line. I'll go check—"

The slam of the hatch cut off his last words.

"Yeah, you go check," the major replied, a drawl replacing the Haederan lilt.

The aeroflyer lurched forward and upward; the interior lights flooded her eyes as the blindfold came off. Avery blinked, her vision adjusting slower than she needed it to. The man she'd thought she'd recognized sat next to her, and she shrank back into her seat before he could hit her again.

He grinned instead.

"Sorry about that"—the drawl grew deeper—"but you almost gave me away in there. I had to shut you up fast. That didn't look like the kind of hospitality I enjoy."

"Hadley." Avery stared at him in relief, then laughed uncontrollably as his words sank in. The cropped hair—within Imperial Haederan Army regulations now—the dark blue eyes, the smirk that couldn't belong to anyone else. He probably thought she was crazy, but maybe she was. "It's really you. I thought you—you just walked right in there and—"

"Yeah. Just walked right in there. Just like that. Gave myself a promotion, too. Here," he said, with a gentle hand on her shoulder. "Lean forward."

"But how did you even—" It was a though she hadn't breathed in an hour, and she gasped for air as he released her wrists and wiped the drying blood from her mouth. "How did you get in there?"

He chuckled and pulled a cold pack from under her seat. "I told you I don't give away all my secrets. Besides, we're not anywhere close to out of the woods yet. The aeroflyer is only to get us away from the city center, then we hide out for a while. They'll be looking for it."

"Then what?" The ice on her lip was enough to make her feel halfway human again, even if her heart was still racing. "Will we be safe wherever we're going?"

"Should be, but no idea for how long. They've shut Cadena down, and I doubt the rest of the planet is in much better shape."

He leaned his head back and closed his eyes, and she tried not to gawk at the moss green Haederan uniform he wore. How was it possible for him to be so calm after what he'd just done? She was going to ruin his almost-jovial mood though. She had to tell him before she forgot, or before the Haederans caught up to them.

No mistakes this time, right?

"Hadley—" She set the ice on the seat and intertwined her fingers. "I had some information for you before this all happened.

It's important. More than important—all on a disk. I gave it to Drex the night of the attack on Alcaris, and he said he'd get it somewhere safe. I have to find it."

"What was on it?"

"Not now. Not here." She shook her head. "It's too critical. When we get somewhere safe, I'll tell you."

"Any idea of where he stashed it?" Hadley didn't sound as angry as he should have.

"I don't know." Avery rested her head in her hands. The adrenaline wearing off, and now her head ached, along with the rest of her. "I can barely think right now. Maybe—his family had a cabin up in the Pelancos. It's the only place I can think of that would be safe. Otherwise, I don't know. It seemed like a good idea at the time, but . . ."

"Then it's as good a place as any for us to head if we can get out of the city." Hadley shot her a look of concern. "Are you all right besides the obvious?"

"I'm—"

No, I am not all right.

There were certain things a person knew without having to think about them, and one of those things she knew now was that she would relive each one of those images as soon as she fell asleep.

The suffocating prison cell.

Screaming at the door as the walls closed in around her.

The guards. Everything they'd done to her.

Chase. Her memory was so full of holes and blackness that she couldn't remember how much she'd told him. Only that it had been too much from the start.

But Hadley didn't need to know any of that yet, and she was glad he couldn't see the guilt on her face.

"I'm fine," she stammered. "I—I will be fine."

The first was an obvious lie since her left eye was still swollen completely shut, and the second, she didn't know. Maybe she'd never be fine again.

"If you're not, it's all right." he said. "We can fix the physical injuries, and the rest . . . we'll handle it." He patted her on the shoulder as the night outside grew brighter and the aeroflyer landed so gently she barely felt it. "We'll figure it out. I promise. Stay here."

Being alone was the last thing she wanted, but she leaned back and did what he ordered. He had to feel responsible for what had happened to her, but this disaster wasn't his fault. If the Commonwealth hadn't recruited her, she'd have antagonized the Haederans anyway. She'd have ended up in the same position. No, a worse one. Maybe already dead.

She glanced out the window as she contemplated that ghastly idea. They'd entered an enclosed garage, and Hadley was back in less than thirty seconds, Feye behind him.

Feye's eyes went wide when he saw her. "We can't take her anywhere looking like that—if she can even walk more than twenty meters," he protested to Hadley. "Look at her. They'll spot her from a klick away and so will anyone else with half a brain."

Her hands felt into her lap, and she looked away.

I do look that bad.

"I walked more than twenty meters to get to this aeroflyer," she pointed out, brushing a finger over her face.

Feye flinched.

"We're waiting here until it settles down out there anyway, so it's academic. She'll be fine, sir." Hadley sounded more annoyed than she'd ever heard him. "Look, let her get cleaned up. If I'm not back in two hours, you know the plan."

She gave Feye a questioning look as he helped her off the transport.

"He's going to ditch the flyer," he said. "Let's get inside and discuss what happens next."

CHAPTER TWENTY-TWO

S<small>HE SHOULDN'T HAVE LOOKED IN THE MIRROR SHE'D FOUND RESTING</small> behind a stack of crates.

Her entire jaw was red, and the bruise that would doubtless appear in a few days would likely be even more impressive. Had it been necessary for Hadley to hit her so hard? Probably, but Avery flinched anyway as she touched a gentle finger to it. Ice would have to do for now.

The rest of her injuries, especially her eye? Well, time would have to heal her eye unless Hadley was carrying half a hospital around with him. And there was no hospital in the room where Feye had dumped her.

Clean was a generous term for the space, in what looked to have been a storage building before becoming a Commonwealth safe house. A thick coat of dust covered the crates and furniture, the floor even more so. Worst, there were no windows—a necessary security measure but confining all the same. How long had Hadley spent in Cadena setting up this building and everything else he needed for this operation?

Feye cleared his throat behind her, and she spun around, forcing a laugh.

"I feel like I've been hit by a starship," she said, smoothing out the sleeves of the clothing he'd given her earlier. The pants were a little large, and the tunic, edged in fine leather, was more elegant than she thought appropriate for an escape, but they looked and smelled clean. Wherever Feye had gotten them, they were a gift. "How long was I there?"

He handed her more ice, then brushed the dust from a chair and sat next to her. "Just over nine standard weeks."

She choked down irritation that he'd used Commonwealth time. Right now, that was too difficult to calculate. Nine standard weeks was what? Six Asrian weeks? Closer to seven?

Too long, that's how long.

"I'm sorry it took so long to get you out," he went on. "It took a while to figure out where you were, and things aren't going so well in Cadena right now. It was hard to get near the building."

"Perrin made it clear what would happen if I didn't play by his rules. I suppose he's made good on his threat." Avery tossed the ice pack from hand to hand, then stuck it against her eye. She didn't deserve the ice, much less Feye's kindness. "How bad is it?"

"They've brought more troops in, shut all the businesses down again." His face grew grim. "And detained all the Defense Forces personnel they'd released after the invasion. That's made it difficult to get good information."

The ice fell into her lap. All except Merritt and the others who had been with him that night, Feye meant. Merritt's plan, failure though it had been, had the Haederans worried. She should have been thrilled to hear it, but the implications were grave enough to send a wave of dizziness through her. The Haederans wouldn't let the Defense Forces' actions go unpunished, and she couldn't let them penalize Asria further.

Feye continued, oblivious to her anguish. "I've also heard rumors they've brought some of their fleet back into orbit, but it's hard to confirm anything like that from down here. They haven't been bombing anything, but I'm not sure I'd rule it out at this point. Perrin threatens it publicly more and more every day."

Her stomach was a rock. Feye certainly knew how to make an unpleasant situation worse. She needed out of this room that reminded her too much of the one in which she'd spent too many hours with Chase, but at the same time, she didn't want to leave what passed for relative safety. The Haederans could be waiting for her as soon as she stepped outside.

Like they'd be polite enough to wait for you to leave . . .

"How long are we staying here?" she asked. "It can't be as safe as Hadley thinks it is."

"Only a few days. We need to give them time to move the search away from the city center and give us a clear path out of town. But we've got to find that chip, if it's as important as Zenos said it was."

"It is." She didn't want to talk about the chip, not then. "Major Feye, how long have you been doing this?"

"Seventeen years." He squinted at her question. Maybe it was too personal for him. Maybe no one had ever asked him. "I can't remember much before that. It's like it was someone else's life. Someone else's mind-numbingly dull life."

"A dull life sounds good to me right now. Have you ever . . . failed?"

"No. And we're not going to this time, either."

His answer was certain, but dread surged in her chest.

"How could you be so certain? They won't stop looking for me. Most of the people in this town know me by sight, as do half the people we'd run into in the settlements outside the capital. I can't trust any of them anymore. I can't stay here, and I don't think Hadley actually has any idea how to get us off Asria." The room spun. "The Haederan blockade—nothing's been able to get past it since the invasion. And if things are worse in Cadena than they were before, I don't see how we'll get out of this."

"We'll get out of here." Feye leaned back and regarded her with caution. "Even off Asria if that's what you want."

"How?"

"Can't say."

Avery swore, surprising herself that she was worried enough to do so. "You can't expect me to follow you halfway across the planet without giving me some assurance you actually have a plan."

"I have a plan."

"You'll forgive me, sir, if I'm not the trusting type anymore. Just you?"

Feye looked toward the ceiling, like he was fed up with her questions. "Zenos and I have worked together for a long time. He has his skill set, and I have mine. Setting up dead drops and off-world evacuations are some of mine."

His matter-of-factness settled her nerves. A bit. Maybe it was just the relentless exhaustion.

"What's his?" she asked.

"Acting. He can blend in most anywhere. Useful, no?"

"I think useful is an understatement, at least in my limited experience." Avery forced a smile. The movement pulled at her torn lip, and she slapped the ice back on. "I can believe he fooled the Haederans, but he fooled me, and I've known him for years."

Feye laughed at that. "And survival."

Hadley broke in from behind him. "And ditching vehicles used in jailbreaks."

She recoiled from the figure coming through the doorway. Hadley had changed out of the Haederan uniform, but the blue knit shirt he now wore had caught her attention in the worst way possible.

"Blue's still too close to green for you. Good to know—I'll change when I can." He collapsed on the floor next to her and tossed her a tablet. "I want to let you get some sleep, but let's talk about that cabin while we have a chance. We should be safe here, but if we have to leave in a hurry, I want some idea of where we're headed next."

She glanced from Feye to him, that familiar heat building behind her eyelids.

"Captain, wait. There's something else I need to tell you before we talk about the cabin, and you're probably going to want to take me right back to the Haederans when I do." She took a deep breath. A flashback, she could manage, but this . . . "I—I told them where to find you. And—and so many other things. I'm so sorry. I have no excuse."

"Not fine, then," he said to Feye, who lifted a nonchalant shoulder in reply. "I didn't think she was."

"I am fine." Not that they'd believe her. "It's just that they told me—" Her voice cracked. She would never forget Chase's words. She was a traitor—wasn't that what he'd said? "He told me I'd betrayed the Commonwealth, and I suppose I did. I know what I said to them was wrong, and I'll take full responsibility for it."

"How did you betray anyone?" Hadley scrunched his face in curiosity. "By giving them outdated information to buy yourself time and keep them from gaining more critical intelligence?" He smiled, although it was strained. "Nothing wrong with that."

"I—" She'd been nearly certain Hadley and Feye would be gone, and maybe that was close enough. It wasn't good enough for her conscience, not even close, but it seemed enough for Hadley, and maybe that was all that mattered. Maybe she'd believe it herself one day. Eventually. "Yes. I suppose that's what happened."

"But I'm curious," Hadley said. "Who's he?"

"What?" Avery gave him a wary look. "He?"

"This isn't an interrogation. Call it personal curiosity. You said *he* once and *they* every other time."

"One of their intelligence people." She scrunched her hair with her hands. Hadley did love information. "Gareth Chase."

"Ah." Hadley gave Feye a sideways look. "Colonel Gareth Chase."

"On Asria? In Cadena? I doubt that." Feye shook his head. "You're mistaken, Zenos. You don't know who or what you saw there."

Hadley gave him a sharp look, and he retreated down the

corridor, pale. Avery watched him go, comprehension dawning. Comprehension and something else . . . anger?

"You know him," she said. "How?"

"Know of him would be a more accurate way of putting it for most of us, but yes." Hadley's eyes searched the dim hallway, but Feye didn't come back. "I'm just surprised he's here, to be completely honest. They don't like to get mixed up in military operations."

She didn't need to ask who *they* were. It was an insult, sending their secret police to an occupied planet.

We don't belong to the Haederan Empire. We will never belong to you.

"But they are military," she said. "Aren't they?"

"Well, yes, mostly. I didn't mean to imply otherwise. But you know how the Haederan Empire is. That would be too much power for mere civilians." Hadley put a fist to his mouth and gnawed on a knuckle, thinking. "Some Haederan military commands just have less oversight than most. This one skips most of the military hierarchy, and that lets them move around and do what they want, where they want. You can imagine the alarm that causes within the regular Haederan service. And Chase is up for the next head of their interstellar counterintelligence division, you know." His face grew reflective. "He doesn't want to make a mistake here."

Avery rubbed her eyes. "What does *less oversight than most* mean?"

Hadley's lip curled upward. "They report directly to the Haederan emperor."

"*Chisho*, Hadley, why are you telling me this?" She jumped to her feet and paced in front of him. There it was. There was the anger that had been boiling inside her, and like always, it was more comfortable than fear. If being angry was all it took to be fine, maybe she would survive after all.

"I was afraid of him before I knew that. And he's been following me around for months! Why didn't you tell me? You never saw him, with me or anyone else? I couldn't get him to leave me alone when he first showed up. You must have seen something. Someone must have seen something!"

"Did you—" Hadley's eyes crinkled. "Did you just swear in Old Ventanan?"

Avery slapped a hand over her mouth. Her mother would never have approved of that part of her education.

"Don't look so surprised." She unmuffled her mouth. "I curse in Voirian and three other archaic languages, too. The academy was educational in multiple ways."

"Right. Well, I'm impressed." Hadley laughed. "Anyway, we didn't know Chase was on the planet. He didn't get where he's at by being overly visible. Besides, information's been scarce since the invasion, and Feye couldn't follow you without arousing suspicion. If we'd have known the Haederans were that suspicious of you, we wouldn't have set this up, I swear to you. We would have called you off. I promise." He ran his hands through his hair, as if that settled everything, and yawned. "So the cabin, then."

* * *

It'd taken two hours of mapping and explaining the route before Hadley had let her sleep. Feye hadn't come back until the very end, looking shaken, like he'd spent their entire discussion being sick. He'd helped Hadley take photo after photo of her injuries, and once they'd released her from the not-an-interrogation, Avery had crashed so hard that it had been a full six hours before she woke to the sound of something hitting the floor.

Rolling toward the sound, she rubbed the red mark where her broken ribs still smarted. The Imperial Security medic had done more to fix her injuries than she'd expected, but even though the springs of the worn cot in a small closet off the main room had dug into her all night, she didn't care. Sharp springs or not, it had been like sleeping on a cloud compared to the weeks she spent sleeping on solid concrete with half-healed ribs.

"Feeling better? You look it." Hadley was crouched across the room, tossing gear into a faded bag that looked like he'd purchased it from a beggar on the street.

Avery nodded. "A bit."

"Good, because we're out of here. Feye noticed movement toward this district a few hours ago. I think we've got some time, but we need to move out. You ready to get going?"

Her eyes went wide. The Haederans had found them so soon? Hadley and Feye had promised this place was safe.

"Yes." She pried herself to her feet and stretched the best she could to hide the fear that was welling up in her soul. "I'm—I'm pretty stiff, but I'm ready."

Hadley tossed her a holster and pistol. After Avery took one last look in the mirror at her disheveled curls and swollen lip, she headed out through the narrow hallway. They slipped out the back door in the silver evening light into one of the poorer districts of the capital.

She had visited this place before with Uncle Victor, over fifteen years ago, was it? He'd believed it was important to introduce her and Quen to the less wealthy areas of Cadena, so each year they'd made personal deliveries of food and other supplies on the king's birthday. She'd looked forward to it each time, and although her mother had protested at first, Uncle Victor had convinced her it was necessary training for her children's future.

She narrowed her eyes at the memory, and even more at what Drex had said about him—that hating him wouldn't change anything he'd done. *You need to pray for him instead*, he'd said. *It'll eat you up, otherwise.*

He was right on an intellectual level, but naturally the concept was easier for Drex to accept. Drex's family had not done such a terrible and unforgiveable thing to their planet.

She debated the idea as she followed Hadley and Feye down the alley. They hadn't gone a half kilometer when she walked straight into Hadley's back, lost in thoughts of Victor and of Drex's impossible standards. Hadley shoved her sideways into the nearest doorway without a second glance. Feye flattened himself against a door across the alley and put a finger to his lips. Did he think she was thoughtless enough to make a sound?

"Twenty of them, Haederan Army, moving down the main road." Hadley backed in next to her and pointed down the alley. "I don't think they saw us."

"You don't *think* they saw us?"

She fiddled with the pistol holstered under her shirt instead— she hadn't fired an Asrian one in years. For the hundredth time since they'd left Hadley's safe house, she wished they could carry the Commonwealth firearms she'd used at the academy. If the Haederans caught them with one of those though . . . there would be no way to bluff their way out.

"Well, they haven't begun firing," Hadley murmured. "They're knocking on doors. If someone saw you, what are the odds they'd keep quiet about it?"

"I don't know. A few months before, no one would've informed on me, but now—here, I think they'd probably say something. Fear and coercion change things."

"Forget fear. Money buys information, too."

"Especially in this part of the capital," Avery admitted. She slumped against the door, dismayed at the very thought.

"We don't have time to wait and can't take the chance they'll turn this way." He shot a look at Feye, who nodded. "He's going to distract them while we move down the other way. When he does, run south."

She grimaced and clenched her hands at her sides. "When he does what?"

Hadley nodded across the street at Feye, who was already making his way north toward the main road, doorway to doorway. "You'll know."

Avery squinted at him in confusion. Deep silence filled the air, the last moment of consciousness before plunging over the waterfall. A detonation, louder than she'd ever imagined, filled her ears, and she smashed into the door, collapsing to her knees as she did. Hadley grabbed her by the arm and shouted something into her ear. Somehow, she found her feet, and he pushed her forward, away from the pile of lumber and steel that had fallen where Feye had been standing.

And then she ran.

CHAPTER TWENTY-THREE

The ground crunched under Avery's feet as she and Hadley made their way through the outskirts of another tiny settlement. Feye had disappeared immediately on the other side of the—larger than necessary, in her opinion—explosion he'd set off in Cadena, but he would catch up with them before too long. Yet there was always the chance he'd injured himself while causing the distraction that had set fire to half an empty block—or that he'd been captured.

Or perhaps not. The inferno had preoccupied the soldiers too much to continue their door-to-door search for her, and Feye looked just Asrian enough to blend in. He would be fine. Everything would be fine, including her aching eye.

She shivered in the cool air and trotted to catch up to Hadley. "Another half kilometer and we're into the foothills."

"And past visual range of anyone in Cadena."

Avery nodded, even though he couldn't see the slight gesture in the dark. "Once we make it over the first hill, they won't be able to see us except with infrared cameras. There's a good chance they'll mistake two signals for wildlife. We'll have to take the long, wandering route up to make sure that's how we look."

The very idea made her feet hurt, along with the rest of her.

Ice, more Sennyl, and an ultrarestore machine—that was what she needed. And rest, lots of rest. A hike up a mountain? Not so much.

"We'll get some rest before we start up."

"Good." She exhaled, too loudly, and his footsteps stopped.

"You can tell me if you're not up to this," Hadley replied. "From the map you sketched, it doesn't look like it's the easiest way up."

Avery tried to laugh, but the sound caught in her throat as she looked up at the pine forests in the higher altitudes of the Pelancos. The woods were thousands of feet up, but that was where Drex's cabin was—and it would be their best protection from an air search. Still, it would be a long climb.

"I've done it a few times." She concentrated on the dark hill looming before her. It didn't take her mind off Chase and the past few months. Left foot forward, right foot forward, repeat. "But you're right, I was in much better shape," she admitted.

A flash of light caught her attention, at first diffuse over the pitch-black mountains. Within minutes it lit up the sky, and rumbling rolled across the summit. A storm would make the cool dangerous, and they had little in the way of spare clothing.

Hadley pulled a glowing map from a pocket and slipped next to her. "If we make it to the first canyon, is there anywhere we can take shelter?"

"There are some overhangs, if you want to take the chance of being washed away by a flood." She blew out a sigh through pursed lips. "The flash floods here are notorious."

"Ever seen one?"

"No, but I've heard stories. The canyons are especially dangerous—no one would be caught in one during a storm unless they had no other choice. Which, I suppose, we don't."

"We'll have to chance it," he replied. "If we get soaked in this weather, hypothermia is certain. Let's head on up."

* * *

Lightning splintered the sky almost once a second by the time they reached the nearest canyon, but the rain was only a light drizzle as the ground became rocky and steep. Still, as Avery searched for a protected spot among the scrub brush, the temperature fell even further. She hadn't been able to stop shivering for an hour, and for the first time since her escape, she wished they'd never left Cadena.

"Right there. Two o'clock, see that ledge? That looks good." Hadley pointed up the canyon, then frowned at her. "Hey. I know that look. You're safer out here in a thunderstorm than in a city of Haederans looking for you, you know."

"Maybe." She squinted above her, into the darkness. Still blurrier than she could afford. "But I'm not quite ready to admit you're right yet."

"One day you'll learn," he replied, "that I'm right about everything."

Giving him a look, she scurried up the cliff face and into the small cave where he'd pointed. The outcropping was high enough to keep them safe from any flooding, yet small enough to keep them warm—she would never admit it in front of him, but Hadley had picked a good one. He tossed their packs up, and she dug through his until she found the shelter canvas. She helped him hang it from the top of the ledge, anchored with heavy stones, then marveled, as she always did, at how the black tarp faded to match the tawny rocks surrounding them.

"There," he said. "No one will see that unless they're right on top of us. Sorry we can't use the ignitor can, but I don't want that much light until we turn away from the city."

"The heat might bring half the rocks down on us anyway," Avery replied, rubbing her hands together. Good reason or not, she was freezing. The heat would have been nice on her skin. "And I've had a bad enough time lately."

"You won't get any argument from me." He handed her a bar of pressed beans, then regarded her with interest as she took a bite. "You really have been up here a lot."

"Hmmm." She finished the rest of the bar in one swallow, then tentatively reached an arm over her head, stretching her sore ribs. "I had a normal life, before a few months ago. When—you know, that. My parents moved us to the palace when I was eight at my uncle's request, but I still had freedom. They let Quen and me do most anything we wanted."

"But you left Asria anyway."

Almost the same words Chase had said to her, so long ago.

Then let me guess—you left for Ventana IV as soon as possible.

How was it possible to remember that when she couldn't remember what he'd done to her in that cell?

"I said a lot, not enough." Her voice strengthened. She could talk about palace life. Just not . . . after. "It got worse as I got older, especially after Quen left, because they were afraid I'd disappear like him. It took years of petitioning the senate before they approved my waiver to attend the academy, and I spent those years imagining what my life would be like in ten years if I stayed."

She traced Merritt's initials in the thin layer of sand on the ground. "When they finally approved it, I ran as fast as I could onto the next transport to Ventana, even though they weren't expecting me on-planet for another six months. I didn't plan to be back here for a long time. Living here was suffocating even before the Haederans arrived—I wanted to be off somewhere making a difference." A laugh escaped, blown into nothingness by the relentless thunder. "That sounds idealistic, doesn't it?"

"Perhaps." Hadley considered the question. "But maybe you're meant to make a difference somewhere else—there's more to life than stars. Not that I think you pilot types would ever believe anything is more important than flying. And I imagine you left quite a few broken hearts on Ventana IV, too."

The blood drained from her face as she brushed away the letters in the sand.

Hadley's cheeks reddened. "I'm sorry. That was inappropriate."

"No. It's not that at all." Avery shook her head, finding even more sore muscles. "There was someone here, on Asria. He was involved in the Defense Forces' effort to retake Alcaris." Had Merritt been gone months already? It didn't seem possible.

Hadley rubbed his face. "*Ku*—Sorry. What happened there was unconscionable."

So, he'd heard the same story Perrin had told her. In a perverse way, it was good to get confirmation of what had happened.

"You don't need to apologize," she replied. "You didn't know about him. And you certainly didn't murder him. Merritt and I— we've known each other for years, since I was eighteen. When I left Asria, I didn't think he'd ever forgive me. He'd spent years begging me to stay, and he asked me to consider the Defense Forces instead of the Commonwealth Navy. I had to leave, and his asking made me feel even more trapped."

She sighed and twisted her ring. "Things would have been so different if I'd done what he suggested instead of leaving Asria. The day I left, he called me self-centered, and I told him I'd rather die than live out my life on a planet halfway to nowhere. We didn't talk for a year after that, and even then, it was a polite distance. Anyway, none of that matters now."

"What happened won't go unpunished," Hadley said. "I promise you that."

"How?" She threw her hands in the air. "The Commonwealth won't ever find out what happened there. Beyond that, they think we've happily accepted Haederan occupation. You and I will die out here, or at least we'll die trying to leave the planet. And the Haederans will go on murdering my people, and there's nothing I can do about it."

Hadley leaned against the cave's wall, then leaned forward, grimacing at the dampness. "First, I doubt the Commonwealth honestly believes the vote happened under anything other than duress—and you can make sure they know the truth once you reach Ventana. Second, Major Feye is an absolute genius at plane-tary escapes. I trust him with my life. Have for years. You'll see."

"Then why don't you know what he's planning?"

"Don't ask questions you don't want to know the answer to." Hadley grinned. "Look, I don't need to know, and that keeps everyone safer if things go all to hell. It's a system that's worked for the two of us for as long as we've been working together."

"That is not reassuring."

"I know. But it should be." He shook her shoulder. "Hey. I can't have you freezing up on me out here."

Avery shook her head. "I won't."

She hoped she sounded more certain than she felt.

* * *

She and Hadley left before daybreak, planning to crest the first foothill before the sun came up. The canyon was cool and dark, the walls soaking from the storms of the evening before. A pale sunrise showed over the top of the ridge, scattering rays over the boulders and down the canyon. They walked in silence for an hour, and it was so peaceful the past few months might as well have been a nightmare. At one point, so convinced she was hiking alone through the mountains, she twisted backward, only to see Hadley picking his way through a dense grove of cactus.

Her shoulders sank.

No, not a nightmare.

Clenching her newly blistered fingers, Avery focused on the route in front her once more. She had wanted to follow one of the many trails that dotted the lower Pelanco Mountains outside Cadena, but following the canyon kept them hidden—and safe. That knowledge didn't stop her sore muscles from screaming at her to slow down as the incline steepened. Hadley had estimated two hours over the nearest ridge, then another five to Drex's cabin.

Seven hours of walking.

She tried not to think about seven more hours of scrambling over rock. The stone was shredding her hands, her eye stung in the morning glare, and her ribs ached each time she took a deep breath. Soon Hadley's climbing ability outpaced her as he worked ahead to clear their path. The rising sun filled the canyon with warmth, enough that she wished for the cold of the evening before. Desperate to fill the silence that allowed too many memories to surface, she called up toward him at last.

"So, what about you? You heard my life's story last night. What's yours?"

Hadley swiveled to look at her as he tested the stability of a higher rock, an odd look on his face.

"You really want to know?"

"Sure. Why not? You must hide so much of your life by necessity, and the few things you can talk about must be enlightening."

"I can't believe you care." Hadley laughed. "You're too standoffish."

Standoffish? No one had ever described her like that before. Usually, people considered her too friendly. Mother and Father hadn't allowed her to be shy growing up—so where had Hadley gotten that idea?

Right.

Because she hadn't thrown herself at him on Ventana IV like half the other cadets. That should make more sense to him now—not that she would have considered it even if Merritt hadn't been in the picture. She'd been too driven, and romance, especially a forbidden one with an officer, was an unnecessary distraction at the academy.

"I'm not standoffish," she insisted, scrambling up to his side. "And I want to know."

He chuckled, quieter that time. "There's not much to tell. You know I grew up on Voirs. My family isn't wealthy, and I wanted to study engineering." It was a testament to his affability that his reference to wealth didn't sound demeaning or directed at her. "I couldn't afford the universities on Voirs, so you know, same old story. Trade a few years of your life to the Commonwealth for some education."

"You're nowhere close to working in engineering. There has to be a story there."

"You're pretty clever. And to think you didn't want to work for me." Hadley ignored her eye roll. "Six weeks after graduating, they recruited me for this. I think it had to do with my charm and good looks." He grinned. "Or it was my language abilities, I don't know. I've been doing it ever since."

"When you aren't preying on unsuspecting cadets."

"Best to get them before they get too spoiled out there with the fleet." He vented a dramatic sigh, and Avery shook her head. He wasn't too far off the mark with that comment. "Too bad pilot candidates are off limits for me. I guess we spend too much time and coin training you to pull you off for Special Operations Forces. That's what they tell me anyway. It would've saved me a lot of time recruiting you on Asria if I could have gotten you on Ventana."

A laugh bubbled up in her chest, and just the sound felt good. Lighthearted joking meant life might end up all right after all.

"Speaking of that," she began. "Last night, Major Feye said the two of you have never been unsuccessful. Is that true?"

Hadley glanced beside him, sharp, all joking gone. "What did he tell you?"

"Just that." Avery tripped on some loose gravel, slicing a thin line across her palm as she reached out to keep from falling.

So it wasn't true.

Hadley turned back to her and perched on a ledge to stretch his legs out.

"It's not true," he said, after a few moments of kicking his legs up and down, "but I'm not surprised he didn't tell you the truth. A few years ago, we had an op go bad in the Litan Sector. Technical malfunction of a courier ship. It wasn't anyone's fault. I spent three days floating in the emergency bay hoping the shielding would hold. Came out of it with nothing worse than a fresh fear of space travel and weightlessness. I'll get over it someday, and in the meantime, drugs help if I have to do anything interstellar."

That explained his phobia—no wonder he thought fighters were terrifying. Would she be able to fly again after an accident serious enough to blast a hole in her fighter? Probably not. She wasn't even sure she could get in a fighter again with her newly acquired claustrophobia—one more thing she'd never forgive Chase for.

"But Major Feye . . ." Hadley stared up the canyon, and when he looked at her again, he was devoid of emotion, once more the officer who had coerced her in that basement in Cadena. "He was thrown free and picked up by a passing Haederan spacecraft. He spent five months on Haedera. I guess I don't need to tell you what that was like for him."

Five months . . .

Another memory rose out of nowhere. Her second year on Ventana, rumors had flown—among most of the women and more than a few of the men—when Captain Hadley hadn't returned from one of his many recruiting trips as scheduled. It'd taken threats and a half-believed official story of health issues to quash the gossip for more than a few days. How naïve they'd all been.

"So yes," Hadley replied. He resumed his ascent up the canyon, and she scrambled to follow him, lost in the past. "We've had one spectacular failure, one we were fortunate to live through. But it won't happen again."

CHAPTER TWENTY-FOUR

By the time Drex's cabin came into view, Avery could scarcely take another step, and sitting flat on the ground was the bliss she'd been waiting for. The blisters on her heels had merged, and her hands hadn't fared much better. She'd wrapped them in dermtape as they exited the canyon, but there was no way the cuts and scrapes would heal fast enough to make the rest of the trip painless. Drex would have pain medicine in the cabin's med kit though, and that one thought kept her moving toward it.

Hadley shook his head from the cliff above her and drew the portable scanner back down. From over the nearest ridge, the small wooden structure rested on pilings above the rocky, bare ground. Still there, still in one piece, even though she was afraid she'd imagined it.

"Only one person up there," he whispered down at her. "We have to take the chance that it's Feye. If it's not—"

A sharp crack interrupted him, echoing across the ridge. Avery fell to her stomach, hands over her head, then coughed, blowing out a mouthful of arid dirt. Hadley's profanity was drowned out in a sound like a tree falling.

And then, silence.

Had the falling tree sound been a shot?

She turned her head to the side and brushed her hair from the cheek. The pine trees above her remained, as steady as ever. No downed tree. No Haederans with rifles surrounding them. With immense caution, she pushed herself to her knees and looked around.

The cliff Hadley had been standing on was missing.

The vision in her left eye blurred as she scrambled downward, toward the blue fabric wedged between the rocks below. Hadley himself had tumbled almost three meters, landing on a small ledge just a hair's distance from a longer drop. He rolled to his back and threw an arm over his forehead.

"Can you move?" she call toward him, under her breath. "On second thought—don't try."

The ground creaked once more, as she slid down on her side, settling next to him. Pebbles plummeted down the slope, coming to rest in a boulder field below.

"I think I broke my ankle." Hadley grimaced as he sat up. "And that's not the worst part."

"Yeah, I can tell what the worst part is." Avery pulled him closer by his sleeve. "Can you stand?"

"If my choices are standing up or falling down a mountain, yes."

He winced as she pulled him halfway to a standing position and took his pack off for him. She hated to leave it down the cliff, but she couldn't lift him with the extra weight—and if she couldn't retrieve it later, no one else needed to get their hands on his gear. Who knew what he had stashed in that bag? Nothing the Haederans needed to get their hands on, certainly.

"Stay there," she said. "I'm going to get higher up and pull you out."

She ignored the pessimistic look on his face and struggled back to where she'd been sitting when he'd fallen. From that vantage point, the drop didn't look as bad. When Hadley stood with his good foot on his pack, she reached his hands and pulled him up, though not without using the rest of the energy she had.

He fell to his knees, and she collapsed on the ground next to him, wondering when the next ten hours of sleep and a shower would be.

"We can't stay here." Hadley ignored her discomfort, secure in his welfare now. "That might not be Feye in the cabin, and we need to know sooner rather than later if it's not."

"Fine." Avery threw an arm under his shoulder and eyed the cabin. Just a few more meters, and there would be water, rest, medicine. *Kusir*, but she needed a break—and to not be lifting his weight with healed rib fractures. "Come on."

The door to the cabin swung open.

She dropped Hadley to the ground and raised her pistol, but it was Feye who walked out the door. She could have collapsed in relief but stumbled inside without a word to search for the med kit. It wasn't an easy quest, since the contents of the closet were all strewn out on the floor. The kit she pulled out of the pile had seen better days, and even worse—there was no ultrarestore machine.

Hadley shot her a mock glare as he limped in, leaning against Feye. "You dropped me. Was that payback for hitting you?"

"Now that you mention it, you owe me for that." Avery ran her tongue over her lip. Still sore. "But if dropping you was payback, then you've paid me in full plus some. Unfortunately, there's nothing to heal your ankle with. You'll just have to wrap it —let's hope it's just sprained."

"Great." Hadley limped to the sole bed and collapsed, then grimaced as he handed him what little Sennyl she'd picked out of the kit. "Better than nothing," he said to the pills.

"Maybe an ultrarestore machine will still show up." She turned her attention to Feye. "Did you find the chip? Where's Drex? If he didn't make it up there, we'll have wasted the past few days for no reason."

"Nothing except getting out of Cadena undetected," Hadley added. "Don't forget that."

She waved off his comment.

"No." Feye shook his head. "And I've been searching for the

damn thing since I got here. Someone else got here first, unfor-tunately."

For the first time, Avery saw the clutter in front of the closet for what it was. The untidiness of the entire cabin, in fact. The med kit scattered all over, the piles of wood strewn near the fire-place, and the sheets in a pile next to the bed. Someone had searched the cabin and hadn't bothered to put anything back where it belonged.

The Haederans.

The Haederans had beaten them to Drex's cabin.

"I'd like to look again though, now that you're here to help." Looking older than he had when she'd met him—or maybe just more exhausted—Feye tossed her a roll of dermtape. "If you've been here, maybe you've got some idea of secure storage places."

She ripped off a long piece of tape for her hands, then wound the rest around Hadley's swollen ankle. Maybe she'd been wrong about where Drex had fled, and he hadn't come all this way up the mountain. He might still be hiding somewhere in Cadena. How were they supposed to find him if he was?

"But what about Drex?" she repeated. "Any sign he was even here?"

Feye glanced at Hadley, and dread trickled through her again. Was this her life from now on—a continual series of events to be feared?

"Tell me." Her voice shook at the order.

He sank to the bed next to Hadley's feet. "Drex was already dead when I arrived. Shot. It was too late, and there was nothing I could do. I'm sorry."

Avery stood there, staring at them both, holding the empty roll of dermtape, trying to conjure up some sort of emotion. But perhaps more surprising than his news about Drex was the fact she felt nothing at all—just a cold detachment where grief ought to be.

* * *

She hadn't remembered that the woods were so full of the constant noise of birds and insects, but it was good to have something to concentrate on as she gazed out over the darkening mountain. Even something as simple as how loud the woods were at night. Anything to take her mind off Drex, for it was impossible to believe he was gone now, just like Merritt. Two constants in her life. Solid as granite, like the mountains below her feet. Now she was alone.

Don't be so dramatic, Lady Avery. Drex's words, spoken to a crying child as she watched her parents leave Sabino on holiday, were clear even now. *You're never alone, not really.*

"You're wrong, Drex," she said out loud. "Even now. Look how far away Ventana is."

It rose in the east as she sat there, shimmering on the horizon. Ridiculing her. Clear, yes, like all the stars were this far from civilization, but so many light-years away, as if she'd never been there at all and would never visit again. Alone? Yes. Drex couldn't argue with that.

She craned her neck to spot Haedera's star, straight above, bright white in the late evening sky. Strange how beautiful a star could appear if you knew nothing about the people that called its system home. Five thousand years ago, could anyone have predicted the Haederan Empire would control Asria? Of course not. Five thousand years ago, people had scarcely known what stars were. They certainly hadn't known about stealth technology, orbital bombers, and data chips.

If she ever made it off Asria, she could tell the Commonwealth the Haederans had stealth technology, but without the chip, they'd have no idea how to duplicate it—and they needed to know how. Right now, they were Merritt's first experimental spacecraft, a one seat flying machine with a top speed of fifty, going up against his Banshee. The Commonwealth had no chance with such a technological disparity.

Footsteps broke through the sound of birds, and she turned to see Hadley limping toward her, leaning on a shovel for support.

"You should be off that ankle," she called out.

"Nonsense." He settled down next to her. "I feel fine, thanks to you."

"You're lying. I can tell you're in pain." She turned her stare back over the ridge. "Besides, we were just lucky."

"Maybe." He shifted and stuck his bad leg out in front of him, looking uncomfortable despite his claim of health. "I looked around. Whoever was here is long gone."

"Imperial Security, I assume." Icy dread slunk down her spine. Chase had been here. "So now what?"

"They have what they want." Hadley looked thoughtful. "Most of it, anyway. And since they weren't lying in wait for you, I think we'll be safe here for a while. We all need some rest. Tomorrow Feye and I will take care of things, and we'll move out the day after."

"You won't be able to walk in a day and a half."

"Do you think this is the worst injury I've ever had?" An amused expression she hadn't seen since Ventana crossed his face. "I'll be as good as new."

"So we'll go where?" she asked. "And why? We can't get that data out now. The Haederans can invade world after world, and we won't be able to stop them."

"No," he admitted, "but they can't spread their fleet out as thin as they think they can. Eventually, even if we can't track them, they won't be able to control every system they conquer, and their empire will come crashing down."

"You can call me a cynic all you want, but the Haederans know war. The First Haederan Empire was how many star systems? Fifty-seven?" She scrunched her hair in frustration. Academics seemed so unimportant now. "It doesn't matter— they've conquered more systems in the past than they hold now. They've done it before, and they can do it again. You're too opti- mistic, Captain."

"And you're a cynic." He burst into laughter, then gestured up at Haedera in what she was certain was a Voirian insult. "Me? I wouldn't say optimistic. Hopeful, maybe."

Avery followed his gaze to the sky, black now, with thousands more stars appearing. She'd always loved the unimpeded view from the mountains, had sat in this same spot for hours as a child, dreaming about what it would be like to explore the worlds circling those twinkling stars. How innocent she'd been. How things changed in just a few years. Instead of stars above her, the Haederans had bombers in orbit. She might see them streaking across the night sky if she looked for them—which she refused to do. She focused on Ventana instead, rising into the darkness.

The Commonwealth would come soon.

"I'm headed inside. You're right—I think it's time for more pain meds." Hadley pushed himself up with the shovel. "Will you be all right out here?"

Avery nodded at Feye's rifle across her lap.

"All right," he replied. "But don't stay out too late, Lieutenant."

* * *

They buried Drex the next morning under a tall pine tree east of the cabin. Avery watched dry-eyed as the two Commonwealth officers dug through the rocky ground. She'd wanted to help, had offered to help, but they'd insisted on doing it alone, even though Hadley wasn't much use. Could it be guilt? There was definite guilt in Feye's eyes, but he couldn't blame himself. This wasn't his fault.

Everyone knew whose fault it was.

Hadley leaned his shovel against a nearby tree and shuffled back to the cabin, putting more weight on his bad ankle than he had the day before. Feye followed; neither looked at her.

She forced herself to move forward and kneel before the pile of rocks.

"I'm sorry this is the best we could do, Drex. And I know you would want me to pray, but I don't know what to say, so I hope you'll be fine with me just saying thank you. For your service to Asria, and to Father, and to me. I won't forget it. I promise you that."

She wiped the tears away. "I'm sorry I lied to you about working for the Commonwealth. I can't make any excuses for what I did, and I'm so, so sorry. If only I could turn back time, and it kills me that I can't."

How true was that? There wasn't much she would have done differently. Maybe she'd have told him. Maybe she wouldn't have. She tucked her legs into a position that didn't put as much pressure on the bruises.

"But I suppose I can tell you this now." A smile spread across her face at the memory, though she tried to quash it. "Do you remember that time we were about to leave Sabino to visit Cadena and someone had sabotaged the aeroflyer? You were screaming because you thought it was the hooligans from the estate down the road, the ones that kept sneaking over and getting drunk on our berries."

A laugh burst through. Drex had been furious that day, and at thirteen, his temper had terrified her.

"I was too afraid to tell you or Father that I'd been trying to figure out how the thrusters worked and I'd made a complete mess of it. I meant to tell you one of these days but it never came up. I guess I'm sorry for that too, but I know you'll forgive me for that one."

She spun again at the cough behind her. Hadley was pointing at the lengthening shadows through the pines, the rifle slung over his shoulder. He nodded at the pleading look on her face and leaned against a tree to wait.

"I wish I could sit here all day and tell you stories, but we need to get moving again." She closed her eyes and tried to blink away the tears. "Holy One, Father, grant him your mercy and peace. I'll see you later, Drex."

CHAPTER TWENTY-FIVE

AVERY PICKED HER WAY THROUGH THE LOOSE ROCK AND FALLEN TREE limbs covering the far side of the summit, wondering why she'd ever thought walking through the woods was recreation. Her pack seemed heavier than it had two days before, and the rough terrain and her thin shoes didn't help her pace, especially after she'd needed to assist Hadley up a particular steep segment of the trail. Never again would she take a hot shower, hot food, or cold water for granted. Or pain meds, for that matter. Her ribs didn't ache this very second, but there was a certain stiffness that made the guards' treatment impossible to forget.

She frowned as she watched Feye, who moved as silently as though he'd grown up in the wilderness, and even Hadley, walking better than her after their latest break. Guilt and a sense of ineptitude took over until she remembered Hadley was afraid of spaceflight—and then she wasn't successful at hiding a quiet laugh.

"What's so funny?" Feye almost snapped the question at her. Natural at this or not, maybe he wasn't enjoying their walk, either.

Avery opened her mouth to reply when movement in the trees ahead drew her attention. She stiffened and sunk behind a pine, pulling out her pistol as the first bullet tore by. A second grazed the tree as she scanned through the underbrush for their attackers, that one too close to her head.

The Haederans were trying to kill them.

She lowered herself to the ground, wishing she had firearms training beyond what the academy had provided—Father had always refused beyond what little Drex had taught her. The Rendon family had more than enough guards for protection, he'd contended. Now Hadley had the group's only rifle, and she couldn't see where he'd disappeared to. Holding her breath, she peered around the tree and was rewarded with another shot in her direction.

A twig snapped in front of her. She brought the pistol up, but in her awkward position the shot went wide. Catching Feye's eye, she cringed and moved to a better angle—her poor aim would have disappointed Drex.

But before she could fire again, Hadley's command echoed through the woods.

"Drop it. Now."

Avery stiffened at his order, but he'd climbed to his feet ten meters in front of her, his pistol at the head of a child no more than fifteen. It might not have been a Haederan patrol, but she didn't trust either of them to not fire an accidental shot. Her hold on her own gun didn't waver as she strode toward them.

"Let her go," she called out, remembering at the last second to avoid his name. She blinked, but her vision turned hazy, even as she rubbed her left eyes. "I doubt she's trying to kill us."

"Fair enough argument." Hadley lowered his pistol a fraction and leaned against the nearest tree. "I'm guessing she's one of yours."

One of hers.

One of the many cracks in her soul mended itself. The girl did look Asrian, with light eyes and the tall stature of most Cadena residents. The sleek russet curls that tumbled over her shoulders were odd for this part of the planet, but not impossible. But Asrian or not, she wasn't a Haederan soldier.

Avery shoved the gun back in her holster and held her hands in front of her as she drew closer. "What's your name?"

The girl's apprehensive eyes darted from her to Hadley to Feye like a wounded animal.

"I wouldn't test him," Avery added, leaning her head toward Hadley. "Or the other one."

"Elsbet." The girl's chin went up. "And I live here. I haven't done anything wrong."

"You were shooting at us," Hadley interrupted.

"I thought you were Haederan." Elsbet's shoulders dropped. "I thought perhaps—"

"You thought wrong," Feye replied. He took the rifle from Hadley and slung it behind his back again, and Avery read the relief on Elsbet's face.

"Then who are you?" the girl asked. "Their soldiers have been all over the woods around here, and no one important comes across the mountains this way. It's much too remote."

Beside Avery, Hadley laughed.

* * *

Feye hadn't wanted to involve the girl further, but she'd insisted they follow her back to her house for a proper meal and shelter for the night. Hadley had argued against her help the most, which in some paradoxical manner meant his ankle was bothering him more than he'd ever admit. But there was another storm coming, Elsbet pointed out, and the Haederans had been patrolling the woods just the day before. They'd be safer with her family in Summerhaven, a resort town for the wealthy on the far side of the mountains from the capital.

At that moment, Avery didn't particularly care if the Haederans came back or not. Her skin stung from her first hot shower in weeks by the time she joined Hadley and Feye in the small but immaculate living room. It seemed safe enough, but she stayed away from the windows all the same. The part-time residents who lived in Cadena the rest of the year might recognize her.

Elsbet's mother placed the last cup of tea in front of Hadley. "We only came up here a few weeks ago," she said. "We thought it would be safer than Cadena, but they came through here three days ago. They were looking for you, Your Highness." She glanced at Avery as she sat, but there was no malice in her eyes, only deep sorrow. "When my husband said that you hadn't been here, that no one had seen you—I hear that shot every time I close my eyes."

Avery's stomach twisted in guilt. These people had nothing to do with her, and yet there was more death. Her fault. She'd failed them.

"I'm sorry," she replied. "I know those words will never be enough to make up for what you've lost, and I would do anything to take that back if I could. Whoever is responsible will pay for what they've done."

"You don't need to apologize for what happened." Elsbet's mother tried to smile, but the reaction wouldn't appear. "He'd have said it if you were hidden in our cellar, and I would have too. I still would."

Avery shook her head. Too many people were already in trouble because of her. "We'll be out of here as quickly as we can. I don't want to cause more trouble." She looked at Feye for confirmation. "Just some supplies, I suppose."

He nodded. "Food's the easiest thing to carry. I assume the Haederans didn't leave any weapons in town?"

Elsbet's mother shook her head. "I doubt it. But you can take the car."

Avery gnawed on her lip. They could move faster in a car, but they'd be easier to spot. Her feet wanted a ride though, and Hadley had never answered her question about their ultimate destination. It could be weeks of walking before they reached wherever they were going. Maybe longer, with his injury—and hers. She would never admit it to him and Feye, but her ribs hadn't stopped throbbing.

"I don't want to leave you without transport, but it would be helpful," Feye replied.

Elsbet dashed into the room from wherever she'd been eavesdropping on their conversation. "You won't get far if they see any of you driving," she said. "I can take you as far as you need to go, then find my own way back here, or Cadena if it comes to it."

"That's appreciated, but unnecessary." Avery shook her head. "The Haederans won't hesitate to execute everyone in this town if they find out you crossed them."

"Hang on." Hadley sounded thoughtful. "She's got a point."

"She's fifteen," Avery pointed out. "So no, she doesn't."

A look of annoyance crossed his face, and he glanced at Elsbet's mother. "Can you give us a few minutes?" As soon as the two women left the room, he faced Avery. "Look, I know you don't like it, but it's our best chance to get where we're going."

"And her father just died for no reason at all." Her breath grew short. Had Elsbet seen him fall to the ground like she'd seen Gavni? "I won't be responsible for more deaths, especially of a child. It's too risky."

"Not that risky," Feye cut in, "but if we see anything we don't like, we'll send her back up here and start walking again. I don't like it either, but we're running out of options. Unless you'd like to hike for another three weeks—and I don't need to remind you we don't have that much time."

Avery sank her teeth into her bottom lip and focused on the silk rug, patterned in the same cerulean asters she was so used to seeing in the palace. Was it a sign? Or simply a lovely carpet Elsbet's mother had picked up somewhere in Cadena?

Who cared?

They were right.

"She goes straight home if we run into anything problematic," she said.

Feye nodded. "Agreed."

* * *

Avery woke to the sound of rocks crunching under tires. The car slowed as she tore herself from dreams of Merritt and blinked away the last of her sleep. Elsbet had pulled off the narrow dirt road and stopped in the surrounding scrub. It wasn't tall enough to hide the car, and Avery shot Hadley a questioning look.

"Checkpoint ahead." Beside her, his face was grim.

"We can't have gotten far." She rubbed her face. Her feet had appreciated the ride. "So now we walk."

"For a while. Elsbet's going to make it through and pick us up on the other side."

Wide-awake at that, she sprang out of the car after him and trapped him against the door. On the other side, Feye was wiping down fingerprints.

"Hadley, no. Absolutely not. You agreed to send her home if we ran into this."

"It was her idea to try. And her mother sanctioned it, in case you've forgotten."

"I don't care if it was her idea! I don't want her anywhere near them, Hadley."

His hands flexed at his sides. "That's not your call, Lieutenant."

Her entire body tensed. Was it worth reminding him that Lieutenant Rendon wasn't her only title—that it was, in fact, the least important title of them all? Was it worth reminding him it was likely he was arguing with the queen of Asria? But then, this was Hadley she was talking to. She'd be wasting her breath.

"I don't like it," she said. "At all."

"You don't have to." He tossed her pack to her and walked up the hill, away from the road.

She looked at Feye in amazement as she picked it up from where she'd let it hit the ground in front of her. With her eye the way it was, catching anything would be out of the question for a while.

"He doesn't listen to anyone, does he?" she asked.

"Don't look at me." Feye shrugged. "I wanted to sneak all of us through in the car."

"They have scanners—they'd find us in an instant. You're both mad." Feeling foolish at the way she had to balance oddly to keep from aggravating her injuries, she jogged to catch up. "But you were kidding, weren't you?"

"Just trying to lighten the mood." Feye grinned as they caught up to Hadley, who was picking his way up the rocks and through the scrub, trying to parallel the road now disappearing beneath them.

"If you two are done laughing about our predicament, the checkpoint appears to be another klick north," Hadley said. "Elsbet will give us a ten-minute head start, and if we can keep the trail going this way, we can monitor things from up here."

It was a good plan, as much as she hated to agree with anything he said. The boulders would hide them, and the troops at the checkpoint wouldn't be looking straight up.

"Maybe take them all out?" Feye patted the rifle, sounding all too pleased with his plan.

"Good idea." Hadley rolled his shoulders and focused up the trail. "If we can."

Avery hung back as they deliberated. Their casual talk of taking lives was more than she could handle, especially after Drex. Disgust welled up in her throat, and she looked into the sky, shivering despite the warm day.

You'd be taking lives right now as well, coward.

The voice was so real at first that she looked around for the source. Her conscience was right though, and a wave of shame washed over her as she slunk by another boulder, trying to distract herself from reality. There was no way she could judge Hadley and Feye for the same thing she'd been prepared to do from a spacecraft and would have done without a second thought. At least they'd seen the people they'd killed, hadn't they?

But when the Haederan checkpoint came into view fifteen minutes later, it became obvious Feye wouldn't be doing any shooting. At least twenty men in Haederan green surrounded each side of the road, excessive for the limited traffic that crossed the mountains this time of year. Yes, the Haederans were as serious about their search as Elsbet had claimed. More disturbing than the troops was the aeroflyer parked nearby, since the dwindling pines at their lower elevation had left them with precious little protection from an air search. They'd be all too easy to spot from above.

"There's no way Elsbet's getting through there." Avery slipped down behind one of the large boulders, then, closing her eyes, waited for the sound of the flyer lifting off. "This was a terrible idea."

"Relax," Hadley replied, sinking down next to her. "They're not after her." He looked at Feye. "Twenty-eight of them, sir, plus the aeroflyer. What do you say?"

"I say we sit tight and see what happens. I don't like those odds."

"Agreed." Hadley fiddled with his chronometer. "Should only be another few minutes. She gets through, we keep moving. Much too open out here for my comfort."

The crunch of gravel drifted upward. Avery held her breath, though all she wanted to do was look around the boulder. Could the Haederans also hear them all the way up on the cliff? She pressed her lips closed and forced a few quick, shallow breaths.

"Don't hyperventilate on me." Dimples formed in Feye's cheeks. "They might not be after her, but believe me, they're not looking up here right now either."

Irritated at her nervousness, Avery stuck her head around the boulder despite her nerves. The cliffs from the other side of the road shaded the checkpoint, and she squinted in the dim light. Troops swarmed the car, and one man pulled the driver's door open. They would pull Elsbet out and do stars knew what to her —but no, she was getting out on her own. Head high, she gestured up the mountain and back down, then nodded, more composed than Avery would have been in her situation. Two rifle-toting Haederans approached, and the figure beside them—

Chase.

The rocks swayed under her, and she laid her forehead against the boulder to stop the dizziness. He wasn't supposed to be here. She wasn't ever supposed to see him again. Not the man responsible for the bruises that made her flinch each time she stumbled on a loose rock.

"That's him." Unable to say more, she clutched at Hadley's arm. He shot her an irritated glare that dissipated when she pointed below them. "Chase is here, right down there," she managed. "I didn't realize he'd be following me that closely. He can't see me. You can't let him see me."

Hadley gave Feye a pointed look. It must have been an unspoken and unorthodox order, for Feye raised his rifle. Time stopped, and the breeze picked up as he aimed. It was so easy to make her nightmares go away forever. So easy to make *him* go away forever.

But would he? Would the nightmares end if he was dead? Would her vision return to normal, her ribs stopped aching whenever she took a deep breath?

I don't know the right decision. Help me.

The sun warmed her cheeks, bringing her back to the present. Not to the cell in Cadena but the mountains she loved, on the planet she still had a chance at saving.

And then she knew.

"Don't," she whispered. "Don't do it."

"Why the hell not?" Hadley looked at her like she'd finally broken right there in front of him. "I know you haven't forgotten what he did to you. What he did to—" He broke off at Feye's quelling stare, but the exasperation on his face didn't fade.

"Because—" She turned her head so he couldn't see the tears that had welled up. Hadley would never understand, because even she couldn't fathom her sudden compulsion to save the life of her enemy. The person who had nearly destroyed her. "Because if you do that, they'll know we're up here, and then they'll kill her. He's not worth her life."

Hadley's jaw grew rigid. "Best do what she says, sir." He snorted. "Asrians. You'd better hope you don't live to regret your mercy, Your Highness."

She didn't feel merciful as she pressed her forehead against the side of the rock and trembled. Only drained and spent of all strength as she watched four soldiers swarm the car with scanners. Front seat, then back seat, with the cargo area receiving extra scrutiny. Chase observed every bit of the search. Minutes ticked by, and finally the Haederans backed away from the car and nodded to Elsbet.

Hadley shifted beside her. "I think we'll be all right now."

He sounded relieved, like he'd been holding his breath, too. The sound of the car's engine and tires crunching over gravel filled the air again, and Feye waved them on. They walked for fifteen minutes, sometimes half-crawling to stand below the line of boulders that blocked Hadley's makeshift trail from the road, before he stopped them. The checkpoint was out of view, and the noise of the roadster had disappeared five minutes before. There was no way the Haederans could see them, and all she wanted to do was keep moving.

Hadley held his hands up in a plea. "I know," he said, meeting her eyes, "but we'll be moving again in a minute. We need to discuss our next step before we meet up with the girl again." He looked at Feye, as if he weren't sure of disclosing what he was about to say. "You asked what the plan was now that we lost the chip."

"And you didn't answer," Avery replied. "Since we can't wander the mountains forever, I assume you're going to tell me now."

He scratched at the stubble that had appeared in the past few days. "We're headed to Villiers."

"Villiers? But it's gone." She furrowed her brow. Villiers, the last-chance, underground Defense Forces base thought to be impenetrable, had been destroyed in the invasion. Hadley hadn't known that—another setback.

His mouth quirked up in the expression that had always attracted women to him on Ventana, and somehow, the remembrance was soothing this time instead of exasperating.

"Only the top levels," he replied with a familiar, smug expression.

"And you know this how? Weren't you and Major Feye"—she motioned to him with her head—"trapped in Cadena during the attack? Anyway, you're Commonwealth Navy, not Defense Forces."

"I know everything." Hadley lifted a shoulder. "Defense Forces or not."

"I ought to be used to your secrets by now." She sighed. "It'll be safe there for Elsbet if we can't send her home?"

"All those people down there probably report to you now. You tell me."

Avery nodded slowly. If Villiers still existed—which she doubted—it would be safe enough until things in Summerhaven and Cadena settled down. Had Elsbet's mother suspected she was sending her daughter toward better shelter than she could provide?

"But the chip," she said. "It's gone."

Hadley glanced at Feye with an expression she didn't like, then Feye shifted his weight to one side and spoke.

"We're going to find it."

She burst out laughing, but neither of them looked like they were joking.

"Are you serious?" she replied. "That's impossible. It's long gone."

"Then we'll head back to Cadena and find your contact. I'm sure he's got the information stored somewhere."

"You make that sound so easy. How much time will that take? What if the Haederans have already found—" Panic built up within her, tempered only by the fact Hadley didn't know Cameron was a woman. That made the scientist somewhat safer, at least. "Every day that goes by, every week—"

"Do you have a better idea?" Hadley asked. "Besides searching all over a planet for a chip the size of my fingernail?"

"No," Avery admitted. "But if you're doing that, then I'm going back with you. You'll need my help."

He ignored her and limped away. Avery darted after him, but he stopped and waved her off.

"Look," he said. "I know you want to see this thing through, but you can't go back to Cadena. That's not an option we can entertain—we can move about a thousand times more freely without you, and like it or not, you're in danger there. We can't be responsible for you being apprehended, either. One, I like you too much, and two, I like my career even more."

She exhaled. It was true. The Haederans who hadn't recognized her before would be watching for her now. The locals would be, too. Going back to Cadena now was just a dream.

"You're right," she replied. "But I don't like it."

"Then I'll make a deal with you." Hadley put a hand on her shoulder, and she gave a small shake of her head. Comforting or not, the gesture was another burden. "Stay at Villiers. Let us do this alone. If we get back with the information, we might need your help to get it off the planet—we had to destroy all the comm equipment when we left the first safe house, so we're back to the old-fashioned ways of getting data out now. Then, if you still want to come with us, you can."

"I'll do whatever you need me to do." How different from her reaction to Hadley's first request, so long ago. The tension dissipated from her neck, and she looked away, out over the mountains, toward Cadena. "As long as it hurts them."

"It will." His grip on her shoulder tightened, and he nodded. "I promise you that."

CHAPTER TWENTY-SIX

Scrub brush flew by as they tore down the deserted road; the spice of cresite bushes filtered through the car's vents. Avery focused on inhaling it—she'd stopped trying to imagine what could be left of Villiers. Hadley had said the top ten levels had taken the most damage, but a passageway known only to the highest levels of the Asrian military had survived. A passageway that linked the main side of the base to an even lower section the Defense Forces had never thought they'd have to use. A level shielded by lead and concrete.

One day, she'd make Hadley tell her how he knew so much for someone who had only visited Asria twice.

She shifted again as she tried to find a position that didn't put pressure on her ribs, striking Feye with her foot. Hadley had promised it wouldn't be more than another twenty minutes until they reached their destination, but she was certain he'd said that an hour ago. As she closed her eyes in another attempt at sleep, the car came to a halt.

"Here we are," Hadley said, gesturing to Elsbet out with his chin. "As far as we can drive, at least. We'll follow the trail another half klick east. I'd recommend keeping your hands visible as you head through those boulders."

"Then what?"

"They'll find us," he replied.

"And if they don't? You haven't actually convinced me that any part of Villiers survived the bombing. We could be wandering out in the desert looking for something that didn't exist, for all you know."

"Oh, I'm certain they'll find us," Feye replied. "They're not leaving their last stronghold unguarded, even from a small group. We could be a small assassin team, for all they know."

Fantastic.

"Then I'll just pray they don't shoot us first." Avery swung her feet out, then froze. "Hold on. I've got to go alone."

"I don't think so." Hadley rubbed his nose with the heel of his palm, then tossed his own pistol into the car next to Feye's. "We're not leaving you now."

"Last stronghold, remember?" She grinned at him, and it felt like her first smile in years. Finally, an obstacle Hadley, even with all his planning, hadn't considered. "You want to deal with the sensors? They've got to have them absolutely littering the canyons around here."

"Ah. Set to kill anyone who isn't carrying some gene or another that only Asrians possess, naturally." Hadley looked flustered he hadn't thought of it first. "Innovative Asrian technology. If only it worked on a large-scale invasion. Then you can be my guest, Lieutenant."

"See you soon," she said with a wave. "I'll be back for you as soon as I can."

Still grinning at him, she dropped her pistol on the floor and stepped out of the car, careful to avoid the thorns on the nearby cresite bushes. The trail Hadley referred to was about a hundred meters away, leading east through rolling hills covered in small boulders. She looked back as she walked, wishing she didn't have to find her way through the canyon alone, and her grin disappeared. But Hadley and Feye were leaning against the car with Elsbet protected in between them, talking and laughing, and even though she shook her head at their frivolity, it lifted her spirits once more. If they weren't worried, she wouldn't be, either.

If only she could convince herself of that.

The trail disappeared after it curved, and she had to scramble over large boulders as the terrain became more rugged. Still raw from climbing up the canyon outside Cadena with Hadley, her hands protested, so she flopped on the ground and examined them.

Villiers, she realized as she dug the dirt from under her nails, might be more of a prison than Cadena had been, and though, yes, she'd be safer, she'd still be trapped. It was hard to admit she was jealous of Hadley and Feye's ability to leave. With a sigh, she tried to wipe the dirt from her hands once more and pushed herself to her feet, tired of the dirt and grime that surrounded her. Time to move on, time to find out if Hadley was correct about what remained of the base. She scrambled across the final few boulders, and as she did, the ruins of Villiers came into view.

It had never been much from the surface, just a few outbuildings, security posts, and fences, but even those were long gone now, absolute destruction left in their place. The structures were gone; not even mangled concrete and steel remained. Craters dotted the landscape, at least a half kilometer wide, deep and razor-sharp, incongruous with the rolling hills and curving canyons of the desert. The shock wave must have killed everything that had been living within the crater, for even the spice of cresite was missing here, replaced by something metallic and warm.

Her heart sank. Cadena had seen its share of damage, but not like this. Hadley had been so certain, but he was wrong. No one could have survived an attack like this. No one and nothing. And now—she would have to make her way back to the car, would have to convince Feye to allow her to accompany him back to Cadena. Hadley would argue, but he'd relent. What other choice was there?

A hawk appeared in the distance, soaring on the other side of the crater, catching updraft after updraft. It dove toward the ground twice, then, perhaps finding nothing either, alighted on a boulder halfway down. Avery waved at it, and it cocked its head and flew off with a resounding screech.

"Thanks for that," she said out loud. "I suppose I'll just sit here a while and catch my breath. Stare at the destruction a bit longer. I'm sorry about that too, you know. I hope you can find another home." Feeling foolish she was talking to an animal who wasn't even visible anymore, she wrapped her arms around her knees and gazed out over the devastation.

She was still staring at the crater when they found her.

* * *

After assuring Avery that Elsbet would be suitably lodged, a Defense Forces lieutenant escorted her, Hadley, and Feye straight to a conference room on one of the upper levels. As far as Avery was concerned, upper levels or not, the room was still a grave, covered by hundreds of feet of solid rock. She would never stop missing the emptiness and expansiveness of deep space.

Still, everything was familiar, from the uniforms to the gray walls, and that familiarity eased her worries more than her newfound security. Even the conference room table was the same one found in every Defense Forces base she'd ever visited, though the full-wall viewing screen across from the door was nonstandard. Someone had programmed it to mimic an Istakian Ocean trench, and it was hard for her to tear her gaze away from the scores of vibrant fish swimming across the azure water—water that looked like it might wash away the evils of the past months if she watched it long enough.

It was just too bad that General Dade Cevall was eyeing her from across the table with the disapproving expression he was. She'd never met Teruel's second-in-command before, but it was plain he viewed her as if she were a misbehaving child. Avoiding his glare, she watched the fish and waited on the reprimand to come.

But instead of addressing her, Cevall turned his gaze to Hadley and Feye. The two stood against the wall next to the door, as if they regretted their entire decision to head for Villiers and meant to escape as soon as possible. In Hadley's case, escape would be slow—his weight was on his uninjured leg.

"Well? What do you have to say for yourselves? The two of you conducted operations on Asria"—Cevall raised his voice—"on a sovereign planet, without our knowledge or permission. You violated I don't even know how many agreements and treaties and might as well been responsible for Lady Avery's arrest yourselves. I don't care that you conducted a successful rescue operation. Who authorized this?"

Feye cleared his throat, as if he planned to point out, like Hadley had coolly informed her not so long ago, that Asria was not as self-governing at the moment as its subjects would prefer to believe. Instead, he swallowed any protest.

"General Torin did, sir."

Hadley opened his mouth, likely to add his disagreement about sovereignty, but Cevall cut him off with a wave.

"Save your breath, Captain. Nothing you have to say will convince me this mess was the right thing to do. I don't want to hear anyone's reasoning. That includes Lew Torin, who will hear from me as soon as we can get a better signal out of this place. If anyone should know better . . ." Cevall's voice softened; the lines in his forehead relaxed. "But I will assume this was all done in good faith. The Holy One knows we need the help. However, you may let Torin know that the Asrian senate—"

He raised his voice in emphasis as Hadley opened his mouth again. "Yes, even now—does not appreciate the Commonwealth's interference in internal matters, especially those of the royal family. They—*she*—are off limits from now on. No exceptions. Is that understood?"

He was shouting by the end of his reprimand, and Avery

winced. So, none of this was about the Commonwealth Navy working on Asria without permission. It was about the Commonwealth recruiting her in the first place. Would Cevall listen to her defend Hadley and Feye? Even General Torin? She owed them enough to try.

"General Cevall, it was my decision to help." A small lie, but she could overlook Hadley's threat now. "The dissolution of the senate effectively canceled any of their wishes for me as they pertain to the Commonwealth. And regardless of what those wishes might or might not have been, I do not answer, and have never answered, to the Royal Asrian Defense Forces."

There. That should stop him in his tracks.

Cevall spun toward her. "No, you certainly do not, Your Majesty."

And thank all that is sacred for that fact, he clearly wanted to add, but she could only focus on his last two words.

"So it's true." Her mouth went dry.

Cevall gave Hadley one last scowl and picked up the tablet resting across from her. "I was very sorry to hear about your parents. Your loss is a great loss for Asria as well." He shook his head. "Shot trying to escape Sabino. Not a fair end. I wish things had been different for both, and you."

Avery narrowed her eyes at his abrupt change in topic. "Thank you."

"With your father gone, you're aware of where that leaves Asria." Cevall pushed the tablet across the table. "I'm sure you knew this was coming."

"I suppose I did." With a shaking finger, she pulled the document toward her. Grant Baylen's untidy scrawl stared back at her, sealing the senate's secret and anonymous vote.

Then it was done. Just as she'd feared, like she'd told Merritt, the senate had preemptively approved her weeks ago, as soon as her father had disappeared and Perrin's rage had turned personal. She only wished someone had told her first. Warned her it was coming. The practice of confirming heirs had fallen out of favor centuries before, with the only genuine candidates coming from the Rendon family, but—but it would have been wonderful to have been *told*.

Her heart thumped as she pushed the tablet aside and looked at Cevall to speak the trained reply in a daze. "And I am honored to serve Asria for the rest of my days."

Hadley winked at her over the general's balding head, and she glared at his audacity. Cevall visibly relaxed at her answer. What would he have done if she'd refused? Could she have refused? Judging by the way he'd sunk into his chair, the outcome had worried him.

He rubbed his neck, and his lined face grew grim. "You realize the Haederans will view this as treason."

Avery couldn't help her laugh. "General, I think it's far too late for me to be worrying about what they think of me. They can view it however they want." And Cevall would release the information to them, of course. Anything to let the Haederans think their grip on the planet was tenuous, however optimistic that hope might be. Her smile faded. "When are we doing this?"

"Right now, if you're willing. I'll just go find another witness. But first, there's one more thing I think you'd like to discuss— immediately. And alone." Cevall glanced at Hadley and Feye. "Give us a minute please, gentlemen."

With them gone, she felt more vulnerable than she had in a long time. "What's so important they couldn't hear?" she asked as soon as the door closed.

"You can fill them in later, but I didn't think you'd want them hearing this. At least, not all of it." Cevall dragged a lukewarm cup of coffee toward him. "About six months ago, we had some trouble. There was some . . . well, let's call it dissent, shall we? A group of my people weren't entirely thrilled with how the king was handling things."

Avery rubbed at a cut on her forearm. "What things?

"Well, one thing in particular, I suppose. He wanted to pull Asria out of the Commonwealth." Cevall sounded as matter-of-fact as if he'd just said the dull, ash-colored ceiling above was gray.

"I don't believe that." She managed to control her laugh that time. "It doesn't even make sense. Uncle Victor never said anything about it. He supported me going to the academy. He even pulled strings in the senate to have my waiver pushed through. And even if he'd wanted to withdraw, that's not his decision to make. You know the royal family has never had enough influence over the senate to swing a vote like that. Certainly not one person."

"You can believe it or not, but it's true, and certain people in the Defense Forces felt his views were worth removing him over. Your father was always the more vocal supporter of the Commonwealth, and they preferred that."

"Remove him?" She flushed in anger, though whether it was over the situation or being forced to defend Uncle Victor, she didn't know. "Even if he'd been anti-Commonwealth, that's no excuse for treason. You knew about this? Teruel knew about this?"

"We handled it internally as soon as we found out, but things like that are hard to keep quiet. We tried everything we could to keep the news from spreading, but the rumors got back to him. I can't blame him for being worried a coup was imminent." Cevall paused, thinking. "He left a week after we first heard the rumor. Intel thinks it's possible he struck a deal with the Haederan Empire that would allow him to come back to rule Asria as a Haederan territory without the influence of the Commonwealth in his way."

"And a Haederan invasion would have been the perfect way to dismantle the Asrian military he was allegedly so afraid of." That time, she rubbed her eyes. It was too much information at once. "Do you know this, or are you guessing?"

"It's an outcome predicted by people more skilled at political games than you or I, Your Majesty."

Of course.

"So where does that leave us now?"

"Exactly where it left us before." Cevall sounded all too certain about that statement. "It doesn't matter why or how it happened, but your uncle abdicated, violating long-standing Asrian law and tradition, and he committed treason by fleeing to Haedera and giving them who knows how much information on our defensive capabilities. I am sorry that anyone in the Defense Forces had any part in initially creating this situation, and I assure you it will never happen again, but it doesn't change the outcome here."

"Don't take this personally, General, but I'm skeptical of that reassurance." She ran her finger around Merritt's ring. "Did Merritt know about any of this?"

"No." Cevall didn't hesitate. "Teruel sent him off Asria as soon as the news broke. He knew Parker was too well connected to the royal family and didn't want any mistakes during the investigation—there could be no accusations of favoritism or anything else. Parker respected the king, although I know he'd have disagreed with his views on the Commonwealth had he known about them." Cevall twirled his pen. "Or maybe he did. Like I said, things are hard to keep quiet, and the king had become more and more vocal about withdrawal over the past few years."

Avery bit her lip harder than she intended. That was why Merritt had been away on *Palafox* when she'd returned to Asria. Teruel's plan meant this scandal wouldn't tarnish his memory. Something to be grateful for, at least.

Small mercies.

Cevall noticed her look and stood to pace the room, waving a hand in frustration. "I can see you don't believe me, but you don't have to. He'll tell you the same thing, and I—excuse my directness, Your Majesty—I know you won't have any trouble believing him."

"I'm sorry?" She must be more tired than she'd thought, because Cevall wasn't making any sense. "Who will tell me the same thing?"

Cevall looked at her like she hadn't been paying attention to a word he'd said. "Colonel Parker, of course."

Cevall doesn't know Merritt is dead.

"General, Merritt is—" She couldn't say the word. She could scarcely think it. "He was at Alcaris when they tried to take it back."

"Yes. And I know you must be terribly worried about him, but even a Haederan prison is better than the alternative. This war will end eventually."

Her mouth dropped open, and it took a fair amount of effort to close it. *A Haederan prison?* But Merritt was dead. Perrin had said so. He'd said they were all dead. She still had his stars in her pocket; she'd seen his token sitting in Baylen's hand. So there was no way Cevall could be saying Merritt was—why was she so dizzy all of a sudden?

"Are you all right?" a voice asked.

Cevall sounded worried, but so very far away, like he was at the end of a long tunnel. He'd stopped his pacing in front of the fish, and the contrast between his uniform and the tranquility of the ocean made reality twist painfully around her. Moving her chest in and out was the only thing she could focus on.

Reality warped again as she sucked in a breath; she couldn't form words. Perrin had never shown her definitive proof. She and Baylen had accepted his story at face value. But why? What had Perrin said to convince them so easily? She couldn't remember details from that hazy night that felt like it was a year ago, only that they'd believed everything he'd said.

Why did we believe him?

"Merritt is—" She gasped for air that wouldn't come. "Merritt is alive?"

"You didn't know?"

Avery pulled out the stars and slid them across the table. "The night it happened, Perrin told me he was dead. That they were all dead. He gave these to me, showed us his authorization token. I had no reason to question him."

It suddenly occurred to her that she'd misspoken, in the most inexplicable way possible. Perrin hadn't given them to her—he'd used them to taunt her, then taken them and Merritt's ring from her hands right before the soldiers had handcuffed her and dragged her from the library.

It had been *Chase* who'd given them back.

But why?

"Taln Perrin is a liar and a coward. You must know that by now, Your Majesty." Cevall gave the stars the briefest look, then shrugged, as if their very existence in Villiers mystified him. "Some survived. Far fewer than I would have hoped for, naturally, but yes, Colonel Parker was among them."

The spinning room ground to a halt as she pressed her palms on the table.

"You know this for a fact?" she asked.

"Yes. The Haederans are playing it straight now as far as prisoners go. Imperial Haederan Army prisoners anyway." He shot an outraged look at an exposed bruise on her wrist, and Avery pulled her sleeve over it. "We've been able to confirm their list is accurate."

Cevall sounded like he couldn't believe it either—and he left no doubt that something terrible had happened that night at Alcaris. She didn't want to know details, didn't think she could handle more bad news that very second, but it was her obligation to ask. The queen's obligation now.

"Playing it straight now?" A muted joy threatened to overtake her thoughts, and she forced it away. It would be a long a while before Merritt's arms were around her again. "What's that supposed to mean? What really happened at Alcaris, General?"

Cevall hesitated. "The Haederans were waiting for them when they entered the hangar looking for the Nightflares. Which weren't there, by the way. We don't know how the intel about that was so wrong. Seven were killed in the initial attack and two-thirds of the prisoners were executed that night. From what we understand, the Haederans made the mistake of informing the Commonwealth—as a warning, I assume. The outrage on Ventana was—" He blew out a breath. "Well, I suspect they became anxious about their own people in Commonwealth hands after that."

Two-thirds. Not all, as Perrin had claimed. Still, so many lives wasted for no reason.

"I see. Then can we get this oath over with now?" she asked. "I want to hear everything else after that. It sounds like there's a lot to discuss."

Cevall nodded and left the room. He was back in less than five minutes with Hadley trailing behind him, plus the lieutenant from earlier who was meant to stand in for the entire Asrian senate as a witness while Avery took her oath. The young woman looked daunted at the responsibility, and Avery supposed she didn't look much better. Was it even a binding oath? Perhaps not, but legalities could wait for another day. All her worries could wait for another day.

Because Merritt was alive.

CHAPTER TWENTY-SEVEN

HER FIRST FEW HOURS AS THE QUEEN OF ASRIA WENT NOTHING LIKE they would have if circumstances had been different, and for that, Avery was glad. Somber occasion or not, it would have required her to receive each senator at the palace, a tradition that took over two days. Instead of that personal hell, Cevall ushered her to empty quarters another five levels down to wait. Alone. For what, she hadn't figured out yet. It wasn't as though the queen of an occupied planet with a price on her head had much to do but wait.

Still, even with the wild cylva she'd swiped from the greenhouse that sprawled across the level just below her, the rooms reminded her too much of the cell in Cadena. There was no need for windows under hundreds of feet of solid bedrock, and the drab gray walls and floor, which hadn't bothered her in the conference room, made the bedroom feel like a prison cell—a dark one. But turning the lights on only reminded her of Chase and that bright room. Of promises and misplaced trust and the way he'd clucked at her injuries and made her promise not to earn any more.

The doorbell beeped as she dimmed the lights halfway and stuck her nose in the glass of cut cylva blooms. With more reluctance than seemed appropriate, she opened the door, expecting to the find the lieutenant in charge of her new internal security team —the woman had scarcely let Avery have a moment's peace in hours.

"Am I interrupting anything?" It was Feye instead of the uninvited lieutenant who grinned at her from the corridor. "Your Majesty."

"Not you, too." Setting the flowers on the nearest table, Avery smiled back and waved him inside. She could handle the gray room if she wasn't alone. "And no, you're not interrupting anything—none of them know what to do with me. I think they're all afraid to talk to me, and to be honest, I don't want to talk to any of them right now."

"Well," Feye began, as he stopped just inside the open door, his back rigid, "I'm not sure you'll want to talk to me either after what I have to tell you."

"I doubt that. I owe you more than I ever thought possible. Without you, I'd still be—" *In that room with Chase, desperate for a safer ally.* Her forehead creased and a more mechanical smile appeared. "Anyway, what's going on?"

Feye let his breath out, then reached in his chest pocket and pulled out an item so small she didn't recognize it at first. When she did, she reached for it without thinking.

He was holding the chip she'd made from Cameron Pernella's data, all those weeks ago.

The chip he'd said the Haederans had taken from Drex in his cabin.

"I'm sure you have a good explanation for this." Heat blossomed in her cheeks, but whether it was anger or fear, she couldn't decide.

Feye handed the chip over to her and rubbed his face. Razors were plentiful at Villiers, but the stubble suggested he hadn't bothered to find one yet.

"When I got to the cabin," he began, "Drex was already dead, but the chip was still there. He'd hidden it well enough that the Haederans hadn't found it, though you saw they tried their best.

It took me hours to search that place—it wasn't until just before you and Zenos showed up that I found it under a loose floorboard by the fireplace."

"And you didn't mention that you had it all this time. You're right—I'm not sure I want to talk to you right now. Why didn't you say anything this about before?"

"Well, because you'll dislike this part of what we needed to discuss even more." He avoided her stare. "Do you remember when you asked me if we'd ever had an unsuccessful mission?"

"Yes."

"I didn't tell you the truth."

"I know." At his shocked look, she added, "Hadley told me what happened to you both a few years ago, and I—I suppose I understand why you didn't say anything."

"He did? What did he tell you?"

"He wasn't specific," she lied. How was she supposed to discuss what Hadley had told her, especially with the man who had lived through it? It was painful enough just to think about it —but on the other hand, there was a certain kinship between them now, an experience that would forever tie them together in a strange way. "Just that a mission went wrong, and . . ." She held out an awkward hand in sympathy.

"Yes. And." Feye began to pace, and his pacing made her stomach churn. "It's strange how he came out of that mess just fine, isn't it?"

"I—"

Dread.

It had become a living a thing, and Avery collapsed in the desk chair as the same terror she'd become all too familiar with washed over her. No, the story hadn't sounded strange when Hadley had first told it, but now that Feye mentioned it . . . yes. Either Hadley was the most fortunate person in the galaxy—and she didn't believe in luck anymore—or he hadn't told her *everything*.

"I'm sure he told you it was an accident," he went on. "But it wasn't, I'm sure of that now. He set us up from the beginning. He planned the whole thing."

She blinked at him, then drew a light finger over the left eye when the extra tears didn't clear the shadows that hung in front of her.

"What exactly are you saying?" she asked.

A pointless question, for she already knew.

"I'm saying that I think he's been working for the Haederans for quite some time. There was no way I could let him get his hands on that, not if you ever wanted it to be of any use to anyone." Feye jerked his head at the chip in her hand. "I'm sorry for hiding this from you, but I couldn't let you know I'd found it until we got somewhere safe. I couldn't risk him finding out I had it, and it was impossible to talk to you alone out there without him overhearing."

The chair was the only thing holding her up now. "Then what really happened in the Litan Sector?" she asked. "You've got to tell me now."

Feye didn't go into much detail, just like Hadley hadn't, but the details he gave were damning, from Hadley's unusual insistence on programming the navigation systems to the fact he'd been running what he had called *routine checks* on the emergency life support systems when the accident happened. It was all too convenient to be a simple accident.

"Can you prove this?" she asked. Hadley had saved her life—but had he also set this entire thing in motion? Was he really a Haederan agent? "I assume you can, if you're making this accusation."

"I think I can now. It's taken a while. But he's too well trained to leave much of a trail, so maybe I can't. Ironic we trained him to do that, isn't it?"

"So now what? This can't stay here." Avery glanced at the chip in her hand, then set it aside. So much trouble over one tiny piece of metal and plastic. "It needs to get to Ventana—or at least off Asria."

"It does. But it won't be easy, especially now. Zenos wasn't kidding when he said things weren't going well on-world anymore." Feye scoffed. "No thanks to him. It'll be hard to get off the planet."

"Then I'm going with you. I'd wanted to stay at Villiers in case there was any additional information about Merritt, but this needs to be done. Let me help."

"No." Feye wrinkled his nose. "Absolutely not."

"I don't care how dangerous it is. You planned this out for two people, and you need my help. I know you can fly, but . . ."

"Lieutenant, listen to me. First, you can barely see, and second, I guarantee you won't want anything to do with this plan."

"I'm fine." She didn't care if he knew it was a lie. "And why not? It can't be any wilder than anything you've asked me to do before, and I agreed to those things."

He sighed once more and ran a hand all over his head, then looked down at her.

"Because I'm going to steal a Haederan ship from Alcaris and sneak through the blockade with it," he said. "If you're ready for that, you're welcome to come along."

* * *

Feye retreated to prepare for his escape, leaving Avery to stare in silence at the chip on her desk. Was it best to tell him what was on it? No one but Cameron Pernella and herself knew it was possible to track the Haederan stealth ships, but intuition told her, once again, that it needed to stay a secret for now. She'd been so close to telling Hadley, after all—and what a disaster that would have been. No, everything would need to remain a secret, at least for now.

With one last glance at the relative—though claustrophobic—safety of her quarters, Avery headed down the hall to meet Feye near one of the emergency lifts. He'd claimed it would be no problem to sneak out, but she made it only twenty meters when

Hadley turned the corner, headed straight for her. She ducked her chin, thankful Feye had taken care of all the gear, and prayed he would pass her by, but he stopped her with a light hand on her arm.

"You don't look well," he said. "Is everything all right?"

Traitor.

She'd been on the edge of holding on before, and seeing him right in front of her sent her tumbling over. *Kusir*, he would turn her over to the Haederans now if he had half the chance.

"I'm just tired. And overwhelmed." She managed a smile. "It's been a long day. Lots of news. Lots of changes. And that room, it's so small—I just needed to go for a walk."

"You should get some rest. Or see the doctor. You've been through a lot, and it looks like you're limping again."

"I saw the doctors earlier. They fixed the superficial wounds, at least." She wouldn't mention to him that she'd sobbed the entire time they'd examined her and treated the rest of her injuries —or that they'd informed her the vision issues might be permanent. Some memories were too dark and too fresh. "And I'll get some rest after I get some fresh air. Besides, Cevall wanted to see me about—about some things," she finished lamely.

"I'll check on you later?"

"Yes. Later." She forced her smile wider. He looked and sounded concerned, but it had to be an act. He was only trying to keep her in her quarters, prevent her from impeding whatever he had planned. She'd never allow that to happen. "That would be nice."

Relief drifted through her as Hadley nodded and continued walking in the direction he'd been headed, humming under his breath. Hadley, humming? Was he that confident he'd find the chip and destroy it? It was a depressing implication, and she couldn't keep her mind off him the entire way to Feye's meeting point. What could have caused him to do this? Money? A woman? Several women? It was Hadley, after all.

Avery shook off the thought. She'd known him for over three

years on Ventana, though never very well, true. His reputation with the Commonwealth was spotless though, and she'd trusted him with her life over the past few months. None of it made any sense, but that was how double agents worked, wasn't it? The Haederans would never turn an untrusted operative. That would be a waste of their energy.

Feye nodded a silent greeting as she approached, then looked back at the box he'd plugged into the small control console near the emergency lift.

"Your Defense Forces are serious about their security," he said. "They've got enough cameras here to fill a small cruiser, but I think I've got them all disabled."

"You think?" She hadn't meant to sound so doubtful. "And won't they notice they aren't working?"

"Sure." Feye grinned. "But I've overridden their caution and warning systems. Anyway, they aren't looking for anyone leaving —only trying to enter. And that's yet another unique set of codes."

He punched a button on the console and the lift door opened. He waved her by, and she stepped inside. No one followed, no footsteps were even audible around the corner before the door closed, and before she was ready, her ears popped as the lift glided upward and stopped at the surface.

Feye motioned her to the side and handed her a large backpack. "This part's tricky," he said under his breath. "I can fool the lift cameras and sensors, but not the blast door. Too many backup sensor systems. Once I get it open, we need to run, and there's still a chance your security people will be fast enough to catch us. The car's two klicks north over the boulder field. I'll meet you there if we're separated. Ready?"

Avery nodded, and when the large blast door slid to the side, she dashed into the sunlight.

CHAPTER TWENTY-EIGHT

IT HAD, IN THE END, BEEN A SIMPLE ESCAPE. THE VILLIERS SENSORS hadn't been programmed for targets heading *away* from the base, and Elsbet's family car was still parked where they'd left it, somehow scorching in the low autumn sun. Able to relax at last, Avery rested in the front seat while Feye drove—the warmth was a welcome change from the insidious and cave-like chill of Villiers. When she woke from a nap she hadn't planned, they were three hours from the base, unpursued by Defense Forces security or anyone else. The silence was comfortable for another few hours, she too tired to talk, and Feye . . .

Well, how much of his reserve was his natural personality and how much was the same familiar terror that must haunt his dreams, too? What had Chase done to him? Had he once had the same bruises as she, the same anxiety in small rooms? Would he ever be able to move past his experience with the Haederans?

Or had he always been this quiet and introspective?

Probably not.

"What do you plan on doing once you're off Asria?" she asked, closing her eyes. It was strange how little she knew about his life beyond what Hadley had told her.

"I'm going on a long vacation." Feye spoke the hope deadpan, then grinned sideways at her. "Somewhere not occupied by the Haederan Empire."

"That sounds nice. If limited at this point in time."

A vacation sounded perfect to her, too, definitely somewhere with Merritt, maybe off-planet. But that was impossible now. Duty called, and the most she should hope for now was a few hours carved out for herself, with security close by. She had responsibilities now.

Responsibilities she'd walked away from, before and now.

Through the painful remorse, an unexpected anxiety materialized, and she sat upright, stiff with unease.

"Major. The checkpoints."

How had neither one of them thought of it before now? It should have been obvious after the checkpoint they'd encountered on the way to Villiers. She and Feye would never make it anywhere near Cadena without the Haederans spotting them, not even close.

Feye chuckled and reached for a small notepad in his jacket. "Don't worry about that. They won't be looking for anyone headed into the capital, especially on the major roads. That checkpoint we saw was in the middle of the mountains, right? And they were specifically looking for you headed toward Villiers. I doubt a single Haederan expects you to walk right back into the capital. Certainly not Gareth Chase . . ." His voice trailed off, and he handed the notepad over. "These are rough schematics of the Haederan spacecraft we'll find at Alcaris. Sorry it's not much, but it should be enough for you. Best get studying."

Squinting, Avery gritted her teeth and thumbed through the paper. The notes were written in what she assumed was Feye's scribbling, and it was disappointing to see the systems and checklists for the Haederan ships differed from anything else she'd flown before, Asrian or Commonwealth. The good news was that Feye appeared to have known what information was necessary. In a perfect world, she'd have wanted more—he hadn't copied down emergency procedures—but it would be enough if nothing went wrong.

"It would be nice if my vision wasn't so blurry. How did you get this, anyway?" she asked, flipping through the checklists for what looked like one of the Haederans' newest fighters, one that had only been rumored about at the academy. It wasn't data one could learn from hanging out in the Blue Room, eavesdropping on Haederan troops.

Feye looked at her, his expression blank.

"Right. Never mind."

The simple vulnerability of information she'd always thought secure terrified her. If Feye had gotten his hands on these checklists, how much did the Haederans know about Commonwealth technology? They'd known how to get past Asria's defenses. Technology helped, but double agents like Hadley played a part, too—and she had the unsettling realization that the Haederans didn't just have agents in the Commonwealth military. No doubt they existed in the Royal Asrian Defense Forces, too. Hadley had probably had help with his plot, even at Villiers.

"I hope you told someone at Villiers about your suspicion," she said. "If Hadley comes after us, if he's able to warn the Haederans what you're up to . . ."

"I told someone."

He didn't seem inclined to say anything else on the matter, so she tilted her head at him and vented a dramatic sigh.

"And?"

"I left everything I have on him in my quarters. They'll find it when they discover we're gone. If you're worried that he'll come after us, don't be—your Defense Forces will handle him."

"Good. So, let's talk about Zenos Hadley. Why'd he do it? You must have some idea."

"How would I know?" Feye's response was sharper than it should have been for a question he should have seen coming. "Because he's rotten." He softened when he saw her reaction, close to tears. "Look, I really have no idea. People do all sorts of things you would never expect. Even people you've trusted for years."

"I thought I knew him. Not well enough, obviously. It surprises me, though maybe it shouldn't." Avery pushed her hair behind her ears. The tears, so easy to fall since her imprisonment, were insistent. "I suppose my uncle did the same thing, though— and I've known and trusted him more than I ever considered trusting Hadley. Is there no one worth trusting anymore?"

"For what it's worth," Feye said, focusing out the front window, "it surprised me too."

* * *

Avery leaned against the fence line of Alcaris's perimeter in the black fatigues Feye had packed for her. While she held a small light in her trembling hand, Feye sketched a crude map into the dirt for her to follow. If her nerves hadn't been in such terrible shape, she might have laughed at his antiquated method of navigation, so much like the treasure maps she and Quen used to draw as children. After he gave her time to study it, he destroyed the drawing with the toe of his boot, and she felt just as incompetent as she had the first time she sat in the pilot's seat of a spacecraft. He had his reasons for everything he did, and she knew nothing.

She repeated the route to herself over and over, memorizing it in case they were separated. They would go through the Alcaris's main perimeter fence, into a service tunnel near a cooling pond, then six hundred paces through the tunnel and up a ladder to an access panel. That access panel, Feye claimed, led into a locked upstairs gallery that ran parallel to the hangar. There they would wait until the guards changed shifts, leaving the ships unprotected for no less than thirty seconds.

It sounded simple, but getting to a ship was the straightforward part. Even if she could fly a Haederan ship with no prior training, even if her vision cooperated enough to see the instrument panel, even if they weren't shot down as soon as they launched from Alcaris, even though they had the Haederan Navy codes that were supposed to guarantee otherwise, there was no assurance they could bluff their way through the Haederan blockade. Feye was confident about that part though, as long as she could fly the ship.

As she ran through the checklists in her mind, Feye knelt beside her and pulled a small explosive cartridge from his pack. She was about to protest about the noise when there was a small pop and flash of red light.

"That's it?" she asked.

"I can be discreet enough when I'm not trying to create a diversion." A grin spread across Feye's face, just visible in the blackness. "You know, like the one outside the palace the night we met."

Avery quashed her uneasiness and followed him through the small hole in the fence anyway, judging each step before she took it. It was too dark to see anything she might trip over, and if she stepped into a hole and twisted an ankle, there would be no way to limp out.

Easy prey.

The service tunnel was a short fifty meters past the fence, the entrance a small door on the side of a rolling knoll. Feye put a finger to a sensor on the side of the door, and she gasped when the door popped open at his fingerprint.

"I don't even want to know how you did that." Even a Commonwealth officer shouldn't have that kind of access to a Defense Forces base.

He put a finger to his lips. "Silence from here on out."

Silence, she could handle. She climbed down the ladder after him, relieved to find the tunnel was high and wide, and well-lit with small lights every two meters. Feye might not be happy about the illumination—she was sure he wasn't—but it kept her apprehension at bay, and she needed all the help she could get. They jogged through the tunnel, and it was less than ten minutes before they were standing in front of the access panel that led into the hallway just outside Alcaris's main hangar.

"Are you ready for this?" Feye spoke under his breath, but his speech bounced off every surface in the tunnel that grew smaller by the minute.

Avery nodded, although every instinct, along with her now-throbbing ribs—told her to turn around and head back the way she came. Was it too late? She glanced back down the tunnel, but he was already working on unlocking the large door.

The access panel popped out with a clang she was certain had alerted the entire base, but Feye's scanners still showed nothing. The corridor was still empty, the whir of electrical equipment somewhere in the distance the only sound. Her chest tightened. Despite the quiet, she wanted nothing more than to turn around and head back into the mountains, back to Villiers, back to safety.

But it was too late for that now. Too late to turn around, too late to abandon her duty to the Commonwealth. Avery whispered a quiet prayer for peace before she climbed through the hole in the wall after Feye. He gave her a quick smile as she helped him reattached the panel, and a bit of the anxiety faded away as she worked.

It'd been a long trip, yes, but everything was going according to plan. A dozen Haederan ships were waiting downstairs. Soon enough she'd be soaring through space in one of them, carrying the most valuable payload she'd ever carried. Just a few more minutes. Everything would be fine.

But when she crept down the hallway behind Feye and stuck her head over the ledge to look into the hangar below, it was obvious his plan wouldn't be as difficult as she'd had first thought.

It would be worse.

CHAPTER TWENTY-NINE

AVERY SLUMPED ON THE GROUND NEXT TO FEYE AND CLOSED HER eyes.

There were five Haederan fighters down there, true.

Five Haederan fighters surrounded by dozens of troops. It would take a miracle for even half of them to leave during a shift change, and that was something they didn't look like they were planning to do soon.

"You didn't say the hangar would be guarded like this," she whispered. "We'll never get to one of those fighters without them seeing us. How did this happen? You said security would be light!"

Something strange and cold touched her soul. His claim no longer made sense. After the Defense Forces' attempt to take back the base, the Haederans would have tripled their security.

"You're right." The curt, abrupt Feye she was so familiar with was back. She hadn't missed that version of him at all. "I don't think we'll make it to a ship."

"Then I hope you have an alternate plan. Going back the way we came sounds good to me—unless they've already been alerted to our presence in the tunnels."

"Yes, I have an alternate plan."

Her heart slowed; her stomach settled. Of course he had another idea. Someone like him would always have a contingency plan—more than one, probably. She just needed to trust him more.

"Then now would be a great time to let me know what that is," she replied.

Before Feye could reply, footsteps sounded in the stairwell at the end of the gallery. Heavy-booted footsteps, an entire squad of them.

The Haederans were on their way up.

How had they known?

Even as she asked herself, she knew the answer.

"Well, it's not one you're going to like." Feye's voice took on an edge she'd never heard before. "Stand up. Slowly."

Heedless of the Haederans soldiers below—and the ones in the stairwell—Avery complied, more out of bewilderment than a desire to follow his order.

"What—" she began.

"Silence." The edge became arctic as he raised his stun pistol. "Turn around and put your hands on your head. No arguing. I don't want to have to shoot you."

She lifted them slowly as she turned to look over the edge of the gallery wall, though her entire body was numb. Had she done what he'd demanded? She didn't know, couldn't feel her limbs at all. Feye stepped forward and relieved her of her pistol and the chip before backing away again, so perhaps she had.

The same strange paradox of existence grabbed her, one she'd noticed months before in the palace foyer as she listened to Feye's catchy breathing behind her: his presence was sharper than it should be possible for a person to be, while the rest of the world had become a silent blur. The footsteps on the stairs disappeared for a moment, and her spinning mind caught up.

Everything he'd said about Hadley, it was him. It was him all along, and she'd gone along with it to her death.

"Why?" she asked over her shoulder. "Why did you do this?"

"It happened just like Zenos said." Feye steadied the pistol and took a step toward her. "A technical malfunction. An accident. It was no one's fault, least of all his. After the salvage ship recovered what was left, the incident board determined it was a bad reactant thruster that caused the explosion. Some sort of propellant leak, they said. I was grateful the Haederans had picked me up instead of leaving me out there to die. We weren't at war then, not really, and I thought—I thought I was safe. I figured they'd detain me a few days, ask me a few questions, rough me up a bit, let me go. Instead . . ."

His voice wavered just enough Avery thought he might help her escape back through the access tunnel, but it strengthened again, filled with the past.

"It didn't matter in the end. The Commonwealth left me there to rot. They knew where I was and what was happening to me, the entire time, and they did nothing but lodge a few official protests. You think the Haederans cared about a few politely worded diplomatic requests? 'Give us our man back, or else?'" He barked out a laugh. "Or else we'll send another complaint in a few days? Yes, so persuasive. So effective. Five months. You—they held you for a few weeks. You don't know what it was like."

No, she couldn't imagine what they'd done to Feye on Haedera to convince him to do this. How they must have threatened him. The mind games that Chase must have played—because Feye's accusation against the Commonwealth left no doubt Gareth Chase had been involved. Imperial Security would have seen Feye as an unbelievable opportunity. The perfect chance to insert an agent into a part of the Commonwealth Navy that was difficult, if not impossible, to fracture. Chase would have salivated over the prospect.

"You're right." She had to change his mind before those boots got closer. "I don't know what it was like, but you know I can understand, at least a little. What I do know is that you don't really want to do this. It's not too late to get out of here. I'll make sure no one ever knows what happened. I'll help you get off Asria, whatever you need. I'll tell them the Haederans killed you or make up some other story to explain your disappearance. Something, anything you want."

Avery glanced behind her at the access panel, but Feye and his pistol were between her and it. She'd never make it before he got a shot off.

"It's too late to change anything," he replied. "And you'd best not turn around again."

As if to confirm his claim, the first Haederan soldiers advanced through the door, swarming the gallery so quickly she couldn't even count them all. The Haederan who reached them first was a young Imperial Security Command captain, and as Feye handed the chip and their pistols over to him without a word, her knees threatened to buckle under her.

Two soldiers spun her face-first against the cool wall before she could collapse, then searched her violently enough that there would be even more bruises tomorrow—if there was a tomorrow, which she was beginning to doubt. Still, she ground her heels into the floor as they pulled her hands behind her and handcuffed her. They wouldn't drag her away. Not without more answers. Feye owed her that much.

"You were supposed to drop her off at the checkpoint outside Cadena." The captain tossed the chip to the floor and crushed it with his boot as she watched in horror, the last of her hope disappearing into dust. "What happened?"

Feye shrugged, coolness personified. "She was suspicious. I had to act like we were going to get off-planet. Did you want me to lose her out there in the mountains if she decided she didn't trust me?"

The captain narrowed his eyes, then shrugged. "Hardly. But I was afraid you wouldn't go through with it. Can't blame me for being concerned when you two didn't show up as planned."

"I told you I'd hand her over, Linden. You didn't give me much of a choice when you tracked me down in Cadena. And Villiers."

"No, I suppose I didn't," Linden replied. "Still, you never know."

"You do when there aren't any alternatives. You made that clear enough." Feye glanced at Avery, avoiding her eyes. "Now what about her? I held up my end of the agreement, and you gave me your word you wouldn't harm her if I did." He shook his head, his jaw tight. "She doesn't know anything. Didn't know anything to begin with. We only used her for her position."

Right. Avery made a noise somewhere between a cough and a whimper.

"Things change." Linden gazed at her with disinterest. "He's waiting downstairs. What happens to her now is up to him."

There was no question of who he was talking about, and she couldn't, she just couldn't . . .

"Please help." Her pride was gone, crushed along with the chip that lay in pieces on the floor. She would plead with him if that was what it took. "Major, please." Maybe that would jar him out of it, though there wasn't a solitary thing he could do to help her now. "You don't want to do this."

Feye looked away, and Linden's disinterest turned to outright hostility.

"She's only trying to screw with your mind," the Haederan said. "Don't listen to her. You did the right thing. The only thing." He jerked his chin at the soldiers holding her. "Take her downstairs." Then, as if in deference to Feye's appeal, he added, "I expect her to be in the same condition she is now when she reaches the shuttle."

"I wish things had ended differently." Feye raised his hands toward Avery. "Believe me, when I said it was too late . . ." He took a deep breath. "It was too late as soon as that hull exploded."

He turned toward the door, Linden beside him. The soldiers pulled her after them. She dug her feet harder into the floor, and as she opened her mouth to scream at Feye to stop, he lunged sideways toward Linden's hand, still holding his pistol at his side. The scream burst through. Feye and Linden were a blur. A shot resonated through the gallery, so loud the pain in her ears rebounded through her entire body.

Avery stopped her struggle, focused on the pain in her side.

They had shot her.

No matter that Linden had just ordered them to treat her with care, she'd pushed them too far this time, and they'd shot her. The air disappeared, and she sucked in another breath, the pain retreating as fast as it'd appeared.

And when she blinked—

When she blinked, it was Feye who lay on the floor, unmoving. Linden was holstering his own weapon, and Feye's lay on ground, untouched.

Maybe that had been his intent all along. Perhaps he'd known he wouldn't be able to live with what he'd done. Maybe she'd changed his mind, and he'd died trying to help her. So much doubt. There was no way to know, but even Feye deserved better than this. Better than all of it.

With strength she didn't know she had, she tore herself away from the soldiers and knelt beside him before they could stop her. He was already gone, the burn mark in the center of his chest the only sign of what had happened. It was useless, but she tried to free her hands to touch him, give herself one last hope he was alive.

There was no fury, no anger as she stared at his motionless chest, just grief that left her empty. She wanted to hate him, tried to hate him, but as hard as she tried, the feeling wouldn't come. A ragged sob broke through as she willed him to breathe again, and she didn't care that the Haederans could hear it. They needed to know someone was mourning him.

"I'm sorry. I'm so sorry." Her tears dampened his shirt as the shadows of the soldiers appeared on the wall in front of her. "Holy One, please forgive him."

The unwelcome prayer was a near whisper as they yanked her back up.

CHAPTER THIRTY

SPACE WAS COLD. IT HAD BEEN MONTHS SINCE SHE'D BEEN OFF THE planet, and Avery had forgotten just how cold it was. Her teeth chattered in the thin air of the transport, and the black fatigues might as well have been paper for as well they were keeping her warm. Yes, perhaps the shivering was fear, but she needed to believe it was only the chill of the Haederan shuttle.

She gripped her fingers together behind her back as the morning sky became darker instead of lighter, and her racing heart told her that idea was nothing more than denial. Chase and Linden sat across from her, a Haederan Army soldier beside her. There was no hope. No way out. No way to keep them from taking her . . . where?

The stars burst out as they climbed higher, and she tried to avoid Chase's inquisitive stare. Avery counted them as they appeared, resolving not to give him the satisfaction of seeing her fear. For there were dozens of reasons they could be taking her off Asria, and none of them ended well for her. Execution? If that was their plan, they were taking their time. They could shove her out the airlock now and be done with it. Perhaps they were taking her to Haedera like Chase had threatened. It was the only option that made sense.

"I'm curious," he said, as she counted star seventy-eight. It might have been Dasia, but her celestial navigation was fuzzy. Everything in this new nightmare was fuzzy, even her vision and his voice. "Who else knows how to duplicate the verium technology?"

Startled by his question, the first words he'd spoken to her since they boarded the ship, she met his eyes. There was no malice there, and the lack of cruelty made the ship spin about her.

"Ah." He laughed softly at her silence, after a brief glance next to him at Linden. "You're so easy to read. It's almost too easy, really. You didn't tell anyone else what you learned, did you?"

With growing dread, she realized why he liked the idea so much. No one else knew what she'd learned. No one else knew what Cameron had told her about the verium-enhanced fuel, and now that knowledge would die with her. She should have made the copy she'd planned to make at Villiers. No matter how long it would've delayed her and Feye's breakout, she should have done it.

She sank back in her seat. It was possible that Hadley might find Cameron, but he didn't know her identity—and he was without a doubt still detained deep underground at Villiers. Would the Defense Forces release him in enough time to make a difference?

No. Of course they wouldn't—Hadley couldn't prove his innocence. It was his word against Feye's, and Feye had spun a brilliant story. So brilliant even she'd fallen for it. The information he'd left in his quarters that accused Hadley of espionage must have included pages upon pages of falsehoods, creative and impossible to prove wrong without her testimony.

Her eyes became wet at the thought, and she tried to wipe them on her shoulder. There wasn't any point in pretending to be brave any longer. Not even in front of Chase.

"I didn't think so." Chase nodded. "And since I don't need to worry about you anymore, that leaves only your source. A physicist, am I right? I'm sure he won't be difficult to find and silence."

His gaze became more thoughtful. "You'll help with that, of course. We can talk about how to find him on the way to Haedera."

Again, there was no surprise at his statement, not even fear, only detachment. Her life had ended when she'd left Villiers with Feye. There was nothing to do now except protect Cameron. Chase's oh-so-Haederan assumption that her physicist source was a man wouldn't shield the scientist for long.

"And once we arrive . . ." he went on. "Well, you do make quite the valuable hostage, Your Majesty. I'm sure we can think of some other use for you. Who knows? You might even grow to enjoy Haedera. Your uncle certainly has." He leaned back in his harness, his satisfaction obvious.

Avery bit the inside of her lip and tasted blood. Then they knew that, too. Cevall had said the Asrian government would announce her new status, but he'd planned on her being safe at Villiers when it happened. He'd never planned on the Haederans knowing like *this*.

"Colonel?"

Her breathing slowed as the pilot broke in over the intercom.

"Go ahead." Chase's eyes never left hers.

"You have a priority comm from *Stargazer* waiting, sir."

"Right," Chase said to the ceiling microphone. He leaned forward and patted her knee before unlatching himself. "I'm looking forward to our trip."

Avery looked back out the window. Seventy-eight *was* Dasia. She was sure of it now, even though she could scarcely see it.

Seventy-nine.

Eighty.

Eighty-one.

Chase disappeared to the flight deck, and she leaned her head against the bulkhead. Of course Feye had told the Haederans what was on the chip. She ought to have known. But what had Chase said? He'd only mentioned *duplicating* the verium technology. Was it possible Feye hadn't told his handlers everything? Was it possible he hadn't told the Haederans their ships were traceable, even with the verium-enhanced fuel?

No, that was a ridiculous thought. Feye had told them everything—Chase was only warming up to it.

He was back sooner than she'd hoped and shrugged at Linden as he strapped himself back in. "Change in plans. I'm headed to *Stargazer*. They're hot about something." His tone suggested that whatever they wanted to discuss was not hot to him. Bureaucracy knew no planetary boundaries, it seemed. "Stars know what, but I'll try to make it fast."

"Sir, are you sure that's such a good idea?" Linden glanced across at Avery. "What about her?"

"She's one prisoner, Captain. You can't handle one prisoner, especially one recovering from a few broken ribs? I would think you'd be able to, since you effectively halved your responsibilities back at Alcaris. What do you think she's going to do, hijack an entire cruiser?"

"She escaped once already." Linden looked doubtful, and despite her fear, Avery fought a childish longing to stick her tongue out at him. "Major Feye said she can be . . . evasive."

"I'd hardly call that an escape," Chase said dryly. He shot her a look that said, *I know exactly how that happened, and it won't happen again.* "In fact, I wouldn't call it an escape at all. Anyway, half of the party responsible for that is dead, and the other half is being detained by his own people. You needn't worry about her. What you need to worry about is your incident report. I want it first thing when I return."

* * *

Chase departed on a transport *Stargazer* sent to dock with them, and Avery breathed easier without him staring at her. She moved her fingers to keep her blood flowing. The cold air was an annoyance, but her numb hands and sore wrists were making her miserable. Then, as the shuttle slowed to dock with a ship so large she couldn't see the entirety of it through the small window over Linden's head, a loose piece of metal, maybe a broken part of the harness for the adjacent seat, stuck out behind her. Avery quietly shifted back against the seat, trying to hide her endeavor, and grabbed it with chilled fingertips. If she worked at the handcuffs long enough, she'd be able to pick them. She'd never let them transfer her to a courier ship, not without a fight.

Linden, apparently displeased at Chase's change in plans, refused to look at her, but the Haederan guard next to her shook his head.

"You're wasting your time." Perhaps thinking she was trying to slip out of the handcuffs, he reached behind her—Avery clenched her fingers around the metal fragment—and tightened them further. "Don't try that again."

She flinched both at his touch and the sudden metallic cold that cut through the lack of sensation, then froze as the shuttle landed with a gentle bump. Out of time, out of options.

The pilot pulled the main door open, and Linden roused himself from his pondering as new, cool air filled the shuttle.

"Take her to holding cell six," he told the guard next to her. "I'll meet you there. I have some incident paperwork to do first, it seems." He pulled a small tablet from his pocket and waved the guard off, head down.

Incident paperwork. What a less-than-charming way of saying, *I have to explain to my superiors why I shot one of my own agents.* And for Linden to leave her with one guard to escort her—well, it was one thing to know there was no chance of escape, but quite another to have the enemy reinforce that despondency with their lack of concern. Avery flexed her fingers again, trying to bend the piece of metal behind her to just the right angle.

There.

"On your feet."

Her knees wobbled as the soldier helped her stand. Metal slipped against her wrist as she did, and Avery forced all expression except fear from her face. She didn't dare move her hands yet, but the desperate feeling of five minutes before had faded in a heartbeat. He led her off the shuttle into a large hangar bay, and she fought a grin at the sight.

Her left wrist was almost free, and seven unguarded Haederan interceptors were parked not ten meters from where she stood.

CHAPTER THIRTY-ONE

AVERY'S BREATH CAUGHT, AND SHE HELD IT, AS IF THE SOLDIER NEXT to her could read her mind if he saw her take another one. There wasn't any time to come up with a plan, but she had an idea, the slimmest thought. Before she could think better of it, she twisted her left wrist down and gasped as the blood rushed back.

The guard noticed her movement at once. His hand went to his stun pistol as he opened his mouth to raise the alarm, but Avery elbowed him in the throat before he made a sound. His warning turned to a harsh gasp as he fell to the deck, a hand at his throat.

Adrenaline surged through her, and she seized his stun pistol from its holster while he twitched on the deck, gasping for air. One inaudible shot to the chest was all it took, and he became silent, his breath shallow. She searched his pockets for the hand-cuff key while she debated dragging him somewhere they couldn't see from the command window above, but there wasn't time. If Haederan security saw him lying here, then they saw him. She'd just have to be gone before they did.

Key in her palm, she fled toward the nearest fighter, praying the canopy would be unlocked. In less than a second she had it open, but her shaking legs wouldn't allow her to climb inside. She placed a foot on the hold and leaned her forehead against the side of the ship.

Move.

Shouts echoed from somewhere behind her and bounced off the walls of the hangar bay. They'd found the guard already? The answer gave her enough strength to claw the rest of the way up the side of the fighter with her arms. She ducked into the spacecraft as the shouts grew louder. Closer.

Shouts yes, but no shots—the Haederans hadn't seen her yet. They would have fired at her already, or at least the fighter, if they had. She crouched as low as possible in the single seat and pushed the button to lower the canopy. Her breathing and her heart refused to slow. She wasn't running anymore. Why was her breath so short? She had to recover, for there would be precious little time to rest before security began checking down the line of spacecraft, searching one fighter at a time. And once they noticed this was the only one with a lowered canopy . . .

Avery glanced up at the canopy that held her captive and began to sweat. Dizziness washed over her, along with anger that her ever-increasing fear of small spaces now included spacecraft. Her first love. Her life. She fanned a hand in front of her face, desperate to stop the heat that threatened to devour her whole. If she passed out, there would be no escape. She'd be trapped just as surely as she'd been trapped in that cell.

Memories of her first flight in the Dragonfly emerged from the depths of her mind. The same panic. She'd gotten past that fear, hadn't she? Just like a Commonwealth ship, this small Haederan fighter wouldn't feel this confining in open space. It couldn't possibly. She just had to get out of the hangar.

That reminder worked—at least enough for her to inspect the panel. It was the same model stationed at Alcaris, one of the fighters Feye had given her information on. Even more amazing, his notes and schematics appeared to be accurate.

Her gaze flickered between the engine start and pressurization switches. Had Feye known he was giving her a way to escape?

That made little sense for someone who'd destroyed any chance the Commonwealth had at defeating the Haederans. It made even less sense for someone who had walked her straight back to the enemy.

She blinked at the controls. But had he really? He could have just as easily turned her in as soon as she walked out of her first meeting with him and Hadley—and yet Chase hadn't shown up in Cadena for weeks after that. No, Feye must have been conflicted about the whole thing.

"Clear the bay!" Linden's shouts were audible through the closed canopy. "Thirty seconds!"

Avery snapped back to the present. Thirty seconds? The smile that had flitted on her lips when she'd first stepped foot in the hangar bay broke through.

They're going to depressurize the hangar.

It was the right thing to do if you were trying to find someone hiding in the hangar bay.

It was the wrong thing to do if you wanted to prevent someone from stealing a ship.

It would be a narrow window. Too soon, and the Haederans would see her. Too late, and they'd succeed in lowering the atmosphere enough for her to pass out. A heavy mist drifted over the canopy, and she strapped herself in and began flipping switches at the same time. There were a few for which she didn't know the purpose—they weren't on Feye's schematic—she didn't dare touch those.

The engines screamed to life, no doubt alerting everyone on the same level that a ship was departing, but her breath came easier as the oxygen generators came online. If it was anything like a Commonwealth ship, the signature of the fighter would be matched to the door, so she guided the ship toward it, grateful the Haederans had evacuated the hangar. Indeed, the door slid open as she did, and she slammed against the back of her seat as the fighter flashed out the egress hole and into open space.

They'd made her escape . . . almost easy?

Avery choked out a laugh as her claustrophobia vanished along with the cruiser, already a hundred klicks back. The Haederans had made wrong decision after wrong decision today. She was about to celebrate by removing the right handcuff from her wrist when the targeting display beeped: three other fighters behind her.

Kusir.

The curse was followed by several more as she threw the ship into a dive and dragged her finger along the weapons display. Worse than her pursuers' existence was the fact that Feye's instructions had included nothing on Haederan weapons systems —she'd have to outrun them if she couldn't figure it out. Dismayed, she increased the power another five percent, all too wary of overspeeding the engines in an unfamiliar ship. Numbers flashed in front of her, and she focused on them, tried to identify them, tried to learn.

The fighters kept an even pace with her as she accelerated.

More speed.

Well, more speed wouldn't be a problem in this spacecraft. She searched her memory, trying to recall how the hyperlight system worked. A small head start at that kind of speed, and even more combat maneuvers—Commonwealth ones the Haederan Empire might not be familiar with—well, that just might be enough to lose them.

A shock wave jolted her, slamming her head against the ceiling. The targeting display indicated two of the three ships had fired at her. Well, not *at* her, but close by. Either they'd missed, or they'd made sure they hadn't hit her, and Haederan pilots missed their targets as infrequently as Commonwealth ones did. Did they want her alive or their fighter back intact? She increased the engines another five percent, then put the fighter into a dive so precipitous it lifted her off the seat.

All three ships drew back.

No time to wait.

Avery reached above her head and opened the cover of the

hyperlight engine switch, then flicked it upward, turning back toward the Haederan cruiser and plunging at the same time. As responsive as if she'd spoken to it in her mind, the fighter flung itself forward, pressing her against the harness she hadn't tightened in her haste to take off. Adrenaline masked most of the pain around her sore ribs, and she yanked the harness back against her chest and took a deep breath as the stars outside disappeared into a haze of black.

Safe.

For a while, at least.

Avery yawned and undid the harness to stretch her cramped muscles. It was a luxury she couldn't well afford since they'd be after her soon enough, but she was too stiff not to do it. The targeting systems were still clear, the other three Haederan fighters a good distance back, and—

And on the same course she'd been on before entering hyperspace? Hadn't they seen her turn?

It didn't matter. At twice the speed of light, she was widening the gap between them at an astonishing rate. Asria disappeared behind her, a dot the size of her fingernail, then was gone. She was outside the system now, headed into infinity, and the Haederan fighters no longer appeared on her targeting screen. With any luck, they were proceeding back to the cruiser, or at the very least, still pursuing in her original direction.

She pulled the handcuff key from her pocket and slipped the restraint off her right wrist. That was physical relief, at least, but now she was in deep space on a ship intended for no more than a two-hour sortie.

Fuel.

She had to check fuel first.

A new target appeared above her as she flipped through the propulsion system screens. A curse on her lips, Avery strapped herself back into the seat and tried to swallow. With Feye's limited notes, she didn't understand the notation on the targeting display, and she couldn't risk changing any parameters in the system to identify it. Still, it had to be a Haederan ship. And even as fast as she was flying, the crew would have already picked her up on their scanners.

Hope slipped away for the last time. She sat motionless and stared at the screen, waiting for the first jolt of a tow beam, as the targeting screen blurred in front of her. She rubbed her eyes to sharpen the image, but it remained fuzzy as a gray shadow fell across the entire cockpit.

Too fast.

She was going too fast. Too fast in an unfamiliar ship.

Or was she going too slow? She didn't know. She had to do something, but she couldn't remember what—couldn't remember being this tired in a long time.

Slow down, that was it. But she couldn't remember how to do it, no longer able to picture the checklists in her mind. Her hand reached out in the pattern that would have worked in the Dragon-fly. Reaching for something . . .

The oxygen mask.

She slapped it against her face and sucked in a breath. The leaden persisted feeling, now in her limbs along with her vision. A stroke?

Emergency lever.

That was what she'd wanted, wasn't it? There must be an emergency kill switch for the hyperlight engine somewhere. Dropping the mask to her lap, she fumbled along the side control panel for a control that felt like—yes, that had to be it, a red glow visible through the intensifying fog. Avery jammed her finger against it, praying the Haederans would grant her even a small measure of mercy when they captured the fighter.

If not . . .

The Holy One will.

A familiar whine screeched in her ears as the hyperlight engine spun down. The stars reappeared all around her, brilliant pinpoints as blurry as the interior of the fighter.

And her vision went black.

CHAPTER THIRTY-TWO

Avery woke up coughing. Somehow, she'd expected to see the fabled golden light of the Holy One, but there was nothing around her but gray. She rubbed her eyes again, harder this time, and tried to focus. No, her vision had cleared. It was the walls, a blue-gray, smooth paneling which meant—which meant she was on a ship. The continuous thrum of an environmental system confirmed it. She had seen no other ships on the targeting screen, so it had to be the same one she'd seen before blacking out.

Haederan, of course.

She closed her eyes against the throbbing headache and reached a hand up to massage her forehead. It didn't help, and the ache increased at her touch. Or maybe at the knowledge she hadn't escaped after all.

"You're awake. How do you feel?"

Avery started at the words and pushed herself up to look toward the feminine voice. A woman about ten years older than herself sat on a chair pulled down from the wall, watching her intently. She reminded Avery of Hadley, though it was impossible to explain why. They didn't look or sound a bit alike. With short blond hair and dark eyes, the woman didn't appear Voirian and didn't sound Voirian. Her consonants were harsh, strident; the opposite of Hadley's softer dialect.

Then what was it about her? Instead of a uniform, she wore a plain gray jumpsuit that might have been purchased on any orbital station across the quadrant, but Avery wasn't fooled. Surprised, perhaps, by the lack of military insignia, but not fooled.

She thought of Chase.

Of the military police uniform he'd been wearing.

No, nothing the Haederans did anymore would surprise her.

"Where am I?" she managed to ask.

"You didn't respond to any of our calls, so we had no choice but to pull you and your ship aboard. You'll be fine, although it wasn't too smart to be flying a spacecraft with a malfunctioning pressurization system and a disconnected oxygen mask. A few more minutes of that, and we wouldn't be talking right now." The stranger paused. "Who are you? And what were you doing in a Haederan fighter?" She held up a hand. "Don't even try to tell me you were supposed to be flying it."

Avery looked up at the ceiling. This woman didn't know who she was? That was baffling. Well, she'd discover her identity in the next few hours. The Haederan cruiser—and Chase—wouldn't have wasted any time alerting their nearby ships about their stolen fighter and escaped prisoner. The sinking feeling in her stomach overwhelmed any relief at being alive. She'd rather be dead than Chase's prisoner again.

"I'm not going to tell you anything." It would have been a stronger declaration had her voice not shook. "About who I am or what I was doing."

"Then you'll stay here until you decide differently," the woman said sharply. Her face softened, changing to something like sympathy. "Look, I don't care who you are, but you aren't getting that fighter back. And how you get out of here depends on what you tell me." She looked Avery up and down. "Whatever you were trying to do, I've got to tell you, you should have prepared better."

"Best laid plans." Avery ran her hands down the filthy black fatigues, and the faintest twinkle of hope sprang up. "I'll tell you everything if you tell me where I am and who you are."

The stranger smiled. "Well, that won't happen just yet. At least not until you can convince me you aren't a threat to this ship."

Avery clenched her teeth together. "Believe me," she ground out, exacerbating the pain in her temples, "no one with a headache like I have is a threat to anyone."

It was only the hypoxia, though—she'd feel better in a few minutes. Still, there was a ghastly hum somewhere in the background, and it hadn't stopped since she'd woken up. The noise pressed into her skull like a vise. Fifteen seconds on, fifteen seconds off. Fifteen seconds on, fifteen seconds off. The cadence made her want to scream.

On and off.

Regular.

Regular?

She inhaled more precious oxygen, gasping away the nothingness of space. Through the pounding, the wildest idea floated into her mind, and without warning she was swimming through an emotion that had taken over all rational thought—though whether that emotion was relief or fear, she couldn't decide. Only moments before she'd resigned herself to the worst kind of captivity, and now . . . now she could scarcely believe where her own imagination had taken her.

Holy One, have mercy. Could it possibly be?

The air conditioning in the prison in Cadena had been irregularly scheduled. The Haederans had taken away every way to mark time, down to the most imaginative method. It was something she'd observed her first hour there and dismissed just as quickly as an irreversible fact of her imprisonment.

And there was something else.

Right.

The way Hadley had been transmitting information off Asria. She'd guessed he'd been relaying his data to a ship right outside the Asrian system—and he and Feye had never verified it.

Now they wouldn't have to.

"I—This is a Commonwealth scout ship, isn't it?" she blurted out.

Kusir, she sounded insane. Hypoxia did that to a person, didn't it? The Commonwealth would never be here, not this close to Haederan-held space. Even if they were, she wouldn't have been lucky enough to stumble upon them. But who else would be out this way? It wasn't an established long-range route, was it? There was no way to know without star charts, not now.

"That's an interesting guess." The stranger's face became unreadable once more.

That was it.

That was why she seemed so much like Hadley. It wasn't her looks or her voice or even the way she held herself. It was that same blank expression that said nothing, yet said everything if one knew what they were looking for.

Special Operations Forces must teach them that.

"Then I'm right," Avery replied, too tired to think of what she'd do next if she was wrong and too tired to be enthusiastic if she was correct.

The woman hesitated.

"All right." She smiled again, but it was a false one, the kind that stopped before it reached the eyes. "You're right, but that's all you get until you answer my questions."

Avery swallowed hard. "I stole the fighter from a Haederan cruiser in orbit around Asria."

"I figured as much. And you are?"

She glanced at the ceiling, then the floor.

Nothing left to lose.

"My name is Lieutenant Avery Rendon."

"Can you prove that? You understand I can't just take your word for it."

"My biometrics are on file." Hope turned to irritation. "You're more than welcome to check."

"We don't have access to that kind of information here. Limited comms. You understand." The woman smiled as she stood to go. "But I'll see what I can find out."

If this was a Commonwealth ship, they would have access to that kind of information, wouldn't they? The seed of doubt grew again, and she had to know for sure, right then. The words tumbled out before she could stop them.

"Elex Feye was working for the Haederans, you know," she said to the woman's gray-clad back in the doorway. "Your failure to realize that he was compromised over two years ago prevented you from getting any useful information out of Asria and almost got me killed. So I don't know who you are or where you came from, but you will not treat me as if I'm the problem here."

The stranger stiffened for a long moment. Slowly, she turned to stare at Avery, wide-eyed.

"He what?"

There was no mistaking her comprehension and shock, and it meant only one thing.

Avery was safe.

CHAPTER THIRTY-THREE

THE COMMONWEALTH SCOUT SHIP *TRIPHANE* WAS A PALACE compared to how she had been living for the past few months, except maybe for the short time at Villiers—though naturally, the underground Defense Forces base didn't have the expansive views of space like the ones *Triphane* had from each window of her wardroom. Unlike the stark cabin in which she'd awoken, the wardroom was homey, with a small kitchen, and sofas that lined the wall opposite the windows. Exhausted as she was, Avery might have stared at the stars for hours.

But Major Brodie Malvern of the Commonwealth Special Operations Forces, who'd admitted her name once she'd identified Avery, had other ideas, too impatient for a full account of everything that had happened on Asria. Much too impatient to let her gaze out windows.

Feeling like she was on display in a museum, Avery shrank back in her seat in fatigue when Malvern led three others into the already cramped room—more of Hadley's special operations friends. All she wanted was a two-day nap, and even with tea and the shot of oxygen Malvern had provided, she struggled to stay awake while she recounted the past few weeks.

"But Hadley will be fine," she finished. "Unhappy and uncomfortable perhaps, but fine." Luckily for him, the Defense Forces would leave his fate to the Commonwealth, and he'd spend whatever time in their custody safe, if displeased—for he was no doubt imprisoned somewhere deep in Villiers, protesting his innocence to anyone who would listen. She sighed and massaged her wrist. "But the data isn't replaceable."

"The data itself isn't, no." Malvern looked thoughtful as she poured herself another glass of sparkling water. "The chip is, though."

"I don't understand. The chip is gone, the data's gone."

And Drex died for nothing.

"You didn't know?" Malvern gave a slow shake of her head. "You were even luckier than I thought."

"Know what?" Avery pulled her own glass closer. "What's going on?"

Malvern's thoughtfulness changed to absolute giddiness, an emotion Avery wasn't sure she'd ever feel again.

"You didn't wonder why those fighters couldn't follow you into hyperspace?" Malvern asked.

"Of course, but—but nothing made sense to me when I was sitting in that ship." The pressurization leak had been that slow, that insidious. The confusion happened to better pilots than her, all the time. "I simply assumed they—"

She slammed her mouth shut.

Wait.

Was Malvern saying there was an actual reason the Haederans hadn't followed her?

No. She'd said they *couldn't* have followed her.

Her breath caught.

But that wasn't possible. She wasn't that lucky. The fighters on that cruiser couldn't have had the verium stealth technology. But they had to be somewhere, didn't they? Why not the ship Chase had taken her to?

"I'm guessing by that look on your face you've figured it out." Malvern glanced at the others and laughed. "We don't need your chip, Lieutenant Rendon, because you brought us the real thing. It won't take too much effort to reverse engineer that interceptor and develop our own verium fuel. We'll have stealth technology as good as theirs in no time. Probably better."

Avery grasped at the cup of water next to her, took a long drink, then ran her finger along the edge. Anything to stall.

"But surely the Haederans can track their own ships," she said at last. "They'd have never designed them without that."

"Only with a unique transponder which was disabled."

She hadn't known such a thing existed. One of the switches she hadn't been familiar with, one Feye's notes hadn't mentioned, had probably controlled that system. His unintentional omission had saved her.

"Even, so, it's not completely effective," she reminded Malvern. "They'll still be able to track us if we can get it working on our own ships. Feye must have told them what their own hyperspace signatures look like."

Avery's forehead creased as her certainty grew. Chase hadn't mentioned that, and he'd told her almost everything at the end.

Feye hadn't told the Haederans a word about it.

Her heart began to race with joy, but she wouldn't tell Malvern her suspicion. Every officer sitting in this room already thought she was too trusting and naïve. It was best to assume the Haederans knew everything—at least, that was what Malvern would claim.

"It's not perfect," Malvern agreed. "But it won't be as easy for them to track us as it is right now. It levels the playing field by I don't even know how many orders of magnitude."

Avery could have collapsed in relief, right there in front of them all. Malvern was right—it certainly did. Maybe it would be enough to turn the tide of the war, even if it was too late for Asria.

"What about Feye?" she asked. "How did this happen? We should have recognized something was wrong with him long before now, right? There had to have been some kind of hint.

Wasn't he put through dozens of tests once he returned from Haedera?"

The captain in the opposite corner—who hadn't introduced himself, and Avery hadn't asked—cleared his throat. "He passed every single medical and psychological evaluation after the Litan debacle," he replied. "Extensive ones. But some poor decisions were made. Mistakes."

"Poor decisions? I can understand that. But mistakes?" It wasn't her business, and Avery doubted they'd tell her anything, but they owed her some explanation.

He looked to Malvern, who nodded her consent.

"He has a sister, a research scientist at the habitat on Iythea." The captain raised his hands in hesitation, then took a sip of neon liquor to delay his news even further. "You remember how early Iythea was taken in the Haederans' latest expansion. That part was coincidental, but once the Haederans found out she was related to one of their sources, she was the perfect leverage with which to keep pressing him. We didn't know about that part until an auto-send message came through from him earlier today. There's one for you as well, Lieutenant, whenever you'd like to read it."

"It sounds like he knew he wouldn't make it off Asria alive." Her gut tightened. "What about his sister?"

The looks they gave each other were depressing.

"We don't know," Malvern admitted. "It's been months since we've gotten any information off Iythea. Our agent there has been silent since just after the invasion."

"Oh." Avery shook her head. She could fill in the rest. "Major Feye gave me the data I needed to operate the fighter. I believe he did it on purpose to give me a chance at escape. Perhaps he even knew he was giving me a chance to deliver the verium technology."

The temperature in the room dropped a few degrees, and she wrapped her arms around herself. Knowing she wouldn't like what she saw there, she met Malvern's disbelieving eyes.

"I suppose it's possible, but it's more likely he was trying to get you to trust him." Malvern's face was hard. "Don't read too much into it."

"I won't." She'd never convince them, but she had to believe it, if only for herself. "What happens now?"

"We've sent a message to Ventana asking for emergency assistance. We couldn't give any details, so I'm hopeful they'll be nosy enough to send someone to rendezvous before too long and find out what we want. They can pick up the fighter while they're at it. In the meantime, *Triphane* is at your disposal. Make yourself comfortable. As soon as we can get a ship here, we'll get you home."

"Home?"

"Ventana IV, of course."

"Ma'am—" Avery tapped a finger on the table. How was she supposed to phrase this? "With all due respect to you and General Torin, Ventana is not my home, and my father—my father is dead." Malvern could connect those dots herself.

"I see." Malvern looked like she couldn't believe what she'd just heard. "You're saying you want to go back to Asria."

"I do." She hadn't realized that was exactly what she wanted until she heard the wish out loud. "I would be safe enough if I could get to Villiers somehow."

Were those words coming out of her mouth? Only months ago, the Asrian senate had practically dragged her off Ventana at gunpoint, and now the Commonwealth would have to drag her back—for no one on Ventana would ever let her do something as irrational as returning to Asria.

Malvern exchanged a look with the other three. "I think it's a bad idea, but we'll send a message to General Torin once a ship gets here." She hesitated. "Are you sure you don't want to stay? Eventually the fleet will be here. If you want to fly in the attack, it would be an excellent opportunity. We could hold you back far enough to keep your security people happy but give you a chance to be involved."

"I'm sure." Avery smiled. "It's time to go home."

* * *

It was hours before she forced herself to pull up Feye's auto-message in the gray cabin. After locking the door and staring at the tablet for well over five minutes, she wound her hands around her cup of hot tea to ward off the chill of deep space as she read.

Lieutenant Rendon,

As I write this, you are about to become the queen of Asria and I am about to betray you. I hope beyond hope that you're reading this now, because if you are, it means I have failed. It means you are safe and I am not.

I'm sure you've already heard of my sordid background from someone—a lot of someones—so I won't bore you with the details. I'll only say I didn't escape from Haedera, but I'm sure you've figured that out on your own.

As for the rest, I'll just say I screwed up, and I wish more than anything I could turn back time and make everything go away. But I can't. All I can do now is try to mitigate the damage I've done. I pray it's enough.

You're probably wondering if I'm the one who tipped the Haederans off about you. If it was I who told Gareth Chase you were working for the Commonwealth. I've done a lot of things I'm ashamed of, but I didn't do that.

When Zenos and I arrived on Asria prior to the invasion, I thought I could ignore the situation, ignore them. That maybe they—that maybe he—would forget about me. I was as surprised as anyone when we heard you had been arrested. Then Rhys Linden tracked me down and asked why I hadn't turned you in first. I had no choice but to do what they wanted after that.

Imperial Security didn't kill Drex. He had the chip, so I took it from him and then I killed him. I hoped once it was gone, it would be the end. Until Linden contacted me here at Villiers and told me I had to hand you over along with it. That unless I did—

well, there's nothing I can say to justify myself to you. There's nothing I can say to justify any of what I did.

I read everything on the chip when I took it from Drex. I know what's on there. I've already transmitted part of it, the verium technology plans, the part they already know. That should satisfy them for a while, and Chase won't bother you about the rest. I didn't tell them we—though I suppose I don't have the right to say we anymore—I didn't tell them the Commonwealth can trace their ships, even with the verium technology. I'll destroy that data myself before I let them find out that part. I'll kill myself before I let that happen—before I tell Chase about it. You know I would tell them everything, eventually, whether or not I wanted to. It's not enough to make up for what I've done, but maybe it's a start.

I don't deserve your mercy, but I hope one day you can forgive me.

The tea was lukewarm when she finished reading it through the second time. Avery drank it in one swallow, then read it through a third and fourth time. It was a long while before she could comprehend the underlying meaning in his words: The Commonwealth could track Haederan ships, and the Haederan Empire didn't know a thing about it.

Eventually—quickly, if the engineers were as good as Malvern hoped—the Commonwealth would duplicate the verium technology and then the Commonwealth ships would disappear. For a while, at least. The Commonwealth and its member planets had just vaulted from a level playing field to somewhere far above.

And a double agent—a traitor—had sacrificed himself to keep that secret.

* * *

Avery never expected to meet Lew Torin in person, but the general himself kicked back in a chair across from her in the wardroom as she sat, his tense shoulders belying his casual attitude. He'd arrived on a courier ship earlier that afternoon, and no one could have been more stunned to see a Haederan fighter moored at the docking bay of *Triphane* than he was.

He was perhaps more stunned that the young lieutenant he'd recruited through Hadley now claimed to be the queen of Asria. Stunned and more than a little guilty over that turn of events, Avery was certain.

"I wish you would reconsider," he said to her, fresh from a closed-door meeting with Malvern. "We could use you on Ventana—and you'd be safe there. But I won't stop you."

With his words, the future she'd visualized upon waking that morning—an isolated life on Ventana, watching her planet decline from a distance—fell away like a heavy curtain, leaving terrified anticipation in its place.

"I can go home?" she asked.

Malvern raised her eyebrows. "It's not the Commonwealth's call anymore, given the new circumstances, Your Majesty."

"I understand your desire and need to go home—to be with your people," Torin added. "Whatever you need, we'll try to help, although it might be some time before we can figure out how to get you back down there. Quite possibly you'll have to wait until the Haederans open trade on Asria again, and that could be months. I can't jeopardize Commonwealth personnel to get you back before then. And being on Asria will be risky. If they apprehend you again—" He spread his hands in concern.

"I know what will happen to me."

Her voice was raspy to her own ears. Torin didn't need to give details—the Haederans would never forgive her for what she'd done. Never. There would be no grace, no mercy, no second chance to play their game.

She stared at the stars outside, imagining what it would be like to float between them, consciousness lasting just long enough for the fear to take hold.

No.

No more fear, wasn't that what she'd decided? There wasn't anything to fear any longer. Certainly not something as temporary and fleeting as death. It was just another curtain to be pulled back. And who waited for her on the other side when the time came . . .

He'll wait for you as long as it takes . . . He wants reconciliation, Chase had contended that first night in the temple. She hated that the revelation had come from him. Always would.

But he'd been right.

Malvern latched onto her outward distress like a starving takair. "You're welcome to stay here on the ship," she said, "but it really would be safer to transfer you to Ventana, at least for a while. No one would blame you for taking shelter away from the war."

Avery focused on the stars. If she ran away to Ventana, even for her own safety, the odds of ever making it home dropped to near zero. she couldn't risk becoming a virtual prisoner on Ventana. To sit in Commonwealth military housing day by day, isolated and useless, dreaming of everything she wanted and could never have again . . .

No, she would never go back.

"I'll wait," she said. "Here. For as long as it takes."

Malvern and Torin nodded their unhappy leave, but Avery barely noticed their departure. The floor-to-ceiling windows in the wardroom caught her eye, a million slivers of hope glittering deep in the void. She searched until she saw Asria and its star, dim sparks in the distance. They were so far away that her little finger covered them both, but she could *feel* the pull.

Merritt was there too, somewhere under the Asrian skies.

Her life. Her future.

Home.

ACKNOWLEDGMENTS

I am beyond blessed to have had some of the most amazing and supportive people helping me through this writing journey.

Kate, instead of laughing your head off when I told you I'd written a novel (although you may have done that as well), you've talked me off the ledge more times than I can count, including on the eve of publishing. I'm so happy I trusted you with it!

Beth, I'm not sure how you did it, but you convinced me that I have an ounce of creativity in me from all the way across the Atlantic. Rainbows, man. Rainbows. Keep them coming.

Meghan, I can't thank you enough for the amazing critiques you've given me over the past year. For the pep talks, the plot hole finding, and incredible support you've had for this project—even if you love its antagonist a little too much!

Andy, thank you for patiently answering my zillion questions about war, the military, and how one might bomb a planet if one was so inclined . . . And for being the most amazing husband I could ask for. I love you.

And last, but by no means the least: A million thanks and all the glory to the Lord, who dragged me kicking and screaming down this path—and then gave me the courage to share the story.

ALSO BY ANNE WHEELER

'Last Mission'

'Leaving Humanity'

Crownkeeper

Crownkeeper Novellas

Treason's Crown

War's Crown

Queen's Crown

Shadows of War

Asrian Skies

Unbroken Fire

Shattered Honor

Faded Embers

The Star Realm Saga

The Stars Wait Not

ABOUT THE AUTHOR

Anne Wheeler grew up with her nose in a book but earned two degrees in aviation before it occurred to her she was allowed to write her own. When not working, moving, or writing her next novel, she can be found planning her next escape to the desert—camera gear included. She currently lives in Georgia with her husband, son, and herd of cats.

For more information:
www.anne-wheeler.com